'Written well, fast paced and had me hooked from the start! … A gripping story with an unexpected outcome' Gemma's Book Review

'I found myself burning through the pages to the satisfying conclusion. Highly recommended' Bookie Wookie

'Kjell Ola Dahl has once again gripped me from start to finish, hooking me wholeheartedly with his beautiful writing and complex plot' Ronnie Turner

'Kjell's writing is amazing as it keeps you tense throughout and you just never know where it is going to end' The Secret World of a Book Blogger

'Each move is planned, no loose ends are left to ponder over, and the intimacy between the characters and the reader makes you want to come back for more' Cheryl M-M's Book Blog

'Kjell's style of writing is relaxed and allows you to get to know the characters, but don't be fooled, it had my heart pumping … I promise you will be hooked!' Wrong Side of Forty

'A compelling and complex book that will have you chomping down on your nails, waiting to see what happens … Brilliant stuff' Jen Med's Book Review

'Kjell Ola Dahl has delivered a complex, tightly plotted crime book, full of tension, suspense, twists and atmosphere' Emma's Bookish Corner

'He spins his tale with ease and keeps you guessing up until the very end. Intricately plotted … with a satisfying ending that leaves you satiated' Where the Reader Grows

'I was gripped' Portable Magic

'If you are a fan of Nordic Noir or like intriguing crime mysteries then you will love this book' Over the Rainbow Book Blog

'There is an evocative richness to Kjell Ola Dahl's writing … The complexities of the plot may demand the reader's full attention but they are rewarded with an engrossing and beautifully crafted novel … it is a book that captivated me from the very first page through to the startling finale' Hair Past a Freckle

'Thrilling and complex … an enthralling read' The Quiet Knitter

'I loved the plot in this book and the writing style was excellent! … A thoroughly enjoyable read' Donna's Book Blog

'I thought Dahl got the pacing of the novel just right, hooking me into the story from the very first page' My Bookish Blogspot

THE COURIER

KJELL OLA DAHL

Translated by Don Bartlett

ORENDA
BOOKS

Orenda Books
16 Carson Road
West Dulwich
London SE21 8HU
www.orendabooks.co.uk

First published in Norwegian as *Kureren* in 2015 by Gyldendal, Norway
First published in the United Kingdom by Orenda Books 2019
Copyright © Kjell Ola Dahl 2015
English language translation copyright © Don Bartlett 2018

Reprinted 2020

ISBN 978-1-912374-43-4
eISBN 978-1-912374-44-1

Typeset in Garamond by MacGuru Ltd
Printed and bound by 4edge Limited, UK

This book has been translated with financial support from NORLA

For sales and distribution, please contact: *info@orendabooks.co.uk*

PRAISE FOR K

'Absorbing, heart-rending and perfectly plotted. Kjell Ola Dahl's *The Courier* passes seamlessly from the present to the dark past of WWII. Fabulous!' Denzil Meyrick

'Kjell Ola Dahl is an exceptionally talented writer and manages to set a gripping sto   st a backdrop of global menace and terror that perfectly blends the hist   with the thrill of fiction in an authoritative manner. *The Courier* sits up ther with my favourites of the historical fiction genre like *Fatherland, Gorky Park* ai   *All The Light We Cannot See* … One of the best reads of the genre' Mumb.   , about…

'*The Cou ier* is a literary spy thriller, perfect for John Le Carré fans … But this is far more   an a thriller and murder mystery. It's also a heartbreaking read, as Ester learns m   e about what happened to her family and her childhood friend. The ending b   ght tears to my eyes' Off-the-Shelf Books

'Each sen ence is like a gunshot. The gaps and the spaces left by the things unsaid let my ir   ;ination run wild and I felt the horror and disbelief for myself … This is a brilli   t thr ler wrapped up in a piece of exquisite historical fiction with meticulo s plot ng and great characterisation' Beverley Has Read

'*The Cou   ir* wa   ntrancing and I ponder scenes in my mind even weeks after reading i The t   .sion and the spiralling plot were mesmerising, giving a true sense of the lo   ty an   sses of war. Brilliant!' Amazon Reader

'Kjell Ol   Dahl's novels are superb. If you haven't read one, you need to – right now' Wi .m Ryan

'A chillin   iov l about betrayal' *Sunday Times*

'More th   gripping' European Literature Network

'The perf   t example of why Nordic Noir has become such a popular genre' *Re   er's Digest*

'Utterly c   ivincing' *Publishers Weekly*

'If you ha   never sampled Dahl, now is the time to try' *Daily Mail*

'Skilful b   d of police procedural and psychological insight' Crime Fiction Lover

'Further   ents Dahl as the Godfather of Nordic Noir, reminding readers why they fell   ve with the genre in the first place' Culturefly

'Fiercely   erful and convincing' LoveReading

'Kjell Ola Dahl's fine style and intricate plotting are superb … never letting go of the tension … a dark and complex story, and convincing characters presented in excellent prose' Crime Review

'Dahl is such a talented writer whose writing is powerful and so convincing … the only fault being the crime gets solved and life moves on!' Nudge Books

'Suspenseful, beautifully and clearly written, with a sure-footed plot, this is a book that thrills' Live and Deadly

'Intelligently crafted and infused with a truly unique personality' Crime by the Book

'With the Scandinavian crime market positively bursting at the seams … Dahl firmly remains one of the frontrunners' Raven Crime Reads

'It demanded to be picked up and devoured, such was the appeal of its characters, themes, story and delivery' Café Thinking

'Kjell Ola Dahl writes wonderfully and it's clear why he is regarded so highly within the genre' Have Books Will Read

'This is a dark, emotive and twisty mystery that has been tightly woven, full of surprises and lovable characters – such a fab treat for fans of Nordic Noir!' Chillers, Killers & Thrillers

'Well written, quickly paced, Dahl's series fits the traditional police detective model (think Michael Connelly, and Karen Slaughter)' Kingdom Books

'As soon as I started reading, I felt like I was in the company of old friends' Steph's Book Blog

'A beautifully atmospheric mystery' Liz Loves Books

'Winds its way around, leaving you guessing and counter-guessing, never knowing where you will end up' Bloomin' Brilliant Books

'Twisty and incredibly well-written story, full of suspense and intrigue and it had me glued to the pages!' Novel Deelights

'Full of plot, twists and tales, this kept me intrigued from the first to last page – I wanted to keep going until I found out what had happened … Clever, twisty tale' Harry's Book Club

'Extremely gripping … fast paced and exceptionally tense' Misti Moo Book Reviews

'Fast paced with a huge amount of twists and turns, yet easy to follow … If you like novels where the story is gripping and the writing is so good that you actually feel like you are in the place it is set then I would highly recommend Kjell Ola Dahl' A Crime Reader's Blog

THE COURIER

Revenge is a faithless servant

Oslo, August 2015

Turid switches off the radio. She revels in the silence and places her hand on the tablecloth where the morning sun shining through the window has formed a square. It is hot. She likes the feel of it. Robert has left the newspapers on the table. She pulls the *Aftenposten* over. Leafs through. News, travel, articles about new TV series.

Her eye is caught by an article on what you can pick up at auctions. At first she focuses on the photo, then she skims the text: 'You can still find treasures at Norwegian auctions. The unique bracelet pictured is valued at more than a hundred thousand kroner.' She looks at the photo again. Turid sits up, removes her glasses, cleans them on her sleeve and puts them back on. 'Auctioneer Guri Holter makes no secret of the fact that her firm is proud to be able to display this attraction. The piece of jewellery is expected to exceed the estimate. "We've already received some serious offers," Holter says.'

This is crazy, Turid thinks. Price is one thing, but putting it up for sale?

It is forty-eight years since she last saw her bracelet. She had been wearing it on her wrist then.

Turid gets up from the kitchen chair. She looks at the wall clock over the stove. It is ten o'clock. She faces the window and looks outside. She can see Robert's back, bent over the flowerbed in front of the laburnum by the fence. She is upset, but doesn't want to tell Robert, not yet. She goes upstairs and into her old study. She makes for the filing cabinet squeezed against the wall beside the desk. Robert always complains that she never throws anything away. Hmm, Turid says to herself. Let's see if this quirk of mine can come in handy. It takes her only a few minutes to find the document she is after.

She sends herself a critical glance in the mirror. She can't go out looking like this.

Half an hour later she meets Robert in the doorway. She had hoped to avoid him; when he works in the garden he generally uses the veranda door. But today, for some reason, he has chosen to walk around the house to come in. His gardening gloves are filthy with soil and he wipes his face with his forearm. 'Are you off out?'

'A little trip to town,' she says.

'Have you been texted some offers again?'

She nods with a smile. 'Christmas presents, Robert. Sale on woollen undies.'

Resigned, he shakes his head and goes inside.

Turid walks to the metro station, angry with herself because she so often decides to lie to Robert in such situations. But he wouldn't have accepted a short explanation. He would have started to ask questions. She has no answers and so wants to avoid the questions.

When she sees a couple of familiar faces in the crowd waiting on the platform she realises she still wants to be alone. She crosses the rails and heads towards the single taxi at the rank nearby. She opens the rear door and gets in. The driver folds the newspaper he has been reading and looks at her questioningly in the mirror. 'Tollboden offices please,' she says, taking out her phone where she has the address. 'In fact, it's in Tollbugate.'

Guri Holter turns out to be a woman between forty and fifty. She is wearing a grey woollen dress – which is a bit tight, considering how many kilos she is carrying around her stomach – and a pink, faux-silk shawl. Obviously chosen to add colour, Turid thinks, and considers it a poor decision. Pink is too insistent. The shawl lies on her shoulders and screams out that she is covering her double chin and wrinkled neck. Her hair is cut into a fringe but is bristly on top. Probably the latest fashion, Turid thinks. Guri Holter looks modern to the nth degree. The rings on her fingers are adorned with large, amorphous gems. Works of art. Then she sees that Guri Holter has long nails, filed round, varnished in the same shade of pink as her shawl. Guri, it seems, is the punctilious type, with an eye for detail, Turid concludes.

The immense hall in Tollboden has a high ceiling, so every sound echoes. Doors slam. Turid's heels click-clack on the floor as though she were a freshly shod horse on its way across cobblestones. A pneumatic drill is making a racket outside the open window. As if thinking the same, Guri Holter closes the window and with her back to Turid asks how she can help.

Turid explains that she has come about the bracelet pictured in the *Aftenposten*.

Guri Holter says she can tender an offer on the phone or via the internet.

Turid shakes her head. 'The bracelet was stolen. This is theft. You can't sell items belonging to someone else.'

Now Guri has nothing to say. She looks at her with a serious, quizzical expression.

Turid opens her handbag and passes her the papers.

But Guri Holter refuses to take them. She looks back up at Turid. 'I don't understand. What are you suggesting?'

'This is a police report. I reported the jewellery stolen at the end of the 1960s. I had no real hope of ever getting it back, but I reported the theft, thinking that a situation like this might arise.' Turid shakes the papers to encourage the woman to take them. 'There's a detailed description in these documents from back then. Also of the engravings.'

Guri Holter casts a glance over the papers again, still without taking them. Looks up. She deliberates. 'I don't know enough about this,' she says. 'If you want us to withdraw this item from the auction, I think you'd better contact the police.' Again she deliberates. 'Or a lawyer.'

Turid eyes her wearily. Considering whether to tell her or not, whether to embarrass Guri Holter by telling her *she* is a lawyer. Retired, it is true to say, but nevertheless. Turid decides to remain silent. Instead she wonders what the smartest thing to do would be – beyond what she has already done. Report the incident? Next step: demand the bracelet back? Not right here, though. That would be too hysterical. Let Guri Holter do a bit of investigation first.

'Yes,' Guri Holter says. 'Perhaps a lawyer is best. I don't know what the police can do really in this sort of case. In fact, I've never been involved in a situation like this before. And you claim the jewellery's yours? Did you buy it?'

Turid shakes her head. 'It's an heirloom. One of the very few things I was left by my mother.'

Turid has nothing else of any value to add. She knows only that she wants to get to the bottom of this. And she wants to stop the sale. The two women stand staring at each other.

At length it is Guri Holter who speaks up. 'I think the best option for you is to contact a lawyer. I'll take up the matter with management, and we'll get in touch with you in the next day or so.'

Turid looks at this woman and has the same feeling she has when she goes to her GP and tells him about her dizzy spells. The doctor doesn't believe her. The doctor interrupts her. This woman doesn't believe her. Guri Holter interrupts her. Guri Holter wants her out of the room, out of the office, out of this dreadful building. Turid passes the papers to her again.

Guri Holter holds up her hands in defence. 'I don't know if…'

'Take them, if you want my name and address.'

Guri Holter takes the papers and Turid turns without another word. She thinks of her mother and all the injustice that has never been redressed. As she carefully descends the staircase, step by step, she knows she has made up her mind. This time she is going to win. For her mother's sake.

Outside, she stands squinting into the bright light. Strolls down to the renovated Oslo East station, which is now home to shops, restaurants and bars, enters and finds a free table. She calls up the contacts list on her phone. There is only one person she knows who can make things happen in a case such as this. She rings Hans Grabbe and can hear from his answer that he is driving.

He shouts and his voice sounds euphorically happy. Turid realises it is Friday. Presumably Hans is on his way to his beach chalet in Tjøme.

'Jewellery? Can't you get someone in the office to deal with this, Turid?'

Turid won't take no for an answer, however. She insists she wants Hans to take the case. 'This is about my mother.'

Hans whinnies. 'Which one of your mothers, Turid?'

'My biological mother, Hans. The one who was murdered.'

Oslo, October 1942

1

Her front wheel is stuck in the tram rail. She wiggles the handlebars, but it is too late. She is going to fall. The wheel continues to follow the rail, her bicycle tips to the side, and she jumps off, runs a few steps so as not to lose balance, slips and almost lands on her backside, but manages to stay on her feet as her bike clatters onto the cobblestones. What a fool I must look, she thinks. The silence behind her tells her everyone is watching, all the passengers waiting at the tram stop. Ester brushes down her clothes without taking any notice, without looking at them.

Then a hand lifts her bicycle. A green sleeve. A uniform. A soldier. A gun barrel points over his shoulder, straight at her. Ester's attention is drawn to the round hole in the barrel. He speaks, but she doesn't catch a word of what he says. At last he stands up. The barrel points upwards. She takes her bike and says thank you, first in Norwegian, then in German and finally in English. Apparently the last causes some merriment. In German he says: 'Can't you see that I'm German?' He laughs. Odd laughter. His wide mouth produces brief squeaking noises, like a bike wheel rubbing. He looks pleasant enough. Innocent, she thinks. Bit stupid. If only he knew who he was wasting his gallant manners on.

She places her left foot on the pedal, pushes, sits on the saddle and freewheels down to the Royal Palace without a single glance behind her. Approaching the crossroads by Parkveien, she brakes in case there are cars coming. None she can see. Bears left, pedals harder, rounds the park, has to brake for a man running across the street, then continues into Sven Bruns gate with the wind in her hair. Brakes on the descent. Slows down to take the bend to the right in Pilestredet. The clouds part so she now has the sun in her face. It is low, an October sun. She glances down at her skirt. A stain. She folds the hem over to hide it, baring her legs to above the knee; she hears a wolf whistle. She turns her head. Sees two German soldiers on the corner, whooping. She almost falls off again, but regains control and lets go of her hem. More wolf whistles. She turns towards her block of flats. Brakes. Gets off her bike. Leans it against the wall. Breathes hard through her mouth and listens. She counts in her head while looking at the piles of wet leaves and inhaling the smell of burnt coke. A magpie is on the rubbish bins, hopping from lid to lid. It flaps its wings and flies off. Ester holds her breath to make sure she captures all the sounds. Nothing happening in the entrance, no footsteps – nor in the block. She does a quick scan then walks over to the nearest bin and the brick behind it, against the wall. She holds her breath again, this time to avoid the stench coming from the bin. Then she flips off her shoe and takes out the papers; she hides them under the brick, puts her shoe back on and can't get away fast enough.

Pedalling has become harder. She should have gone to Kirkeristen first. She would have had the whole day to deliver the papers then. It was the practical Ester who told herself the papers had to be delivered and that as the block of flats in Pilestredet was on the way, she could go there first. But now her fears are mounting. The fears that she doesn't have enough time. There are very few people in the streets. It is early. Perhaps not early enough, though. Ester sees clocks everywhere. Above jewellers' shops, on church towers. On the neon sign advertising Freia chocolate. She tries to concentrate on other matters. Cycles up Apotekergata and turns down to the marketplace. Soon she is racing along towards the cathedral. Her eyes are drawn by the clock on the tower. She jumps off her bike at the corner of Glasmagasinet, the department store. Glances both ways and runs across the street, dragging her bike. Pulls up sharply when she sees uniformed men outside the shop. Hovers for a moment, then continues walking. Pushes her bike past the shop windows, slowly, so as not to attract attention. Squeezes the brake as the road slopes downwards. One of the soldiers is sticking a poster to a shop window. He runs his hand across the poster and is satisfied with the result. Steps back.

Jüdisches Geschäft. Jewish shop.

Ester screws up her eyes and reads the poster again. And once more. Then loud shouts are heard from inside the shop. A man wearing civilian clothing – it is Dad – is dragged through the door. A man in a dark-blue uniform is hauling him outside. Ester stands watching. They are shouting in Norwegian. They tell him to be still, even though he isn't moving. He looks lost. His jacket is open and he is bare-headed; his hat is in his hands. As the policeman lets go he totters. Falls to his knees. He gets up and tries to brush the dirt from his trousers. The second policeman grabs him again and shoves him into the back of the police van by the kerb. The rear door slams shut. As though he has been swallowed by iron jaws.

Ester can see part of her father's face through the bars on the window. The hairline, the fringe over his forehead and the top of his glasses. That is when he sees her. They exchange looks. His hand grasps a bar on the door. She closes her eyes and regrets that she has seen this. She wishes she had spared him the humiliation.

So she doesn't immediately hear the policeman shouting. The man in the dark-blue uniform points. She doesn't understand. Takes one hand from the handlebars of her bicycle and points to herself. Me?

'Yes, you!'

Ester is rooted to the spot. All she can do is stand and stare at the man waving his arms. Then she clicks.

'Get out of the way!'

The police van is trying to reverse and she is in the way.

Lowering her head, she pulls her bike up onto the pavement. The mudguards clattering. The van sets off in the direction of the eastern railway line, rounds a corner and is lost from view. She casts a glance over her shoulder. A small group of police officers is still outside the shop. One of them pushes inquisitive onlookers away. Another seals the shop entrance with chains and a padlock. A third paints something on the door in white:

Closed (Jew).

Ester trundles her bike down Torggata. Stops. She has no idea where she is going. Someone behind her almost collides with the bike, curses and carries on. Ester looks around. The world hasn't changed. People on the pavement are scurrying to and fro. Outside the entrance to Christiania Steam Kitchen a woman is sweeping. A barber is putting a sign outside his shop. This is what dying is like, she thinks. You have gone and the world doesn't care. You die and others eat pastries. She keeps walking with her hands on the handlebars, and all she can feel is that she is cold. She leans her bike against her hip and lets go of the handlebars. Her hands are trembling. She has stopped by the kiosk with the Tenor throat pastilles advertisement on the roof. A woman carrying a shopping net emerges from the subway under Folketeateret. Out of the corner of her eye Ester registers the buxom figure. A familiar sight. The waddle, the arm outstretched as if for balance, and the funny hat. It is Ada, who lives across the corridor from her.

Ada approaches, clasps her arm and tells Ester not to go home. Ester answers like a machine. She knows. She was there when they turned up early this morning. Ada looks around to check no one is listening. 'Have you got somewhere to go?' she whispers. 'To hide from the police?'

Ester racks her brain, nods. 'I think so.'

Ada gives her a hug. Her body is large and soft. The embrace prevents Ester from moving and her bike clatters to the ground. She bends down and lifts it up, nods again and assures her: 'I know where I can go.'

2

The bike clanks as she pedals. The incline in Uelands gate gets steeper and steeper, but Ester stays seated on the saddle, pumping hard with both legs. She approaches the camp filled with lorries and German soldiers. Looks down at the front wheel and mudguard, which is askew. The pedal scrapes against a bump in the chain guard every time her foot goes round. She hasn't noticed it before. It must have happened in Youngstorget when Ada hugged her and the bike fell. She is hot. The hill is getting even steeper. She is moving more and more slowly. But she doesn't want to dismount; she doesn't want to stop in front of the soldiers.

At last she is at the top, and now it is easier. She continues past the monumental staircase known locally as 'the Wolf Steps'. The trees in the St Hanshaugen district have red crowns. She turns left. Another incline. But after that the road is down all the way so she freewheels to the block of flats.

She climbs the stairs and knocks on the door of a first-floor flat. Three quick taps, then a pause, one short tap and three thumps with longer intervals.

Silence inside the flat.

At last she hears a knob turn inside, the door opens and Åse is standing there with a baby girl in her arms. 'It's Ester,' Åse says over her shoulder and holds open the door.

Normally Ester would have spoken in baby language, tweaked Turid's cheek and tickled her. But not today. Ester goes in and undoes her shoes.

'Ester?'

She can't bear to meet her friend's worried eyes at first. Instead she goes into the kitchen. Gerhard is there in his three-quarter-length breeches and woollen jumper. He seems to be on his way out.

Gerhard takes a pile of newspapers from the cupboard, and it is clear they have been stuffed in there a moment before. 'What a fright you gave us,' he says, picking up a little suitcase, laying it on the table and filling it with the newspapers.

Ester takes a copy. Reads without registering a word. Noticing only that it looks different. No title on the front page.

'Where's the name of the paper?'

'They've decided to remove it.'

'Why?'

'Because of the new regulation. Death penalty.'

'They think I risk less if I deliver papers without a title?'

Gerhard shrugs. 'If you're caught, you have an argument. You didn't know you were delivering newspapers.'

Ester slumps down on a kitchen chair. She studies the floor, still sensing Åse's eyes on her.

'Ester, what's the matter?'

She takes a deep breath. 'They've arrested my father.'

Now she has said it. The catastrophe is out in the open.

The kitchen has gone quiet.

'The Germans?' Gerhard breaks the silence.

'Quisling's Hirden thugs and the police. They're arresting Jews. They came to the flat early today to arrest Dad, but he wasn't there. He's been sleeping in the shop since the vandalism started. I hurried over to warn him, but I was too late. I had to stand there watching him being arrested. They've closed the shop. Locked it up with chains and a padlock.'

No one speaks. Ester can feel herself becoming irritated by this mixture of silence, sympathy and impotence.

'They're throwing us out of the flat. Mum's gone to Gran's, and I can't stay in my own home.'

The two of them stare at Ester in disbelief.

'It's true. We've been thrown out. Now Norway's like Germany.'

Åse passes her baby to Gerhard. She crouches down in front of Ester and places her hands on her knees.

'You can stay here.'

Ester shakes her head.

Åse insists. 'You can stay here. No one here knows you. No one here knows you've got a Jewish passport.'

Ester shakes her head. 'Then they'll come here, and you'll be arrested.' Even though both Åse and Ester know that to be true, it feels brutal to be so dismissive. She adds: 'Living beside a camp full of Germans would be a daily nightmare, anyway.'

'You can stay here until you've had time to think, at least.' Åse gets up and cradles her baby again.

Gerhard closes the suitcase containing the copies of the *London News*. He stands with his hands on the lid, as if in deep thought. Finally he says: 'It's fine by me if you stay here with Åse for a few days. I have to go away.'

Stay here for a few days? What about the days afterwards? What about the rest of my life? Ester thinks.

'But perhaps you should drop the paper run tomorrow?'

Ester shakes her head.

Åse interjects: 'I can take the suitcase for you tomorrow.' She turns to Ester. 'You can look after Turid while I do the run.'

'No, Åse. My contact doesn't know you.'

'Ester's right,' Gerhard says. 'Her contact will take it as a provocation if you or someone else strolls up. There's no point.'

Åse nods. She understands. 'But you'll stay here until tomorrow, won't you?'

Ester nods. 'Definitely.'

Åse says she just has to change the tiny tot.

Ester asks if she can do it. 'I'd like to have something else to think about.'

She takes the baby into her small room. Lays Turid down carefully on the changing table. Her little face beams. Her feet kick out clumsily as her unbelievably tiny digits clasp Ester's forefinger. The tiny tot is ticklish. She makes funny baby grimaces, which end in a howl of delight.

The nappy is heavy and wet. Ester undoes it and takes a new one from the shelf under the table. Sprinkles talcum powder over Turid's bottom and secures her clean nappy. She hears Åse and Gerhard whispering outside.

Ester picks up the little one and she beams back a toothless smile.

Despite herself, Ester listens in. The voices have become slightly sharper.

They are having a row, Ester thinks, and it is because of her, and she regrets having come, regrets having unloaded her problems on these two people, who have enough to deal with already.

It goes quiet again.

Then Åse tries to talk in a normal voice. Theatrical, thinks Ester, who knows most of the timbres in her friend's vocal range. Åse asks Gerhard if he knows when he will be back. Gerhard answers in forced tones that she knows very well she mustn't ask. Afterwards the door slams shut and Gerhard's footsteps can be heard going down the staircase.

Ester has finished, but isn't sure whether she should leave the room at once. There is something very private about the silence outside. When finally she opens the door, the tap is running in the kitchen and Åse is standing with her back to her. Ester suspects she has been crying and now she is washing her face.

Ester leaves her friend in peace. Goes into the sitting room. Lays Turid on the carpet and takes the rattle from the floor. Shakes it above her cheery face. She becomes aware of a movement in the doorway. Åse is there, watching, her expression overwrought and her thoughts miles away.

Ester asks Åse if she can walk down the streets unmolested, with the Germans around, or indeed generally.

'Why do you ask?'

'Because you're the prettiest girl I know. I think the Germans occupied the country just to catch you.'

They exchange looks. Åse forces a sad smile before she joins them in the sitting room.

3

When at last she hears some noise in the kitchen, Ester pulls at the cord to the spring and lets go. The blackout blind rolls up with a bang. But the room is no lighter. It is still grey outside, neither night nor day. An October morning. She swings her legs out of bed. Sits for a while, staring vacantly into the air before getting up, collecting her clothes from the armchair and going into the kitchen.

Åse is sitting at the table, breastfeeding.

'Sleep well?'

'Not really, no. I didn't sleep a wink all night.' Ester goes to the sink and fills a glass of water from the tap. She puts down the glass and stares at the wall. Not wanting to express her worst thoughts: that she stopped on the way, that she might have arrived at Kirkeristen earlier, that things would be different if she didn't keep making mistakes. But then she feels Åse's eyes on her. 'What is it?' Ester asks.

'You're completely out of it. Didn't you hear?'

'Hear what?'

'I said I've heated some ersatz coffee.'

Ester smiles, but is not interested. 'You know, I was never very fond of proper coffee either.'

She can see her father's eyes through the bars in the iron door; this image has haunted her all night.

Åse passes her a jug. It contains hot water. Ester takes the jug back to her room and fills the bowl in the corner. Looks at herself in the narrow mirror perched on the dressing table against the wall. She warms her hands in the hot water, splashes a little over her face and wishes she had her toothbrush with her. Lost in thought again, she manages to drag herself away and put on woollen stockings, a skirt, a blouse and a jumper.

When they are sitting either side of the table afterwards, she says lying awake and thinking has in fact been useful.

Åse is sympathetic. 'What do you think they'll do?'

Ester is at a loss to know what to say. This is not something she wants to talk about.

'To your father.'

Ester doesn't wish to speculate. She has been wondering about it all night. Perhaps it will boil down to a charge connected with his business; perhaps they questioned him for a few hours, then let him go. These thoughts went through her mind, but with little conviction, because the sign on the window told a different story.

Eviction from his home, the closing down of the shop. What happened the day before was a further turn of the screw. Ester cannot convince herself it will be the last.

Åse squeezes her hand.

They exchange looks.

Ester says that now, for her, there is only one solution. 'I have to get to Sweden. As soon as possible.'

Åse places Turid over her shoulder to burp her. Pats her little back gently. No burp. She stands up and swings round, but the child shakes her head; she's not in tune with her mother's plan.

'Are you sure?'

Ester has never been surer of anything. 'They say we don't own our possessions. My father's driven off in a police van, and they barred the doors of the shop with iron chains. It's only a question of time before they come for me.'

Åse is silent.

They look at each other again, and Ester doesn't know what to say to lighten the atmosphere.

'But how will you get to Sweden?'

'The people I talked about, in Carl Berners plass. But I need money. Clothes. I have to go home and pack. Dad doesn't need his money now.'

'What if—?'

Ester interrupts her. 'I have to do this!'

She can hear how harsh and irritated her voice is. But she has had enough of talking now, and gets up and goes into the hallway. Finds her shoes. Slips her feet in. Goes out to the stairwell. The toilet is free. She enters, fastens the hook on the door and leans against it. Some things can be said. Not everything, though. When Ester is overcome by despair, like now, she stands and waits for it to pass. The walls in the little room appear to be pulsating. She sits down on the seat. What happened the previous day is a link in a longer chain that started years before. What she has to do today is react while she still can. She has to defy them, she has to go home and pack, get ready for the journey.

Ester glances at her watch. Sees that she has to hurry.

She leaves the toilet and goes back to the flat, into the kitchen. Washes her hands in the sink, then takes the suitcase containing the newspapers.

'Are you sure you want to do that today, Ester?'

Åse has put Turid down.

'I can't not do it. Someone's waiting for me.' Ester gives her friend a hug. It turns into a long embrace.

Åse swallows. 'Will I see you before you go?'

They look at each other, and Ester senses that she has to be honest. 'I don't know.'

Neither of them speaks. Åse's eyes are moist and shiny.

Ester picks up the suitcase. 'In a way it's wonderful too, knowing this is the last time. I'm afraid I have to go.'

Then she is out of the door.

4

She kicks the bulge on the chain guard with her heel, lifts the rear wheel and revolves the pedal once. No scraping sound. Attaches the suitcase to the luggage rack with leather straps. Tucks her fingers up inside the sleeves of her jumper as she sits on the bike. The temperature must have sunk to zero during the night. Every breath she exhales is a white cloud. People are going to work. Crowds are waiting at the tram stops. Ester is frozen and alternates between keeping one hand on the handlebars and one in her jacket pocket. A bell rings. She is passed by two cyclists in a hurry. The pedalling gets her circulation going. Soon she is hot. On the slope down to Bislett she can hold the handlebars with both hands, no problem. The wind catches her hair and her eyes begin to water. A lorry with German soldiers in the back passes. One of them waves to her. She looks down and concentrates on maintaining her speed, which she can do until Hegdehaugsveien starts to rise. She hears the clatter of the tram behind her and moves onto the pavement. Jumps off and waits for the tram to pass before she continues. The day is brighter now, but it is still grey and chilly.

She stands on the pedals for more traction up the hill. She feels hungry. She should have eaten something at Åse's, but didn't have the heart to take food from her. However, she does have food in the cupboard at home. As soon as she thinks about home she has doubts. Could they have changed the lock to the flat? No, they are not that quick, she thinks. There aren't that many of them. It occurs to her in a flash that they might have used chains and a padlock, as they did with the shop, but she dismisses the idea. She will go in, gorge herself, make a packed lunch and get her clothes. Again she has a nagging doubt. How will they react at the plant nursery if I just roll up? Can't be helped. I will have to take the risk. I will pass on Dad's regards. It was him who gave me the man's name. He had planned that we should all escape together. I will have to say that, tell them what has happened. Now there are only three of us – Mum, Gran and I. Again the self-reproach comes flooding back, and she pedals harder; pedals like a woman possessed to expel these thoughts from her mind.

She looks behind her before crossing over to the other side of the street as she approaches Valkyrie plass. Stands on the pedals and freewheels the remaining metres to the metro station entrance. Places the bike against the brick wall by the staircase going down. She is concentrating, even though her movements are familiar and drilled. She loosens the strap over the suitcase on the luggage rack, feels the same stabbing pain in her stomach she has every time she does this. As always, she thinks *someone* is watching. *Someone* has seen everything. *Someone* has watched her come here on the same days, on her bike, carrying a suitcase, rucksack or bag – *some* collaborator in pursuit of a privilege or more ration vouchers. *Someone* who is thinking: *Her. There's something funny about her.* As always, Ester straightens up and scans her surroundings to locate this spy, but she doesn't see him, she sees no one. So she takes the suitcase with her down the underground staircase.

On the landing where the stairs divide to lead down to the two platforms, she stops and peers over the wall. The platform to the right is empty. But it shouldn't be. She doesn't like what she sees and glances at the station clock.

It is the correct time. The minute hand jumps. Then there is a click in the air, above her shoulder, like someone invisible snapping their fingers. Ester has a nasty feeling and a chill runs down her backbone. The suitcase is suddenly very heavy.

Ester tells herself it is her; she is early. Warily, she descends the steps to the platform on the right, where the air is raw and there is the usual draught through the tunnel. Her skirt flaps. She walks slowly along the platform to the bench. Sits down. There is total silence, apart from a distant hum from an oncoming train. This is presumably the one she will catch. The one she would have caught if the other woman had been here. So what should she do if the woman doesn't appear?

Ester lifts her head and stares straight ahead. On the opposite platform there are a few people. One of them is reading a newspaper; a man is standing with his hands in his pockets. Ester lets her eyes drift to the right and on the bench she sees a woman.

As the woman turns her head, Ester sees it is the one she has been expecting.

Ester stands up and waves.

The woman quickly looks away.

At that moment the roar of forced air and the squeal of brakes grow, and the train bursts into the station and stops in front of Ester.

For an instant there is total silence again until the doors open.

No one gets out.

Something is happening on the opposite platform. Through the carriage windows she sees a man looking at her as he runs back down the platform to the steps.

Then Ester realises what has happened.

Now she will be arrested.

Ester weighs up her options. Back the same way she came? But then she would run straight into the arms of the man who is bounding up the steps on the opposite side. There is only one possibility.

She leaves the suitcase where it is. Breathing heavily, legs like jelly, she walks across the platform and into the carriage.

The train is still stationary.

She hears the man's footsteps on the stairs. The clatter gets louder. His steps are a drumbeat. Getting louder and louder.

Ester glances at the sliding door between compartments. But she doesn't dare turn her back on the drumming feet. She stands looking out at the staircase. A foot appears and a breeches-clad leg.

With a thud the doors slam shut.

The carriage jerks as it moves off. It trundles forwards, slowly, much too slowly. Now the man is on the platform and looking straight at Ester through the glass door as she backs against the opposite wall. She meets his cold eyes as he bangs his fists on the door, but the train doesn't stop. The man runs alongside the carriage, banging on the door, but now the speed of the train is greater than that of the man. The distance between the man and the carriage increases. Then the carriage is in the tunnel and in darkness.

Ester grabs a strap hanging from the ceiling to prevent herself from falling. She can taste blood in her mouth. There is a bang and Ester's knees give way.

It is the conductor opening the door to the compartment. Legs apart, wearing a uniform. He asks where she is going.

5

Ester pays, but stands by the door, ready to get off at the next station. Impatiently she waits for the train to stop and the doors to open. At long last the train pulls into Majorstua. She jumps off, runs along the platform and down the steps to the subway leading to the other side. She breathes through her open mouth as she runs up the stairs to the opposite platform.

Here she forces herself to walk slowly, trying to breathe normally, and strolls as calmly as she can back to the station building. Glances left. Sees a man sprinting down the slope to the platform on the opposite side. Could this be the same man? Could he have run that fast?

Ester forces herself to walk even more slowly.

The man is wearing a cap. Ploughing his way through, he looks like the man from Valkrie plass. Breeches. It must be him. He must have turned immediately, shot back up the stairs and run along the street. And now he is walking along the platform, scanning the crowd. He stops, shades his eyes and searches for the train she took. She doesn't look in his direction. Ester stares at the ground. She will soon be gone. She joins a crowd of passengers.

The bike, she thinks.

But she can't go and fetch it; not now. Åse can do that, perhaps tonight. Perhaps tomorrow.

6

The bare branches of the treetops stretch out to the sky. Ester wades through leaves along Kirkeveien. It is like shuffling through coloured paper. On another day she would have kicked at the leaves and rejoiced at the different hues. Now she is walking with her eyes peeled and her ears pricked. The motor of a machine drones and some workers are shouting to one another. They are building pillars for a gate into Vigeland Sculpture Park. Ester has to pass through a group of German soldiers. She looks down as she steals between the uniformed backs, trying to think about something else. But she can't. Even when she thinks she has left them behind she doesn't dare look up to check. She studies her shoes. They are wearing badly. Her father tried to drum it into her: *Save your shoes, Ester. Catch the tram, cycle, walk as little as possible.*

She carries on, her eyes boring into the pavement. Turns left into Frognerveien. Now she is taking her old school route back home. Yesterday seems a very long time ago. Only when she turns into Eckersbergs gate does she lift her head, slow down and look around her. Everything seems normal and still. Nobody is on the street, no cars.

She stops outside the entrance to number ten. Checks again. Looks up and down the street.

She walks past the entrance. Stops. Thinking once again that the arrest of her father was an attempt to frighten him. That they checked his papers and let him go in the evening or the night. Perhaps he is already at home. Perhaps everyone is. Waiting for her.

As she visualises this, she knows it is a dream. Wishful thinking. She looks up at the windows of their flat. Everything looks normal.

She makes a decision. Goes to the entrance. Opens the door. Enters. Inhales the familiar atmosphere of the stairwell of her home. But her state of mind is the same. The fear is still there. It feels as if she is wrapped in a cloak of unease.

She hesitates on the first landing. Takes a deep breath and forces herself to go up to the next floor. Passes the doors and continues upwards.

She stops on the landing at the top and takes in the sight before her.

She is not sure what she expected, but it definitely wasn't this. The door to the family's flat has been smashed open. Ester registers what she sees with the same dead eyes she has seen everything since her father was dragged into the police vehicle. White splinters stick out from the door frame, there is a hole where the lock should be and the door is open.

The sight of the splintered door frame is the irrefutable proof. Her wishes will not come true. Her father has not been released. Her mother is still with her grandmother. And Quisling's paramilitaries have been here again. They have forced their way in, smashed the door. In her mind's eye Ester can see the crows, the black crows with greasy beaks, hopping around on the bodies in the forest.

She observes the destroyed door and listens. All she can hear is the usual silence in the stairwell. She raises a hand, touches the door and pushes it. The hinges squeal. She walks in. Again she stops and listens. The hallway looks as it always does. Mum's elegant coat and dad's light gabardine hang where they usually do, and there is not a sound to be heard.

But they have been here. They have destroyed the door. Forced their way in. It strikes her that they still might be inside, just in a different room. So she stands still and listens, but hears nothing. And tells herself that those who broke in wouldn't be so quiet. Unless…

Unless they are waiting for her.

She makes herself move on. Pushes open the door and goes into her father's study. Here, things are strewn across the floor, papers are scattered around his filing cabinet, the drawers have been pulled out. The bottle of ink on his desk has been knocked over. A very black stain has spread across the inset writing pad and the woodwork. The drawers have been smashed. There are white splinters around the locks. Her foot slips on a piece of paper. The noise makes her freeze. She is still for a few seconds. Curiosity drives her on. She supresses her fear and continues over to the desk. Takes hold of a drawer. Pulls it right out. It is empty. Her heart sinks when she sees this. Nevertheless she has to check. She runs a hand carefully over it. Next drawer. Puts a hand in and searches in vain. Desperation clouds her eyes. How will she and the others get away now?

She hears a thud in the adjacent room.

She quickly crouches behind the desk. Stays stock still. Listens to her heart pounding. Whoever is in there must be able to hear her heart, smell her fear, smell her sweat, she thinks. Whoever is in there is bound to know where she is hiding.

The door creaks as it swings open. But she hears no footsteps. The silence persists. Why has no one come in? She hugs her knees so hard it hurts.

It really hurts.

Was the noise she heard just her imagination?

At length she makes herself stick out her head and have a look.

The ginger cat is sitting in the doorway. When it sees her it gets up and comes in through the door. Strolls over with its tail in the air, rubs up against her legs and starts purring.

The relief turns to a groan as she staggers out. Grabs Puss. Stands up with the cat in her arms and buries her face in its fur. She laughs out loud. 'So it was you, was it?'

Ester feels braver now that she is no longer on her own. She goes into the room with the grand piano. The family's polished, gleaming, nut-brown Steinway. The sight of the piano is like looking at a picture of another era – the era before yesterday. She can see her grandmother on the piano stool, her father with a pipe in the corner of his mouth, listening to the music with his eyes closed. Now I am the little match girl, now it is me, dreaming about the comforts that once existed.

She has to speak to them.

She puts the cat down on the lid over the keys. Turns to the telephone. Lifts the receiver, dials and asks the switchboard for a number.

Ester breathes out and closes her eyes when she finally hears her mother's voice:

'Thank God, Ester. I thought something had happened to you. But where on earth have you been? We were so frightened for you.'

'They took Dad,' Ester says, fighting to keep her voice under control. 'I didn't get here in time.' She is aware the woman on the switchboard will be listening. Someone has probably been informed that the Lemkovs' telephone is not private.

Her mother says she knows. 'The police told us when they came here, to Gran's.'

Ester says she saw her father being arrested; she arrived just a bit too late. She tries to stop herself, but can't. She starts crying and blames herself for making the situation worse with her snivelling. She doesn't want her mother to console her. There are others who need that comfort more.

'It's not your fault, Ester.'

She can't waste valuable time making her mother say silly things, Ester thinks. She has to be strong. She has to pull herself together.

Her mother asks if she is still there.

Ester says they have been here; the front door is smashed to pieces. 'I think they broke in. Dad's desk has been broken into and all the contents have gone.'

Her mother says nothing. Eventually she asks: 'Everything? You know what I mean. Has all *that* gone?'

'Yes.'

'Is there no end to this evil?' The despair in her mother's voice makes more of an impact than her words.

Ester takes a deep breath. 'Mum, we have to get out. We have to go – now.'

'I can't leave Dad, Ester. Not until I know more about what they want to do to him. If they've stolen things from the desk, we're poor. Can you have a look for my jewellery?'

Ester puts down the receiver and goes into her parents' bedroom. The cat is sitting on the piano, watching her pass. It is happy. It is kneading the piano with its front paws. It thinks the world is as it was yesterday. That it will continue to be like this for ever.

Ester is in the bedroom. At once she sees what has happened. She goes back, lifts the receiver. Takes a deep breath.

'It's gone.'

Ester hears a vehicle stop outside.

She knows what it is. Nevertheless she puts down the receiver and looks outside. She is right. Uniformed men.

She lifts the receiver again. 'Mum, I have to go. They've come back.' She hangs up. Meets the cat's eyes. Makes a decision and takes it in her arms. Leaves through the battered door.

At that moment the front door downstairs bangs.

7

Ester lets the door close without making a noise. Stands motionless with the cat in her arms.

She looks down. Dark-blue uniform sleeves on the banister. The stomping of feet echoes against the walls.

Then the neighbour's door slides open. Ada is in the doorway. She beckons Ester over. Ester goes in. Ada closes the door without a sound. Locks it.

The two of them say nothing, just stand holding each other. The cat starts purring again. Ester lets it go. It strolls through Ada's flat with its tail in the air.

Ester flips up a corner of the curtain over the glass in the door. She stands on tiptoes and gazes out. Two men in Norwegian Nazi uniform and one man in civvies study the smashed door frame. Ester's calf muscles begin to ache. At last all three men go into the flat. Ester gives Ada a hug, takes a deep breath and frees herself from her arms.

Ada shakes her head. Tries to hold her back.

Ester mouths: *I have to go.* She lowers her head. Remembers something. Mouths again: *Take care of Puss!*

Ada nods. Twists the lock and opens the door without a sound.

Ester slips out onto the staircase. She glides down, staying close to the wall so that the steps don't creak.

Downstairs at last. She runs to the front door and tears it open.

A black car is parked by the kerb. A man in a dark-blue uniform is smoking a cigarette and leaning against the bonnet. Ester notices too late. It is not a good idea to turn around now. She continues straight on, breathing deeply. Turns left. She is about to pass the car and the man in the uniform. Then she sees a polished black boot – it is stretched out in front of her, blocking her path.

She stops.

The man in the uniform locks his narrowed eyes on her and clamps his lips around a cigarette. His skin is pale and he has pimples around his mouth and by his temple. He is young, perhaps younger than her. A farmhand, she thinks. Eighteen maybe, possibly nineteen. Someone who can stop her simply by raising a leg. He has probably done the same to many others. Who knows what horrors this poor boy has already committed? She looks him in the eye. Meets the self-assured gaze and observes he is puffing on the cigarette in a pseudo-macho way. She can see that appearing nonchalant comes at a cost.

Again she looks at the raised boot and says nothing. Then she feels a slap on her bottom as he lowers his boot. She carries on her way, head down. Her backside burns where he struck her. I should have hit him back, she reflects, slapped his face. Is it suspicious not to react?

Her neck is burning too. From his eyes – or something. She crosses the street. Continues down the pavement on the opposite side. The crossroads is ahead.

A tram rattles past along Frognerveien. The noise means that she can't hear what is happening further away. The tram is soon out of view. Two more metres. Now she finally dares glance over her shoulder. The two Hirden men and the one in civvies have emerged from the block of flats. All four are standing by the car and watching her. She forces herself to walk slowly over the final stretch. Rounds the corner. Out of sight. She breaks into a run. The tram is heading for the stop by Frogner cinema. She speeds up, crosses Odins gate. The tram has stopped. She is panting and crosses the next side street. She couldn't care less what she looks like. She is going to catch that tram. She strides out. The tram sets off. She is going to make it. Ups her speed again. Steadies herself and jumps onto the platform at the back. Tastes blood in her mouth, stands there, chest heaving, recovering. The distance from the corner of Eckersbergs gate grows and grows, and there is not a uniform in sight.

Oslo, October 1942

1

Åse holds a hanging strap as the tram crawls into Carl Berners plass. It stops. She manoeuvres the pram to the door. The conductor is a bit slow. He is making his way through the passengers, but can't get to her. Two men vie to help her with the pram. In the end she lets go and allows them to take control. She thanks them and waits until the tram has moved off before heading towards the crossroads by Trond-heimsveien. Here she has to wait. A police officer is directing traffic. Soon he raises a palm to the line of cars. They stop and she sends him a questioning look. He nods briefly. She pushes the pram across and walks up the hills to Hasle, stopping for breathers on the way. The pram is heavy. Fortunately her baby is still asleep. From the corner of the pram hangs a shopping net, which swings to and fro in time with her strides. She turns into Hekkveien. Now and then she holds the net to stop it banging against the pram and waking her child. She comes to a halt. The linden hedge is still covered with yellow leaves, and behind it she can glimpse the roofs of two greenhouses. She turns into the gravel drive of the nursery. Comes off the drive and aims for the space between the greenhouses. Here the flagstones are uneven. The wheels get stuck in the gaps between them, and Åse has to push hard to make any progress.

She has to pass a lorry. The generator is smoking. A man is loading sacks of generator fuel onto the back. Åse steers the pram past and heads towards a line of cold frames. Two young men are walking either side of them. They lift the glazed lid from each in turn and carry it to a pile. They place the glass on the pile, turn and go back for the next. The sound is monotonous: the crunch of footsteps on gravel and a little clunk as the lid falls into position. One of the young men leans forwards and checks that the last lid fits snuggly onto the previous one. Both glance at her furtively.

Åse sits down on the bench by the entrance to a greenhouse. The man with the sacks of kindling has finished. Åse says hello. The man pretends he has seen her only now. He has red hair and freckles. A red fringe curls over his forehead. He stops in front of Åse, who has crossed her legs and is rocking the pram.

Åse points to the pram and puts a forefinger to her lips. 'I've got a little something for Ester,' she whispers.

The man goes to a small shed, which appears to be leaning against the hedge behind the plot. The door is crooked. One hinge is almost hanging off. He goes in. Comes back out, followed by an athletic man wearing work pants and high boots.

Åse gets up.

The man proffers a muscular hand. 'Alf Syversen.'

Åse grips his hand and says her name.

Syversen asks how he can help.

She repeats that she wants to see Ester.

He looks at her. 'There's no Ester here.'

Åse is puzzled. 'No Hilde either?'

'Hilde?'

'Hilde Larsen. Dark hair, long. My height, slim, about twenty…'

Syversen shakes his head. 'Afraid not. There's no one here but us.' He points to the boys moving the cold-frame lids, the man with freckles and himself.

Åse looks down, thinking, so that is that, we won't meet again. She fights her emotions. Unhooks the shopping net. 'Then I'd like to ask you a favour. Please could you give this to her from me.'

He raises a palm, not wanting to take it.

'She needs it.'

'I can't give something to someone who isn't here.'

They stand looking at each other. She searches his gaze, but fails to find any understanding or sympathy.

'I just wanted to say goodbye,' she says. 'Properly. The last time we met went so fast.'

He turns away from her. He leaves.

Åse watches the broad back and shoulders, wondering for a moment if he was right – she had been imagining things.

At any rate, she wasn't going to get anywhere with him. She pushes the pram back the same way she came. Turns when she hears someone running.

It is the man with the freckles. He says he will help her past the lorry, grabs the pram and pushes. It is tight and they have to coax it through. Turid wakes up. Starts whimpering. They reach the entrance. She wants to thank the young man, but Turid is bawling now. She asks him to wait and lifts the child onto her shoulder, mumbles reassuring phrases and rocks her.

Finally Turid is quiet and Åse puts her down again.

The young man has gone. Åse walks down Hekkveien towards Carl Berners plass. It is only when she reaches the tram stop that she realises what is different. The shopping net with the clothes and food for Ester has gone.

2

Åse puts a hand in the pocket of her woollen jacket for what must be the tenth time. Counts up the ration vouchers and stuffs them back. Leans over the pram to confirm the tiny tot is asleep. The queue is slow. She has been standing outside the shop for an hour and a half. But now there are only a few people ahead of her. A little boy of four or five is sitting on the step in front of the door. He yawns and rests his head on his hands. Åse thinks he is a good boy to have waited for so long without complaint. She leans over the pram again. Turid is still asleep. The doorbell jingles. The woman coming out seems angry. This is a bad sign. Åse has been uneasy for a while. The queue is moving faster now, and the people emerging have lean shopping nets and grumpy expressions on their faces. She guesses there is no more meat. But she won't leave. She has been waiting here for so long that she is going to try, to ask, when it is her turn.

A man comes round the bend from Frølichbyen. There is something familiar about his gait. The way he moves his legs. She watches him. They wave to each other at the same moment. It is Erik.

There are only two people in front of Åse in the queue as Erik crosses the street and they say hi.

Another woman leaves the shop. One person left in front of Åse.

Erik stops and tells Åse her mother sends her love and he has something from her.

'Have you got time to wait? It's my turn soon.'

He lifts his hand. 'I'll drop by later.'

It is Åse's turn. She puts the brake on the pram. 'When?'

But Erik is already well down the road.

3

Åse has had the blackout blind up for a long time as she puts Turid in the cradle. She is spreading the cover over the baby when there is a knock at the door. She switches off the light and goes out, leaving the door to Turid's room ajar. She listens for a few seconds for any noises. There is another knock and all is quiet in the bedroom. She goes into the hall and waits. No coded knock. It might be Erik. Perhaps he knows Gerhard isn't at home, she thinks, but represses the thought at once. She opens the door a fraction.

Erik is taking off his rucksack.

She opens the door fully and lets him in.

'Any luck at the shop?' Erik puts the rucksack on the floor. Bends down and loosens his shoelaces.

'I got some flour and potatoes,' she says. 'So I haven't got much to offer you.'

'My treat,' he says. He shakes the rucksack.

She can't help but smile. 'When Turid's bigger you can have a permanent job here, as Santa.'

'Your mother sends her love,' he says, getting to his feet. 'By the way, love from Gerhard as well.'

Åse looks at him in surprise.

Erik opens the rucksack and winks. 'Secret. Hush-hush!'

He imitates Gerhard. Åse has to smile, even though she does dislike people mimicking others.

She wants to know more. 'Did he say when he was coming home?'

Erik straightens up. Looks at her.

There is a slightly uncomfortable silence and she feels she has to do something; she looks away. Goes to the window for some air. Remembers the blackout and turns back to him.

He says: 'Sorry. Wasn't thinking. We should say as little as possible to one another. Forget what I said.' Then he smiles and rummages in the rucksack. 'Look what I've got!'

But Åse can't move on from the atmosphere. 'Was it a long time ago?'

'Was what a long time ago?'

'When you saw Gerhard?'

'Early this morning.' Erik puts the contents of the rucksack on the table: a small tub of milk, cheese, bread and something bigger wrapped in brown paper. He points to it. 'Shank of lamb,' he says. 'From your mum. But what have we got here…?' With an even bigger smile on his face he lifts up first a dark, elegant bottle of fortified wine. Then a box of what must be chocolates. And a carton of cigarettes.

Åse gapes at the bounty, overwhelmed.

But he hasn't finished yet. Another bottle appears. 'Scotch.'

She smiles.

He winks at her. 'Shall we have a taste?'

'Where did you get it from?'

Typical Erik. Things he can't say, he acts. He stretches out his arms to the side, hums engine noises and imitates a plane in the sky.

'An airdrop?'

Erik puts a finger to his lips again. 'Shhhh!! Are you crazy?'

Erik lifts the first bottle: Harvey's Bristol Cream. 'But we need something to drink it in,' he says, pulling off the cork. 'Sherry, Åse. Drunk by the finer ladies of England!' He holds the bottle to her nose. 'Smell.'

4

Erik can't take his eyes off Åse's face as she sniffs the Bristol Cream. The high forehead with the finely drawn eyebrows, the cheekbones and the nose; he can barely look at her lips, they are like a wound in her face. Now they spread into a smile and his heart beats faster.

'I've never tasted sherry.'

'Then it's about time you did,' he says, having cleared his throat to make his voice carry. He swallows. 'Glasses.'

Åse gets up, moving supplely and soundlessly across the floor. She fetches two glasses from the kitchen cupboard. Puts them on the table and folds her hands in her lap.

Erik fills one glass. Sets the bottle down and twists off the cork of the whisky bottle. 'If you're going to drink like a queen, I'm going to drink like a king.'

Åse smiles again, revealing her pearly-white teeth. When she closes her mouth his senses are reeling.

She sips from her glass. Nods contentedly, raises her glass and studies the colour of the sherry.

Then she remembers something, stands up and listens at the door behind them. 'Have to keep an ear open for Turid.'

Erik finishes his glass. Theatrically shakes his jowls and gasps for breath.

She comes back, sits down and takes another sip.

He feels the fire from the whisky spread through his stomach and enjoys it. Leans back against the wall and feels how good it is to be in her company, here and now.

As usual she is curious as to what is happening at home and what he can tell her. Who has hitched up with whom? He tells her that her mother occasionally has help at the farm – a widow from Skrautvål. But her mother always asks after her.

He fills both of their glasses.

She has turned serious.

He doesn't like it when she turns serious. But there is nothing he can do about it. 'She asks if you have everything you need.'

Åse looks down.

'And of course she asks when you're going to come to your senses and move back home.'

She doesn't say anything now either. So they sit there, silent, lost in thought. Her with her eyes inwards. Him with his eyes on her. He doesn't want her to be sad and unthinkingly grips her hand.

She stands up quickly and frees her hand as though it were burning. 'No one can turn back time, Erik.'

She sits down again.

He listens for the baby's cries, but there is total silence.

Erik leans forwards in the chair. 'Åse.'

She puts down her glass. 'Yes?'

'Isn't it difficult, being alone so much of the time, with a baby and all that?'

The thick plait slips off her shoulder. 'I'm not in the mood to discuss things like that.'

'Åse?'

'Yes?'

'Can I ask you a deeply personal question?'

She beams a smile again. 'Ask away. I'll say if it's too personal.'

'Why are you and Gerhard still not married?'

'We'll get married when the war's over.'

'What if the war never ends?'

She is the one to look away. But her smile is condescending now, and he doesn't care for it much. 'Gerhard's sure the war will be over by next summer. He says no one can withstand the terrible Siberian winter. The Red Army is falling back, as the tsar's soldiers did against Napoleon. The Germans will fail. It's pointless declaring war against nature. Hitler thinks he can defeat God.'

Erik doesn't like to hear Gerhard's profundities. He says; 'Let's not talk about Gerhard now.'

'Fine.'

'Or Hitler.'

'Nor Hitler.'

'Can I ask you another personal question?'

Åse nods.

A sound reaches them from the bedroom. 'I have to see to the baby.' She stands up.

He grabs her hand and holds her back.

Åse stands still.

He gets to his feet and spins her round. They are the same height. But she is looking at the floor. He places a finger under her chin and raises it. They look each other in the eye.

She says: 'I think I'm a bit drunk.'

'Me too.' He can hear his voice is hoarse. He has to swallow.

Then he holds her face with both hands and tries to press his lips against hers.

She pushes him away and shakes her head.

The sound in the bedroom turns to crying.

Erik grins and clings to her. 'I want to dance.'

He leads her across the floor. Forces her arm up and out. His knee between hers. Swings her around.

She uses the next swing to break free.

But he doesn't let go. It becomes a wrestling match.

Åse falls. Her head hits the edge of the stove. She lies motionless on the floor.

Erik kneels down. 'Åse?'

He bends over her. 'Åse!' He shakes her, thinking no one has ever seen a more beautiful creature. The buttons of her blouse are threatening to burst. Her skirt has ridden up, revealing stocking tops against a background of white thighs. He lifts his hand, the movement isn't his; his hand is being steered by the Maker, three fingertips against this milky skin.

She opens her eyes.

He takes away his fingers.

She looks at his hand. 'Budge, Erik.'

He doesn't.

'Erik! Move!'

He puts a finger to his mouth. 'Shhh.'

She listens and they exchange looks. Once again all is quiet behind the door where Turid is asleep.

5

Åse can feel eyes on her. She is dreaming and knows she is, and at the same time she has two worries. One is the staring eyes. The other is an absence. My child, she thinks. It is not the eyes she should be dreaming about but Turid. She should be listening because Turid may need something.

She opens her eyes.

At that moment she hears a noise.

It is a familiar sound.

She is lying in bed in the semi-darkness, listening for snuffles from her daughter. But the child is quiet. Then she knows what the noise was. A door. It was the door closing. She sits up in bed with a start. She gropes to the left. Feels Erik's shoulder. He is here, lying on his side. He stirs and grunts in his sleep.

Erik is here. So it can't have been him.

Åse looks at the sitting-room door. There is a light on behind it. She is breathing through an open mouth now; her mind is working feverishly. Did she remember to switch off the light? She tells herself she must have left it on.

She knows there shouldn't be a light on behind the door. She manages to swing her legs out of bed and stand on the floor, knowing fear has not deceived her. She did switch off the light. She always switches off the light. Something is very wrong. Perhaps that is exactly why she is moving. It is the certainty that her child is in a different room that pushes her on, that forces her towards the sitting-room door, even though she has apprehensions and she fears that they will be confirmed. She is naked, but couldn't care less. She just wants the pain in her chest to go. She doesn't want a dry mouth, doesn't want to fight to control her breathing. And hopes against hope that she is wrong, that everything is fine and the sound of a door closing was part of her dream. No one has been here, no one has stood over the bed looking at her. No one knows what you had the temerity to do in the night, no one, she tells herself. She opens the door without making a sound and glides out of the bedroom.

At first glance everything looks as it did when she and Erik left the room a few hours previously. Åse strides over to the other door, which is ajar, as it should be. She pushes it inwards. Quietly. She tiptoes in and leans over the cradle. Turid is sleeping soundly. Åse holds her hand over her face, and feels the puffs of breath on her palm. She resists the temptation to lift her up. She backs slowly out of the room and gently pulls the door to, but leaves it open a crack.

She turns round and takes two steps, then freezes.

The ashtray. There are cigarette ends in the ashtray.

Now Åse is wide awake. Now she can also smell the smoke. That is new. No one smoked in this room last night.

But someone sat here smoking while she and Erik slept in the adjacent room. She looks into the hallway, looks at the front door. The person who sat here let himself in with a key.

Åse, still naked, stands bent over, almost doubled up in the chilly room. She knows the nightmare hasn't even started yet. The dream wasn't lying. He did stand over the bed staring at her. The door she heard closing wasn't part of a dream. She looks at the blackout blind. A thought strikes her. She has no idea what time it is. But she does know it is night. She can feel it is because she has scarcely slept.

Where is he now? Outside the door, in the stairwell? In the yard?

Åse is sure of one thing. Erik has to get away before he returns.

Oslo, November 1967

1

Her flared white trousers flap as she walks. Her plimsolls are closer to grey than white. She is wearing a tight, pink woollen jumper under a well-worn military jacket. She is carrying a shopping net. Erik knows the net contains a law book, a pencil case and an exercise book. He knows her everyday routine.

She waits until the tram has left before she rushes across the rails. At that moment, in the way she moves, she is the spitting image of her mother. Erik thinks she rushes in a controlled manner – as if she lets her legs do the running while her torso strolls, slightly bent over. Of all the mannerisms she has inherited from her mother this is the one he appreciates most. Watching her through the large sitting-room window as she hurries up Slemdalsveien, it strikes him how strange it will be when, one day, she moves out. He hopes that won't be for a while. She still has two semesters left of her course, and at this moment she doesn't have a steady boyfriend.

Turid stops by the line of post boxes. She puts a hand inside theirs and takes out the contents. Pushes a strand of hair behind her ear and then flicks through the mail while ambling to the front entrance of their semi-detached house.

She stops by the door. Reads the address on one envelope again. Then she stuffs the rest under her arm and opens this one. Studying the letter, she opens the wrought-iron gate as if on autopilot. This is when she usually looks up at him in the window and waves. Not today. She dawdles towards the door, engrossed in her reading.

Erik goes back to his chair and sits down with the newspaper.

Turid is now in the hallway. Grete sticks her head in from the kitchen.

'What are you looking at?' she asks.

'A photo of my mum.'

'Me?'

'No, Åse.'

Erik lays down the newspaper. He sees his daughter pass the photo to Grete.

'You're so like her,' says Grete. 'Look, Erik.'

Erik gets up joins them and looks at the photo Grete is holding. It is old and worn, dog-eared and scratched.

'Where did you get it?'

'Came in the post.'

He arches both eyebrows and all three of them exchange glances. 'Who sent it?'

'No idea.' Turid passes him the envelope. It is addressed to her. Both the name and address are written in black capitals. The envelope has a stamp, but there is no sender's name.

'Any letter with it?'

Turid shakes her head. 'Odd, isn't it? Hm? Sending me a photo of her in the post?' Turid looks from one to the other. 'Why do that?'

Erik can feel himself becoming annoyed. 'Don't ask me. No one here sent that letter.'

Turid eyes him. Now it is her turn to become annoyed. 'It's my mother, and someone has sent me a photo of her. What's your problem?'

He opens his palms. 'Nothing.'

Turid snatches back the photo. 'That's mine.'

'By all means. I wasn't planning to steal it.'

'Stop it, both of you,' Grete says, and adds: 'Arna rang. She's got an extra shift and will eat at work.'

She talks to her husband's back. He is on his way to the kitchen table.

'That photo,' her daughter whispers to her. 'I don't understand.'

Erik slides down onto the chair. 'You're not the only one.'

Grete puts a casserole dish on the table. Fish balls in white sauce. Then she brings a pan of potatoes. 'There'll probably be more letters,' she says. 'There's bound to be an explanation.'

Erik spears a potato with his fork and starts peeling it. 'Someone might've found this old photo and thought you should have it.'

Grete gets up and fetches the dish of grated carrot. 'Almost forgot this.'

The atmosphere during the meal is not as Erik had imagined it would be, if indeed he had imagined anything. He tries to think of something to say that would make sitting there more congenial. But he can't. He looks at Grete and Turid, who are both picking at their food as though their thoughts were elsewhere. He is ill at ease and he wonders whether he is the one who has caused this tense silence, even though he doesn't want it himself. He would like to do something to lighten the atmosphere. He has tried before in such situations, but usually he fails.

'It was taken before she had you,' Grete says.

Turid looks up. 'Can you see that?'

'You're not in the picture. That was Åse in a nutshell. She never let you out of her sight, not for one second.'

Turid falls into a deep reverie.

'Perhaps my father took the photo,' she says.

'Perhaps,' Grete says, winking at her.

'Anyway, it wasn't him who sent it. That's for sure,' Erik chips in. 'I imagine the person who put that in the post box must've been alive, don't you think?'

Oslo, October 1942

1

Sverre Fenstad sits on the stool. It has accompanied him everywhere. His grandfather made it for his fourth birthday. A birch seat with four round legs, lathe-turned and neatly inset. It has moved with him to all his homes, then been stuffed into attics and cellars. Now it has a use again, after thirty years.

He leans forwards. With his penknife he loosens a plank in the floor. Lifts the plank carefully and leans it against the attic storeroom wall without making a sound. In the hollow under the floor are all the parts. He takes them out one by one and calmly assembles them. Two batteries, which he connects to two leads. Which he connects to the radio valves. Then he attaches the twined leads to the headphones, which he hooks over his ears.

A door shuts outside the storeroom.

He takes off the headphones. Not stirring from the stool, he raises a hand and opens the door a fraction. The reflection from the bulb on the untreated wood in the drying loft creates a cosy, yellow atmosphere.

He hears footsteps and narrows the crack in the door. A plump woman with a washing basket under her arm has come into the loft. She stops by the first washing line. Starts hanging clothes, humming as she does so.

Sverre Fenstad likes her. He likes her curves, likes the fact that she doesn't know she is being observed. Her body is hidden behind sheets and duvets. Fingers run along the washing line. And underneath them her calves. Like a dance in a dream, Sverre muses, following the movement of her ankles. Her buxom figure reappears. The basket is empty. She leaves.

He sits still until he hears the attic door closing. Then he puts his headphones back on, twists the knob and waits. It takes the radio time to warm up, but soon there is a low buzz. He has to fine-tune.

Searching. It is the noise of German jammers. A voice from Berlin, whistling, short snatches of melody. Until he finds London and he can hear nothing. He checks his watch. A few more minutes. He takes a pencil he from behind his ear. Licks the tip. Digs out the piece of paper from the breast pocket of his shirt. There's the signal – da-da-da *Dah* – the opening to Beethoven's Fifth Symphony. Followed by the reader's voice. Sverre notes down the codes.

Finally he stuffs the piece of paper back into his shirt pocket. He switches off the radio. Removes the headphones. Rolls up the leads. Undoes the batteries and the valve unit. Puts everything back in the hollow. Gets up and replaces the plank. Checks the join, then leaves the storeroom, clicks the padlock and is off.

He goes downstairs to his own flat, but stops on the landing above – there is a man sitting outside his door with a rucksack between his legs.

Sverre regrets putting the paper with the codes in his pocket. He should have learned them by heart and then burned the paper. But he doesn't hesitate any longer. He continues down the stairs at the same pace as before and the man looks up. Sverre Fenstad is relieved. It is Gerhard. Gerhard Falkum – codename: Old Boy. Sverre stops by his feet. But he says nothing. He unlocks the flat and holds the door open.

Fenstad closes the door behind them. He is annoyed at Gerhard for coming here like this. It shouldn't happen.

But before he can say anything, his guest speaks. His voice is low and tremulous. 'I know coming here is against the rules, but I have no one else to turn to.'

Gerhard passes him a rolled-up newspaper.

Sverre unfolds it. The evening edition of *Aftenposten*. The annoyance grows. 'I've got it here.'

'Read,' Gerhard says, pointing to a news item on the front page.

'I've read it. It's about a dead person.'

'It's Åse.'

Sverre looks from the newspaper to Gerhard and realises how stressed his guest is. The situation is quite different from what he imagined.

'Åse's the dead person.'

Gerhard's face is drawn, his eyes burning and the hand holding the newspaper shaky.

'The police were in the block when I arrived. I have no idea what happened. I didn't know anything had happened. Suddenly there's a Gestapo officer in the doorway, and the woman next door shouts that I'm the husband of the woman who's dead. I'm standing there with my rucksack on my back. Containing my gun. I had to run for it.'

Gerhard sways. He holds the door frame.

Sverre Fenstad reacts. Opens the door to the kitchen. 'Here. Take a seat.'

They go into the kitchen where the blackout blind has already been pulled down.

'I don't know what happened to Åse and Turid, Sverre. I don't know what's going on.'

'Number Thirteen,' Sverre replied automatically. 'Don't use my name.' At once he realises his response is ridiculous. After all, he is at home in his own flat. And he is correcting a man who has lost his partner and suffering from a terrible shock. The situation is dramatic. The Gestapo are obviously after Gerhard Falkum. And he has come here.

Gerhard can't tell him anything for certain. That means neither he, Sverre, nor Gerhard, nor anyone else knows the extent of the incident. Sverre is in urgent need of information. At the same time he can see the state Gerhard is in and sympathises with him. In Oslo they are fighting a war, day in, day out. Then a disaster befalls an innocent woman, a young mother. *Found dead.* What is the story behind those words?

'Could she have committed suicide?'

'Why on earth would Åse take her own life?'

Sverre is about to say something, but Gerhard carries on.

'We have a daughter. She never lets the child out of her sight. Why kill herself?'

'What about her health?'

'What? Åse's as strong as an ox.'

Surely a housewife can't die in her own home, Sverre thinks. He says: 'You know what this must mean, don't you?'

'What?'

'Someone must've murdered her.'

Sverre sees the colour drain from Gerhard's face. Sverre turns away, staring at the wall and thinking all manner of dreadful thoughts while listening with half an ear to Gerhard blaming himself, saying he shouldn't have been in the mountains. He should have been with Åse and his child. Taking care of them.

Thoughts race through Sverre's mind. A young mother, strong – partner of a well-trusted resistance man – is dead and the Gestapo are involved. Could the Nazis be behind it? But in what way and why?'

'We know nothing,' Sverre says, as much to himself as his guest. He fixes his eyes on Gerhard again. 'Are you sure the Gestapo were there?'

'Of course I'm sure.'

Sverre raises both hands in defence. 'It's just so odd. It doesn't matter whether there's been an accident or not, if people die it's a police case. Not for the Norwegian Sipo.'

'The man was Gestapo. He was wearing the uniform and he spoke German.'

'But why the Gestapo?'

'How should I know?!'

Sverre raises his hands again. 'What I'm trying to get at is what might've happened.'

Gerhard stands up and grips the edge of the table. 'When I left there was a suitcase full of copies of *London News* in the kitchen – but Hilde came before I left.'

'Hilde?'

'The courier. Ester.'

'Ah, of course.'

'She came to pick up the suitcase. Ester's reliable. She must've taken it with her. I'm sure there wasn't a single copy in the flat.'

'Weapons?'

'A gun. But well hidden.'

'Nothing the police might've found while searching the flat?'

'If they did they would've had to dismantle the fireproof wall. For all I know, they might've done. I don't know.'

A silence settles over them. Sverre takes a deep breath, but is unable to repress an accusatory tone as he says: 'You ran off with the Gestapo at your heels and of all places you chose to come here, to me!'

They look into each other's eyes. Sverre sees that Gerhard has to compose himself. He can literally hear the man on the chair counting to ten before answering: 'I can promise you one thing, Sverre. No one followed me here. This all happened several hours ago. I've been lying low and intentionally waited until it was dark.'

'How long did you have to wait in the stairwell?'

'Two or three minutes. Max.'

'Anyone pass you while you were waiting?'

Gerhard shakes his head.

Sverre goes quiet again, reflecting. 'We have to know more. For the moment it's best if you stay here.' He looks at his watch and calculates how much he can achieve in the course of the day and evening. He makes a decision. Then he goes from room to room checking all the blinds are down. Finally he turns off the light in the sitting room. He calls into the kitchen.

'If you're tired you can sleep in the guest room.'

He indicates the door and opens it so that Gerhard can see. 'The bed's made.'

He kicks off his slippers and sticks his feet in a pair of brown walking shoes in the hall. 'Don't sit up waiting for me.'

Gerhard's eyes widen. 'What are you going to do? Where are you going?'

'Out,' Sverre Fenstad says, taking the coat hanging on the hat stand. 'I'll see what I can find out.'

2

There is a loud buzz of conversation around the tables. Sverre is sitting on his own. He fidgets with the cutlery. Thinking that, if nothing else, it will give the appearance of some sort of eccentricity. Sitting, eyes downcast, he swaps the positions of the knife and fork; immersed in thought, seemingly unconcerned, Sverre Fenstad, a Mr No One at a table in Studia restaurant in Observatoriegata 2. He has taken a seat at the back of the room, a corner table for four with high chairs. Sitting on the edge of his seat, he can see the front door. Fidgeting with his cutlery is his response to the curiosity he occasionally senses from the customers in the line of tables for two. Most are German officers accompanied by their Norwegian mistresses. Sverre stands out, a man with no uniform, no conversation and no lady. He looks up, scans the room, avoiding eye contact. Time to swap the knife and fork again. At least it helps with the waiting.

Finally there is activity around the head waiter's chair at the entrance. Sverre smiles at Vera as she enters. She is wearing a tight, short-sleeved, apricot dress that suits her very well. Her gloves are the same colour as the dress. Her heels make her as tall as the head waiter. She isn't wearing a hat. Her blonde hair is held in place with slides and reveals a fullish neck. A wake of glances and admiring looks follows her as she winds her way between the tables.

Sverre Fenstad stands up. 'Dear Vera, how nice that you could come.' He pushes the table aside to make room for her.

'Not bad,' she says, dropping into the seat by the window. 'Inviting me to dinner in the lions' den.'

He bares his teeth in a brief grin. 'You know, lions are not known to eat other lions.'

She pulls off her gloves. He marvels at her small, slim fingers. 'You look wonderful in that dress,' he says, taking her hand.

'Let's not get carried away, shall we,' she says in a low voice. 'Many of the people sitting around us know me, and they're bound to be curious as to who you are.'

He lets go of her hand. 'It's because you have such beautiful hands. They remind me of graceful female kittens.'

She laughs and spreads the serviette over her lap. 'Heinrich says they remind him of a hen's claws.'

He likes her laughter. It sounds like the ice melting in spring, he thinks, or the murmur of wine being poured. 'No breeding,' Sverre says with a smile. 'You're much too good for him, Vera.'

A waiter appears at the table.

Fenstad passes the waiter the menu and an impressive stack of ration vouchers: 'We'll have what we agreed.'

Vera's eyes widen.

'But what will he say to this?' Sverre asks.

'What will who say to what?'

'What will … Heinrich say to you being busy tonight?'

'He won't get the chance to voice an opinion. There have to be limits.' Now, when she laughs, there is a flash of gold in the corner of her red lips. 'Joking aside, he has other things on his mind. A new girl's started in the office. Lillemor. She's just nineteen years old. The two of them are head over heels in love with each other.'

The officer at the neighbouring table apologises to his table companion, gets up and goes to the toilet.

Sverre watches him.

'A krone for your thoughts, Sverre.'

'I don't think about anything other than what I asked you to investigate.'

'Shall we change places?' she says.

'Of course.'

He stands up and waits with his back to the room until she has sat down again. She arranges the serviette and scours the room from under lowered eyelids.

'Just to be on the safe side,' she says, and adds: 'Little pitchers have big ears, as my mother used to say. It's my job to file the documents. So I've also read them. And I was a fly on the wall during a top-level conversation.' Vera's mouth flashes again. Then she leans forwards across the table: 'The woman was in bed when she was found. The neighbour who found her lives opposite. She'd heard the child crying and thought it strange the front door was open. The poor baby wasn't even a year old. They say the mother was suffocated, the poor dear.' Vera shivers.

Sverre looks up and Vera straightens her back as the food arrives on the table.

The waiter says he hopes they will enjoy it.

Vera answers she is sure they will.

The waiter withdraws. She looks down at the plate and raises her eyes: 'What have we ordered?'

'French is not my strong suit,' Sverre says, and adds: 'But it looks good. And the mood of the customers around us suggests it *will* be good.' He lowers his voice: 'Why hasn't news of the murder reached the press?'

'They're still discussing how best to handle this case.' Then she mouths the word *propaganda*.

He looks up.

'American cigarettes had been smoked and British sherry drunk in the flat. That and Scotch.'

He needs a little time to digest this information before he again raises his eyes and sends her a serious look. 'Are they sure this is Åse Lajord?'

'One hundred percent. Her mother has come from Valdres to identify her formally. What I'm trying to say is that, as far as death and destruction go, there are creative spirits in the admin department.'

'Spirits?'

'Such as Heinrich Fehlis and Siegfried Fehmer.'

Sverre strokes Vera's forearm.

'If you carry on like this, your food's going to get cold,' she says with a wry smile.

'Why are the top Nazis interested in this case?'

'The neighbour who found the poor mother alerted the police and they examined the flat. When they found those very unusual items, they called in our Norwegian Gestapo, the Stapo, who are thorough. They found a gun – hidden in the fireproof wall. The neighbours thought the couple were married. But they weren't, even though the man the dead woman lived with is the child's father, apparently. That self-same father has disappeared. Now you have to eat, Sverre.'

They eat. There is a commotion by the entrance. Vera looks up. Sverre turns to glance at the door.

A highly decorated German officer enters. Several of the customers jump to their feet and raise a glass. They clap.

'Anyone you know?'

Vera shakes her head, but uses the fuss to lean forwards and say: 'What made Heinrich Fehlis interested in the case was the gun. He's ordered SS-Hauptscharführer Gustav Barschdorf to act as a consultant to the Stapo.'

'Just because of this wretched gun?'

'There's more. The man of the house, Falkum – the one who's legged it – is a commie.'

Sverre shakes his head in desperation. 'Fantasy, Vera.'

'You can believe what you like. At any rate he was a volunteer in the Spanish civil war. Barschdorf considers him a terrorist, and thinks he has some link with Asbjørn Sunde, the man known as Osvald – the terrorist who planted those bombs in Oslo East and West stations in February.'

Fenstad leans back.

'That's given you something to think about now, hasn't it?'

'How did they find out the man had been in the International Brigade?'

'The files.'

'Which files?'

'We have a Minister of Police who was very interested in Norwegian Bolsheviks long before Germany saved us from the British invasion.' She smiles. 'That last bit's irony.'

'Do you think he was under surveillance?'

'Not recently.' Vera shrugs. 'But he was before. His name's in the private files of our Nasjonal Samling party man, Jonas Lie. Falkum sailed with the Wilhelmsen Line until October '36. Then he's supposed to have made contact with a German communist agent. Afterwards he enrolled with the International Brigade. He served on the side of the Spanish Republic for a little more than a year, but was injured at the battle of Brunete. Then he was discharged.'

'My impression is that Sipo, the Gestapo really, are not actually interested in the murder,' she says. 'They want to use the case against the resistance folk. There'll be an official search for Gerhard Falkum. Which will lead to arrests, whatever happens. Look around you. No, don't turn. My point is that there's no shortage of informers.'

Fenstad nods pensively. 'What about the child?'

'I believe she's been placed in a children's home.'

'Children deserve better.'

Vera smiles. 'I can hear you care about this child.'

Sverre looks down. 'Someone told me the deceased's mother lives on a smallholding in Valdes. The child would be better off there.' He lifts his head. 'Could you use your influence in that direction?'

Vera looks at him quizzically and winks. '*Someone* told you?'

Sverre smiles back without answering.

'I can't promise anything. Lillemor's the apple of his eye now.'

A silence descends over them.

Vera looks up. 'What are you going to do later this evening?'

'Do? I'm all yours, Vera.'

She lowers her gaze. 'I almost believe you, Sverre. You're a good actor.'

'Actor?'

'What does Lillian say about you leaving home tonight?'

'Lillian lives in the country with our child. It's best like that.'

They exchange glances and let the silence speak.

Vera straightens her back again. The newly arrived German officer has taken to his feet and demands the restaurant clientele's full attention.

There is a hush. Vera listens. Sverre leans back and thinks about the sad fate of Åse Lajord while the officer talks about the Führer's advances on the eastern front.

Finally the officer raises his glass and proposes a toast. Other officers follow suit.

Vera raises her glass. She and Sverre exchange glances. She tilts her head peremptorily. Dutifully he raises his glass too.

There is a scraping of chairs closer to the exit. Laughter rings out. The officer standing up is drunk and almost falls. Sverre sees what is happening in the mirror on the wall. The officer begins to sing.

Vera and Sverre exchange glances once again. Vera laughs and swings her arms in time.

'*Heute wollen wir ein Liedchen singen, Trinken wollen wir den kühlen Wein…*'

The 'England Lied' continues, and it isn't long before several officers strike up the refrain. '*Wir fahren, wir fahren, ja, wir fahren…*'

The officer who started singing raises his arms. The song dies and the officer roars: '*Gegen Stalingrad!*'

The officers in the restaurant cheer and laugh. Vera laughs along and winks at Sverre.

The singalong carries on. More people stand up. The singing is so loud the room echoes. The waiters stop working and politely withdraw to the kitchen.

The officer at the neighbouring table motions to Vera and Sverre: *Stand up and join in!*

Vera gets up. Again she glares at Sverre, who rolls his eyes and laboriously staggers to his feet. When the refrain comes they clink their glasses with their arms entwined.

3

Sverre Fenstad wakes in the middle of the night. At first he doesn't know where he is. Then he recognises the contours of the ceiling lamp. He is lying beside Vera in her double bed. He listens to her breathing. She is asleep. Carefully, he raises the blanket and gets up. From the end of the bed he watches her. She is mumbling in her sleep. Her curves are clearly visible beneath the bed linen. He walks naked into the sitting room. Their clothes are on the floor. He finds his trousers, shirt and jumper. Puts them on. A cough causes him to turn.

Vera is standing in the bedroom door.

'You'll get cold, Vera.'

'Are you sure there isn't a curfew?'

He has to smile.

'When will you be back?'

'Soon,' he says, slipping his feet into his shoes.

'Come here.'

He goes over to her.

She wraps her arms around his neck. Her body is warm from bed. She mumbles against his mouth: 'Do you have to go already?'

He smiles.

She smiles back.

'Believe me. I do,' he whispers.

4

Outside, the night is so black he has to stand still for a good while until his eyes get used to the darkness. It is anything but easy to find his bearings. But he has been here before. Finally he can make out the kerb and begins to walk along Hegermanns gate. Passes the dried-up bronze Bull Fountain that appears from nowhere like a towering colossus. Oslo is still. Three years ago, he had been in the same place, in the same state. He and Vera had been making love for hours. It had been an autumn night, like now. He was on his way home. Although the city was still and sleepy, it glittered like a starry sky. Now it is all dark. As though the city were a wounded animal in hiding. He walks on beneath the extinguished street lights. The white lamp posts are all that help him find the way. Whenever one appears he counts the paces to the next. He follows the lamp posts and emerges in Vogts gate. Stops and waits. Hears rather than sees a taxi coming. The car has hoods over the head-lamps and a wood-gas generator on the side. Sverre Fenstad steps into the street with his arm raised. The taxi stops.

He unlocks the door as quietly as he can. The ride in the taxi has woken him up. He goes into the kitchen. Washes his hands and face in the sink. Cleans his teeth. There is a strip of light under the door to the room where Gerhard is. Either he is still awake or he has fallen asleep with the light on.

Sverre pauses for thought. How little we know about each other. So Gerhard is a communist with war experience. His mind churns as it has done since he left Vera's soft embraces. He has a problem which, if Vera is right, will grow and grow in the days to come. Sverre dries his hands. He goes to the door of the guest room. Hesitates. Lifts a hand to knock, but lowers it again. He and Gerhard can have this conversation tomorrow. He turns to go to bed as the door is wrenched open.

'Well?'

Gerhard is dressed. He has a cigarette in the corner of his mouth and blue smoke billows through the door.

'You haven't been to bed?'

Gerhard turns back into the room and stubs out the cigarette in a makeshift ashtray on the chair. A saucer.

Sverre wonders how to phrase this and clears his throat.

Gerhard is motionless, as though dreading what is to come.

'There's no doubt that the dead person is Åse.'

Gerhard is still motionless.

'The good news is that your child's in good hands.'

A twitch runs through Gerhard's body. He puts a hand through his hair.

'Åse was murdered, Gerhard. They think she was suffocated.'

Gerhard leans against the wall. 'Suffocated?'

They look at each other.

Gerhard speaks first. He blinks to check his emotion. 'And Turid, my daughter?'

We'll have to take this one step at a time, Sverre thinks. 'She's just fine.'

'But where is she?'

'With her grandmother, Åse's mother.'

Sverre tells Gerhard all he knows without hiding anything. He tells him what the police found in the flat, about the Gestapo's role in the investigation. What their thoughts are.

'So it's obvious someone visited her,' he concludes. 'Who could that have been?'

Gerhard looks blankly into the air. 'Who? How should I know? I was in the mountains for a few days.'

Sverre Fenstad inhales and puts his hands in his pockets. He is about say something, but hesitates.

'Come on,' Gerhard says.

Sverre is still hesitant.

'Say it.'

'You and I know who has the best access to booze and cigarettes,' Sverre says.

They stand their ground, looking at each other.

'What are you trying to imply?'

Sverre chooses to keep his own counsel. Gerhard knows as well as he does how German officers go about bagging a Norwegian woman.

'Actually I cannot understand how you can entertain such an idea,' Gerhard says at length. 'And right now I'll turn a blind eye. The reason you can think like that is simply that you didn't know her. Believe me. It's out of the question, Sverre. I hope you realise that. You can get that idea out of your head this minute.'

Again they measure each other up in the dim light. 'I'll soon find out more about how the police are working,' Sverre says eventually. 'I have a reliable source. By the way, there's one thing you'll have to prepare yourself for.'

'Oh, yes?'

'You'll have to cross the border.'

Gerhard eyes him in silence.

'And at once,' Sverre says. 'I'll review the possibilities tomorrow.' He is aware of Gerhard's tense looks. 'What's the matter?'

'Why should I go to Sweden?'

'Because there are several reasons why the Gestapo want to get their hands on you.'

'Several?'

'You were in the International Brigade.'

'So what?'

'So was Osvald.'

'What's he got to do with me?'

'The Gestapo are trying to exploit this case to their own advantage. They found your gun in the wall. They're going to plug that for all it's worth and connect you with other cases. For the Gestapo the flat's now home to a terrorist. The murder of a young mother, an innocent woman, took place in that nest. The Gestapo are chomping at the bit to broadcast to the Norwegian people that you – a terrorist – are nothing but a murderer who killed the mother of his own daughter and left the child by the corpse. Not only will they be able to blacken what we do, they'll also use propaganda to catch as many of us as they can. They're hoping informers will grass on us and I think they're right – unfortunately.'

Gerhard looks sombrely into the air.

'If you're caught and questioned, you constitute a risk for many others.'

'No one will be able to force me to divulge a thing.'

'Nevertheless, there's a lot at stake for many of us now. It's safest for everyone if you escape, and Sweden's the only good card we have.'

'I don't want to.'

'It doesn't matter what you want.'

Gerhard takes a step forwards. He is angry. But Sverre is not about to give way. They stand eyeball to eyeball, and Gerhard says: 'I can't.'

'Why not?'

'You know why. I have a daughter who's just lost her mother.'

'Your daughter's fine.'

'How can you say that? Now she only has me, and I'm not with her.'

'Gerhard. We're at war. The child has been taken care of.'

'But Åse's mother is ill.'

'Your daughter will be much better off in the country than you can imagine. I've done the same myself. I've packed my wife and son off. They live with my in-laws in Kvam. They're safe there. Your child will get enough milk and food and loads of love at her grandmother's.'

Gerhard looks at him without saying a word.

'I can promise you one thing. I'll do everything in my power as far as your daughter's concerned.'

Gerhard still looks doubtful.

Sverre fixes him with an icy stare and decides the moment has arrived. 'Do any of our people know about your sympathies?'

'Sympathies?'

'Spain. You risked your life to fight for the socialist republic. A man like you must have strong sympathies for the Reds.'

'You probably won't understand, but this comes with your mother's milk.'

Sverre has nothing to say to that. They hold each other's gaze, for a long time.

In the end it is Gerhard who speaks. His voice has assumed a sharp undertone: 'I'm fighting for my fatherland now, Sverre. Like you.'

Sverre raises a calming hand. 'The thing is that the political side of all this gives the Gestapo a good hand if they want to blacken your name. What the Germans are best at is hating Jews and communists.'

'But you and I don't believe the Nazis' lies, do we, now.'

The same furious undertone. Sverre Fenstad looks down. He turns and walks to the hallway. 'You can stay here until we arrange transport and a guide across the border. Now let's try and get a bit of shut-eye.'

1

Sverre Fenstad is sewing. He uses the thimble to press the needle through the leather, then holds the pliers to coax the needle out before tying the thread in a tight knot, making sure the pelt covers the seam, and preparing for the next stitch. He is bent over his old desk, concentrating hard, surrounded by everything he needs: the bottles of glue and solvent, bobbins, needles, awls, small scalpels, an ashtray and a cup of coffee. He enjoys sitting like this with the smell of glue, leather and alcohol, even if his back aches and his eyes are tired from concentrating so hard. This is how a hobby should be, he reflects. A hobby should create calm, keep every other intrusion at arm's length and give you the satisfaction of mastering an activity.

He straightens his back and looks at the capercaillie on the chest of drawers. It is stretching its neck, head back, beak open, tail feathers fanned out, as if ready to lunge. You almost expect it to start strutting around. The otter, which he has attached to a tree root, seems to be smiling. The otter is playful. It is funny. Sverre is busy now with the biggest challenge he has ever faced. It is a rare pelt. A male lynx that was shot in Vassfaret more than a year ago. The hunter wants to decorate his mountain cabin with the trophy. Sverre pushes back the chair and gets up. He notices only now that the record has stopped playing. The stylus hasn't risen as it should, instead it is jumping rhythmically on the inside groove. He goes over to the record player and lifts the pick-up. Places it carefully on the support. Discovers that he hasn't closed the tube of glue. Goes back and screws the lid on. Lifts the cup. The coffee is cold. He pats his breast pocket, but the pouch of tobacco isn't there.

He can't be bothered to look for it. He stares through the basement window.

The shadows of Sognsvann Line carriages glide under the light illuminating the platform on Nordberg station. The metro train stops and stands still during the time it takes for the doors to open and close again before the row of lit windows moves on and is lost behind the trees. On the platform is the silhouette of one person. It is a man. He walks slowly down the ramp from the platform and disappears out of the light. To reappear under a lamp post in Holsteinveien. He is coming closer. The man seems to be on his way to Sverre's front gate.

Sverre listens intently.

And sure enough. He hears footsteps outside. And then the bell rings.

Sverre grips the stick leaning against the desk and hobbles slowly up to the ground floor. He continues into the hallway and opens the door.

The man on the doorstep could be around fifty. He is a head taller than Sverre. Muscular chest. He stands with his hands in the pockets of a blue poplin coat; he has a plain hat on his head. The face has deep furrows around the mouth and marked lines around the eyes.

'Sverre,' the man says. 'You've changed.'

'Do we know each other?'

'We did, once upon a time.'

At that moment the man grimaces. Sverre Fenstad angles his head at the sight of a familiar mannerism and recognises the features of the narrow head. 'Gerhard?' he says tentatively, until he is sure of himself: 'Gerhard Falkum?'

Sverre places the stick against the door frame and proffers a hand, but the man keeps his in his coat pocket.

'It's a long time since anyone called me Gerhard. Most say Gary.'

Sverre doesn't take offence. He grasps the stick and mumbles a 'come in'.

Gerhard lays his hat on the pouffe inside the door. He has black, slicked-back hair; only around his temples are there specks of grey. He unbuttons his coat, but keeps it on.

At first Sverre thinks he should pass him a coat hanger, but decides to let his guest make his own decisions. Instead he shows him into the sitting room. He is puzzled by the visit and at a loss as to know what to do; he ends up by opening the cabinet in the shelving unit. This is where he keeps his collection of brandy. Five or six bottles. He brings out the Hennessy. He takes two brandy glasses from the adjacent cabinet and pours.

With his back to his guest, he says: 'I thought you were dead.' He turns back to the guest. 'We all thought you were.' He hands him a glass.

The situation with the glasses is a little strange as the other man has kept his coat on. But Gerhard takes the glass and looks around. With his free hand he picks up a photograph from a shelf. Studies it.

'As you can see, I'm alive,' he says in a low voice, showing the photograph to his host. 'Your wife?'

Sverre takes it and nods. 'Lillian's dead. Cancer.'

'And the child?'

'A son. He's a lawyer and … a state secretary.'

'Power stays in the family?'

Sverre puts the photograph back and inhales, but doesn't answer. He doesn't like being interviewed in this way.

It is the guest who breaks the silence. 'Grandchildren?'

Sverre angles his head, enquiringly.

'Has the state secretary given you any grandchildren?'

'No, not yet. I think they're waiting.'

'So he's married?'

'He is, yes. *Skål.*'

Gerhard raises his glass, but doesn't drink.

They stand looking at each other, glasses in hand. Sverre enjoys the taste of the brandy as he tries to read his guest's eyes. Falkum just looks at him, neutral and expectant. Those bluish-grey eyes focused and unmoving.

In the end it is Sverre who resumes the conversation. 'How long has it been?'

'About twenty-five years.'

'Imagine. Twenty-five years.'

The guest nods.

'But what have you been doing all this time?'

Gerhard looks down into his drink without answering. He raises his eyes and studies Sverre with the same expectant gaze.

'Where have you been living?'

'In the States.' His pronunciation is so American that Sverre waits for him to continue. But he doesn't.

'Where in the States?'

The guest turns and takes in the room around him again.

Sverre himself looks at the room and its interior with a critical eye because it is being inspected by someone else. Some of the books in the shelving unit aren't straight and some are piled up. The landscape painting from Fåvang has dust on the frame. There is a little spider's web in the corner. The lithograph by Espolin Johnson is hard to decipher. The seat and arms of the wing chair in the corner are threadbare. The other armchair, a leather one, is facing the wrong way – at the television instead of the coffee table. Old newspapers on the table. Sverre has never been good at either decorating or tidying up.

'Minnesota.'

'So you live there? I've got family in Minnesota. Duluth.'

'I live in Minneapolis.'

Sverre smiles at the pronunciation and intonation. 'You talk like a born-and-bred American. What do you do there?'

'I have a garage.' He corrects himself: 'Gas station – petrol station.'

'But this isn't the first time you've been to Norway in all these years, is it?'

'In fact, it is. The first time.'

The gurgle of the bottle is all that can be heard as Sverre pours himself a refill. He looks at his guest's glass. It is still full. He puts down the bottle. Swirls the brandy round in his glass and watches it. At length he raises his eyes. They look at each other.

Silence is allowed to reign for some tense seconds until Sverre takes a deep breath and steels himself: 'Do you bear grudges, Gerhard?'

The other man looks down. 'Grudges? What about?'

'About how things turned out back then?'

'You're talking in riddles, Sverre.'

This time Sverre chooses his words with care. 'We heard you died in battle. That you were a gunner and were killed during a raid over Germany.' He pauses, then raises his head. 'And your remains were never found. That's the official story. But I happen to know this story was fabricated by the legation in Stockholm. I also read an unofficial report at the time. The kind of document that's burned after reading. It said you'd died in a different way.'

Gerhard eyes him frostily.

'We never questioned the reports,' says Sverre.

The other man is still silent.

'And now here you are, still alive and kicking, many years later.'

Sverre decides he has spoken for long enough.

It works. Gerhard finally clears his throat and says: 'Do I bear a grudge? I'm not sure that's the right expression.'

Sverre nods thoughtfully. Unable to find the words or an angle that could lighten the atmosphere or prompt his guest. Instead they stare at each other.

Sverre Fenstad turns the leather chair towards the coffee table and sits down. Points to the wing chair. 'Don't you want to sit down?'

Gerhard perches on the edge and looks at him.

Sverre searches for words, but gives up. And goes straight to the heart of the matter. 'What actually happened?'

'That day?'

Fenstad nods. 'The day we thought you died.'

Gerhard smiles, eyes downcast. 'That part of history stays with me, Sverre.'

Another silence.

'But you must've travelled quite a bit that year, from Sweden all the way to America.' Sverre pauses. He waits for his guest to answer. But the man looks back at him with an equally blank expression.

'While all our people assumed you were dead.'

Not even now does Gerhard open his mouth.

'And you stayed there, in America.'

Sverre looks away, composes himself and asks the question that has been on his mind the whole time. 'May I ask what brought you here?' He raises his eyes again and meets those of his guest. They are as hard as before.

'I suppose neither of us would've believed,' Gerhard says, 'that after you helped me get to the Swedish border our reunion would be so cold?'

Sverre opts to remain silent.

'Why don't you say anything?'

'What should I say? You're the one who's said this reunion is cold. I seem to remember I offered to shake hands with you.'

'You're wondering why I've come? I want to find out who killed Åse.'

Sverre takes a sip of his brandy. He doesn't know what he expected. Not this anyway.

'When she died I started a life I didn't want, but couldn't escape.'

'Are you bitter?'

'Not anymore. Not after accepting that things developed in the way they did.'

Sverre considers this answer and the period of time it covers. 'The Nazis weren't able to clear up the mystery. How are you planning to tackle it, so many years later?'

'It must've been someone she knew well. Åse would never have let a stranger in. But the police wore blinders. They'd made up their minds I was the murderer. When I left for Sweden I wasn't able to direct the police to who might've done it. So the case was never solved.'

'And do you know who did it now?'

Gerhard doesn't answer.

'A lot of years have passed.'

'So?'

'The person who killed her could be dead.'

Gerhard's mouth twitches, as if Sverre has made an involuntary witticism.

'Have you had any contact with your daughter?'

'Not yet. But that's also my reason for coming here. I don't want to burst in on her. I'd like to ask you a favour. To ask if you'd be my go-between. I'd like to have a chat with the couple who adopted her at that time. To fix it so I can meet her.'

'Erik and Grete Heggen,' Sverre says, feeling some surprise once again. Why is he asking me to do this? he thinks, and formulates another question for himself: why has the man come here at all?

Sverre continues: 'Of course I can talk to them, but I can't promise anything. You realise that, don't you?'

Gerhard fixes him with a long stare, so long that Sverre wonders if he has said something wrong.

Gerhard gets up. 'I'm staying at the Continental. The name's Gary Larson and I'll wait for a call from you there.' He goes to the door.

Sverre makes a move to accompany him.

'Don't move,' Gerhard says, stopping by the sitting-room door. He takes Sverre's walking stick from the door frame. 'Stuff has happened to you too since then,' he says. 'We all have our little secrets.'

'This is no secret,' Sverre says, sitting down again. 'I was run over.'

'Long time ago?'

'During the war.'

Gerhard's smile is chilly. 'War injury: car accident. Was the enemy involved?'

Sverre says nothing. He has no wish to prolong Gerhard's visit.

Gerhard puts the stick back, then leaves without another word.

As the front door clicks shut Sverre notices that his guest's glass is untouched.

He stares into the middle distance. When he finally moves it is to reach forwards for his guest's glass and pour the contents into his own.

2

Gerhard surveys the half-full auditorium of Saga cinema. He is sitting on his own in a box at the back of the room. It suits him to be alone, at a distance from the others. The voice of Bibi Andersson fills the room, and her face the screen. Gerhard doesn't see her. He just looks at Turid's shoulders and the back of her head. She is sitting in the third row, beside a slightly younger woman Gerhard assumes is her sister. When everyone was in the foyer, waiting to get in, he could see a likeness between the younger woman and the parents. The two sisters in the third row are doing the same as everyone else there: looking up at Bibi Andersson telling Liv Ullmann about an erotic experience. The audience is absolutely hushed. Not a single rustle of sweet papers, not a snigger, not a cough is heard, only Bibi Andersson's voice talking about when she was first married and went to the beach with a girlfriend. They sunbathed in the nude. Two small boys spied on them. Bibi Andersson talks about her excitement at the boys' desire and what she made one of the boys do to her.

Gerhard shifts his eyes to the screen. Bibi Andersson is drawing breath and Liv Ullmann's face, behind her, is blurred.

He looks for the silhouettes of the two sisters again.

The two of them exchange glances and pull a face.

Gerhard sees this, and imagining he is sitting with them, he pulls a face too, and shares a secret pleasure in listening to these words that border on insanity.

Then something seems to be happening at the front. Something he has been waiting for. Turid has turned her head and is casting a glance over her shoulder. It makes him happy that she can feel the energy coming from him; and when she turns, he smiles. He doesn't like the cinema darkness, though; doesn't like sitting here and being invisible to her. Nevertheless, he is there. He waves, even though he knows that all Turid can see is darkened heads over the rows of seats and specks of dust dancing in a yellow beam of light from the projector room above them.

When the film has finished Gerhard waits in the darkness of the box until the two women pass him on their way out. Then he weaves his way forwards until he is walking behind them. He follows them out of the cinema.

Arna asks what Turid thinks.

Turid says she isn't going to talk about what Arna wants her to talk about.

Arna grins. 'But what do you think?'

Turid says she thinks the scene with the shard of glass was terrible. 'Why's that?'

Turid says that it's the evil behind it that makes her feel nauseous.

The two women turn right towards the stairs down to Nasjonalteatret metro station. On their way they go into a kiosk. Gerhard does the same. It is packed with people. Gerhard stands behind them in the queue.

The man in front of the women has finished, and Arna steps back to let him through. She bumps into Gerhard and exclaims, 'Oh, my god.'

He stops her from falling.

'Sorry', Arna almost shouts, and the two sisters look at each other and burst into laughter.

Gerhard beams back. He is still smiling as they both buy a hot dog from the assistant in the kiosk. Turid wants only mustard on hers. Arna has both ketchup and mustard. Gerhard moves aside to let them past. He watches them as they enter the metro station. He cranes his neck and doesn't hear what the assistant says to him. A young boy in the queue behind Gerhard pushes to the front and says he wants two sausages in one roll. The assistant is polite and repeats his question to Gerhard. Does he want anything?

Gerhard doesn't hear him. He is making his way out.

Outside, on the pavement, he stops and reflects. He has seen her. But is that enough? He lifts his hand and examines his fingers. They are not trembling. Focus, he tells himself, focus. No drinking now, no self-pity. Not yet. He feels a hot jet washing through his body. It isn't enough.

3

Sverre Fenstad tells the taxi driver to wait, opens the door and climbs out. He straightens up and gazes across a chaotic building site. Between the wooden shuttering, from which reinforced-steel bars poke into the air, waiting for concrete to be poured, there is a big orange Brøyt digger working.

Sverre crosses the piles of earth, heading for the digger. He slips in the mud and uses his stick to prevent himself from falling. He stops. Looks around. Wearing a white shirt and tie under his coat, trousers with a crease in and galoshes over his black shoes, he looks out of place. He carries on. The stick is muddy now. The digger has a set of two metal wheels under one part and a set of smaller rubber wheels under the other. The engine is mounted in a huge box behind the driver's cab, and is the same size. The bucket has teeth that at first seem to claw at the ground – apparently without meeting any resistance – before they tear up a massive rock and a tree stump, which vainly clings to the soil by its white roots. These are snapped like rotten twine and disappear in the mass of earth in the bucket, which rotates on its own axis and despatches the contents, with a noise like a thunderclap, onto the back of a Magirus Deutz truck, which sways under the weight of rocks and earth and tree stumps.

Sverre Fenstad stands watching the machine at work. When the lorry is full the digger driver signals to the man in the lorry. The engine roars into life and the lorry departs.

Sverre waves to the man in the digger cab. The machine stops. The cab door opens.

Erik Heggen jumps out. He is wearing a red-checked flannel shirt, grey work pants and high boots.

'Fenstad?' he shouts. 'Damned if it isn't you. How long has it been?'

'Much too long, Erik.'

They shake hands heartily. Erik's hair is thinning. His shirt is only half buttoned up and his boots are grey with caked mud.

Erik smiles. 'I know where you've been. Not exactly my circles though.'

Sverre smiles back.

They stand side by side, surveying the site.

Erik takes a yellow packet of chewing gum from his breast pocket. Juicy Fruit. Peels off the paper with coarse fingers.

He offers the packet to Sverre, who declines. Instead Sverre takes out a red-and-grey pouch of tobacco. Asbjørnsen's mix. 'What's it going to be here?'

'Housing blocks,' Erik says, folding the flat stick of chewing gum and putting it into his mouth. 'High rises, the kind where folk live in tiny boxes and chuck their rubbish down a chute.'

Sverre licks the glue on the cigarette paper and looks around. Some distance away a cement lorry pumps its load into the jagged shuttering. In their line of vision there are walls of yellow wooden shutters and reinforced steel mesh. 'Take a few years, won't it?

'Nah, it's quick, this is.' Erik smiles and chews. He waves to a lorry driver, who waves back.

Sverre takes a lighter from his pocket and puffs life into his roll-up. He blows some smoke through his nose and has to shout over the racket made by a passing lorry. 'I'm always impressed by building sites like this. By what is possible. By what hard work…' He lowers his voice as the engine noise stops. 'What hard work produces in terms of houses, roads, schools, shops and so on. It must be good to be part of this. Forming the landscape, seeing the forest and fields turn into town.'

Erik nods. 'We're born with it,' he says. 'Just watch kids in the sandpit. They're lost in their own worlds as soon as they flatten out a road between two mounds of sand.' His lips part in a wry smile, then he blows a bubble with the chewing gum.

Silence reigns. The man in work clothes waits to hear the reason for the visit, and the man in office clothing struggles to find the words to explain.

'Actually this visit is to do with your daughter, Turid.'

'What about her?'

Sverre points to a metal wheel that has no muck or soil on. 'Perhaps you'd like to sit down, Erik.'

'Why?'

'You adopted her in 1943, didn't you?'

'Forty-four. When her grandmother died and it was clear Gerhard Falkum had been shot down over Germany.'

'That's the point, Erik. Turns out Falkum's alive.'

Erik looks at him without speaking. His eyes look not so much shocked as distant.

'He's here in Oslo and wants to meet his daughter.'

Slowly Erik's shoulders droop and he sits down on the metal wheel. His jaws churn. He swallows. 'Well, I'm damned,' he says softly.

Sverre remains quiet. He has said the same several times to himself.

'In Oslo? Where in Oslo?'

'He's staying at a hotel. I've spoken to him. It's Gerhard alright. No doubt about it.'

Erik chews thoughtfully. Blows a bubble, which bursts.

Sverre clears his throat.

Erik looks up. 'Yes?'

'Does Turid know the Nazis suspected Gerhard of killing Åse?'

Erik shakes his head. 'It was bad enough losing her mother. The story we told her about Gerhard Falkum is that he had to escape to Sweden long before Åse was killed.'

Sverre gazes at the machines working. A tipper truck on its way down a slope is tilting so far over it looks as if it is going to topple.

'Then he died in battle.'

The truck straightens up and trundles along on an even keel across the ridge.

'Anyway, some parts of that story will have to be rewritten now.' Erik gets up. 'But do you think he could've done it?'

'Done what?' Sverre takes the roll-up from his mouth and glares at the end of it. He flicks off the ash and takes another puff.

'Do you think Gerhard killed her?'

Sverre shakes his head.

Erik looks away. Sverre follows his gaze. A lorry is climbing the mound of earth. The back and the cab are rocking from side to side, as if it were a toy being pushed by a rough, invisible hand.

'I think he did,' Erik says, clambering back into his cab.

Sverre smiles patronisingly. 'You think he killed the mother of his own child?'

Erik grasps the ignition switch with his right hand and looks through the steel frame that constitutes the machine's windscreen, lost in a distant memory.

'While their baby was in the flat? And then he left her there with the corpse?'

'Who else could it have been?'

'Gerhard thinks he knows who it was. At least that was how it seemed.'

Erik sends him a morose look.

Sverre shrugs. 'Our theory at the time was that it must've been a German officer or some high-ranking Norwegian Nazi. Someone she knew, more or less. He brought some goodies for a woman who barely owned a button in the world. Perhaps he went there because he suspected her or Gerhard.' Sverre flicks the half-smoked roll-up into a ditch. He has to shout to be heard over the din of an approaching lorry. 'Or he was just drooling over her,' he shouts. 'Åse was quite a looker. Everyone could see that. That night she was on her own. Which means he could do as he pleased. Once inside the door he headed for the bedroom. Afterwards he killed her to hide the crime. The police were blinkered in their search for Gerhard so the real murderer couldn't be caught – they never looked for him.'

The last words are drowned in the roar of the digger starting up. Erik holds both hands on the levers. Sverre Fenstad almost has to jump clear as the bucket swings towards him. The two of them exchange glances. Erik waves and is once again concentrated on his work.

Stockholm, December 1942

1

The typewriter roller grips the paper. She twists it until a white strip is visible above the keys. It is crooked. She straightens the paper and takes out the cards with the names on and starts typing. She hears footsteps on the stairs. She recognises them. It is Markus with the post. Ester can visualise him – in his uniform with the Norwegian flag on his sleeve. The short hair and the pointed nose; the angular body and the legs that bound up the stairs in long strides. She likes Markus. The door opens.

The first thing he says is: 'Hi, Ester.'

'Hi,' she says, looking up as her right hand bangs the roller back to start a new line and her fingers find the rhythm once again.

'How do you do that?' he asks from somewhere behind her.

She stops tapping. 'I went on a course once. Besides, it helps if you can play the piano.' She regrets her response immediately. Markus comes from the East End of Oslo and probably thinks playing the piano is snobbish. He has played centre-forward for Dæhlenengen and can reel off *ad nauseam* the results of the AIF league 1939 season.

The dismissive comment about playing the piano fails to materialise. 'Can you read music?'

She swivels round on her chair and looks at him.

He is holding out a letter.

The handwriting is unmistakeable. Ester snatches the letter and turns it over. No doubt about it. The envelope has been opened.

Censorship, she thinks, and is annoyed. Someone already knows what her mother wants to say to her. They have weighed up and assessed the contents and graciously allowed it through. Ester has strong opinions about this. She can – at a pinch – understand how people can join the far-right Nasjonal Samling party and make themselves believe the arguments of Quisling, Irgens, Riisnæs, Meidell and whatever they are called, but opening other people's letters … That is dirty.

She forces herself to stay calm. On the one hand, it is reassuring to receive letters. Simply holding one in your hands takes a burden from your shoulders and dampens any fears that the rumours are true. However, she still dreads reading the letter. She dreads bad news. And she doesn't want to share it with anyone. She wants to react to it alone. She puts it down and pulls her chair in to continue doing her work.

Ester types away doggedly, hardly aware now which keys her fingers are striking. After a while she looks up and finds Markus watching her with both hands in his pockets.

'Anything I can do for you?'

'Well, look at *him*!'

Mildred appears from behind them, tickles Markus with both her hands and asks him if he thinks he is allowed to have favourites in the office.

Ester grasps the opportunity, takes the letter, wriggles past them and into the little snack room. Closes the door. Sits down. Rips open the envelope with a tremulous forefinger. Unfolds the sheet of paper and looks at the date. It is more than three weeks old. But old news is better than no news.

Dear Ester,

I'm told that your journey went well. That was so good to hear. We have been worried about you. Mostly, though, I am happy you have got away. It gives me some peace of mind to know you are in a safe place and can move around without being frightened, without being noticed or feeling in other ways that you are valued less than the rest. I am sure you have written to us, but now the situation is such that hardly any post gets through. It is safest to send news via friends.

Things here have taken a turn for the worse. The flat and our possessions have been confiscated and we, Gran and I, have to report to the police. It is humiliating, but still better than being in prison, as Dad has been for three weeks. Night after night Gran and I have discussed what to do, weighed up the pros and cons, but we have decided to wait before we follow you. Gran isn't sure that she could manage the trip now it is getting colder and winter is approaching. It is no joke covering large distances at her age. She and I are living with fru Gleichmann in Tøberg now. Her husband has also been arrested. Dad and Gleichmann are both in Berg Prison, outside the town. Here in Tønsberg we have each other, and I hope I will have the chance to visit Dad soon.

   My dearest daughter, you have always been capable, strong, proud and intelligent. I am sure someone in Stockholm will find a use for you, a job. I am…

That is all there is. The second sheet is missing. They have removed it!

Ester takes all of this in. Whether it is the censorship or the content of the letter she was allowed to see that increases the pressure behind her eyes she cannot say. What is important is that all three of them are alive.

Eventually she gets up and examines her face in the mirror above the washbasin. Washes. Blows her nose. Blinks. Her eyes are still red around the edges. Nothing she can do about that. She takes a deep breath. Opens the door and walks past the other girls. Markus has gone, fortunately. She looks down. Sits at her desk. Someone coughs. Ester looks up.

2

Torgersen is standing in the doorway to his office. He says he has to talk to her. He ignores the others in the outer room, all of whom are following the conversation with interest. He coughs again. 'Privately.'

Ester stands up. Follows her boss into his office.

Torgersen resumes his place behind the desk. He is the kind of man who is always correctly dressed – in a dark suit with a waistcoat, a watch chain over his stomach. He is in his late fifties. He has short grey hair, a sensitive mouth and round frameless glasses. The eyes behind the lenses are blue and cold.

'Ester, I need to ask you a different type of favour today.'

Ester waits quietly.

'A job. It might take you a little beyond your working hours.'

As if that matters, she thinks, and says: 'That's fine. I haven't got anything else to do.'

'There's a resistance man I understand you know: Gerhard Falkum.'

Surprised, she looks up. She nods.

'Falkum's come to the refugee centre in Södermanland.'

Ester sinks down onto Torgersen's soft visitor's chair while he tells her what he has been told by his contacts in the Swedish police. 'They – the police, that is – want to remove him from the centre and question him here in Stockholm.'

'But why?'

'He's wanted by the Norwegian police.'

'There are lots of Norwegians here who are.'

'This is a bit different. Kripo in Oslo suspect him of murder.'

'What!'

'A civilian. A woman. Murdered.'

'Gerhard? I don't believe that.'

'It's a complicated case, Ester. This might be Nazi provocation. We don't know much. Barely anything; and that's highly problematic because Falkum's an important person for us. He's trusted.'

'But who's the dead woman?'

'Her name's Åse Lajord.'

Ester gasps. 'I know Åse. I know her well. I mean, I knew her...' She whispers the last words.

'My sympathies, Ester. I'm sorry to be the bearer of bad news. But I didn't know.'

'Of course not.'

Ester struggles to believe what she has heard and has the same sinking feeling she had when she was reading her mother's letter. She has to force herself to straighten up, to be present.

'As this concerns a serious crime – the murder of a civilian – no one can know how the Swedish authorities will react. I presume there's little to fear. But you can never be totally sure. Falkum's a highly trusted man with a great knowledge of resistance work in Norway, especially about how Milorg is organised. The last thing the legation here wants is a situation where extradition to Norway becomes an issue.' Torgersen leans back in his chair and closes his eyes as if searching for the right words.

'The reason I'm asking you this favour is that you know Falkum. I'd like you to go to the refugee centre and bring him back to Stockholm before the Swedish police can react. I think I've managed to delay any reaction from the police, but for no more than a day or two.'

Torgersen fidgets restlessly with the edge of the desk. 'The way I see it is that Falkum's a capable sort. The challenge is to get him to be a team player.'

She nods.

'I've organised a car and a driver. Go there. Use us, the office, to gain access. Sort out the practical details with the driver. We have to make an attempt, and this is the best we can do, the situation being what it is.'

Ester nods again and takes a deep breath. 'When do you want me to go?'

'Can you travel now, as quickly as possible?'

She nods again.

'Then there are a couple of items here.' He rummages through a desk drawer. Hands her a passport and a little box. '*Le bon dieu* is in the detail, as Flaubert once said.'

3

The dark shadows of trees flicker past. The frost has left a layer of rime on the fields and ice across the water. Ester is sitting on the back seat of a Ford, which is moving at a considerable speed. The driver is in his forties. A taciturn man. Twice she has tried to initiate conversation, but with no response, other than a cool look in the mirror. He doesn't like this situation, she thinks. He doesn't trust me. He thinks I am small fry, too young, inexperienced and stupid. Besides, I am a woman. He thinks this is irresponsible.

On the other hand, he may appreciate silence. It is good not to have to talk when your mind is circling around the incomprehensible. It is one thing to tell yourself this is the way things are now. But to visualise it? Åse was strong; she believed in herself, lived with a man she loved without being married to him, bore and gave birth to a child at a time of occupation, insecurity and shortages. Ester admired her courage, will power – her refusal to let others govern her life; her refusal to let life stop. The Germans may have taken control of Norway, but they never controlled her. A sudden memory flashes in front of her: her and Åse hanging over the fence of the pig pen and feeding their sow with chickweed, and the pig that attacked them when there was nothing left to eat. The hysterical panic when Åse lifted her by the legs and she almost fell into the pig pen. How old were they then? Eleven? Twelve?

Then she remembers their embrace when she was keen to get away and deliver the newspapers. Ester closes her eyes. Now she can't see Åse anymore, only dad's fingers on the bars of the police van. She is back in the confusion and shock of waking up in the darkness, as mum leans over her in bed. Torn from her sleep, she hears harsh voices behind her mother as she whispers: *The police are here. They say they're going to arrest Dad. Hurry to the shop and tell them what's going on.*

Ester wrings her hands in her lap as the old panic sets in. What if the rumours are true? What if it is the same with her parents as it was with Åse – that they never meet again?

She tells herself she has to concentrate on things it is possible to do something about. Gerhard is her concern now. Immediately an unease creeps in again. What has happened to the child? Could he really have left his daughter – a daughter now without a mother – in Norway? But if there are two of them, how will she get them out of the camp unobserved?

She takes a deep breath to try and compose herself and earns another look in the mirror from the driver.

The sun is low and shines from behind tall tree trunks with next to no undergrowth – pine trees: elegant skirts against the sky. She recognises this countryside and realises they are getting close.

The driver stops twenty to thirty metres from the gate. Finally he opens his mouth. He speaks facing the windscreen. 'You'd better get out here. Think that's the best.' Then he turns and looks at her, silent and expectant. Ester realises he is waiting for what she has to say.

'Behind the sports ground,' she says.

He nods.

'But it might well take time.'

His cool expression softens. 'Time is something we have enough of.'

She opens the door. Quickly collects her papers. Shuts the door, but hesitates when she sees a movement ahead.

The driver rolls down the window. He winks at her. 'She who wants to reach the source has to swim against the current,' he says. 'You'll do just fine.' He winks again.

Ester puts on a weak smile, then fills her lungs with air and starts walking.

4

The camp manager is a friendly man in his sixties. He wears a wig, she notices. Because her focus is now on him, she supposes. The last time she was here the focus was on everything else around her. She tries not to stare at the brown toupee balanced on his pate like a slightly too-small beret. He has grey sideburns and white stubble. But he is polite and says he remembers her. She doesn't believe that for a moment. Ester tells him she has come on behalf of Torgersen. And it seems that, unwittingly, she has used the magic word – as soon as she mentions the name Torgersen the manager is all ears. She takes out a piece of paper and a pencil. Tells him that Torgersen is writing a report for the legation. With this in mind she would like to interview a random selection of Norwegian refugees about their experience of the situation. 'It won't take long,' she assures him.

'Take all the time you need.' The manager is kindness itself. Could he read the report when it is finished? Naturally.

She walks slowly along the path following a stream of people drifting towards the building that constitutes the central hub of the place. They are independent here. Most have community duties. And new refugees keep arriving from across the border.

She waits until she is certain everyone has gone into the refectory. Then she walks to the door, enters and stands on the platform inside, surveying the assembled crowd. Meat soup is on the menu. The women in white aprons ladle it from big pots into bowls. At the long tables they sit close together, line upon line of men and women eating.

From where she is standing she can be seen by everyone in the room. She has chosen this position intentionally. She lets her eyes wander from table to table and finally sees him watching her. He is sitting almost at the back, by the wall. His spoon hand hovers over his bowl. After exchanging looks he puts down the spoon.

She beckons and goes outside.

She moves away from the building, and walks over to the tall elm tree she always liked to be near when she herself was staying here. She takes off a glove and feels the bark, looks up at the gallimaufry of black branches – thick tapering lines that at the very top are like a spider's web. She is dreading meeting Gerhard, but can feel her body calming down, here under the tree. She turns only when she hears his footsteps on the gravel.

They look at each other without saying a word. In the end she takes two steps forwards and hugs him.

His body is as stiff as a poker.

She backs away and has to blink tears from her eyes. 'I was rather dreading seeing you again.' She could now say it's *nice* to see him again, but she refrains. Silence is eloquent enough. It is a good silence.

He asks if she has heard about Åse.

She nods and moves towards the bench beneath the tree.

They sit down.

'You were one of the people she loved most,' he says.

She has nothing to say in response.

'Perhaps the person she loved most of all,' he says.

Her daughter, Turid, she thinks. And she loved you, Gerhard, and her mother. But Ester is frightened her voice will fail her if she says what she thinks.

'She's supposed to have been suffocated,' he says. 'That's all I've heard. But no one knows if there was a break-in or an assault, or if it was the work of a nutter.'

She knows there is more to come and she has to be patient.

He swallows. A lock of hair falls over his forehead. He looks away and runs a hand through his hair.

He tells her that the police were in his flat when he arrived. He had been away for a few days, and he went up the stairs in the same way as he left, with a rucksack on his back. He stopped in his tracks when he saw a Gestapo man in the doorway of his flat. He turned and fled. After all, he had a gun in his rucksack. What he found out afterwards was that someone had paid a call on Åse, someone with rarely seen items from abroad – cigarettes and whisky.

Ester stares into the air and tries to imagine it. Nosy neighbours in the block, men in uniforms. And Åse lying there naked while they tramp around her, talking in strident voices.

Ester becomes aware of a movement on a branch above her head. It is a blue tit. She watches.

Gerhard rubs his hands on his thighs. 'The police would probably have come to their senses if they hadn't found one of my guns in the flat. Then they dug deeper and found my name on a register of people who volunteered for the International Brigade in Spain. Since then they've used the investigation to round up all the Milorg resistance people who came to our flat. I became a wanted man. They stuck posters of me on lamp posts all over the place. That set the informers off. So Sweden was the only solution.'

Ester remembers the moment when the little girl gave a toothless smile, kicked her little feet and gripped her fingers. She manages to say without her voice breaking:

'What's happening with Turid?'

He tells her that Åse's mother is taking care of her. 'So I know she's fine. In the country. Apparently a young mother living nearby has a lot of milk and is breastfeeding our little one too.' He averts his eyes.

All that can be heard is the fluttering of the blue tit as it moves between branches. Then a door shuts in one of the barracks. A man comes out onto the doorstep, lights up a pipe and says something to a figure standing behind an open window.

Ester can't get the image of the little child out of her head. She is there again, in the bathroom – Turid kicking her legs happily and the silence outside the door where Åse and Gerhard whisper words they don't want her to hear.

'You're the priority now,' she says. 'The police here are after you. You're not safe in this camp.'

A woman carries a pile of bed linen along the footpath between the barracks. The man holding the pipe calls to her.

'The resistance committee in Stockholm has decided to give you a new identity. I have a car here. You and I have to travel back to Stockholm. We have to go now.'

He straightens up and eyes her attentively. 'I can see you have a plan.'

'The sports ground,' she says. 'Behind the stand. A car will be waiting there. In an hour from now.' She checks her watch and looks at him.

Ester sees surprise in his eyes. 'Coming?' she asks.

He smiles weakly. 'I'm coming, boss.'

'The driver will wait for you. Do as he says.'

He nods.

'Don't ask questions. Just do as he says.'

He nods again.

'Did you give them your real name?'

He nods once again, and with the same incredulous expression.

She burrows in her bag. Hands him the passport. 'From now on your name's Geir Larsen.'

He opens the passport and sees a photograph of himself. 'How on earth did you get this?'

'The photo was taken here,' she says without expatiating. She doesn't know who their contact in the office is or how the photograph found its way into the passport.

'If you can't get there unseen, you'll have to insist from now on that your real name is Geir Larsen – to everyone here too. Does anyone know you as Gerhard?'

He shrugs. 'Only those in my hut.'

'As I said, if you can't get there unseen...'

'I'll get there.'

'If not, you'll have to get everyone in the hut to keep mum regarding your name. Show them your passport. Your name's Geir Larsen.'

'They've registered me.' He nods towards the admin building.

'They might've had a file on Gerhard Falkum there, but not any longer.'

Again he is amazed.

'You came to Sweden to be reunited with your wife,' she tells him.

'Oh, yes? And who's that?'

'Me. Hilde Larsen.'

'We haven't got rings.'

Ester burrows in her bag again. 'I have a boss who thinks of every-thing.' In her hand are two rings. 'Take one in case we need them.'

She gets up. 'In an hour then. Go and finish eating.'

5

Her visit to the camp has to be justified, so she has conversations with a handful of residents. Afterwards she chats to the manager, who has taken a keen interest in the report. He has a number of suggestions for various areas; he links his hands behind his back and rounds off every sentence by thrusting his chin into the air. She catches herself watching the toupee. It remains in place, and stays there while he accompanies her all the way down to the gate. Here she thanks him and says he has been too kind. He pats her on the shoulder and says it has been a pleasure. She emphasises, on behalf of her employer, how important it is to continue the good work, keeping refugees active, playing sport. He agrees wholeheartedly and says he has plans for a championship. International games. Ester applauds his ideas and promises to mention them to Torgersen. She says she will write up what she has experienced and will perhaps return to correct anything that might be unclear. He says she is welcome to visit again whenever she chooses.

As she approaches the car she becomes nervous; she can only see the driver's silhouette. She gets into the back. The driver starts up.

'So it didn't work?'

The driver shakes his head.

'You mean it *did* go well?'

He turns his head. The blue eyes tell her nothing. The man is from Østfold, that is all she knows. 'So-so.'

They drive in silence for five long minutes before the driver pulls over, stops, gets out and opens the boot.

Gerhard clambers out. His hair is dishevelled and he is carrying a rucksack.

She wriggles over to the other side of the car.

The driver says he could have left the rucksack in the boot.

Gerhard gets in and runs a hand through his hair. 'It was a bit cramped,' is all he says by way of an answer. Then he laughs and looks at her. She smiles back.

The driver starts up again. Gerhard shouts. 'Thank you!'

The driver shrugs without turning.

She assumes it is the driver's presence that makes conversation feel forced. She hasn't got that much to say either. She is staying in a flat, alone for the time being. The idea is that she will share with two other women. They haven't moved in yet. She doesn't know what plans Torgersen has for Gerhard, but the legation has some accommodation at its disposal. He soon stops asking questions.

The driver pulls in to the roadside and stops. He gets out and bangs around. He pulls down a sack of firewood from the roof rack. Then puts wood in the generator. Gerhard rolls down the window and asks if he needs any help. The driver says no, thanks, he is fine. Gerhard draws the fresh air into his lungs. Says Sweden smells of freedom.

She laughs at the association. They exchange glances, and he bursts into laughter too. His dark face opens, his smile reveals a line of white teeth. The smile turns him into a very good-looking man, and she understands why Åse fell in love with him. But the laughter she has released carries a weary capitulation with it. She can't stop the sobs. Tears begin to roll. She hides her face and glances at him, and as they exchange looks again, they both burst into laughter. The door at the front opens. The driver gets in. She meets his cold gaze in the mirror. The laughter dies and she leans back with closed eyes, composes herself and tries to breathe normally.

Night is falling. They drive more slowly now because of the traffic. She sits with her eyes closed. She is glad the job is over and feels calmer than she has for months. As she dozes, her thoughts turn to Åse, and Ester sees, perhaps for the first time, how absurd this situation is. Åse drinking with a stranger. Åse being attacked and killed. Something is utterly wrong. When did the cosy atmosphere turn into violence? Was it something she said, something she did?

Ester opens her eyes and looks at Gerhard.

He feels her gaze. 'What's the matter?'

Ester says nothing and closes her eyes again. Keeps them closed. The monotonous drone of the engine lulls her to sleep.

When she wakes up and looks out, she recognises the contours of the treetops in Gustav Adolf Park. At last the car comes to a halt outside the girls' school in Banérgatan.

Ester and Gerhard wait on the pavement until the driver has left. She crosses the street, indicates the way into the corner block where the legation resides and walks ahead, up the stairs.

The outer room is quiet. But there is still a light in Torgersen's office. That is when a voice says: 'Ester.'

It is Markus.

He is sitting in Mildred's place, looking up from a book he is reading in the light from the street lamp outside.

She walks over to him.

His smile is strained. He looks over her shoulder at Gerhard.

'Wondered if you'd like to go to the cinema with me.'

A part of Ester is still in Oslo, with Åse, the baby and Gerhard. She looks at Markus, but says nothing.

'Later,' he says with a blush.

Ester sees and wants to help him. 'I'll think about it,' she says. Confused, she catches herself again. 'Of course I'd like to go.'

She can feel Gerhard watching them.

Ester walks to Torgersen's door. Knocks.

She hears a curt 'Yes?' from inside.

Opens the door and sticks her head in. 'He's here.'

Torgersen's desk is, as always, covered with papers and memos. He looks up. 'Tell him to come in, Ester.'

She glances back at Gerhard, and beckons him in, holding the door open.

She turns to go back to her desk.

'You come in too, Ester,' Torgersen says.

They both go inside.

Torgersen and Gerhard Falkum shake hands. 'This is unusual, Falkum. You've come to Sweden as a refugee, but you're not safe yet. I'm the first to regret this situation.' He stands, thinking. 'Wouldn't you like to sit down?'

Gerhard chooses one of the wooden chairs.

Torgersen says they are going to try to have Falkum transported to England or Scotland. But no one knows when. Falkum has to be patient. In the meantime he has to stay undercover. He will live under his new name, Geir Larsen, and Ester will escort him to a little bedsit, which he will have at his disposal until further notice.

Gerhard thanks him.

Torgersen scribbles down an address on a slip of paper and passes it, plus a key, to Ester.

'The driver,' she says. 'He's gone.'

'Markus is here. He can drive you,' Torgersen says.

6

Ester watches Torgersen strolling slowly to the crossroads. He doesn't have far to go. He lives in Karlevägen, only a few blocks from the legation office. He walks with his head bowed and his coat almost dragging along the ground. He looks old when he walks like this, crazy in a way.

'So that was that,' Gerhard says.

She turns to him.

'Free, yet not free.' The cheery spirits of the car ride have dissipated now.

'It'll sort itself out, I'm sure.'

Gerhard doesn't answer.

The silence weighs on them. And again she is struck by this energy field between them: in the car her total surrender to laughter, and now these massive quivering vibrations that are stifling any attempt to make conversation.

Then, in the light from the street lamp, she spots some flakes. She throws up her arms. A snow crystal lands on her mitten. 'Look,' she erupts with joy, 'It's snowing!'

He shakes his head at this childish outburst, but can't help smiling.

He is lit up suddenly by a pair of headlights. It is Markus with the car. He stops in front of them.

'There he is,' she says.

Markus jumps out and gallantly opens the door for Ester. He bows theatrically. Gerhard gets in on the other side.

Ester and Gerhard sit side by side at the back. The oppressive silence re-establishes itself. Ester sinks back in her corner, looking out at the traffic and thinking about the people she misses. The next moment she is struck by pangs of conscience. She can see her father in front of her. Unshaven, hungry. Is he cold at night? Do they beat him? And when she thinks along these lines, she understands why her mother and grandmother don't want to travel. Her feelings of guilt – at being the one who escaped, the one who left them behind, grow. Ester knows it is wrong to think like this, but she can't stop herself. With half an ear she hears Gerhard ask Markus why he fled to Sweden.

Markus meets his eyes in the mirror. He says: 'I'd prefer not to talk about it.'

Ester wonders whether the kind of answer Markus just gave is right, whether it is better to keep personal thoughts and emotions to yourself.

The snowflakes blowing across the pavements are like wisps of dust. She closes her eyes and can see Åse's face. She thinks about when Åse went to Syversen's plant nursery with food and clothes. It must have been difficult for her, not only doing without these items, but also managing the pram all the way there. Everyone at Carl Frederiksen's Transport was terrified of being exposed by the Nazis. That was under-standable. Rolf Pettersen and the organisation had been driving refugees over the border to Sweden for a long time. They figured they would be caught sooner or later. A young woman like Åse coming and asking after a friend in hiding could easily have been an enemy. Ester's assur-ances that she was no threat made no difference. No one else but Alf Syversen was allowed to go out and talk to Åse waiting on the bench.

'They've got everything here in Sweden, haven't they.' It's Gerhard's voice again.

'Quite a bit, anyway,' Ester says. She looks through the window. Tries as best she can to answer without revealing her emotional state. 'There's rationing here too.'

Gerhard says he wants to go to the cinema. 'Shall we go to the cinema, Ester?'

We, she thinks, and looks at Markus's neck. He has his eyes on the road and both hands on the wheel.

'Of course,' she says and catches herself. 'We'll have to see. You have to keep a low profile.' And she thinks, now he has me saying it. *We*. That was quick.

Markus brakes and slows down, looking through the side window. 'This is Kammakargatan,' he says. 'And this is number thirty-three.' He stops.

Gerhard sits, looking out, then opens the door.

On the pavement Markus goes to carry Gerhard's rucksack. He shakes his head and snatches it from him. 'I can manage it myself.'

Ester is waiting at the door. She opens it and leads the way inside.

On the ground floor there are names on both the doors to flats. She carries on up to the next floor, annoyed with herself that she forgot to ask Torgersen which flat to go to when she got the key. On this floor there are three doors. The first two have nameplates screwed on between the door panels. The third door has a slip of paper pinned to it. *Larsen*.

She unlocks the door. Lets him go in first. He brushes past her.

Again she is aware of the effect he has on her and steps back a pace to breathe more freely. She hands him the key. 'You'll be fine here.'

Meaningless words, she thinks. I wouldn't be fine here, with bare walls and a hard single bed in the corner. The room was like a prison cell.

A zinc bucket sits on the floor, full of coke. 'There's supposed to be more in the cellar.' She nods towards the bucket, feels the stove, which is cold, and goes to the cupboard in the kitchenette. Sees some tins on the shelves. 'And there's some food here.'

He mumbles a response. Stands by the window and looks out. She goes over to him. Digs in a pocket. 'I almost forgot this.' She holds out a handful of notes. 'Money for bread and so on. I'll have more with me next time.' She thinks: Next time? But there will of course have to be a next time, and it could equally well be her as anyone else.

He pushes her hand away. 'Money is the only thing I have enough of, Ester.'

She puts the notes back in her pocket. Then extends her hand again. 'Ration vouchers,' she says. 'No one can have enough of them.'

He accepts the pile and stuffs them in his pocket.

'When will we see each other again?'

She doesn't know. But feels she has to give an answer. 'In a few days?' She heads for the door.

'Ester!'

She turns.

He is leaning against the wall. Flat stomach, dark, narrow, unshaven face, but good-looking. Black, tousled hair falling over his forehead. Ester understands what Åse fell for.

'Thank you for all your help.'

She looks down.

'It's good to see you again,' he says.

'Good to see you too, Gerhard.'

She lets herself out. Again thinking about Åse as she jogs down the stairs.

On the pavement, she glances up and sees him in the window. She waves.

A movement from above. He waves back.

Markus gallantly opens the door for her again. This time she sits at the front, beside him.

7

Rocky Sullivan is on death row. The priest is begging him. He can still save the poor children from disaster.

Ester is gripped. She is begging him too: *Do it, Rocky, do it! Pleeease!*

You could hear a pin drop in the cinema auditorium. A moment of terror for the audience quivers in the air. Rocky Sullivan leaves; he marches to the place of execution. Passing the terrible electric cables. His face is in focus – it is still evil. The priest reads some holy words over the doomed man.

Ester can't bear to watch. She puts her hands over her eyes. As she peers between her fingers, the priest looks down. Ester grasps Markus's hand and squeezes it without realising how much pressure she exerts. Again she closes her eyes and hopes it is soon over. Markus lets her squeeze without saying a word.

Ester sits back exhausted. 'What an awful story. And it isn't even about wartime!'

People around them start getting up.

'He speaks Yiddish,' Markus says.

'Who does?'

'Cagney. The actor. I've seen a film in which he speaks Yiddish.'

'Is he a Jew?'

Markus shrugs. 'Don't think so.'

When they come out of the Park-Teater it is cold, but still not very late. She doesn't feel like going home at once. They stroll back to the car, along Sturegatan, by the park, and turn into Humlagårdsgatan. Markus stops outside a café. It is full of people and the laughter, and loud voices carry into the street every time the door jingles. He looks at her quizzically and she says: 'Yes, it's nice here.' They go up the steps and inside. At the back, by the wall, there is a table for two free.

The room is chilly and she keeps her jacket on.

He wants to treat her and goes to the counter. Returns with two cream buns and two cups of coffee on a tray. He is excited that they sell genuine coffee, and she hasn't the heart to tell him she doesn't like it.

He asks her what she would most like to do while she is here.

'In Sweden, that is,' he adds.

'Go to a restaurant and dance,' she says.

He licks cream from the corner of his mouth and looks at her. She considers her answer childish. Sometimes, with Markus, she feels stupid. Or perhaps not stupid; immature, rather, she thinks, and feels a need to explain what she has said. 'Not necessarily to dance but to really feel I'm normal, that it's possible to live a perfectly ordinary life, like everyone else.'

He nods. 'Berns,' he says.

'What's Berns?'

'Let's do that when we have enough money. Go dancing at Berns.'

'Deal.'

'But apart from dancing?'

She looks down, thinking he is adapting down to her the way she is adapting up to him. But the question isn't easy to answer. She hasn't spent much time dreaming, not for quite a while. But she thinks she has to say something. She says she would like to drive a car, like him.

'I can teach you.' Markus tells her he learned to drive in his father's Ford. But it was his uncle who taught him. 'My dad can't drive. They say that if he's going to they'll have to clear all the rocks, people and lamp posts from the road. He hits everything he shouldn't. He's like a magnet.'

She imagines a car attracting other cars.

'And that wasn't very practical where we lived.'

'Where is he now?'

Markus looks away at first, then he meets her gaze. 'Do you believe the rumours?'

It is her turn to look away. She watches the people at the neighbouring table. A woman bursts into laughter at something a man says. He chews on his pipe stem and continues talking with the pipe clamped between his teeth, and she laughs even louder. Ester says she isn't in the mood to talk about rumours. 'No rumours,' she repeats.

They sit without speaking, and when the buzz of voices and laughter rises in the room, she feels that she and Markus are the only ones who don't fit in here and that they never will.

He asks if she goes to synagogue.

She shakes her head.

'I never used to either. Before.'

'But you do now?'

He nods.

'Why do you go now?'

'I want to understand.'

They exchange glances, and it is there again – the sense of shared experience. She doesn't need to ask him what it is he wants to understand, and says: 'Do you think it's possible?'

'I do,' he smiles with embarrassment. 'I believe that if there's something I don't understand myself, I have only God to rely on. I have to rely on someone.'

She looks down and sees her grandmother's heavy earnestness in this belief. Ester has always connected religion with a heaviness. But now almost everything's different. She thinks that feeling you can control your own life is a form of self-deception. There are outside forces that keep subjecting you to new tests, whether it is war or escape or…

But does that mean Markus is right? She doesn't know and prefers not to commit to one side or the other. In a way it seems too simple to leave wonder, mystery and doubt to what Markus calls God.

He looks at her. 'What do you think about hope, Ester?'

She doesn't understand what he means.

'It's a feeling, isn't it. A feeling one has from time to time, but only from time to time.'

She nods. 'That's one way of putting it.'

'Hope exists,' Markus says, warming to the topic. 'It's very specific. It's in the synagogue. Hope is with God.'

She is thinking that the fellowship she shares with Markus has its limits, too. But this doesn't upset her. She likes to discover these things.

People are scurrying this way and that past the windows. She lifts her cup and holds it with both hands. It warms them. 'Coffee's good for something then,' she says, and smiles to him across the table.

1

Sverre Fenstad is at work before anyone else, as usual. He unlocks the door, holding the morning edition of *Aftenposten* under his arm. He has read the newspaper on the tram so he puts it on Pia's desk in reception. The building is utterly still. He continues into his office, and switches on the lights as he moves through the room. The first thing he does when he sits behind his desk is to go through the appointments book for the day and the rest of the week, then he looks at his paperwork, putting aside everything that can wait.

Half an hour later he hears Pia letting herself in. As usual, she arrives half an hour later than him and a quarter of an hour before the others. He hears her moving around in the kitchenette, making coffee. When it is finally quiet he presses a button on the intercom and says: 'Fru Moløkken.'

'Coming.'

A cupboard door closes. Then there is the click-clack of her heels on the parquet floor in the corridor. As usual, he is surprised. Thigh-length skirt today; knee-high boots with a fringe. Her footwear reminds him of the shaggy hooves on brewery dray horses in the old days. 'Good morning,' he says.

She reciprocates and goes to the window.

'I don't have to go to court until Thursday.'

'That's correct.'

'Would you mind cancelling all my appointments after lunch today?'

She turns and looks at him in surprise.

'It was a simple question, so just give me a simple answer.'

'Not at all.' Pia Moløkken opens the window a fraction. 'The air's a bit stale in here.' As she stretches up to undo the top clasp, her skirt rides up perilously high, revealing a strip of white flesh above her stocking tops.

Sverre likes what he can see. 'Thank you.' He places a hand on the telephone receiver.

'There we are.' She pulls her skirt down. The leather fringes dance around her calves as she walks. Sverre takes a deep breath. Pia Moløk-ken really is a breath of fresh air in the office, he thinks, waiting until she has closed the door before he picks up the phone.

2

The straps hanging from the bars over the central aisle swing slowly backwards and forwards. The whole carriage rocks as the tram races down the street alongside Frogner Park. Sverre is sitting alone on a seat, thinking that, actually, he doesn't need the stick. On a sunny day like today the pain in his hip is almost non-existent. However, in a way, the stick has become part of me, he muses. Something to lean on. In a metaphorical sense, that is. One probably needs it. I might, anyway. For a fraction of a second he has eye contact with a youth leaning against the stanchion by the door. He is wearing dark flared trousers with a tight-fitting jacket. His hair is uncombed, falling over his shirt collar, and his wispy beard ends in sideburns by his ears.

This is what the war did to us, Sverre thinks, his gloved hands resting on his stick. When peace came it was trivia that took over the public consciousness. Now life isn't about being on the right side, ideologically or nationally. Now it is all about you, your body, whether the length of a man's hair or the length of a woman's skirt.

He catches a glimpse of a Fiat advertisement at the top of a function-alist building by Frogner square. He waits until the tram has passed the entrance to Vigeland Sculpture Park. Then he pulls the cord and gets up. Holding one of the straps as the tram slows down. When the tram stops in Frogner square, Sverre Fenstad is the only passenger to alight. He waits until the tram has departed. Again he can confirm that the pain in his hip is less than expected. Again he thinks that the stick is redundant. Nevertheless, he leans on it when he comes to a halt in front of the entrance and scans the names on the board by the doorbells. He rings one, opens the door and goes in. He can hear a door open higher up in the building. He can visualise her waiting in the doorway but not raising her head until he is almost there.

Then he takes in the sight of her. Ester hasn't changed much. Her facial features are sharper. But it suits her. Her hair is black, no grey streaks, and her figure is still wonderful. She is wearing a red-and-yellow outfit that brings out her golden complexion.

He is slightly out of breath and rests on the top step. There is the sound of a piano coming from her flat.

'Ester,' he says.

She smiles quickly and, as always, he is fascinated by the glimpse of a front tooth that is a little longer than the one next to it.

Sverre takes the last step onto the landing. They observe each other for a few seconds, then Ester turns and holds the door open.

The hallway is airy and impersonal. A large oval mirror covers almost a whole wall. On the opposite side there is a hat shelf. On the floor beneath, a red school satchel.

He hangs his coat on a hook above the satchel.

Ester holds a door open for him. 'Please take a seat for a moment. I have a pupil, but she'll soon have finished.'

He enters what must be the sitting room. It is simply furnished – a sofa and two armchairs. The furniture is heavier and bigger than is the modern fashion. The table is low and made of teak. He is taken aback by the sight of the grand piano. The tones from the adjoining room tell him she has two rather large instruments in a relatively modest flat. There must be a very special explanation. Sverre is fond of dwelling on this kind of mystery.

On one wall hang a woven rug and two framed photographs. One shows a young man in uniform in front of an armoured vehicle. Sverre studies the picture. He has met the soldier once, in Jerusalem, when he was still a young boy. He has become a good-looking young man. His still immature face has inherited his mother's clean features and eyes. In the other photograph he is younger. He and his mother are standing side by side in a busy street. He is looking into the camera with an uncertain expression. Ester has a scarf tied under her chin. The dress and sunglasses make her look like Jackie Kennedy.

Sverre goes to the window. A woman is taking her dog for a walk in Thomas Heftyes gate. A car turns in from Bygdøy allé, drives past in the street below and disappears down Eckersbergs gate. Sverre tries to follow the staccato piano notes from the next room. Recognises the tune they are trying to recreate. A slow, somewhat fractured version of the first movement of the Moonlight Sonata. The sequence of notes stops. He hears Ester and the pupil talking in low voices. He imagines Ester sitting down on the bench to show the pupil how to play. And so she does. Some beautifully clear melodic lines follow. The sequence is repeated three or four times. Then it is the pupil's turn. Slower, out of time. Then there is silence. A door closes. Sverre Fenstad looks out again. Waits. The front door below opens. A girl steps out. She must be twelve or thirteen and has blonde hair and plaits. Her satchel bounces up and down as she breaks into a run. He watches her go down the street. She grips the satchel straps and disappears from view under an awning. Sverre keeps watching. He doesn't turn away until he hears Ester. The door opens. She backs into the room, carrying a tray. She puts down the tray and places cups on the table.

He runs his fingers over the smooth, shiny wood of the grand piano: 'You don't let your pupils play this one, do you?'

'That's my private piano.'

He waits for her to continue. She doesn't.

He watches her pour tea from a brown pot into the two cups. She puts down the pot and tells him to come over and take a seat. She chooses the sofa. He sits opposite her in the broad armchair.

He wastes no time: 'I received a surprising visit the other day.'

'Like me today,' she says.

He arches his eyebrows.

'We haven't seen each other for ages, Sverre.'

'There was a man at the door. Gerhard Falkum.'

He tries to read a reaction in her face. Concluding that if there is one, it is invisible.

'Were you surprised?'

For an instant she smiles and reveals the irregularity in her teeth. 'It was you who received the visitor, not me.'

'At any rate, *I* was surprised.' He thinks back and adds: 'Surprised that he was still alive.'

Ester straightens her back and gazes into the air for a few long seconds. At length she clears her throat. 'Do you take sugar?'

'Yes. Please.'

She goes out.

He lays the stick beside the chair and leans back.

Ester returns with a bowl of sugar. Puts it on the table and sits down.

He takes the bowl and puts a spoonful into his cup. He stirs with downcast eyes, then tastes the tea. It has body and a kind of smoky taste. 'Lapsang?'

She nods and slants her head. 'Are you a tea man, Sverre?'

'That's putting it a little strongly. But I've tasted this one before.' He puts the cup down.

'As Gerhard is alive, someone else must've died,' she says.

He nods.

They look at each other.

'It's a creepy thought,' she adds.

'A lot of water has flowed under the bridge since then, Ester.' Sverre looks up, searching her eyes.

'I was supposed to go with Gerhard,' she says.

'Oh, yes?'

'Yes. Gerhard and I. We were supposed to take the car together. To the house. I thought about what happened. A lot.'

'What were you supposed to do there?'

She looks up. Her eyes are suddenly sharp.

He takes a slightly bigger sip of tea. The silence continues for so long that it becomes slightly uncomfortable.

Sverre becomes aware of a ticking sound. He lifts his head. There is a clock on the wall beside the window. A white dial with black roman figures. 'He lives in America and his name's Gary Larson now.'

Ester smiles, broad and captivating this time.

Sverre angles his head, curious.

'I was the person who gave him the new name and passport. Gary's presumably another version of Geir. It was a new identity for Stockholm: Geir Larsen.'

'He wouldn't tell me how he arrived there, in the States.'

She looks up. 'Did he say anything about what happened that evening?'

Sverre shakes his head.

'Did you ask him?'

He nods.

'Did he say anything at all?'

'He said he came here to find out who killed Åse Lajord. He thinks someone close to him must've done it.'

'I can see why he might think that.'

'Åse had a visitor the night before she was found,' Sverre says. 'The Gestapo made a big deal of finding a bottle of Scotch, a bottle of English sherry and the butts of American cigarettes in the flat. Our theory at the time was that she was killed by a Norwegian Nazi or a German officer. After all, the only people who had access to such goods were the Germans themselves or high-ranking Norwegian Nazis.'

'So you carried out your own investigations?'

'What could we do? The police force was a nest of Nazis. The only conclusion we could come to was that the goods were brought into the flat by the enemy.'

Ester looked at him from the corner of her eye. 'Do you believe that? That a German would drink with Åse in her home, kill her and run around free afterwards? They meted out tough justice, even to their own.'

'That was why we leaned towards the theory that it was a Nasjonal Samling Norwegian. They did absolutely incredible things to incite reactions. Just think of those traitors Rinnan and Pisani.'

Ester raises her eyebrows.

'Rinnan was—'

'I know,' she interrupts. 'But Pisani?'

'A crook who had a relationship with Elna Bruun.'

'Who's Elna Bruun?'

'The wife of Petter Bruun, who was one of the men involved in blowing up the labour exchange in forty-three. Pisani was an informer and a scumbag; it was his activities that led to the arrest of Kåre Brubak. He was almost tortured to death, then sent to Sachsenhausen. Elna Bruun was also arrested.'

'But what's the connection with Åse?' Ester pours herself more tea, lifts the pot towards him with a raised eyebrow.

He shakes his head. 'Still got some, thanks. Pisani used brandy and cigarettes to get close to Elna Bruun – and succeeded. He was a guy she met in the street after her husband had gone underground.'

Ester shakes her head firmly. 'The Åse I knew was not the type to get involved with strangers in the street. I believe it's more likely she opened the door to someone she knew well.'

Silence.

In the end it is Sverre who breaks it: 'Why do you think Gerhard's here now?'

Ester eyes him. 'Didn't you just say why?'

'He's talking, among other things, about meeting his daughter.'

'That's a legitimate reason – and extremely understandable.'

'But why only now? A lot of years have passed. It's a long time to wait to be reunited with your child.'

Ester shrugs. 'Don't ask me.'

He takes a pouch of tobacco from his jacket pocket. Rolls a cigarette. Lights it with a silver lighter he finds in his other pocket.

Ester gets up, goes to the window and opens it.

Sverre reacts. 'Sorry. I didn't ask.'

'No, no, feel free,' she says. 'I like the smell of tobacco.' She goes to the sideboard by the wall, and from one cupboard takes an ashtray, which she places on the table. 'The smell reminds me of my father. He smoked a pipe.'

He studies the ashtray. It is a minor work of art. A carved mermaid wound around a shell. 'Gerhard hasn't contacted you yet?'

Her eyes widen. 'Yet?'

Sverre puts the ashtray down on the table. 'You were our liaison person in Stockholm for Gerhard.'

'Is that what I was?' She shakes her head. 'No, he hasn't been in contact.'

She goes to the window and looks out.

He gazes at her back. 'You lost all your close family, Ester. And on top of that, Åse.'

She turns. 'I don't want to discuss the loss of my nearest and dearest with you, Sverre. Please don't take it personally.'

'Not at all.'

'So you think Gerhard may be right,' he says. 'Åse was killed by someone she knew?'

'Yes, I believe that's possible.'

'What do you base that on?'

'Other things that were happening at the same time. There was so much going on at once. Perhaps that was why I finally decided to cross the border. My cover was blown. I walked straight into an ambush, if I can put it like that. It was pure luck that I got away.'

She sits down on the sofa again.

He flicks ash into the ashtray and waits.

'There was a delivery,' Ester says. '*London News*. I took the newspapers as always. But the police were waiting for me where the handover was meant to take place. My contact was a woman. That morning she turned up on the wrong platform at Valkyrie plass station. I think she did it on purpose to give me a chance. The police pretended to be passengers. Just as they spotted me the train arrived. I jumped on and escaped. I was able to do that because she'd led them to the wrong platform.'

'Do you think this incident has anything to do with Åse being killed?'

She thinks before answering. 'There's something about it. I walked straight into the police that day.'

She lifts her cup. It is empty. She puts it back on the table without bothering with a re-fill. 'Two or three days later I was driven over the border in Rolf Pettersen's lorry. That was a dramatic trip, too. The sacks of kindling for the generator went up in flames – just outside the German camp in Kjeller. Rolf jumped down and did a Nazi salute.' She imitates the straight arm. 'German soldiers put out the fire while twenty-odd Jews lay quaking under the tarpaulins.'

The ticking of the clock on the wall is loud again.

'This incident was just chance, I'm sure, and now that I think about it perhaps everything else was chance too, but…'

They sit for a long time without speaking.

A telephone rings in another room. She lets it ring.

He coughs politely. 'Just answer it.'

She shakes her head. 'I was on the waiting list for that phone for two years. In many ways it was worth the wait, but I refuse to let it interrupt conversations like this one.'

Eventually it stops ringing.

He smiles. 'I could never let a phone ring. Aren't you worried it might've been something important?'

'Important?'

'Your son? What if it was him ringing from Tel Aviv?'

'He's in the military. The little money he earns he spends on other things than ringing his mother.'

They sit in silence until Ester asks: 'Do you ever think about what life has done to us, Sverre?'

Sverre smiles wryly. 'Do you mean what war's done to us?'

'No, I mean what life's done to us – turned us into.'

'I do. Every day, Ester. Every single day.'

After Sverre has gone, Ester stands by the window, looking down. She waits until she sees him emerge in the street below. Watches him lean on his stick and walk in the direction of Frognerveien. She waits until she hears the tram's metal wheels squeal on the rails and stop. She doesn't move until the tram has set off again and she can be sure Sverre is no longer at the tram stop. Only then does she go into the hallway and don her outdoor clothes.

3

Gunnar Wiklund is singing about Ramona on the radio. Ester turns down the volume, as she does whenever she has to concentrate harder on driving – like now, keeping an eye open for a free parking spot. Kvadraturen is full of parked cars. Driving up Kirkegata for the third time, she finally sees an empty space. She switches the radio off and slots in. Gets out. Rummages through her bag for a coin. Inserts it in the parking meter and turns the knob. Half an hour should do it. She walks briskly to Den norske Creditbank. Stops by the kiosk on the corner. She rarely reads weekly magazines and hesitates when it is her turn in the queue. But then she sees the cheerful face of King Olav in the recent edition of *Allers*, asks for this magazine and pays. Slips it under her arm and continues to the bank. Enters. Waits her turn. The woman behind the counter has back-combed blonde hair with so much lacquer it seems to defy gravity.

'How can I help?'

Ester says she wants to open her bank box.

The woman locks her till, signals to the colleague sitting next to her and gets up. She is wearing a tartan-patterned woollen skirt and a pink blouse. She leads the way down to the vault. Ester holds her breath. The woman has been as generous with perfume as she was with the hair spray.

Under the cashier's surveillance Ester opens the door to the cabinet where the boxes are kept and takes out hers. Then goes behind the curtain, where she is alone. She opens the box.

Inside is a short-barrelled revolver.

She removes it and stuffs it in the pocket of her trench coat. Takes the packet of ammunition and drops it into her other pocket.

Stands pensively examining the pile of passports from various countries. Opens the French one. It has run out. She sees how young she was in the photograph. And remembers how old she thought she looked when the photograph was taken.

She flicks through the pile until she finds her Israeli passport. It is still valid. Pensive, she holds onto it while she makes a decision. Then she puts the pile back into the box, closes it, and joins the bank employee waiting in the vault. She pushes the box back in and locks up.

Ester thanks the cashier, goes up the stairs and out of the bank.

4

The centre pages of *Allers* show a picture of King Olav and the Crown Prince. It is evening, they are standing in front of the entrance to the Grand Hotel and both are smiling into the camera. One self-assured and worldly-wise. The other more embarrassed, as though the smile is a nervous, though polite, grimace. Ester has put the magazine on the kitchen table. Now she is taking apart her old Colt Cobra 38 Special and putting the parts on the heads of the king and crown prince. She takes a rag from the cupboard under the sink unit. Then goes into the room where the sewing machine is. Opens the drawer under the needle. Takes out a small bottle of oil. Goes back to the kitchen. Lubricates all the parts of the gun. Reassembles the revolver. Puts it down. Wipes her hands on the rag. Rubs the remains of the oil from the weapon. Rotates the cylinder. Listens to the sound. Gives the cylinder a drop more oil and rotates it again. Listens. Another drop, until she is happy. Holds the gun out straight and pulls the trigger. Once, then again, and one more time.

She flips open the cylinder. Places a bullet in each chamber. She clicks the cylinder back into place and applies the safety catch. Deliberates. Goes back to her study. She removes three volumes of Aschehoug's Encyclopaedia from a shelf on the bookcase and puts the revolver in the void by the wall. Puts the books back into position. Notices the bulge in the line of spines with disapproval. Adjusts the other fifteen volumes until they are all the same distance from the wall. Approves. Goes back. Meets her own eyes in the hallway mirror. Tells herself, yes, this is the right thing to do. Turns away from the mirror to avoid seeing her own doubts. Continues into the kitchen. Folds up the magazine. Puts it in the sitting-room stove and strikes a match. It burns well.

1

A solitary lamp hangs from a cable beneath the arch of the tunnel. The lamp starts to buzz, the light goes out and comes back on. Again it goes dark, then the light flickers, sending a flashing gleam across the platform and stairs.

Further ahead there is a bench by the wall. Ester heads for it, and crosses the platform. Every time the light goes out, she stops so as not to miss her footing and fall onto the rails. When the light returns she carries on. Walking slowly. It feels like treading water, her slow walk to the metro carriage. The carriage door is open. Now she hears footsteps behind her, coming closer. Nevertheless, she can't quicken her pace. All too slowly she lifts her feet and climbs into the carriage. She gasps for air. The sound of footsteps comes even closer. She wants to flee. But her legs are so heavy, she can't even move them now. The footsteps are getting louder. Echoing. She sinks to the floor and holds her hands to her ears. The door closes. A man with blue eyes stands outside. He bangs on the glass of the door. Hard. Repeatedly. At that moment she sits up in bed with a start.

She is bathed in sweat and out of breath. She peers into the darkness. Switches on a light. She gets out of bed, tiptoes into the sitting room. Switches on the light there. Goes to the hall. Takes a deep breath and braces herself. Unlocks the door to the stairs and sets the bolt in such a way that it can't close. Runs into the toilet. Freezing cold. The porcelain of the bowl is cold too. She pees. Hurries back to her flat. Locks the door and runs into the kitchen. Washes her hands. Dashes back to her bedroom. Gets under the duvet and looks at the ceiling. The sheet under the duvet is still warm. She goes to turn out the light, but rolls over the side of the bed first, looks underneath, checks no one is hiding there, then she turns out the light. Lies curled up to regain heat and fall asleep, but remembers she has her back to the door, and that isn't good, so she twists round and switches on the light again to check the door is closed.

She thinks about the dream, about the panic she felt in Valkyrie plass. Reruns what happened. Thinks about her contact, the woman who went down to the wrong platform followed by the police. She must have done that on purpose. To give Ester a chance. Because she herself had been arrested. But why had she been arrested? Could there be any other explanation than it was the work of an informer? *Someone* must have whispered a word into a policeman's ear. Someone who presumably knew there was to be a meeting, a handover of illegal newspapers right there. Or perhaps not? No, Ester has to dismiss any other explanation. She is sure of one thing: the woman could have waited anywhere; the reason she went to the right place but on the wrong platform must have been because the policeman knew about Valkyrie plass. He just didn't know *where* on the station.

Ester lies staring into the darkness as her thoughts churn, the way they do whenever she chews over this incident, knowing she won't go back to sleep. She has had this dream before. She has woken up from this dream before. She has lain in bed looking into the darkness in the same way before. She needs to do something about this, she thinks. To try and make herself stronger. Other people are suffering. She is fine. She is safe. She can't let a nightmare rule her circadian rhythms.

She rolls over onto her back. Sneaks a look at her watch. It is getting on for five in the morning. She has to be up at seven anyway, and now she is wide awake. She sighs, makes a decision and gets up.

2

Ester is usually the person who opens up in the morning. That is why it is generally her who puts on the kettle. The rationing scheme means they have to resort to ersatz coffee. And with Swedish cargo ships being torpedoed, as Torgersen is wont to say, the little coffee there is has to be imported from Argentina. Despite rationing, Mildred always has access to cigarettes. Both Margit and Mildred smoke. For lack of other topics they talk about cigarette brands and how women should hold a cigarette. Margit and Mildred say women can do most things men can do. Then they discuss the purpose of inhaling. Mildred is annoyed that Margit doesn't inhale. 'There's no point smoking if you don't draw the smoke down.' Mildred is experienced and blows smoke through her nose as she speaks.

'But I'm just a social smoker, really,' Margit says.

Ester looks out of the window and sees Torgersen crossing the street. Immediately the smokers scamper about like squirrels, airing the room and rinsing their mouths and emptying ashtrays. When Torgersen opens the door, everyone is sitting at work, deep in concentration.

Ester looks up. She nods to Torgersen, then goes back to her typing.

He hangs his coat on the hat stand.

She sits with her back to him, waiting for the familiar sounds – him going into his office and closing the door behind him. As she hears neither, she turns round. 'Yes?'

'Is Falkum getting on alright?'

Ester is put on the spot. Four days have already passed since she fetched Gerhard from Kjesäter. But she hasn't seen him. 'I think so.'

He looks down. 'Good, Ester, good.' He goes into his office.

She watches the door close. Wonders why Torgersen has asked her about Gerhard. So no one else is keeping in touch with him, and Torgersen assumes it is her job?

I ought to pop round then, she thinks. Today, this afternoon. Now she is unsure. What am I going to do there? Ask him if he has enough money, like an old aunty – if he is remembering to clean his teeth?

At that moment Markus comes into the office. He is breathless and holding an envelope. It is a letter for her.

This startles Ester, and she stands up so quickly her chair teeters threateningly. She reads the name of the sender. It is Ada Vinje. She looks up and meets Markus's questioning gaze. She grimaces. Frightened to open it. Watches Markus as he does his rounds. Turning all the time and looking at her. Then he has finished and motions towards the envelope on the table. Isn't she going to open the letter?

He talks in a low voice and she answers in an equally low tone. 'I'm afraid of what's in it.'

He understands. She can read it in his eyes. Markus is also nervous. The last letter from her mother was already several weeks old. So Ada must be someone who knows why Ester hasn't received any further letters.

Over Markus's shoulder she can see that the others are pretending that they aren't interested. But they are. Everyone is consumed by the rumours and everyone is after news from home. Markus picks up the envelope and passes it to her.

Ester runs a finger along the edge of the flap. In fact it looks unopened. But is that possible? Could this letter of all letters have managed to evade censorship? Her apprehensions have crept up from her stomach and now run along her arms and legs. She stands up. Goes to the window and looks out and down on Karlavägen. A black vehicle races up towards the crossroads. Another emerges from Banérgatan. The lorry brakes and goes into a skid. They are going to crash.

Ester turns quickly and hears the bang at the same moment. She doesn't want to see. In her mind's eye she sees the deer that was run over on their Easter holidays when she turned fifteen. The thud and the deer rolling across the carriageway in such a brutal, uncontrolled fashion, down into the ditch, where its thin legs trembled less and less until they stopped. She opens her eyes. No one else in the room appears to be taking any notice of the noise outside.

That must be a bad omen, she thinks. I go to the window and something like that happens. Her hand on the envelope is shaking. She feels sick and has to support herself.

'What's the matter?'

'A car crash,' she says. 'I can't bear to see it.'

Everyone races past her to the window.

She sits down and rips open the envelope with her forefinger. Slumping down as she reads.

Markus has lost interest in the collision. 'Tell me, Ester; tell me what it says.'

Ester gets to her feet. She staggers towards the dining room.

✳

Markus stands looking down at the letter. He can only read the first line: *Dear Ester.*

He seems to be leaning on the table as his hand spreads out the whole letter:

Dear Ester,

I hope this letter finds you in good health. I will be brief. I truly regret to have to pass on this news. A week ago today a slave ship left Oslo harbour. On board were Norwegian Jews and their German guards. There were as many women and children as men. No distinction was made between the healthy and the sick. No one was travelling of their own will. Everyone had been rounded up by Norwegians and stowed in the miserable hold like goods. During the night our own policemen ordered them out of their beds, young and old alike. Even patients from the hospital were hoisted aboard the ship in their sick beds. Your dear mother, father and grandmother were among them. They were in good health. That is all I know. It is with great sorrow that I have to give you such terrible news. Because it doesn't stop here. A family of Nazi sympathisers has moved into the flat you grew up in and had to flee. They have no sense of shame, not even about using your parents' furniture and things. There are many of us clenching our fists in anger. One day justice will prevail. I know it will, Ester. In Ecclesiastes it says there is a time for everything, a time for war and a time for peace. With God's help there will be a glimpse of hope in the darkness. The Nazis are in trouble on the eastern front. And now winter is around the corner. I dearly hope the rumours from London are correct and the German army will meet the same fate as Napoleon's the last time pride came before a fall on the Russian steppes. Small comfort maybe. But there are many of us who think about you. There are many of us who thank the Lord that you escaped unscathed.

Please, Ester, write and tell us how you are doing.

All the very best wishes, Ada

PS: Your cat has landed on her feet. She is pregnant! Her stomach is bulging like a balloon. This may sound trivial, but good news is good news, however small.

Markus looks up.

Mildred is glaring at him from the window. 'It's not nice to read other people's mail, Markus.'

He doesn't answer. Just stares blindly into the air.

Mildred looks past him and at the closed door to the dining room. It has stayed closed. She looks back at Markus. 'Bad news?'

Markus nods. 'These accursed rumours,' he says. 'You never know what's true and what isn't.'

He turns on his heel and walks out.

Oslo, November 1967

1

It is half past two in the afternoon. Sverre is standing with his back to the heavy door of the National Archives of Norway building, watching the traffic, when the door opens behind him. Only then does he turn.

Vera has become a woman of almost sixty, hair dyed a reddish-brown, glasses on her nose and a chain attached to the frame. She is still wonderfully curvaceous. They hug. Neither of them speaks.

She tightens the belt of her coat.

'Have you finished for the day?'

She shakes her head. 'It's so nice out. Let's go for a little stroll.'

They walk side by side, extolling the mild, sunny autumn. They walk towards the Kontraskjæret area. He asks, and she says she already has a grandchild.

'Astrid was only sixteen, so Tulla is two years old. A young mother. But her husband's a great guy. He's an engineer on a Bergesen Line tanker. Sails for months at a time, so Astrid and Tulla are at home with us a lot.'

He says it must be nice to see time pass and manifest itself in new generations.

'Yes, it's just lovely. Grandchildren are a great gift, Sverre.' Then Vera says she has been following his son and is sure he is going to have a great career as a politician. 'He's inherited his father's wit, intellect and charm.' She winks at him, and he can't help but smile.

They cross the lawns in front of Akershus, stop and look at the view over Honnør Quay, the City Hall and Akers Mekaniske Verksted shipyard. The traffic by the quays is dense. He asks if she would like a cup of coffee at Skansen café, but she suggests a harbour walk instead. They take the steps down to the pavement below. She waits for him as he leans on his stick for the last few. They exchange glances.

'Don't ask,' he says. 'I tell myself every day I'm getting better. This is my life-lie. I'm more dependent on my stick now than the day I was discharged from hospital in 1944.' Sverre takes the last step and he is down. 'The irony was that it was our own boys in the car,' he says. 'Even though I was several hundred metres away, the driver still managed to hit me.'

'Our own boys?'

'They'd liquidated Gunnar Lindvig, the Nasjonal Samling police inspector.'

'You didn't tell me that then.'

He smiles. 'You didn't tell me everything either – then.'

She smiles back.

'The worst thing about the whole business wasn't that I was left with a broken hip. It was worse that Reinhard started up Operation Blumenpflücken. It was an act of revenge that cost a lot of good men their lives.'

'I was still frightened for you,' she says.

'I know. You wrote to me in hospital,' he says.

They are silent as a heavy lorry passes them. 'It's all so long ago,' she says, angling a glance at him. 'And I have to confess I'm keen to find out the real reason for you contacting me now.'

He winks at her. 'Real? Hm. The worst part is how to start,' he admits.

'Get straight to the point,' she says.

His smile is broader. 'Let's go back to 1942,' he says.

She nods.

'October. A young mother's killed in Ila, and the Gestapo reacted.'

'I'll never forget that case. I'd just been dumped. Do you know he had a daughter with her? Fehlis and Lillemor had a child. My God, I've wondered many times what sort of life they had, those officers who bore the responsibility. Heinrich Fehlis lived only thirty-nine years. Imagine living by those absurd ideals. And then he went and killed himself. In the depth of his soul he must always have known how wrong it was, everything they were doing.'

Sverre Fenstad links arms with her, and Vera blinks with emotion as they walk.

'You genuinely loved him, didn't you?' Sverre says at length.

'I genuinely loved you, too.'

The low sun angles in from the south-west. The treetops across Nesoddlandet and Bygdøy still glow orange; they resemble giant light bulbs when the light hits them. A Nesodden ferry is on its way to the quay.

'I had to grass on them when peace came,' she says. 'In Hvalsmoen. I had to wear a veil, but I had to go round and point them out, the ones hiding among the rank and file. Gestapo officers and their lovers. Finn Knutinge Kaas and I did that. He was keen, I can tell you – he even picked out a former girlfriend. All to save his own skin.'

They stand looking at the still water in the harbour. Litter and rubbish float alongside the wall. 'What war does to people,' he sighs.

'He was sentenced to death, Kaas was.'

'And reprieved. Like most of them. Today he's probably a business-man in Germany. Bremen.' Sverre falls silent for a moment. 'Actually he should've died as early as 1943 … I think. He was down to be liqui-dated. Our boys set themselves up in a flat across the street from him. But that night Kaas had a visitor, a woman. The plan was that he'd be shot as he drew the blinds in the morning. And then it was her. Who drew the blinds, I mean.'

They walk on, lost in thought. The ringing of a bell means that the shunter locomotive is on the way. They hurriedly cross the rails and head for a free bench by one of Per Hurum's bronze sculptures of women.

'Perhaps she was lying by the nearest window,' Vera says. 'Or perhaps he was more tired than she was. Fate hangs on such small details, and I spend too much time thinking about them.'

They sit down and without speaking watch the goods wagons clank-ing past.

The last wagon disappears behind Oslo West station. 'The role of chance is interesting,' Sverre says. 'Lillian, my wife, was deeply religious and thought the war was caused by "Evil", literally. She was preoccu-pied with nature's signs. For example, the extremely cold winters during the war, she thought, were a sign that "Evil" had gained the upper hand over or outmanoeuvred "Good".'

She squeezes his arm again and they are silent. In the end it is Vera who speaks first. 'What I remember about the dead mother is that the case was shelved. The man they thought had killed her died himself apparently, in a bombing raid or something like that. He escaped to Sweden after killing her.'

'In the resistance movement we didn't share the Nazi view of the case.'

She turns to him, waiting to hear more.

He smiles weakly. 'Might it be possible to find any of the investigation paperwork now?'

She eyes him. 'We can only try.'

'That would make me very happy. Sipo had something going at Valkyrie plass station at the same time. A courier must've been arrested a little earlier. This woman was supposed to take delivery of a bag of illegal newspapers at the station. She appeared at the station with the policemen in civvies. But she went to the wrong platform, presumably to give the other courier, who had the newspapers, a chance. Do you remember a case like that?'

Vera shakes her head. 'But it might be easier to investigate. I presume the woman will have testified against some of the torturers in the trials after the war.'

2

The fencing piste resounds as her feet accelerate in an attack, but Captain Hanaas parries and ripostes, so she has to retreat. Ester is well aware she is having a bad day. She parries badly and when she does hit, she doesn't hit hard enough to score any points. She is behind the whole time. Barely able to keep her balance when she is in a lunge position. Having lost two training bouts against Hanaas, as she goes into the next, again she isn't concentrating. He immediately has two scoring strikes. The next point is hers, but then he is back like lightning and scores. After a few seconds she loses her balance and oversteps the line. She has to retreat a metre before they can restart. She can't see his expression behind the mask, but she knows he is grinning. Today of all days she could have done with a female opponent, someone who was lighter and smaller than her. But no other women in the Oslo Fencing Club use an épée; and Ester prefers the épée to a foil. They are *en garde* again. She advances rapidly and he backs away. This is more like it. The lost metre is regained. She parries and lunges, but also this strike is too weak to count. She parries again, but he is quick and she feels it when he hits home. So he wins the point. That was that. The first to five and he won.

'*Scheiße.*' She swears in German because it is neutral. Her God doesn't listen to German, whether it is cursing or common sense. She tears off her mask and shakes her hair loose. She could drink a litre of Coke at least. No, a beer. A Danish pilsner from the cellar. That would be something.

Captain Hanaas has also removed his mask. Sweaty, but happy to have beaten her. 'Another one?'

Ester says no. 'It's not my day.' She could add she hasn't had enough sleep and therefore lacks concentration, but she refrains.

She goes to the changing room to shower. Takes off her fencing uniform and fetches a towel from her bag. Stands listening. She can hear water running. Two women are there, at least. They are talking and laughing. As a rule she waits until she can have the shower room to herself. But today she can't be bothered. She will have to lump it. She goes in and hangs her towel on the hook. The two young women are both fit and buxom. Straight away both stare at her scar. Both react in the same way as everyone else. They go quiet. They look away. They look down at the floor and send each other a furtive glance.

Ester turns her back on them and washes. She is soon finished. Before the other two. Dries down with her back to them. After she closes the door, they resume their conversation. Probably they talk about her, about the scar. Ester quickly sets about getting dressed and imagines the conversation they could have had: No, it's not a failed caesarean. And, yes, you're right, I don't want to talk about it. Yes, it does bother me. I can't wear a bikini. I never sunbathe. I don't undress in front of a man with the lights on. In Norway you can't have cosmetic surgery. Yes, I have thought about it – travelling to America and having it done. But it costs a fortune. I'm sure you've read that.

Ester gazes at the wall. It almost cost Ester her life. One second's inattention on 2nd December 1947. Three days after the UN passed the partition plan for Palestine. Jonatan was ten months old. She had something to do, but forgets what. Death leaves no space for trivialities. Ester remembers the awning flapping, which caused her to lift her eyes, which allowed her to see the sun glint on the knife blade, which gave her time to react.

She is slowly putting on her coat now, but hurries when she hears the two young women turn off the water in the shower room. She wants to be gone by the time they come out.

A last check in the mirror and she rushes out of the changing room. Continues towards the front doors of Njårdhallen and her car parked at the back. Captain Hanaas is waiting outside. His face is as red and content as when he placed the final thrust. He has bought a hot dog from the kiosk.

'Same time next week?' he asks, biting off a piece of sausage. She nods and waves, and heads for her car. All she knows for certain about Hanaas is his rank. She assumes he works for the intelligence service. Her assumption is based on his greeting her by name at the first training session. He made no secret about knowing it. But he has never overstepped the mark. Has never mentioned names or events. Has only made the parameters clear: I know who you are.

They have made it a routine to train together. He is in the club more often than she is. But he usually stops his other training to fence with her. When she says he doesn't have to, he grins and says she will have to use a foil if she wants to train with the women. Mostly their bouts end in a draw. Sometimes she wins, and then he leaves under a black cloud.

Ester gets into the car. Her body is pleasantly stiff and sore. She likes the feeling and luxuriates in it for a while. Rummages through the heap of cassettes on the passenger seat. Finds what she is after and puts it into the player. Turns the ignition key. The car starts. Dinah Washington immediately launches into 'Alone'. Ester reverses, humming along. There is something desperate yet satisfying about Dinah's appeals for what might never happen. It is a lone wolf's cry for the moon, Ester thinks. The song is a statement of my own situation, she thinks, and waves to Hanaas, who is going in the opposite direction; he lives in

Bærum, in the Defence quarters in Eiksmarka. She drives out of the Njårdhallen car park, down towards Smestad. Carries on towards Majorstua, turns right by Volvat and drives alongside the Vigeland Sculpture Park home. But she hesitates by Frogner plass. Makes a quick decision and steers hard right to Skøyen. It is worth a try, she muses. Passes the Vigeland Museum thinking, yes, it is actually a damned good plan. Perhaps it's the bouts against Captain Hanaas that have given her the idea. She can't use him, but she can use what he stands for. So all she has to do is find the right man in the right network.

3

Ester turns off the main road by the neogothic palace on the hill, continues down the narrow drive and pulls up in front of the red garage doors marked 82c. She gets out of the car. Stands for a few seconds admiring the embassy building, then ascends the staircase and reports to the duty official. She asks for Rabbi Rebowitz.

'Is he expecting you?'

She shakes her head.

'Name?'

'Lemkov, Ester Lemkov.'

The official is young. His shaved neck looks vulnerable as he leans forwards with the telephone to his ear, and she feels like stroking him. He must be the same age as her son, Jonatan, and she wonders if they have trained together as recruits. He says she can wait inside, then comes out of the duty room and leads the way to the house.

The fire is lit in the huge reception room. Ester stands by the tall windows and looks out. The Bygdøy landscape is aflame with autumn hues, and Oscarshall Palace towers like a fairy-tale castle amid the orgy of colour.

A door opens and Ester turns. A woman peers at her through the narrow opening. Ester doesn't recognise her and makes no attempt to greet her. The door closes. Ester turns back to the window.

She doesn't hear him come in. Senses only that she is no longer alone. When she looks round, he is there, in the middle of the room, wearing a dark suit and a skull cap on his head. The round, rimless glasses give him a somewhat squinting expression.

'It's been a long time, Ester.'

She nods.

'What brings you here?'

'I'd like to ask you a favour, Markus.'

He nods, almost imperceptibly.

'I need some help to investigate something – in America.'

Markus Rebowitz raises both eyebrows.

'A Norwegian is calling himself Gary Larson – an anglicised version of Geir Larsen. He came to Oslo from the USA a few days ago. Apparently he runs a petrol station in Minneapolis. I need to know more about him.'

Rebowitz lowers his gaze and thinks.

'What's the matter?'

'I remember a Geir Larsen from Stockholm. He died.'

'He didn't.'

Markus Rebowitz sucks his teeth. Wry smile. 'You're no longer in service, Ester, and you haven't been for a long time.'

'So?'

'May I ask why you're asking me to do this?'

'It's private.'

'The problem is, we don't do this kind of work for private individuals.'

'I know.'

'Yet you're still here.'

She nods. 'I'm not asking for a big investigation. I just want his story checked, possibly fleshed out. I need to know the details of it. Yes, it's important for me from a personal perspective, and I doubt this will cause either you or the embassy any inconvenience.'

Markus Rebowitz searches her eyes.

'Consider it a personal favour,' Ester continues. 'I want to know what he's living off. Is he married, has he got any children, has anything dramatic happened in his life recently that might've suddenly made him want to travel to Norway? A country he left, using a different identity, many years ago, during the Second World War.'

Markus tilts his head. 'End of forty-two, wasn't it?'

She nods.

'And you want some flesh on this? It could take time.'

'I'm willing to wait.'

'We need more people like you, Ester. You're missed.'

'But I've stopped, Markus. I live a quiet life now. I'd like to carry on like that.'

'When your name was mentioned just now, people's faces lit up, Ester. You're sorely missed.'

'But I'm fine as I am, Markus.'

'Do you give piano lessons?'

'Yes.'

'That must be a big change.'

'For the better, yes. It's different.'

'Your boy's also getting good references,' he says with a smile.

She looks down. 'I hope he avoids having to fight again.' She looks up again and feels she has to explain her negative response. 'There were some tough days this summer.'

He is quiet, and she feels some irritation at having exposed herself in this way. 'It was tough not knowing whether Jonatan was alive or not,' she says finally.

'Of course,' he says.

It is a polite response, but unsympathetic. This embarrasses her – both his lack of interest and the fact that she has been standing here, cheapening her emotions.

'We're an exposed country and an exposed people. Attacks like this will happen again,' he says.

Now it is her turn to answer politely and unsympathetically. 'Of course.' She prepares to leave, faces the door.

'I'll see what I can find out about Larson.'

'I appreciate that, Markus.'

'In return, I expect to see you more often at the synagogue.'

Ester looks down. 'I'll do my best, Markus. I promise I'll do my best.'

Stockholm, December 1942

1

The Swedes say they have never had such a cold December. Ester has wrapped herself in a woollen cloak and wound her scarf around her neck several times. She trudges across Kungsbron Bridge on stiff legs. The cold nips at her face. The freezing air makes her nostrils stick as she breathes in. She has her felt hat pulled down well over her ears. Klara Sjø canal is steaming and there are still open channels, and from chimneys white wisps of smoke rise against the deep-blue sky. She turns left into Vasagatan. She has to step into the road to pass two coalmen shovelling coke down through an opening to a cellar. She wonders which is worse: extreme cold or extreme heat. Her father used to say the cold is fine because you can just wrap up and protect yourself. The heat however … Then her mind goes back to the same thoughts. As they do every day. Where are they? Have they got enough warm clothing? Surely it can't be as cold in Germany as it is here. That is impossible. But then she stops and stares into the distance. She is deluding herself. What would the point be of transporting them out of Norway? She doesn't want to think these thoughts. Instead she represses them, concentrates on walking, telling herself she has to focus on something else, something nice. But what? She looks at the monumental buildings towering up everywhere in this city. Thinking that, despite everything, the world has developed this far. There are generations of people behind towns. They have lived here for hundreds of years. They have built houses and paved streets. They have had children and built schools for the future. War is temporary, a destructive force that will decline because there is nothing positive about destruction. It is as simple as that. As simple as ABC. Call me naïve, she tells herself, continuing down Vasastan. For someone sinking, finding solid ground has meaning. She clings to this thought, and through walking generates some heat. The Roman

Empire survived for as long as the culture held decadence in check. Napoleon was a megalomaniac soldier who was doomed to fail sooner or later. Hitler is a copyist who doesn't even dare stand in the forward column of troops. Everything is in the Allies' favour. Everything except time.

Finally she can turn into Kammakargatan. She walks to number thirty-three, opens the door and enters. Carries on up the stairs. Stops outside the door and knocks. Nothing. She knocks again. And again. In the end she tries the handle. The door isn't locked. She opens it a fraction. Peeps in. 'Hello?'

Would he have left the flat without locking up?

She steps into the hallway.

'Gerhard? It's me. Ester.' She ventures further inside. The door to the sitting room is ajar. The air is cold and clammy. He can't have had the fire lit much. She pushes the door fully open. The hinges scream. She sees a shoe and a trouser leg. A figure is lying face down on the floor. The shoe soles are worn. His arms are out to the sides. As though he has been shot in the back, she thinks, a second before discovering a half-empty bottle of spirits beside his right foot.

'Gerhard!'

She takes off her hat, scarf and mittens. Undoes the lowest buttons of her coat and kneels down. He is lying with his cheek on the floorboards. His breaths coming fast and shallow. He reeks of alcohol and is dribbling. She carefully raises one eyelid. A white eye flickers. What should she do? She gets up and feels the stove. It is ice cold. Her breath is white. Then she sees several empty bottles. One of them is by the wall under the window. There is a half-empty bottle of some shiny spirit on the table.

He groans.

She grips his shoulders and shakes him.

He stirs. Brings his arms closer to his body. Lifts his head very slightly. Tries to force his chest off the floor. Slumps back down. Tries again. His chest rises and he rolls onto his back. The back of his head hits the floor with a bang. The saliva from his mouth becomes a string and sticks in his hair.

'Gerhard! Can you hear me?'

He opens his eyes. Looks at the ceiling. Raises his head and looks at her. His eyes are swimming.

'Can you hear me?'

He holds out his right arm. She takes his hand. Holds it as he struggles to his knees. He is heavy. She pulls his arm.

Finally he is up on his feet, swaying. His eyes are still swimming.

As though he doesn't know me, she thinks.

'What are you doing here?' he says.

'What do you mean?'

The grimace is malicious. 'Are you hard of hearing? I'm asking you what you're doing here.' He falls against the wall. Raises his arm again. His forefinger is pointing at her.

'We agreed that I would come.'

'Can't you knock on the door like other people?'

'I did.'

'But then you marched straight in, anyway.'

'Gerhard, this was an arrangement.'

'Do men just walk in on you if you don't hear them knock?'

'Gerhard, what is it?'

'What is it? That's what I'm wondering.'

'You're drunk!' She doesn't like the harshness of her own voice.

He teeters, but remains on his feet. He stands like this for some time, as if he is slowly returning to this room and the present situation.

She turns her back on him. Shovels coke into the stove and lights it. Soon the flames are roaring.

Without a word he staggers over to the sink. He tears a towel from the hook on the wall and lays it over the plug-hole strainer at the bottom. Turns on the tap. No water comes out. Yes, it does, a drop. Then a drop more. The drops become a trickle. The water starts to run. Soon it is a torrent and fills the sink. When it is full he dunks his whole head in the water. Water splashes onto the floor. But his head stays there, in the water.

Suddenly he straightens up. Water splatters against the mirror and walls.

Ester is splashed in the face. She dries herself with her sleeve as he gasps for air. Then he dunks his head again.

This time his head stays under for even longer.

She takes the full ashtray from the table and empties it into a bin, already brimming with ash and cigarette ends, behind a cupboard door.

She clears away the bottles. Opens the cupboard door. More bottles. Empties.

Gerhard leans against the wall. He is breathing heavily and his hair and chest are wet. He strides across the floor. Takes the half-empty bottle.

'No,' she says.

He eyes her from a distance. Then he seems to make a decision, lets go of the bottle and makes for the cupboard. Rummages around inside. Finds what he is looking for: a bottle of beer.

'No,' she repeats.

'Oh, yes,' he mumbles and knocks back the beer in one draught. Then he gasps and puts the bottle down. Smacks his chest and belches.

She feels the stove. It is beginning to heat up. She breathes out through her mouth. Now her breath is almost invisible. 'Aren't you cold?' she says.

He shakes his head.

'When was the last time you ate?'

He grins.

'What are you laughing at?'

'You're all sweetness and light, aren't you? Even if I punched you in the teeth, you'd be kindness itself. An angel.'

She feels the blood draining from her face. She presses her hands against the wall to stop the terrible shaking. Nevertheless she manages to say in a fairly controlled voice: 'Perhaps I should give you a clout!'

He laughs. His face opens and his mouth becomes all white teeth and charming smile.

It is as though the insult had never been uttered. And she catches herself thinking that this is how it is. The words were never said. What matters is only this smile.

But Gerhard is already somewhere else: 'You should try it. Sit tight doing bugger all. Waiting day in, day out, not knowing what's going on. You should try it some time.'

She takes her scarf, hat and mittens. 'I thought we were going to the cinema.'

That stops him in his tracks. He understands and flashes another smile.

'Of course we are. In fact there's a cinema right here, in Sveavägen.'

'Are you sober?'

'As a newborn babe,' he says, with a stagger. 'Just have to change.'

He pulls off his top clothes. Ester turns and walks to the window. It is dark outside, so she sees a reflection of him in the glass; he is washing under his arms. He is lean with pronounced abdominal muscles and rippling sinews in his arms. Fortunately he keeps his trousers on. Puts on a white singlet he fetches from his rucksack and roots through it until he finds a rollneck jumper.

'Ready, steady, go,' he says, walking to the door, opening it and performing a deep bow. 'After you, fru Larsen.'

2

The lights go on in the auditorium. People get to their feet. Ester remains seated while she gathers her things. When she looks up she sees a bespectacled man staring in their direction. She looks at Gerhard. He stares back at the bespectacled man. They know each other, she thinks, and is aware that now both of them are averting their eyes as though it had been her who broke the contact between them.

She stands up. The question is whether the man has anything to do with the police. She scouts around, but cannot see him in the crowd anymore. The cinema audience metamorphoses into slow-moving matter that flows through the double doors. She and Gerhard walk side by side in the throng. A shy silence prevails as the queue moves out into the night and the cold. Ester puts on her mittens and winds her scarf around her neck. She turns again and scans the people around her, but the man is still nowhere to be seen. I am probably overwrought, she thinks. I am probably seeing ghosts in broad daylight.

✳

They stroll side by side away from the cinema. She ought to say something. But she doesn't know what.

He talks about the film.

Ester listens with half an ear. Several free taxis pass. But she thinks she should accompany him back to the flat. Make sure he stays there. She can hail a taxi in Vasagatan afterwards.

Now Gerhard seems sober and strong again. The outbursts in his flat didn't come from him, she thinks. It was the effect of the alcohol and befuddlement. Now he is polite and imitates the stupid slugger from the film who knocked the hero to the ground again and again. She laughs. She likes being in Gerhard's company when he is like this. He is funny and easy to be with. And then he talks about the argument they had and teases her: 'You're a toughie, Ester. I'm glad you're my childminder.'

'Childminder, my foot.' She elbows him, and he pretends to double up in pain and, smiling, grabs a handful of snow from the banks the plough has left on the pavement and throws it at her. She fends it off and runs away laughing.

They turn into Kammakargatan.

If he invites me up, I must say no, she thinks.

Again he talks about the film. He says the problem with such films is that all the pieces fall into place like they do in patience. Life isn't like that. He doesn't believe the final scene – the two of them riding into the sunset, not a cloud on the horizon.

Ester finds it liberating that he is still preoccupied with the film. It renders him harmless. 'Cinema's a dream world,' she says. 'That's the whole point.'

Once again there is a silence.

'I should never have come here,' he says. 'There are lots of people on the Gestapo lists. But they don't give a damn. They head up into the forests and prepare to strike back. Think of the guys who blew up Oslo East and West stations, or the guys who managed to sink the two German patrol boats in Oslo harbour, or the fire-bomb attack on the timber yard in Lunner.'

Again she is wrong-footed by his sudden turn, the change from merriment to melancholy. And again there is that strength, the power behind the words. She wants to contradict him. 'The Germans take hostages every time,' she says.

'Or think about how they felt, the guys who blew up the German train in Nyland station and hurled fire-bombs at Grua Sawmills,' he says. It's as though he hasn't heard what I said, she thinks.

'The Germans shoot innocents in retaliation.'

He stops and eyes her condescendingly. 'You can't win battles without fighting.'

'Osvald and his ilk think they're doing something useful, but they only make things worse.' She can hear that what she is saying has little substance. But it feels appropriate to contradict him, to resist.

He studies her coldly. And repeats his argument: 'You can't win battles without fighting!'

She falls silent. Gerhard is right of course. But the resistance arguments about independent saboteurs and their attacks also seem sensible. She doesn't want to discuss this. She doesn't want to provoke Gerhard again.

'So what's the pointing of sitting on your arse in a bedsit in Sweden?' Gerhard says. 'If you know the answer, please explain the point to me.'

'You have to think about Turid,' Ester says. 'It was best to come here for her sake.'

'Why?'

'Because your daughter's the most vulnerable hostage in the world.'

He glowers at her for a long time. 'You're right,' he says.

They walk on.

She notices the tension increasing between them and feels the need to release it, to break the silence. But she has no idea how to do it.

He stops again. 'Is anything happening?'

She doesn't understand what he means.

'Is anything happening? Has Torgersen contacted the British? Are they doing anything to move me on?'

She has no answer and doesn't want to have to say so. She walks on, faster this time.

He catches her up. 'Do you know?'

'How should I know? Why are you hassling me? Things take time.'

'Hassling? Me? I haven't spoken to a single person in days, and then I hear I'm hassling!'

'Torgersen isn't lying. Don't forget he got you out of the camp before you were arrested.'

'Him? Torgersen? It was you who came in the car.'

Before she has a chance to contradict him she sees a black car parked outside the entrance to number thirty-three.

He has seen it too. They both stop dead in their tracks.

The car has broad fenders. A light falls from a window onto the sign over the windscreen: *POLIS*.

They look at each other.

'Wait here,' Ester says, and leaves him. Without a look behind she walks to the entrance and enters the building. She goes up the stairs. Two uniformed men are standing outside the door she herself opened a few hours ago. They are knocking on the door and appear impatient. Ester sneaks past them and carries on up to the next floor. Feeling the two men's eyes on her as she turns. There is only one more floor. If she continues she will come to the loft. But she is out of their sight now. There. At last the two men are talking. She stops. Listens. Unable to distinguish the words. There is a slight echo in the stairwell and the policemen are mumbling.

She sits on a step. It is still impossible to distinguish what they are saying. A door opens below. A neighbour, she guesses. Correct. Men talking to a woman. Then a door closes and their footsteps go downstairs. And out.

She waits until she is sure the two policemen have gone. Then she stands up and goes back down.

3

The icy air bites at her cheeks. She stops and orientates herself. The police car has gone. But Gerhard is nowhere to be seen. She walks slowly back to the place where she left him. She is becoming uneasy. Perhaps the police bumped into Gerhard and took him with them?

She looks up and down the street. The smoke from a lorry waiting at the crossroads floats across the pavement. No pedestrians anywhere.

She turns into a narrow street – Sankt Eriksgatan. Walks to the next crossroads. Nobody. She turns left. This road leads to a little park with a few trees. Without thinking she begins to walk in that direction.

As she approaches the trees she spots Gerhard under a street light. He is sitting with another man. They are talking. White, frosty breath swirls above their heads. Gerhard is gesticulating. The man is shaking his head.

She stops and watches them. This man can't be from the police. He is wearing a winter coat, a hat and dark gloves.

The man turns towards her. He is wearing glasses. It is the man she saw in the cinema. Of that there is no doubt. The round, rimless glasses and the narrow mouth are unmistakeable.

The man gets up and leaves. Soon his figure is swallowed up by the darkness of the park.

Gerhard sets off in her direction, out of the trees and across the street. Hands buried in his coat pockets, he is a shadow gliding alongside the house walls.

'Over here, Gerhard.'

He stops and looks at her.

She crosses to his side of the street. 'Who was that?' She is breathless and her tone is harsher than she had intended.

'A man.'

'I could see he was a man. But who?'

'He lives nearby. We chat sometimes.'

She fixes Gerhard with a stare. He looks away and she doesn't believe a word he is saying. Besides, he has been told to keep a low profile. Why would he chat with people in the neighbourhood?

'Did he like the film?' she says.

'Film?'

'He was sitting four rows in front of us. At the cinema.'

Gerhard doesn't answer.

'You didn't see him there?' she says, and she can feel she is on thin ice.

Gerhard is suddenly annoyed. 'He gets me booze,' he says. 'On the black market. Is there anything else you'd like to know?'

They eyeball each other.

Then he bursts into loud laughter. 'Has it struck you that we're behaving like husband and wife,' he grins. 'The way we're arguing.' He starts walking.

She doesn't move, still caught up in the unease and the tension.

He turns and waves. 'Are you planning to stay there?'

She was actually planning to ask him where he was going, but in a way she already knows the answer. She postpones this for another time, follows him and says instead what worries her most: the police outside his door means that they have him on their radar.

'Come on. We have to behave normally in case they're spying on us.'

They reach the street lamp on the corner and stop. They exchange glances again. She knows he knows what she is thinking. He is waiting for her to speak. This amuses him. She doesn't want to say anything, but there is no option. 'Let's go back to mine, in Kungsholmen. You can sleep there tonight.'

He doesn't answer, but looks into her eyes.

She turns and starts walking away.

Oslo, November 1967

1

Sophia Loren is lying with her head on a pillow. She has almond-shaped eyes and a dark shadow over her eyelids. Marlon Brando is standing over her with his arms crossed and a sceptical, almost angry, expression on his face. He is wearing either a blue smock or a dressing gown. Presumably the latter, Ester thinks. Because of the pillow. The backdrop of the poster is an evocative picture of Hong Kong, with skyscrapers and Chinese junks in the harbour. She likes both Brando and Loren. And as the director is Chaplin himself, she thinks that this film might be worth seeing. Another evening. The last performance has almost finished.

She walks away from the entrance to the Klingenberg cinema then ambles back. There is a chill in the air. She sticks her hands in the pockets of her anorak. Actually I should just go in, she tells herself. Go down the stairs, find the table where he's sitting, pull out a chair and say *Nice to see you again*. But she doesn't. Why not? Because he hasn't contacted her. Which means he is either unusually busy here in Oslo or he is avoiding her. But it will soon be two hours since she saw a man very similar to Gerhard leave Hotel Continental and enter the door in front of her. A man who can sit for two hours alone in Rosekjelleren bar on a normal evening can't be that busy. Ester wants to know more. She wants to know what it is that is making him avoid her.

She leans against the wall bearing the poster case and continues to wait. Then she notices two drunks on the opposite pavement staring at her. She turns to the wall and looks straight into the face of a scantily dressed woman. The photograph in the case. She looks at the picture to avoid being chatted up by the two men. That is the disadvantage of leaning against a wall on a dark October evening in Oslo. Despite the fact that she is dressed in trousers and an anorak, they take her for the sort whose services are for sale. How drunk can you be?

Under the photograph of the stripper is the picture of a black drummer. The name: Pete Brown. The poster says he plays with three other men. Arild Bjørk on tenor sax, Lulle Kristoffersen on piano and Hein Paulsen on trumpet. Ester has read the poster probably twenty times and is still wondering why the group doesn't have a bass player. The rhythm section of a jazz band usually has drums and a bass.

A couple walk past her. They stop outside the entrance. The doorman comes out and holds the door open. They go in. Before disappearing behind the door they both look at her.

I am attracting attention, Ester thinks, and moves back a few metres, to the street corner.

2

Gerhard is sitting alone with an almost empty cup of coffee on the table in front of him when a couple come down the stairs and go to the cloakroom.

The lady coming in searches for some eye contact.

Gerhard is looking at the stage. A slightly plump woman is doing a striptease number. She is accompanied by the jazz band. Soon she starts moving wildly to the sound of a vigorous drum roll. A few of the men in the crowd whistle. The dancer turns her back on the audience and fumbles with the hook of her bra while furiously waggling her hips. Finally she manages to undo it. Then she spins round, holds the bra up like a trophy and she is done.

Scattered applause as she trips across the floor on her high heels.

A man from the back shouts: 'Get yer knickers off. Don't be a coward.'

A drunken customer bursts into loud laughter.

The jazz band performs a fanfare.

A spotlight falls onto the stage. Into the light steps an overweight revue artist wearing long underpants, a raffia skirt and a straw hat.

Gerhard sits up.

A heavily made-up woman has stopped by his table. She asks if she can join him.

He shakes his head.

Then she sees he is drinking coffee, rolls her eyes and goes to the next table, where there is another solitary male customer.

The pianist plays the opening to a tune the audience seems to know. There is sporadic clapping.

Gerhard looks at his watch. Gets up, takes his coat from the back of the chair and leaves. As he reaches the stairs the revue artist starts singing. The audience cheers at something on the stage. Gerhard can't be bothered to turn round to look. He shrugs his coat on as he walks up the stairs. The cracked voice of the singer carries up after him, but more and more faintly: it is a pre-war Einar Rose hit.

The doorman steps aside and holds the door open. Gerhard is out. The door slides to behind him. He buttons up his coat. Composes himself before walking down to the crossroads by Håkon VIIs gate and turns right towards Vikaterrassen.

Slowly he walks up the stairs to the 7th June square. Here he stands for a few seconds studying the building housing the Royal Norwegian Ministry of Foreign Affairs. The windows by the entrance are large and reflect the grounds behind him. Gerhard studies the reflection for any movement before continuing to Drammensveien by Abel Hill. He pauses on the pavement and waits for a taxi to pass, then crosses the road and walks among the elm trees in the Palace Gardens.

After he has walked through them he steers right, to the Nisseberget area. Slows his pace and glances over his shoulder. Then he jogs down the steps between the lilac bushes, which still have dense green foliage. He is completely alone. He stops just before the street lamp at the bottom.

He listens for footsteps. But there are none. Then he continues along the pavement in the Palace Gardens. He stops and looks up at the royal palace. His eyes sweep the terrain. He turns and walks on.

Ester has found a bench by the path on top of Abel Hill. From here she has a good view of Nisseberget, the university and Karl Johans gate. She watches Gerhard as he crosses the university square to go into the gardens there. She doesn't move.

He hasn't changed much. Not quite as slim as before – age has played its part. He is still lithe though. The way he walks. Gerhard is in good condition. Spying on him feels strange. Shadowing him and not making her presence known.

But Gerhard has paid a call on Sverre Fenstad. So he must have done some research, skimmed through a telephone directory. Ester refuses to believe that the man down there hasn't searched for her name. He has to know she is alive, lives in Thomas Heftyes gate and has a phone.

Yet he hasn't contacted her.

So what do you want, Ester? she says to herself. Now you have seen him. Now you have rolled back the years. Is that why you are doing this? For your own sake? What do you want to know?

She has no other answer than that there is something wrong if this particular man is avoiding her.

She stands up and cranes her neck to follow his movements. If Gerhard decides to walk through the gardens, he will come out on the other side and she can make a quick dash and catch him up. The other possibility is that the walk in the gardens is another ploy to check that he is not being followed. If that is the case he will turn round. She guesses he will and watches carefully.

Then she sees movement by the entrance to the gardens. A shadow flits back across the university square.

She gives him a good head start, then goes to the steps, runs down and sets off in pursuit.

The night is damp. As Gerhard strolls up Ullevålsveien, there is low-lying mist. He walks along the wall towards the Cemetery of Our Saviour. The wall is succeeded by a fence made of vertical iron spikes. He carries on a few metres. Stops by a narrow gate in the fence. Looks around. Silence. The few illuminated windows in the house on the opposite side of the street tell him how late it is. He opens the gate and the hinges squeal. He slips inside. Stands still and listens for footsteps. When he is sure he is alone, he moves on. Darkness is no obstacle here. He knows the way.

✳

Ester stops and looks up into the darkness. She can see neither
Gerhard nor his shadow. Slowly she crosses Ullevålsveien and treads
warily alongside the cemetery fence. Gerhard is still nowhere to be
seen. No shadows ahead of her. She passes the wrought-iron gate, but
then she reflects on the fact that it wasn't closed and stops. The street
is empty and quiet, and behind her there is an open gate. She turns
and walks back. She slips inside. Stands utterly still, listening. Hears
nothing. The obelisks and gravestones look like frozen shadows in the
darkness. She takes two paces forwards. The gravel crunches under her
shoes. She steps to the side, off the gravel path and onto the grass. She
moves forwards again, parallel with the gravel path, slowly, without
making a sound. Visibility is barely a metre. She stops. Looks back.
She can no longer see the gate. She wonders whether she has made a
mistake by entering the cemetery. If he has come in here, it might be
a diversionary tactic.

Perhaps he has tricked her.

Perhaps he is waiting for her.

She listens, but hears nothing.

She walks on. The mist hangs between the trees and the tall gravestones, which appear suddenly from the gloom. Busts of the deceased
stare blindly into space.

She hears some low, muffled sounds, and stops. Then it is quiet
again. But the noises are confirmation that he is here.

She moves in the direction of the sounds. The moisture on the grass
soaks into her shoes. The terrain rises. She seems to be in an older part
of the cemetery. The gravestones are taller and closer together, the trees
are older. She hears a loud scraping sound. She stops. It came from
close by. Motionless, she listens. Now there is total silence. Then there
is the sound again. And it is gone. It was close enough for her to decide
not to move. She waits. There is a crunch of gravel. Footsteps. They are
coming closer. Ester is paralysed as a shadow takes form in the darkness.
It is a man. It is Gerhard. He passes her less than a metre away. But then
he comes to an abrupt halt and listens.

Ester holds her breath and stands as still as he does.

They are not far from each other. Two silhouettes. Both stationary. He takes a step forwards.

Ester quickly crouches down, hides behind a gravestone. The material of her anorak rustles.

Gerhard jerks his head round.

Slowly he rotates on his own axis, searching the darkness.

Ester hugs her knees, breathing soundlessly through an open mouth. Soon her thighs begin to ache.

At last he starts walking.

She stays in a squat position until she can no longer hear footsteps. Her joints and muscles are stiff, but she forces herself to wait a little longer before she slowly stands up. His shadow is no longer to be seen. She goes back to the entrance, treading carefully, so as not to stumble. The gate is closed. She opens it gently, but the hinges squeal anyway.

1

In the darkness, the bedroom door is framed by a yellow rectangle. Ester lies in bed, waiting for him to switch off the light. But he never does. She falls asleep and wakes with a start. The light is still on. Now she is awake. Knowing that Gerhard is on the sofa in the sitting room, only a few metres away, is having an effect on her. She struggles to fall asleep, hears a creak in the floor and imagines she sees the door handle moving. But it doesn't. The door is still closed. She almost drops off, then comes to and thinks he is standing in the doorway. Again, it is her imagination. She dreams that he comes in and lies next to her. She rolls lazily against his warm body, but wakes when she realises no one is there. She is sweating and ashamed of her own fantasies. Now the light in the sitting room is finally off, and she wonders whether he is also lying awake. Wonders whether he is waiting, listening for the door to open, for the patter of her footsteps across the floor.

She tries to count sheep, but can't concentrate. Gets up, opens the window and draws the icy air down into her lungs, closes the window and goes back to bed. She talks to Åse and is even more ashamed. Åse doesn't answer. She just looks at Ester with a serious expression. Ester now realises she is finally asleep and can feel herself looking forward to being with Åse in her dream. But when she looks for Åse, it is her grandmother and mother she sees. She asks where her father is, but they don't answer.

✳

Gerhard wakes up to the knocking of the radiator under the window. The sofa he is lying on is not a good bed. The base slopes down to the wall. Nevertheless it feels pleasant to lie on your side and doze.

He doesn't have the morning-after-the-night-before feeling. This is different from how he usually feels after a long bender. His mind goes back over events. Soon it will be twenty-four hours since he blacked out. That is probably why. In fact, he feels refreshed. After a while he hears floorboards creaking in Ester's bedroom and the door opens. He observes her though lowered eyelids. Ester tiptoes from her bedroom. Wearing a dressing gown. She rushes through the sitting room into the kitchen. Soon the tap is running. He hears her light the gas and put on a kettle. Then a chair scrapes as she sits at the table. After a while there is another sound, a softer scraping. He wonders what it could be. Of course – a pen on paper. She is writing a letter. The sound of the kettle, a hum that grows louder as the water begins to boil. The click as she puts the pen down on the table. The scraping of the chair as she gets up to stop the kettle boiling over. He lies with his eyes closed, imagining the lid on the kettle rising. Waits for the smell of ersatz coffee. Nothing. Why not? She turns off the gas. A cupboard door. The clink of cups on saucers. A pot filling with a liquid. Of course. Ester drinks tea.

Gerhard opens his eyes. The kitchen door is ajar. He watches her. Every so often she puts down the pen and sips her tea. The low winter sun makes her hair glow.

She licks the envelope and seals it. Gets up. The sunlight outlines her body through the material of her dressing gown. He is happy to lie there looking at her.

But then she opens the kitchen door fully.

He closes his eyes.

Hears her tiptoe into the bathroom. When the door closes he sits up. Puts his feet on the floor.

Gerhard strokes the hair from his forehead. He has to get hold of some hair oil. Runs a hand over the stubble on his chin. It rasps. His razor is in the bedsit. He pulls on his trousers. Letting the braces hang loose. Stands by the window and looks out. The flat has a view of the canal the Swedes call the Klara Sjø. Judging by the height of the sun, it will soon be morning proper. Small clouds float across the sky. They are pink with a yellow aura. The edge of the ice flashes a gleaming gold. The canal is slowly disappearing under the frosty mist sweeping in. The buildings are wreathed in a steaming bank of cloud that drifts on and disappears. As though the remains of the night are being shown the door by the morning sun, he thinks.

He takes a cigarette from the packet on the table and rummages in his pocket for matches. As he pulls them out, the ring he was given by Ester comes too.

First you play at living some sort of life during the German occupation, he thinks, and then the pretence continues here. A ring, a prop – like a ridiculous mask. He slides the ring onto his little finger and lights the cigarette.

The bathroom door opens. Ester comes out with a towel wrapped around her body, like a dark-haired beauty in a daring film.

He turns.

She heads towards her bedroom.

'Ester,' he says. His voice is hoarse.

She turns in the doorway. Her skin is so white and fresh that he instinctively holds his breath. Then she smiles. One of her front teeth is slightly longer than the other.

'Good morning, Gerhard. I've made some tea. It's on the kitchen table. Don't have any coffee, I'm afraid.'

'You're very beautiful, Ester.'

She looks back at him.

He has to clear his throat for his voice to carry. 'I say this because you deserve to hear it. But most of all it's important you understand I'm truly sorry I was so unpleasant to you yesterday. I behaved badly and unreasonably. Such behaviour is unforgivable.'

She stares at him, still not moving.

'Nevertheless, I hope you'll forgive me.'

'You were forgiven ages ago.' She cast her eyes down, slips into her bedroom and closes the door after her.

She can sense it, he thinks. She can feel the desire that has taken root in my heart.

Gerhard rolls the ring between his fingers while listening to the sounds from Ester's bedroom, guessing what she is doing and how she does it.

Oslo, November 1967

1

Sverre can't concentrate on sewing. He presses the needle with the thimble, grips the pliers and pulls it through. He is too heavy-handed. The leather seam tears. He curses. He puts down the pelt and screws the top onto the tube of glue. The music doesn't help either. Energetic violins. The scraping is stressing him. He gets up and turns off the radio. Stands in front of the stereo system thinking, then makes a decision and goes upstairs to the telephone. He rings Ester's number without success. Looks at his watch. It is quite late. But he thinks it is worth a try and calls Hotel Continental. He asks to be put through to Gary Larson's room. He doesn't get an answer this time either. When he puts down the receiver he is even more restless than before he called. It strikes him that it can't be a coincidence that neither Ester nor Gerhard is close to the phone. He goes into the sitting room. Sits beside the television. Switches it on. While it is warming up, he looks at his watch. The news finished a long time ago. The picture appears. It is the test card and there is a hiss. He switches it off. Puts on the radio instead. Waits impatiently for the sound. Then he searches long wave until he finds some muted jazz. Leans back in the chair. But he can't relax even now. He gets up, goes to the phone and rings Hotel Continental again.

Again he is put through to Gary Larson's room. There is a ringing tone. When Gerhard answers, at first Sverre doesn't know what to say.

'Hello?' Gerhard repeats.

'Sverre here. I've been talking to Erik Heggen. By the time he and his wife, Grete, adopted your daughter after the girl's grandmother passed away, Milorg had issued a statement to say that you'd died. The news that you were alive came as a shock to Erik.'

Gerhard says nothing.

'He's worried how Turid will take it. I think it'd be best if you and he met without her being present.'

Gerhard is still silent.

'To prepare for the meeting – for where and how you and Turid should meet.'

Sverre decides to wait for a response this time.

When Gerhard speaks his voice seems to come from far away. 'Listen carefully to what I tell you. My daughter's of age. She doesn't need to take any account of either Erik or you. Or indeed anyone.'

'I'd still like you to work with us.'

Gerhard is quiet, and Sverre senses an opening. 'Especially with regard to the old murder case,' he says. 'You'll need access to police papers and information if you want to find out who killed Åse. In that connection I may be able to help.'

'Sverre, there's an expression they use in the States for what you're doing: you're barking up the wrong tree.'

'Well, I have a certain influence, and what I can offer will make it possible for—' Before Sverre can finish the sentence Gerhard rings off.

Sverre sits looking at the receiver, then sighs and cradles it.

2

The water is boiling hot. It burns her ankles and then up her calves. Ester hesitates. Holds a hand on each side of the bathtub and lowers her body slowly. The heat rises over her knees, thighs, stomach and to her breasts. Finally she lets go and slides under the water. Enjoys the heat as it spreads. Looks up at the ceiling, where the shadows from the flickering candle flit around. She raises a wet hand and lets the water run off before she takes the wine glass from the stool beside the bathtub. Tastes the white wine, beads of condensation pearling on the glass. Nothing is better than this, lying in the bath oblivious of time or place, just enjoying the heat of the water and the taste of grapes and minerals.

The telephone rings in the hall. She puts the glass on the stool and sinks beneath the water. She doesn't want to hear the telephone. When she can no longer breathe and has to come up gasping for air, the telephone is still ringing. She blinks water from her eyes and sticks fingers in her ears.

She removes her fingers. The ringing has stopped. She sips the wine again. The telephone may have gone quiet, but it is still on her mind. It is late. No one rings her at such a late hour. She begins to wonder who could have rung, and this detracts from the joy of lying in the bath and getting warm. As she leans back, she grips her hair and twists it lightly so the water runs off. The telephone rings again. Ester sighs, gets out of the bath, careful not to slip, and takes a towel from the shelf. She lays it down beside the bath. Steps onto it and sends a disapproving glance at her body in the mirror on the door. The shameful red scar glistens. Every time it is as though she can hear the flap of the awning in Jaffa Road. She sees Jonatan's sleeping face in the pram. The sun reflecting on the knife of the man running towards her.

Ester takes the bathrobe hanging from the hook on the door and wraps it around her.

Tells herself she did well. She managed to react. A shameful scar and pain for many years is nothing compared with losing your life or your child.

But how long can you have luck on your side?

She should have thought about that before she went out. Because on a day like that she ought to have known there would be reactions. She glimpses her critical eyes in the mirror again. Should she have stayed indoors? On a day of national celebration?

She walks into the hall. Answers the telephone.

'Sverre Fenstad here. Sorry, but I called earlier without success. This is quite important.'

Ester doesn't have a chance to respond before he carries on:

'Has Gerhard contacted you?'

'No.'

Silence for a few seconds.

'Have you tried to contact him?'

'No.'

Now Sverre Fenstad's silence is longer. At length he coughs. 'I'm ever so slightly uneasy that I don't know Gerhard's agenda.'

'But you told me his plans, didn't you?'

'To clear up a murder that took place during the war? I've offered him help, but he isn't interested. I think he has other plans, but he's keeping them close to his chest.'

'Perhaps he wants to do things his way. It's his business. And in fact it's not strange that he wants contact with his child.'

'I'm afraid there's more to it than that, Ester. He has revenge on his mind. And that could affect us both.'

'Just a moment.' She puts down the receiver and goes into the bathroom. Takes the bottle and the glass. Fills it. Thinking about what Sverre has just said. She carries the glass to the phone. 'Back again.'

'I said it could affect us both.'

'Speak for yourself. But you said something about revenge. I didn't understand that.'

'I had that impression when he was at mine.'

'What would he want to avenge?'

The silence tells her she has touched on a sore point.

She is about to say goodbye, but is not quite quick enough:

'Gerhard's come back to Norway after many years, and you and I are in an odd situation.'

'I'm not. He hasn't contacted me. So he doesn't want to have anything to do with me, which I am the first to respect.'

'He wants to know what happened when Åse died – and you were her best friend and confidante.'

'I think you're blowing this out of proportion, Sverre.'

Ester considers whether to tell Sverre that Gerhard creeps around cemeteries when normal people are in bed. But she holds her tongue. There is something here she should find out for herself. But the unsettled score she has with Gerhard Falkum is private.

'I'm serious.'

Ester takes a sip of wine. 'What if Gerhard actually does just want to be a father to his daughter?'

Sverre is quiet for a long while. 'I have a suggestion,' he says at last.

'OK?'

'We discover what he really wants.'

'Why are you telling me this?'

'You knew Åse, you knew Gerhard, and you were the link between him and Stockholm.'

'I'm a music teacher. Nothing more, nothing less.'

'Ester…'

'You're a man with power. You're on speaking terms with all the cabinet ministers. If you think Gerhard has dubious intentions, you can thwart them with a phone call or by pulling strings, as you've always done.'

Sverre carries on: 'All conflicts can be shown to lead back to people. The same is true of solutions. Gerhard's a man with mental wounds. I understand him and you understand him, and we both know different sides of this case.'

Speak for yourself, she thinks, without bothering to say so again. She puts down her glass. If there is one person whose actions she doesn't understand it is Gerhard Falkum. She opens her bathrobe and examines the scar on her stomach again in the mirror.

'I'd just like to ask you a little favour,' he says. 'Tomorrow, if you have the time and opportunity.'

'And what kind of favour would that be?'

3

The wall clock shows a quarter to ten. Three quarters of an hour have gone since Gerhard Falkum left the breakfast room and took the lift up to his floor. Sverre Fenstad moves from the chair he has been sitting in and goes into the hotel lobby. A newspaper under his arm, he looks for a table in the lounge. Finds one, sits down and orders a coffee. Asks to pay at once – 'Should I have to go suddenly.' The waitress takes the note. She goes to the till and returns with the change.

From the chair where he is sitting now he can keep an eye on the check-in counter, the lift doors and the windows looking out onto Karl Johans gate. There are two receptionists on duty. They are busy. A businessman is checking out and new hotel guests are arriving. The bellboy rolls suitcases into a left-luggage room before accompanying the new guests up the stairs to the breakfast room.

The lift doors open. Two people with suitcases and keys in their hands. But then Sverre catches sight of Gerhard leaving the lift behind them. He is lost in the crowd by the reception desk. Fenstad looks out of the window. Spots Gerhard again, now outside the entrance. He is carrying a briefcase.

Sverre raises the morning edition of *Aftenposten* in front of his face as Gerhard, briefcase under his arm, stops and buttons up his coat. When Sverre lowers the newspaper Gerhard has passed the windows. Sverre cranes his neck and watches him until he rounds the corner.

Then Sverre stands and picks up his stick. He leaves the newspaper and goes to the lift, which is open. He enters. Presses the button for the fifth floor. The doors close. The lift ascends. The doors open and he steps out. He walks down the corridor and passes a cleaning trolley in front of an open door. A chambermaid with bed linen in her hand comes out of the room. Inside there is a food tray on the floor. Half a bottle of champagne and two used plates. He nods to the chambermaid, continues to the corner and turns down the corridor, stopping by the last door. Hangs the stick over his forearm and takes a piece of hard plastic from his pocket. Looks around. No one in sight. He inserts the plastic inside the door by the lock. Slides it down. Wiggles it until he feels the catch. Takes the plastic and pushes the door open. Sverre Fenstad enters Gerhard's room and closes the door behind him.

Ester regrets having agreed to this. She is soon fed up with waiting. Besides, standing at a tram stop with one tram after another passing, and not getting on any of them soon attracts attention. So she uses her imagination as best she can. She studies the film posters in the glass cases outside the Scala, sits on a bench by a rose bush in front of the entrance to Pernille restaurant. Gets up, strolls over to the kiosk beside the entrance to Theater Café. Buys a cone of jelly babies. Returns to the line of cinema posters. She is back at the tram stop when she sees Gerhard outside the hotel entrance. He is walking in the direction of the Odd Fellow building. He looks like a businessman, with his navy-blue coat and a briefcase under his arm. Under the coat he is wearing a suit. Between the lapels a collar and tie are visible.

He goes round the corner, heading for the harbour.

Ester tightens her scarf and puts on sunglasses. She follows him along the pavement, fifty metres behind.

Gerhard passes a flower shop and a gentlemen's hairdresser's before crossing the street outside Saga cinema. He strides past the entrance. He has a clear destination; it's as though he is going to an important meeting.

Gerhard crosses Klingenberggata. On the opposite side he marches into the Thiisgården branch of Andresens Bank.

Ester reaches the bank. Removes her sunglasses. Slowly approaches the front door. Through the windows she can see Gerhard being shown to a staircase in the middle of the room. She can see the silhouette of a figure disappearing down the staircase. What does she feel? The excitement she had felt when she saw Gerhard the evening before has gone. She wonders why that should be. The moment in the cemetery? Or that she is sneaking around after him for the second successive day without making her presence known? Something else? She doesn't know. She goes into the delicatessen opposite the bank.

Sverre Fenstad has entered a large, comfortably furnished hotel room. It is on a corner of the fifth floor and has a balcony. The door to which is open. A suitcase lies on the bench beside the main door. It is empty. On the bedside table there is a novel written by Arild Borgen: *And Night Turned Slowly to Day*. The dust jacket is shiny and the price sticker is still on it. He flicks through the pages. Puts the book back and opens the drawer. Nothing apart from the obligatory New Testament. He goes to the desk. A pile of newspapers and various magazines. He leafs through the pile. No notes. In his mind's eye he sees Gerhard putting the briefcase under his arm. If Gerhard has any important documents, that is where they will be. But Sverre Fenstad isn't going to give up that easily.

He goes into the bathroom. There is a toiletry bag on the shelf under the mirror. He opens it. Sees two bottles. Shakes one of them. Pills. He takes both out and reads the labels. Puts them back. Leaves the bathroom and goes to the wardrobe filling almost one whole wall of the room. Opens the door. Clothes on hangers. He starts thumbing through them systematically.

In the delicatessen Ester stands watching the door to the bank through the shop window. She is still asking herself why she said yes to Sverre. She doesn't like spying on people. Sverre Fenstad is a man with influence. Why not use it? Why this amateur surveillance?

An assistant behind her says: 'Can I help?'

Ester turns to the woman. 'I'm just thinking.'

Other customers are seen to while she stands there. Once again the shop is empty. Finally Gerhard emerges from the bank. Ester gives him a few metres head start, then sets off.

Gerhard walks back the same way he came.

Presumably he is on his way to the hotel and his room. Ester hurries to the telephone booths outside the Saga cinema. There are two, but both are busy.

Stupid, Ester thinks. Stubborn Sverre and all his daft suggestions.

In the left-hand booth there is a teenage girl, eighteen or nineteen, with the receiver held to her ear. She is winding chewing gum around her forefinger as she talks. In the other there is a gentleman skimming through the telephone directory.

Ester knocks on the door.

The man doesn't hear.

The girl in the booth on the left laughs out loud. She hoists herself up onto the shelf with the directories, long legs in a short skirt.

Ester knocks again.

Finally the man reacts. Straightens up and turns.

Ester taps her watch and angles her head.

He opens the door a fraction. 'Are you in a hurry, *frøken*? If so, by all means.' He comes out.

Frøken, Ester thinks, and goes in.

The girl in the mini-skirt laughs so loud the windows vibrate.

Ester has learned the number by heart. Finally she finds a coin in her pocket. The paper cone of sweets comes out with it. She eats a jelly baby and inserts the coin in the machine. The dial moves so slowly. Outside the booth the man smiles at her. A wrinkled face. Grey hair and grey moustache. She opens the door and offers him a sweet. He thanks her and deliberates which one to take. Chooses a red jelly baby and looks for another. At long last the phone rings. It rings for a long time. A voice says Hotel Continental. Ester closes the door and asks to be put through to Gary Larson's room. Looks down at the cone. The man has helped himself to at least five. No red ones left. She looks out. He is walking away.

Gerhard stands reading the headlines of the newspapers on the table in the kiosk. Then he takes the morning edition of *Aftenposten* and pays. Goes into the lobby. Makes his way to the lift. Passing reception.

'Larson?'

Gerhard turns. The receptionist is standing with the receiver under his chin. Gerhard goes to the counter.

'There's a lady on the line asking to be put through to your room. Would you like to take the call in your room?'

Gerhard says he can take it there and then.

The receptionist passes him the receiver.

Gerhard grips it and says his name.

The line is dead.

Gerhard shrugs and passes the phone back. 'Did she leave her name?'

The receptionist shakes his head.

Gerhard goes into the lift, presses the button for the fifth floor. The doors close.

Sverre Fenstad has moved back into the bathroom. From his inside pocket he takes a tool he has brought with him, a small spanner. His fingers work quickly. Sverre knows that a hotel guest can never be absolutely sure of the staff. However virtuous we may appear, we humans,

Sverre thinks, are all voyeurs. We want to know about our neighbours. The more mysterious and closed a person appears, the more our curiosity is piqued. Sverre knows this, he is like that himself now: he wants to get in the room, he wants to lift the duvet, he wants to see who Gerhard really is and he wants to know his secrets. Of course the man who has rented this room also knows this side of human nature. If he really has something he wants to hide he will go to extremes to hide it. The object, if it is an object, won't be in a suitcase, won't be in a pocket and won't be in an envelope in the desk; it will be somewhere the hotel staff either wouldn't think of looking or can't be bothered to look. In all hotel rooms there is a place like that: the cistern in the toilet. Sverre has already loosened the screw holding the lid in place and his fingers are now groping inside. His face breaks into a little smile. It is here. You're getting warm now, Sverre. His forehead is sweating as his fingers grope through the cold water. He can feel something. He digs in his pocket for the other tool he brought. His wet fingers stick to the lining, but eventually he produces a little torch. He shines it into the cistern and peers inside. What he can see is a weapon, a kind of knife – a bayonet or a stiletto. He straightens up and puts the lid back into place. At that moment he hears the rattle of keys outside the door to the hotel room.

Stockholm, December 1942

1

Darkness is falling as Ester clears her desk and gets ready to leave for the day. There is still a light on behind Torgersen's door. Otherwise the office is deserted and quiet. The flames in the stove are roaring and there is a freezing cold draught coming from the window where Ester is standing, looking down on the scene below. Under the street lamps busy people scurry hither and thither despite the cold. Christmas is approaching. On the radio they have been talking about record low temperatures. In Laxbäcken, minus fifty-five has been recorded. The thermometer outside the window where Ester is standing shows a mere minus twenty-four. That is cold enough. The clear, stable weather can only move the cold further south in Europe. She thinks about her parents. What warm clothing do they have?

Torgersen opens the door of his office. She turns and looks at him.

He asks if it is still as cold outside.

She examines the thermometer even though she knows the answer and says minus twenty-four.

He asks why she hasn't left yet.

She says there were a few things that had to be finished. 'But now I'm on my way.'

He praises her work rate.

She looks down, lost for words.

He asks if there is any news about her family.

She says she has reason to believe they are in Germany. Not wishing to say more or reveal her fears. Torgersen looks down. He has never been good at social intimacy. He pats his pockets. Composes himself. There is something he wants to say. She is beginning to know him now.

He looks up and straight at her. He expresses his sympathy.

It is as if she understands what he is thinking and so has to think the same herself. And again she is overcome by the same cold fear of what may happen to them – or may have happened already. It is like an acute stomach ache. She has to take a seat.

'What's the matter, Ester?'

Torgersen is standing in front of her. His eyes are genuinely sympathetic.

She searches for words. In the end she says even just the thought that she left them to come to Sweden while they stayed makes her feel unwell. It feels like betrayal.

'You haven't betrayed them. You did what you held to be right, and that's never a mistake.'

She knows he means what he says and is grateful. He says he is sure her parents are happy that she crossed the border to safety.

Ester thanks him, but says it is hard not to blame herself.

He asks if she is ready for any more jobs.

'What do you mean?'

'You have the best grades for active service.'

'Thank you.'

'Besides, you managed the Kjesäter job brilliantly. To have the initiative and wits to pull off jobs like that unaided is an inestimable gift, Ester.'

She looks down. She has never been good at receiving praise.

'Perhaps some more active service will do you good.'

She looks up. Anything is better than being weighed down by the heavy office air and thinking about everything you don't want to hear concerning your loved ones. Active service is action, planning – a real break from demoralising thoughts. She hears herself say: 'OK. I'd very much like to do active service, as you call it.'

2

She extends a hand holding the money. The taxi driver takes it. The next moment he is out, round the car and opening the door for her. She thanks him, though feels awkward as she does so. She waits until the taxi has gone before she starts walking, keeping her eyes peeled.

If the police are here it is not panic stations. She is working for the Norwegian legation. It is her job to help refugees. It is none of her business what they are wanted for in their homelands. But she doesn't see a police car anywhere. Kammargatan is quiet and there is almost no traffic. She goes up the stairs and lets herself in.

The smell of Gerhard still lingers between the walls.

And the smell of alcohol. There is a bottle behind a chair. The floor underneath is wet. She searches for a cloth, without any luck. So she picks up his rucksack instead. Empty. Goes into the bathroom. Gathers up his toiletries and shaving stuff. Puts everything into the toiletry bag on the shelf. He uses a cutthroat razor to shave. She can imagine it: him stretching his neck, his head to one side, jaw white with shaving foam, contrasting sharply with his black hair. Him slowly running the razor across his cheek. The rasping sound of the sharp razor slowly moving down to his Adam's apple.

She wraps the leather strap around the razor. Puts everything into the bag, along with the toothbrush. Drops the toiletry bag in the rucksack.

A pair of binoculars hangs from the bedhead. They go into the rucksack. Searches for clothes. Sees a little pile and a shopping net. She throws it all on the bed. It is a pathetic sight. One jumper, underwear, woollen socks.

She holds the socks in her hand. The heel has been darned. Åse, she thinks, and imagines Åse's nimble fingers doing the needlework.

Now she feels very near to her. If I turn around now she will be in the doorway, looking at me, Ester thinks. She turns.

The door is as before, closed. The moment has passed. She rolls up the socks. Feels something heavy in one. Sticks her hand in and pulls out two wads of notes. Two compact rolls secured with an elastic band. Green and black. American dollars. She weighs the notes in her hand. It must be quite a lot of money, she thinks. She resists the temptation to remove the elastic bands. Puts the heavy wads back and drops the socks in the rucksack. She does the same with a pair of breeches.

She sits down on the bed and lifts the pillow. Here is his passport. She picks it up. A few negatives fall out. She holds them to the light from the window. Tries to make out the subjects. One is a picture of a middle-aged man. If she tilts the negative, the features become clearer.

The man bears some resemblance to Gerhard. His father, she guesses. In another picture there is a woman holding a child in a christening dress over a font – Åse and Turid? A photo of Åse on her own. The last negatives must be of a cemetery. At any rate, it looks like headstones.

Once again she can feel Åse's presence, as though her friend is sitting beside her. As soon as the thought strikes her she dismisses it and pulls herself together, slips the negatives back into the passport and lays it in the rucksack. She opens the drawer in the bedside table. Inside there is a gun and a cartridge clip. She jumps back and stares down at the weapon. At length she picks up the gun. It is heavy.

There is a knock at the door.

She turns towards it with the gun in her hand. It is a hard, imperious knock, as though whoever it is knows someone is inside. Ester freezes, unsure what to do. There is another knock, like thunder.

Oslo, November 1967

1

Gerhard is taken aback by the sight that meets him in the hotel room. Drawers are open, clothes are scattered everywhere. The newspaper falls to the floor and he looks around. The door bangs. A draught. The balcony door is open. He strides through the room, out onto the balcony. No one there. He spins round. At that moment he hears a door click shut in the room. He goes back in. Through the room. Tears open the door. The corridor outside is empty. He runs. Turns left, then left again, to the lift. There it goes. It is on its way down.

The staircase. He can catch up with the lift. He races down, two or three steps at a time.

On the third floor he sees the roof of the lift; it is only a few metres ahead. He runs even faster.

There. Down in the lobby. He charges over to the lifts. The doors are closed. The sign over the door shows the lift has stopped on the first floor. He runs back to the staircase, races up to the first floor. Looks around. No one. Then he sees a green EXIT sign over a door. He pulls it open. A rear staircase. Now he can hear another door shutting on the floor below. He charges down the stairs. The staircase ends in a door. He opens it and scans Klingenberggata. He sees only strangers rushing past.

He is panting hard. And watching, but doesn't see anyone he knows – no sudden, surprising movements. He turns and goes back up the stairs. Has to wait for the lift. Finally the bell pings and the doors open. He steps inside and goes up to the fifth floor. Back to his room, along the corridor.

Gerhard passes a chambermaid hoovering inside a room. Gerhard stops and goes back. He knocks on the open door.

The maid turns out to be a woman in her late fifties. She looks up. He raises a hand.

She steps on a button on the vacuum cleaner. The noise stops.

Gerhard says: 'Good morning.'

She sends him a questioning look: 'Morning?'

'I'm expecting an old friend. You haven't seen him, have you?'

She shrugs.

'I arrived late and I'm not sure if he's been here or not. Have you seen anyone walk by?'

'I just saw you,' she says. 'And a gentleman with a stick.'

Gerhard nods. 'A stick, OK. That's him. Between fifty and sixty, right? And a little goatee. Bushy eyebrows?'

She nods. 'Yes, he was here and then he left. A few moments ago.'

2

In the oval rear-view mirror Ester sees the crossroads on Kjeld Stubs gate. A young man is pushing a sack trolley stacked with cardboard boxes, holding them steady with his chin. He manoeuvres his way from the little lorry to a shop for boat equipment. Ester shifts her gaze and looks through the windscreen, at the traffic alongside the rock under Akershus Fortress and at the path up to Skansen restaurant.

She has parked at the bottom of Rosenkrantz' gate, by the Holm Hats shop windows. When she looks in the mirror again, the vehicle belonging to the sack-trolley boy has gone. She sees Sverre come round the corner. He stops to check before limping towards the car. He steps into the road. She rolls down the window and looks up at him without speaking.

He leans on his stick, smiling like a clever schoolboy over a chessboard. 'Well?'

'Let me say it,' Ester says. 'You got out before he came back?'

'I did.'

'Was it worth the effort?'

Sverre shrugs. 'Gerhard has an alcohol problem. He takes Antabus for it. If that's combined with alcohol you're really in a bad way. It means he's an alcoholic and he struggles to stay sober. I saw it when he was at my place. He didn't touch the drink I poured him.'

'Were you willing to turn thief to find that out?'

'I didn't steal anything and I'm still not a thief. Where did he go?'

'He went to Andresens Bank, down to the vault. I tried to contact you when he was heading back, but I wasn't put through.'

Sverre frowns. 'The vault? He must have rented a bank box. What does an American tourist want with a bank box in Oslo?'

She opens the door and gets out. Further up the street the lights turn green. A lorry roars past them. She waits until it is quiet again. 'Sverre, this is no good. I can't do this.'

'Take it easy. He didn't notice a thing.'

Ester looks at him patronisingly. While she had been sitting in the car, waiting, she had been wondering whether to tell Sverre about Gerhard's nocturnal visits to the Cemetery of Our Saviour. But she changes her mind now. She doesn't trust Sverre. There is no sense in ransacking Gerhard's room. But Sverre found some sense in it. So there is something he isn't telling her.

'The excitement,' he says, a smile playing on his lips. 'Think of the excitement.'

'Don't you lie to me. If you want me in the team you have to tell me what you're actually after.'

He looks back at her without answering.

'I mean it. This operation was utterly ridiculous. Pulling strings would be much better. If you're frightened that Gerhard's agenda is a threat to someone, there are institutions that can deal with it.'

'The interesting bit is the bank box.'

'What about the bank box?'

'I went through the whole room, all his pockets, and found nothing but coins and fluff. But he left the room with a briefcase, to go to a bank box.'

Ester opens the door and gets in. Turns the ignition key. Starts up.

He bends over further. 'That bank box...'

'I don't want to hear about the bank box. Why did you have to break into his room? What are you after? What's the agenda he has that you're so frightened of? How could this poor man, who has lived in America for years, affect you in any way? A man who gets invited to the Royal Palace?'

Sverre doesn't answer. Instead he stands up straight and takes a step back.

Ester puts the car in gear and pulls away.

3

The gate squeals on its hinges as Ester opens it and enters the Cemetery of Our Saviour. She stops. Ruminates, recalls where she was when she was shadowing Gerhard, then walks in that general direction.

Some workmen are raking leaves from the gravel paths and lawns, putting them into heaps and shovelling them into wheelbarrows.

Ester thinks back to when she was walking between the headstones. She remembers the terrain sloped upwards. There is in fact only one place where it is that steep. As she walks over to it she passes the grave of Edvard Munch. Stops.

She walks back to the part where the ground is flat. The incline is the start of a little wooded mound inside the cemetery. On the opposite side the mound ends at an impressive buttress wall. That is not relevant for her. She heads towards the mound and counts her footsteps. Goes to one side. Opens her eyes. She can't see anything unusual. But she had heard a noise and moved towards it, and if she was standing here and walked on, there is only one way she could have gone. If not, she would have collided with the headstones. She carries on. Moving into the area with the tallest obelisks, where the trees have the thickest trunks. She walks slowly. And notices a footprint in the black earth of a flower bed. The print looks suspiciously like the sole of one of her own casual shoes. She tries to draw a sightline from here. Studies a rock. It could be the one. The rock she crouched behind when Gerhard walked past her.

So where could he have been?

She tries to establish the general area, remembering the silhouette that appeared from out of the mist. She walks in that direction. Passes under an immense treetop. Behind the trunk there is a large commemorative grove. She walks across the flagstones into the grove, which is demarcated by a little wall. There is an old grave. On the ground there is a coffin-shaped stone engraved with a name that has faded so much it is practically illegible. She spells out the name of the person resting here. Alvilde Munthe. The name means nothing to her. The barely legible inscriptions on the plate below the name tell her Alvilde Munthe died many years ago. Long before the war. The flower bed on top of the grave is dry and hard and untouched. No one has tended it for many years. One slate tile is uneven because tree roots are demanding their space. No one could have visited Alvilde Munthe's resting place for a very long time.

Seeing two scratches on the plate, she kneels down. It appears to be made of some kind of metal. She runs her finger along the scratches. They are recent.

She closes her eyes and tries to remember the sounds she heard that night.

Instead she hears a low mumble.

Ester raises her head and sees two women strolling along the path. They are carrying flowers. They move off the path in the direction of a grave nearby. They stoop down over the bed and start weeding the long grass at the edge.

Ester stands up. She casts a final look at the grove. Now she has been here. If necessary, she will come back. She nods to the women as she passes them on her way out.

Stockholm, December 1942

1

There is more knocking at the door, now it is more insistent. Does whoever it is know she is inside? Panic-stricken, Ester shoots glances around the flat. Looks at the gun in her hand. The rucksack, she thinks. Puts the weapon and the cartridge clip inside, shoves the rucksack behind a chair and goes to the door. She opens it. And looks straight into the face of a man. She has seen him before. It is one of the two policemen who were standing outside this flat the other evening. But now he is in civvies.

The woman next door, she thinks, and remembers the voices from when she was sitting on the stairs. The police must have asked her to keep an eye open and tell them if anything happened.

'Tor Jonasson Holmér, Stockholm police,' he says, and asks who she is.

Ester tells him the truth. She works for the Norwegian legation. 'This flat's ours.'

He comes up close to her. She doesn't back away. She looks him in the eye. 'How can I help you, Tor Jonasson Holmér?'

She wins. He takes a step back and a flicker of uncertainty crosses his face, but only for a second. 'Shall we talk inside?'

Ester holds the door open. He is a thin, medium-height man with vulpine features and intense energy. His eyes sweep over the flat. He walks around, examining his surroundings as he speaks.

'I'm looking for the man who's staying here. Gerhard Falkum. A Norwegian.'

'There's no one staying here,' she says to his back.

He turns. In his hand he has a half-full bottle of spirits. 'Is that so?'

'I'm clearing up. Making the flat ready for someone else to move in next week.'

His gaze takes in the rucksack behind the chair.

'So you've no idea where this Gerhard Falkum has gone?'

'I don't know anything about the people who've stayed here or will stay here.'

He looks at her and angles his head. 'Haven't I seen you before?'

'Maybe. Maybe we go to the same synagogue.'

The flicker of uncertainty crosses his face again. 'Oh, so the lady's Jewish?'

'Yes,' she intones. 'The lady is Jewish.'

The atmosphere is less charged now. He has tried to impose his authority on the situation, and she has succeeded in parrying it. He will have to try a fresh angle. She guesses he will go for the rucksack.

Which he does. He lifts it. 'This—'

'Is legation property,' she interrupts coolly. 'If the police are interested in anything pertaining to this flat, you'll have to approach the intelligence office at the legation. I'm sorry, but that's the way it is. The man you're looking for isn't here. I'm only doing my job. Now, may I ask you to leave?'

He puts the rucksack down and smiles to himself. He raises his eyes. 'Have you got any ID?'

It is her turn to bare her teeth. 'No, but if you wait downstairs until I've finished, we can drive back to the legation office. Then you can get confirmation of what I've said and ask more questions. What do you think about that?'

He shakes his head. 'Not necessary.' He goes to the door. 'We in the police are dependent on cooperation at all levels. So – if Gerhard Falkum should appear I assume you or someone at the legation will inform us.'

'Of course, herr Jonasson Holmér.'

She closes the door behind him. Leans back against it and breathes out. She is bathed in sweat, but also surprised at herself. She feels relieved and happy with her performance. However, she isn't very happy that she has had to lie to the police. I will have to take this up with Torgersen, she thinks.

2

She decides to walk to her flat in Kungsholmen and trudges down Vasagatan with the rucksack on her back. She thinks about Åse. Still unable to come to terms with what happened. Why wasn't Åse alone with her child that night? Who was she with? Again she sees Åse on the bench beside her pram in the nursery as Syversen goes out to talk to her. What if she had defied Syversen and gone out to talk to her herself? Would she have found anything out? Ester isn't sure she would. They hadn't been particularly open with each other over the last year.

A freezing cold wind gusts across Skeppsbron Bridge. She speeds up to keep warm. Carries on into Scheelegatan. Goes inside and up the stairs. For a fraction of a second she is surprised when the door opens.

'Fru Larsen,' he says.

She smiles back. Thinking he has seen her coming from the window. He has been waiting.

She takes off the rucksack. 'Here are your things.'

He seems surprised, almost impressed. 'Thank you, fru Larsen.' He opens the rucksack and looks down. Rummages through the clothes. Takes out the woollen socks and squeezes them. She unbuttons her coat and pretends she isn't looking. He grabs the gun and winks at her. 'You think of everything, my dear.' He puts the gun back.

She shakes her head at the affected 'My dear'. He is quick on his feet and helps her remove her coat. Hangs it on a hook and says that this is almost as if they were married properly.

She is hot. Her body reacts to the transition, having walked fast for quite a distance in the extreme cold. She starts sweating. Takes off her boots and walks past him and into the sitting room. Sees how tidy everything is. The positive side is the commitment, the consideration. The negative side is that, whoever does the cleaning also looks as they do it. She can feel she doesn't like that. In a way this little flat contains everything she is now. She doesn't like other people looking in her cupboards and drawers without being invited to do so. She thinks about the Hirden, the NS militia, who invaded her home in Oslo. Has he been through her bedroom as well? No, fortunately, it seems to be how she left it – in a mess. She finds some clean clothes in the wardrobe. Changes into a different blouse. Closes the door after her on her way back to the sitting room.

But he is standing in the corridor in front of her, and she has to stop abruptly to avoid a collision.

We are standing too close, she thinks. She closes her eyes.

He lays a hand on her cheek. Then the other.

Without thinking, she strokes her cheek against his hand. The movement becomes a caress. She almost gives a start at the thought and opens her eyes. They are close to each other. His breath is hot. She should take a long step back now, she thinks, but doesn't move.

It is only when she feels Gerhard's lips on hers that she steps back and frees herself. She does so in panic.

'You smell of fresh air,' he says.

She turns away. Searching for something to talk about, something that can return the situation to what it was before they held each other. But she finds nothing. Eventually she meets his eyes, which are questioning, enquiring, wondering and at the same time appraising.

She grasps his hand. They stand like this, face to face. This silence is more intense than the moment when he held her, and she thinks, now I won't be able to resist.

But his hands don't move. He is about to say something. She places a finger on his lips. She pulls herself together and says:

'They've decided that you should stay in a hotel – Sirena. It's just by Norrmalmstorg. The square.'

He smiles again. 'Are you throwing me out?'

She smiles back, grateful for the gentle reaction. 'The resistance people want you to stay there until further notice. I'll accompany you there.' She adds: 'Afterwards.'

Oslo, November 1967

1

It is afternoon by the time Sverre Fenstad catches the tram home. Once again he sifts through what he has done. Was it right not to tell Ester about the weapon he had found in the cistern? Again he concludes it was, for the time being. Hiding the blade with such care may suggest Gerhard intends to use it – or thinks it might be necessary to do so. Such a conclusion proves that Sverre is right to focus on Gerhard's as yet unknown agenda. Sverre's motto is: keep a cool head. Fishermen are the apostles of patience. Waiting is an art. Waiting until you know more. The same rule applies when information has to be disseminated. Inform when the time is ripe.

Having got off at Nordberg he stands on the platform, watching the tram disappear around the bend before he tackles the hill. As soon as he leaves the platform, he hears a car engine start up. The driver accelerates. Sverre steps back into the snowberry bushes. The car screams to a halt beside him.

Sverre loses balance, but regains it. The car is a white Volvo Amazon. The driver stretches across the passenger seat and rolls down the window.

'Find anything, did you?'

Gerhard's face is distorted into a frozen grimace. 'Find what you were looking for?'

Sverre chooses not to answer. He sets off walking.

Gerhard drives slowly alongside, so close that Sverre is almost shunted off the road.

Gerhard shouts through the window: 'You're a clown, Sverre. Ever heard that before?'

Sverre is silent. He is frightened by Gerhard's fury. He seems so out of control. Sverre just focuses on the weapon in the cistern. The goal is now to reach his front door. Get nearer to people and houses.

Witnesses. In case he has to call for help. Climbing the hill makes him out of breath; his panting means he doesn't catch all Gerhard says. He keeps going. When he is close to his gate he sees people.

A girl in stretch pants and an anorak is walking a cocker spaniel; the dog stops and lifts a rear leg against the gate post.

Sverre stops.

The girl nods to him and pulls at the dog, which resists at first, but then follows happily.

The car has stopped.

Sverre looks for the girl, who turns into a gateway. He wonders if he should talk to her, get her to turn round, come over. But he doesn't. He looks across at the car. Gerhard has also been watching the girl. Now she is nowhere to be seen.

Gerhard opens the car door and steps out. He doesn't move. They glare at each other over the car roof. Finally Gerhard closes the car door.

Sverre casts around the neighbouring houses for help. All his eyes see are empty verandas and blank windows reflecting the sky. No one around.

'You think the world is as it was before,' Gerhard says. 'You think you won the war on your own, don't you. You, with a little help from Max and Kjakan.'

Sverre doesn't answer.

'The Soviets took Berlin with a loss of fifteen million men. A trifle, eh?'

Sverre struggles to control his breathing.

'Did you ever wear a uniform, Sverre?'

Sverre takes a step back towards the gate.

'After victory arrogance is a new and greater opponent. But perhaps you never learned that?'

'What do you want?'

'Don't you think I know who was constantly travelling from Oslo to Stockholm in December forty-two? Don't you think I know what you were doing there?'

Again Sverre's eyes wander to the neighbouring houses. Some lit windows gleam in the afternoon. But still there is no one around.

'And don't you think I intend to do something about it?'

'Is that a threat, Gerhard?'

'Are you anxious?'

Sverre doesn't answer.

'Are you afraid?'

Sverre assumes that, so long as they are standing still, the situation won't degenerate into something nasty.

'Did you ever fire live ammunition during the war, Sverre? I know you pushed a lot of paper. I know you sat with a mask over your face in meetings with people who were playing the same war game as you.'

Sverre Fenstad dangles his hand behind him, finds the catch on the gate and opens it.

'Before you go,' Gerhard says, resting his arms on the car roof. He folds his hands and leans casually against the car, as though this were a cosy chat between two old friends. 'Let me tell you a little story from another war. When we were lying in the trenches by Cordoba, sometimes we were posted as sentries in no-man's land to resist the Moroccans. It was the worst sentry duty you could have. Because if you fell asleep on duty you were done for. It wasn't unusual for us to wake up in the morning and find a comrade with his throat cut. No one wanted this sentry duty…'

'Where are you going with this, Gerhard?'

'If you were ordered to do this duty there was only one way to stay awake all night: you had to put the rifle butt on the ground and the bayonet under your chin.'

Sverre's breathing is normal now. 'I just asked you a question,' he says. 'Are you threatening me?'

Gerhard straightens up. Opens the car door.

Sverre breathes out.

Gerhard points to his chin. 'A bayonet, Sverre, under here.'

He gets in, twists the ignition key and presses the accelerator. The tyres scream as they spin away.

Sverre waits until the car has gone before turning and going indoors. He goes upstairs and into the bathroom to take a shower and change into fresher clothes.

2

The lighter is a silver-coloured Ronson. It makes hardly any noise when the top is pressed, and the yellow gas flame burns equally soundlessly. Its special feature is that the hood over the jet remains open until you close it and smother the flame. This makes the lighter ideal for lighting a pipe or a cigar. It was a present from Lillian almost eleven years ago. Five years before she died. It fits well into his hand and is always with him at work, in his free time and on holiday. Now he is lighting up and puffing at his cigarette – the second he has lit while he has been waiting. Sverre is sitting at the corner table in La Belle Sole and has smoked half the cigarette by the time Vera finally appears. The sight of her takes him back years. He remembers the scene as if it were yesterday – the moment the perfectly shaped diva entered the room and revelled in the hot, admiring gazes that evening in 1942. This is a sort of reprise. The room has barely any customers, and Vera has packed her feminine charisma into an unknown number of kilos and added an aura of grandchildren and exotic cake. He crushes the cigarette in the ashtray, gets up and holds a chair for her, the way he used to do.

Vera strokes his cheek and sits down. 'How amusing that you wanted to meet me here, Sverre.'

Her hat, however, is in the latest fashion, a striped, tight-fitting creation, resembling a helmet. It brings out her facial features in a becoming manner. She looks around. 'But I liked the old furniture better. The high seat-backs were intimate and reminded me of the little compartments on a train.'

'I've always had a soft spot for this place. It's remarkable that a restaurant in Oslo can keep going for more than forty years. I think only the Grand and the Theatercafé can rival it.'

Vera smiles. 'What about Stratos, Cecil or Dovrehallen?'

'Yes, but I used to know the owner, Hans Larsen, quite well. He died earlier this year, you know. He bought the whole block back in 1923, and established the restaurant then. In those days he had a chicken farm across the road, in a kind of barn outside the university library. The menu wasn't very big in those days, remember? So he just walked across the road and twisted the neck of a chicken when he needed one.'

'He'd stopped doing that when we were here. I know the bird that was served in most restaurants during the war was crow.'

Sverre nods. 'Crow's supposed to be a delicacy. If they're cooked well, most animals are good. I've heard they eat dogs in China.'

'Thank you. I prefer fish. The owner must've done too, don't you think?' Vera points to the aquarium taking pride of place in the middle of the room.

The waiter arrives with menus.

Vera asks for a glass of red Martini to start with.

The waiter withdraws.

'You used to be able to point to the fish you wanted served fresh,' Sverre says. 'But Larsen developed personal friendships with the fish. He gave names to the ones that lived longest. Called them Hitler and Stalin, Mons and Betsy. Then it was harder to let them go.'

They sat looking at each other.

'I might've managed to locate the woman you're searching for. The only problem is that she's dead. Would you like the long or the short version?'

'The short one,' he says.

'OK. This woman – Åsta something or other – was a courier. Åsta was arrested in October 1942. Which meant that she testified in many cases against certain top-ranking Nazis in forty-five and forty-six. Among others, Reidar Haaland. When Åsta was arrested she was subjected to a brutal interrogation – by Haaland. I think the case against him will be interesting for you. When Haaland ratcheted up the pressure, she chose to confess – but she also gave false information to make up for the damage her confession caused. She admitted to Haaland that she sometimes worked as a courier. Then he wanted to know who her contact was and when they met. She made up a story about her contact being a man with a cover name of Kåre. This Kåre used to catch the Sognsvann line to the centre of town from Valkyrie plass station. The truth was that that she regularly met a *female* courier working under the cover name of Hilde. Åsta and Hilde always met on the opposite platform. They caught the metro together to Sognsvann. She didn't know Hilde's identity – only her cover name. This Hilde didn't testify. I haven't been able to find out why. Perhaps she's dead. The routine was that, whenever they met, they would sit together on the tram with the bag between them. They always chose a time of the day when there weren't many people around. Hilde always got off at the first stop – Majorstua station. She always left the bag of illegal newspapers behind. Åsta got off at Tåsen station and handed the bag to her contact there.'

'Hilde wasn't dead,' Sverre says. 'She spent a number of years abroad after the war.'

'Ah, that explains it, then. Well, on this particular day Åsta was accompanied to the station by two men: Haaland and a German from the Gestapo. Both wore civvies. She led them down to the wrong platform. The aim was to tell the other courier – Hilde – that their cover had been blown. She would try to talk her way out of it with Haaland afterwards. Hilde appeared on time. However, the two men spotted her. They tried to capture her, but Hilde got away. Afterwards Åsta was again subjected to a brutal interrogation. But she had no idea what Hilde's real identity was. So in the end she was released.'

The waiter brings Vera's Martini. They look up at him.

'Are you ready to order?'

Vera looks across at Sverre. 'I'll have what you're having, as always.'

'I'll have the halibut.'

'Me too.'

'And to drink?'

'The house white – if it's dry.'

'It isn't, but I have a Riesling for the same price. I'd recommend it with halibut.'

'Then we'll take it.'

Sverre waits until the waiter is out of hearing. 'What about the murder of Åse Lajord?'

'I've only just started to look into that. Haven't found anything yet. Don't expect too much, either. The paperwork may've disappeared in the chaos of peace. There was a lot of German propaganda about this case during the war. But I still remember the civil case. You can ask me about that.'

'The civil case?'

'The guardianship. Åse Lajord's mother, Margaret Lajord, was awarded custody of the child. She can thank me for that. And the money.'

'The money?'

'The poor girl must've scraped together a pretty big deposit for her flat, so that was still with the building owner, and there was still rent in credit, and the furniture was worth a bit too. I helped to sell some stuff. Imagine, at that time I did all that for your sake – and you didn't give it a thought.'

'Are you saying the flat belonged to Åse?'

'She rented it. I remember the Gestapo lapped that up. Falkum using the lodgings as a kind of cover made him more suspicious in their eyes. Åse Lajord's mother died of kidney failure in 1944. Before she died, the child was adopted by a younger couple in Valdres. Erik and Grete Heggen. They live here in Oslo, in the Slemdal district. I found his name in the phone directory. Apparently they were childhood friends of the girl who was killed. Oh, and I've just remembered one more restaurant – the Ekeberg. It's been going since 1929, hasn't it?'

The waiter has brought the bottle of wine. She straightens up and falls quiet as he opens it.

3

Gerhard leans back in the driver's seat. He has a grandstand view of the window and Sverre Fenstad sitting inside with a woman. They are eating and laughing together. It almost looks like he is getting her drunk. As soon as the first bottle is empty, another appears on the table. Gerhard leans back again and tips his hat over his eyes. The next time he looks up they are onto the dessert. Fenstad has a cognac and the lady a small glass of a greenish liqueur. Not long to wait now, fortunately. Gerhard takes a pack of cards from his pocket and plays patience on the passenger's seat while keeping an eye on the two of them. The street lamp gives just enough light. He plays Perpetual Motion and, strangely, discards all the cards at the fifth attempt. At that moment Sverre Fenstad and the plump woman are on their way out. He gives them a head start of fifty metres before opening the door and following them.

✻

Vera and Sverre stroll side by side along the tram tracks in Solli plass. It is dark and quiet. They stop by the timetables board. She casts an eye over the times and then looks at her watch. 'I can never remember when they go.'

'You still live in Torshov?'

She nods. 'Fredrik signed up for the OBOS housing co-op when we got married. But he still hasn't been offered the dream flat we're going to live in. Now we've been married for twenty-one years. Altogether I've lived for thirty-two years in Hegermanns gate.'

'You haven't thought of moving to a modern satellite town?'

'No, thank you. High-rises and howling winds? The view I have is still among Oslo's best, and the flat's just the right size.'

They look at each other.

'Now it's as if we're the ones who are married,' she says. 'Our conversation has no energy or excitement.'

He is about to say something.

She places a finger on his lips. 'Here's my tram.' She holds up a hand. They both step back a pace. The tram stops. The door opens. 'It was good to see you again, Sverre,' she says.

He nods. 'I think so, too.'

She gets on.

He stands watching the tram as it pulls away. A single HØKA carriage. It tapers at the back into a square window. Vera stands there. She waves. He raises a hand. Vera and the window become smaller and smaller. Soon she is out of sight.

He takes a deep breath and can feel he is not very steady on his feet. He drank most of the wine and on top of that had two cognacs. He decides to walk it off.

His hip is fine this evening. He barely feels any pain, and there is hardly anyone else out – only the occasional taxi passing. It is so quiet he can hear the click of his own shoes and the tap of his stick between every pace. Then he hears another rhythm. The sound of footsteps. Sverre Fenstad casts a glance over his shoulder.

Some distance behind him, a man in dark clothes and a hat is ambling on the opposite side of the street, in the shade of the trees in the Palace Gardens. He has his hands in his coat pockets. He is no more than an outline, a silhouette against the trees in the park. But the silhouette is unmistakeable.

Sverre walks on. But feels uneasy having Gerhard behind him. He stops and turns around. Gerhard stops too. In the silence they stand staring at each other.

Sverre Fenstad sets off again. But then he thinks: I can't be bothered with this. Gerhard isn't going to try anything here. There are witnesses around. He decides to confront him. He spins around.

But Gerhard has vanished.

4

Sverre can feel a nagging anxiety in his chest now. He walks down the tiled corridor leading to the platform. He glances over his shoulder again and again. Every time he is able to confirm that he is not being followed. A Sognsvann line metro train has just gone. Almost twenty minutes to wait. He finds a free space on a bench. He leans back against the wall and wakes with a start as a dark-red train glides alongside the platform. He quickly checks his watch. He has been asleep for more than ten minutes. His nervousness is mounting. He has lost some of his self-control. The doors slide open and the conductor jumps out. There are still a few minutes left before departure. Sverre Fenstad sits down in the non-smoking compartment at the front of the empty carriage. The conductor and the driver are chatting outside. The driver lights the stub of a roll-up he takes from a matchbox. The conductor comments on the diminutive size. Sverre doesn't hear the response. He has fallen into his own reverie. Remembering the time the air-raid siren went off after the German ammunition dump in Filipstad exploded. The cargo ship *SS Selma* was fully laden with German grenades. It was being unloaded when there was an explosion. Which year was that? Forty-three? Before Christmas? Yes, December forty-three. What a bang! And what panic! Between forty and fifty people were killed, more than four hundred wounded. Grenades were raining down on Oslo. It was a Sunday. He had been out with Vera then as well. Rain and slush. They had been two of several thousand people who came down here afterwards, to the underground. He and Vera had made their way along the rails and found some stairs in the tunnel that led to an exit in Oscars gate. From there they walked around to find out what had happened. It could have been an air raid, or sabotage. But it turned out that Germans themselves caused it.

The door to the driver's cabin closes and soon after the conductor blows his whistle. Sverre puts a hand in his pocket and takes out his ticket.

When the train stops in Valkyrie plass no one gets off or on. Sverre looks out and imagines a young Ester waiting on the platform with illegal newspapers in a bag. He thinks about the magical capacity of towns to remain backdrops for generations of people. Someone stole a first kiss in a place like this. Others had their lives turned upside down by stumbling or meeting a gaze. All the time a place such as this waits patiently for new events from a new narrative.

The train stops at Majorstua. Here the platform is crowded. Sverre looks at his watch and guesses the nine o'clock performance at the Colosseum cinema has just finished. The carriage is crammed full. Sverre moves closer to the window to make more room on the seat. Two middle-aged women sit down and talk about the film. Sverre Fenstad gathers that Elizabeth Taylor and Richard Burton are the main stars. 'Such is love,' says one woman. 'That's how it is. You can't escape the truth.' Her friend is more interested in Taylor's figure. 'Don't you think she's put on weight? She was so attractive when she played Maggie in *Cat on a Hot Tin Roof.* Goodness me, now *that* was a love story.'

Sverre closes his eyes and ears. The train ride is a routine your body adapts to all on its own. He has calmed down, and when sleep comes he does nothing to prevent it. He nods off again and wakes automatically on the incline up to Østhorn station. Now there aren't so many people in the carriage. He waits until the train sets off again. Then he buttons up his coat and gets to his feet. At Nordberg he is the only passenger to alight.

5

Gerhard is standing by the garden gate in front of Sverre's house. The Sognsvann train departs from Nordberg station. A single person comes down the slope to the crossing. Sverre's figure is easily recognisable because of the stick.

Quietly, Gerhard waits until he can hear the rhythmical tap of the stick on the tarmac. Then he crosses the lawn and goes in through the open veranda door. Gerhard goes up the stairs and into Sverre's bathroom. From here he can see down to the gate and the front of the house.

Gerhard looks through the bathroom window as Sverre Fenstad appears behind the hedge. He stops and stands quite still. Sverre has at last seen what has been happening.

When Sverre leaves the station he is thinking about Vera and the times they will never see again. He walks into the light from the street lamp and out again. That is when he notices the light behind the hedge. The discovery causes him to slow down and he feels a cold claw in his lower abdomen. At the garden gate he sees the light is on in the sitting room. He stops. The sitting-room window should *not* be lit. The light is always turned off when he isn't at home.

He stands under the birch tree, looking at the light in the window. It is almost as if the house has become alien to him.

No movements behind the glass that he can discern.

Eventually he treads warily towards the wrought-iron gate in front of the entrance. The gate is wide open. He walks through, leaving it open. Walks around the house, into the garden.

His shoes shuffle through the wet grass as he slowly makes his way along the house wall, rounds the corner and stops. The veranda door is open. It gapes ominously. Sverre starts sweating. The silence is numbing. He looks around. Some windows in the houses nearby are lit, but not a sound can be heard through his open veranda door. He forces himself to step onto the veranda. Tries to tread silently on the tiles. The curtain flaps through the door. He lifts his stick and holds it at the ready, like a club, as he enters.

Stockholm, December 1942

1

Gerhard holds the front door open for her. The cold air hits them. The taxi is waiting by the kerb. The driver sees Gerhard is carrying a rucksack, so he walks around the car and opens the boot. Gerhard shakes his head and puts the rucksack on the rear seat, then gets in. Ester gives the driver the address. Now *he* holds the door open for her.

The car sets off. Ester looks through the window without registering anything but illuminated shop windows and the dark shadows of people on the pavement. She is unsure what is going on between them and considers it positive that Gerhard is moving out. At that moment she notices a shift in atmosphere and turns to him. He says nothing. Just looks at her.

The car pulls up. The driver turns round and announces: 'Hotel Sirena.'

Gerhard opens the door and slips the rucksack onto his back. He asks: 'Are you going to come up with me and have a look?' She agrees and wriggles out of the car. She is about to take money from her bag, but changes her mind. Asks the driver to wait. Avoids eye contact with Gerhard. Instead she looks up at the façade. Dirty, grey building. Dirty windows. The sign above the entrance isn't easy to see. She follows him up the steps and inside.

They enter the reception area. No service. She waits by the lift while he goes to the counter.

There is a bell on the counter. He presses it. No audible response. He turns to her, eyebrows raised. She shrugs. He presses again. No ring, no buzz. He holds the button down.

A door opens and a squat man in trousers, vest and hanging braces comes through the opening behind the counter. He is chewing. Tells Gerhard he can take his finger off the bell now. He takes a ledger from a drawer.

Ester turns her back while Gerhard registers and is given a key.

The lift is a little cage with walls of black steel grating. The door is wrought-iron and closes with a scissor mechanism. They have to stand close to fit in. Ester avoids his gaze as the lift transports them up through the floors. Getting out, Gerhard walks ahead down a narrow corridor smelling of dust and mould. He unlocks the door and enters. Sighs at the sight that meets them inside. A prison bed, a sink, a table and a chair.

'Not exactly an esplanade hotel in St Tropez.'

'Only German soldiers stay there. You wouldn't have liked it any better.'

He grins.

She smiles back.

He eyes her from the side. 'It would be easier to convince the police we're married if we lived together, fru Larsen.'

She doesn't know what to reply. She likes the intimacy, but she doesn't like his references to the relationship. In a way her silence emphasises what she doesn't say. They are standing close. She steps back and says nervously: 'Now, you promise me you won't get drunk again.'

'Ester,' he says, slumping down onto the chair. 'There's something you have to know. I'm not cut out for this.'

She knows what is about to come and she understands.

'I'd rather go back to Norway than stay in a filthy hotel under a false name.'

She looks away. Wanting to reassure him. She knows she isn't allowed to say this, but decides to reveal the plan anyway. 'They're planning to organise Norwegian troops here, in Sweden.'

He gets to his feet, but his eyes are sceptical.

'This is actually confidential information,' she says. 'But there are lots of Norwegians who want to go back and fight. That's why Swedish soldiers are being brought in to train Norwegian troops. The idea is that it will take place in Kjesäter.'

He turns his back on her.

She takes a step forwards, apprehensive.

He turns round. 'And what good is that to me?'

'It means you'll get what you want anyway. Military training. Mobilisation.'

His eyes harden. 'But I was promised transport to England. You heard that yourself. It was a promise.'

She doesn't remember Torgersen's phrasing, but she doesn't want an argument. 'You have to understand that you have to be patient. There are thousands of Norwegian men wanting to enlist and return to fight.'

'Enlist? I don't need any register. I'm signed up. I've been signed up and have fought against the Germans from the very first day!'

'Torgersen's a man of his word. Just be a little patient. It won't be long now. I'm sure of that.'

He shakes his head.

'I'll push, Gerhard. I promise you.'

'The people here are out-and-out amateurs.' He extends an arm to take in the room. 'Look what they do with their resources. Pack me off into this grubby hotel room instead of helping me go to a training camp. Do you really think I can accept this?'

'For Åse's sake.'

He shakes his head.

'For your daughter's sake.'

'Ester, you can see the meaninglessness of this existence. You have to.'

Then she says: 'For my sake.'

He sighs out loud and smiles condescendingly. 'Ester, you must never make a promise you can't keep.'

They exchange glances and she has to look away. She knows all too well that he knows what she is thinking.

'I promise to tell them how hard you think this is,' she says. She can hear in her own ears how empty this promise is, but she needs to talk about something trivial to break out of this intense atmosphere.

She goes to the door. Turns and looks at him. Walks back and gives him a quick, firm hug before leaving and going back to the lift.

She struggles with the concertina door. Can't get it to close completely. The lift won't start. The metal rattles as she pushes the door open and pulls it back with all her strength. The lift still won't budge. Staircase, she thinks. At that moment a door in the corridor opens. A fat woman in a nightie stares at her, a cigarette in the corner of her mouth. She is wearing slippers. In one of them there is a hole and a toe is sticking out.

Ester tries once again to get the lift moving, but nothing happens. The fat woman comes into the corridor. She shuffles over to the lift and presses a button. The lift starts. Ester watches the woman's body disappear. She has a rash on her calves.

In the street, she scans the front of the hotel. Waves up at the window where she thinks Gerhard is, then jumps into the taxi, which immediately draws away.

Oslo, November 1967

1

Sverre pauses inside the veranda door. He stands quite still, listening, but can't hear any unfamiliar sounds. He sees the silhouette of Gerhard following him alongside the Palace Gardens. What if he is waiting for him in his house?

Gerhard must be unbalanced. Sverre has had dealings with such people before. But this man has no limits. He breaks into people's houses. In addition, he is armed. There is one thing Sverre has no doubts about: Gerhard is dangerous.

But he has to control his panic. And then he must search his house with a fine-tooth comb. First of all, he closes the veranda door behind him. Then he goes right into the house and up the stairs.

The hallway is empty. Nothing seems changed. His pulse rate is high when he pushes open his bedroom door. But the room is empty.

The bathroom is empty.

Back down the stairs. The same on the ground floor. No one in the sitting room, no one in the kitchen. Nothing seems to have been touched.

Can Gerhard have left the house with the door open? Is this tit for tat – a threat?

Sverre stands in front of the cellar door. At length he opens it. First, he peers down into the darkness. Then he switches on the light. Sees nothing unusual. The stairs are steep and he has to concentrate not to fall. He stops halfway. Looks back. The door slowly closes.

Sverre continues downwards, step by step. At the bottom he twists the next switch. The neon tube on the ceiling flickers. It won't light up. He studies the hobby-room door as the light struggles to come on. Then there is a bang.

Sverre's heart stops and he falls against the wall.

His forehead scrapes against the coarse brickwork. He gasps for air and claws at the concrete wall, but nothing happens – except the bang growing into a low roar.

He clutches his chest and realises the noise is the central boiler coming on. He breathes through his mouth, regains his balance and doesn't move until he is back to normal. His chest still hurts. The central heating hums, and the marker on the boiler's temperature gauge rises.

He moves forwards and opens the hobby-room door. Turns on the ceiling lamp. Nothing appears to have been touched. Leather, tools and stuffed animals. All the mess is as before. The dust is as before.

He turns round. The pain in his chest is less noticeable as he staggers to the stairs and goes back up. There is nothing out of the ordinary in the house. No drawers opened, no clocks stolen, none of Lillian's silverware in the sideboard has gone, nor the record player or the expensive Tandberg Sølvsuper radio. The wall clock shows it will soon be midnight.

Here, in the hallway, he stops and looks at the telephone.

He flicks through the directory. Finds the number of the police. Deliberates. Changes his mind. Puts the directory back. Takes the little wallet from his inside pocket and finds a private number instead. Looks at the clock. It is past midnight. It is a weekday. He stands up and deliberates. In the end he lifts the receiver and rings Hotel Continental. He asks to speak to Gary Larson. He is put through. The phone rings for a long time. No one answers.

He puts down the receiver. 'Oh Gerhard, Gerhard,' he mumbles, and goes over to the bar. Opens the cabinet. Pours himself a drink from the bottle he offered to Gerhard a few days ago. Drains the glass in one swig. Puts down the glass and goes to the bathroom.

Afterwards he goes back to the telephone. Rings Hotel Continental once again. He is put through to Gary Larson's room. No one answers this time either. He holds the receiver and listens to the constant ringing. He wonders whether not knowing where Gerhard is might be a cause for concern. Ends up telling himself Gerhard has been here to frighten him. As a kind of retaliation for his visit to Gerhard's room. An eye for an eye. Presumably Gerhard is on his way back to the hotel. Or he is intentionally letting the telephone ring because he suspects it is Sverre calling.

Sverre walks through the house one last time, checking that all the doors are locked. The front door, the veranda door. Now that he is sure he is alone, it costs him nothing to go down to the cellar and check the entrance there. The wooden doorframe is damaged. This is where Gerhard broke in, possibly with the help of a jemmy or some other tool. He forced the frame to the side. That won't happen again. The door has two locks: a normal lock and a metal fitting on the inside that can be padlocked. He goes into the hobby room and takes the padlock from the drawer. Locks the door. Now it won't be so easy to break in again. He checks that the windows are properly closed. He stops by the telephone and lifts the receiver. He lays it on the table. The sound of the dialling tone follows him up the stairs.

He gets undressed to go to bed. Opens the bedroom window a little. Changes his mind and closes it. Once again he makes sure the window is closed before he slips under the duvet.

2

A shadow leans over the bed. A figure wearing a balaclava. Sverre tries to raise a hand and push the man away, but can't. He wants to tear off the balaclava, but still he can't move his hand. Sverre realises he is dreaming. As he realises this, the shadow disappears, and Sverre feels cold. It is the cold that has woken him.

He wakes with a start.

The window is wide open.

Sverre is immediately alert and tries to control his breathing. He lies still, listening. It is raining outside. A branch scrapes against the pane. He turns his head carefully. The darkness in the corridor outside the bedroom is a black wall. The door is open.

Someone has opened the bedroom door. Someone has been in here while he has been asleep and opened the window.

Now Sverre hears a strange hissing sound beneath the driving wind and rain, from inside the house, on the floor below.

He tries to slide from under the duvet without rustling the material. Puts his feet on the ground. He stands up and the pain in his hip flares.

He teeters, but manages to stay upright. The floorboards creak as he walks to the wall. He looks over his shoulder as his hand fumbles with the window catch. Grabs it. Closes the window. Limps to the door. Scans the darkness in the corridor outside the bedroom. Listens. Silence – apart from the strange hiss from downstairs.

What is Gerhard up to?

Sverre goes back to the bed. Opens the drawer in the bedside table. Where there is a dagger. He takes it and heads for the dark corridor. Inches alongside the wall, dagger raised, to the staircase.

His mouth is dry. His arms and legs feel numb.

He pauses at the top of the stairs. At the foot, light is coming in – through an open door.

Someone has switched on the light. Someone is still here.

He wants to shout, but his voice won't carry. He is sweating and his dagger hand is trembling.

But he doesn't want to be like this. He needs to have certainty. Needs to know what is going on.

He forces himself to go downstairs. One hand is on the banister. The other is holding the dagger aloft

The hissing is getting louder with every step he takes.

Before he reaches the bottom he sees the telephone receiver is back in position.

He stops on the lowest step, his hand squeezing the banister as he stares at the telephone. The light from the sitting-room doorway falls on it.

Slowly he turns his head to the right.

The sitting-room door is ajar. This is where the hissing is coming from.

He continues to the door and pushes it open with the dagger.

No one there, but the television is on. There is snow on the screen. Noise. He walks in. Switches the television off. There is total silence.

There is a light on in the kitchen. That door is ajar too.

He tries to move without making a sound. The door hinges scream. On the worktop there is a half-empty coffee cup.

The kettle is on the stove. He feels it. It is still warm.

As he places his hand on the kettle the telephone rings. He turns. Goes to the hall and lifts the receiver. 'Hello. Sverre Fenstad here.'

No answer.

'Hello?' he repeats.

A click tells him the caller has hung up.

He cradles the receiver and goes towards the sitting-room door. He sees the outline of a man in the TV screen. His knees give way. He clutches his chest.

But the movements on the screen tell him this pathetic shadow of a person is himself.

He has to lean against the door frame until he is calm again. Then he limps into the sitting room and sits down on the chair in the corner. Here he has a better chance of seeing what is going on than he does in the upstairs bedroom.

He tells himself he has to search the house, thinking at the same time it isn't necessary. The person who has been here has gone. However, Sverre knows he has to strike back. He has to show Gerhard. He has to make him understand that this time he has gone too far.

In fact there is only one thing to do: ring Brustad early tomorrow morning.

Could Brustad have met Gerhard during the war? he reflects. Of course, it is a possibility, but it doesn't necessarily have to be the case. He seems to recall that Brustad was in Oslo all of 1941. Afterwards he was at the intelligence office in Sweden for a short while, before going to London, where he worked as a security officer in intelligence. Sverre doesn't think Brustad knew Gerhard Falkum. Sverre doesn't have to tell the surveillance boss the whole story. It doesn't matter anyway. Brustad never does the dirty work himself.

Sverre Fenstad raises his hand. It is still trembling. The doors and windows were closed when he went to bed. How could Gerhard have got in?

Sverre leans back in the chair and surveys his home. When day breaks, he thinks, when daylight returns, so will serenity, and then I will be able to put this experience behind me.

Stockholm, December 1942

1

They walk past the lines of partition walls. Even though all the booths are empty, Markus chooses the shooting range at the very end.

'We won't be disturbed here.'

She gazes at the targets hanging from the ceiling while Markus takes the weapon apart. The gun is smaller than the one she found in Gerhard's bedside table.

Markus tells her it is a Husqvarna M40.

She notices a crank handle on the wall. The targets can be wound back and forth.

'Pay attention,' Markus reproves. The barrel, the stock, the magazine and the lock lie in pieces on the bench. He shows her which movable parts it is important to lubricate and how the gun works. 'You pull the trigger, the firing pin hits the primer in the cartridge, the powder explodes, the bullet is fired and the force makes this slide backwards. Notice the springs. The empty cartridge case is ejected and the next one is pushed up by the magazine. They call this gun a Lahti.'

He shows her how to load the magazine. Eight shots. He tells her to push the magazine in.

She holds the gun. Presses.

'You have to use a little strength.'

He takes it back and does it. The magazine clicks into place. He cocks the gun. Takes out the magazine and passes it back. 'Your turn.'

She tries again. Likes the feel of the gun in her hand. Pushes the magazine in. Cocks the gun.

He nods. Takes the gun back from her. Applies the safety catch and afterwards shows her how to hold it. 'With both hands. Hold your arms out at shoulder height. Look at the angle between my upper arm and chest.'

She looks. Lifts her own arms and compares.

'Feet well apart. That'll give you good balance. Slight bend in the knees, so you're supple. Straight back. In that way the gun's stable and the chances of hitting with several shots are that much greater.'

She nods again.

'Try to imagine a straight line between your nose, the sights on the gun and the target. Try.'

She tries.

He asks her what she is doing on Friday.

She lowers the gun.

He repeats the question.

She says she is going to the synagogue.

His face brightens. 'Good. Then we can go together!'

She has to smile when he laughs. Markus has an infectious laugh. But she doesn't respond to his invitation. She takes the weapon.

'Ear defenders.'

She puts down the gun and places the defenders over her ears.

He nods.

She holds the gun with both hands outstretched as he has shown her. The target has been drawn onto the chest region of a man in silhouette. She tries to pull the trigger.

'Release the safety catch first.'

She smiles sheepishly, does as he says and lifts the gun again. Pulls the trigger, but doesn't manage to stifle a squeal as her hands fly into the air.

Markus grins.

Ester blushes. I'm a fool, she thinks.

'You felt it then. You have to be the boss. You have to control the gun. Hold it down.'

Ester can feel the blush is still there.

Once again she holds the weapon with both hands and her arms outstretched. Focuses on the target. Fires three shots. The impact of the shots tears at her arms. She knows she has missed the target, but not a sound escapes her mouth.

Markus nods acknowledgement. She takes off the ear defenders.

He takes the gun and applies the safety catch. 'It's hot. Feel.'

She feels.

'The heat affects the metal. It can become unstable. That's why lubrication and cleaning are so incredibly important.'

She gives a start when a shot goes off somewhere behind them in the cellar.

'You have to get used to the noise down here,' he says, loading the magazine.

Ester cranes her neck. A man emerges from a booth further down. Now he is standing with his back to them. He is wearing only a singlet on his chest, and the muscles in his upper arms and back ripple as he forces cartridges into the magazine. He turns and fiddles with the gun. There is something familiar about his profile.

'Do you know everyone here?' she asks.

Markus shakes his head.

She motions her head towards the man in the singlet and arches both eyebrows.

Markus shakes his head and whispers. 'English. SIS. Secret Intelligence Service. He's an English intelligence officer.'

She stares at the furthest booth again. The man puts the ear defenders over his head and readies himself. Then she recognises him. Round, rimless glasses and a narrow mouth. It is the man from the cinema. The man Gerhard spoke with in Tegnérlunden after she had gone to see what the police were doing in Kammakargatan 33.

He looks up and their eyes meet.

He shows no sign of recognition. A second later and he is hidden by the booth wall. A quick series of shots. Then it is quiet and the target glides back to the booth.

'There are lots of Englishmen in Stockholm,' Markus whispers with a grin. 'Very hush-hush because of the war. But you get used to them,' he says, passing her the gun. 'Come on. Another round.'

2

Snow is falling fast. Her whole field of vision is obscured by thick, white stripes angling downwards. The world is disappearing. Cars stand askew, their wheels spinning. Trams have come to a halt as the conductors work with crowbars and gas flames on the rails to remove the ice and snow from the points. A man in a winter coat with his collar up and his hat pulled down over his forehead is shovelling snow from a car parked by the pavement. Ester is overjoyed that she can walk to work. Even if that, too, is sometimes a trial. The snowploughs churn the snow onto the pavement so that the road is the only viable place to walk. Until a bus races along and she has to leap for her life and wade through deep snow again.

On her way up the steps to the intelligence office she has to slow down. She is walking behind a snow-covered back she seems to recognise. When he turns to brush the snow off his shoulders there is no doubt:

'Number Thirteen,' she says.

Sverre Fenstad beams. 'Ester!'

'But what are you doing here?' she says, genuinely surprised. 'Don't tell me you've had to leave Norway, too!'

He shakes his head. 'I have a meeting.'

'But what's happened?'

'Nothing special. Those of us at home just have to coordinate with those of you here in Sweden now and then. We're going to see each other many times. But I'm going back tonight or tomorrow.'

He opens the door and holds it for her. 'Ladies first.'

They go inside.

In the office Torgersen is waiting.

While they are hanging up their clothes, Sverre whispers: 'You're looking good, Ester.'

'Thank you, and the same to you.'

Sverre thrusts a hand into his inside jacket pocket and pulls out a letter. 'For you, from Åse Lajord's mother.'

She takes it and studies the envelope. When she looks up, Sverre Fenstad has gone into Torgersen's office.

Ester becomes aware of an unfamiliar scent in the office. It is after-shave. It smells like lemon. It is only now that she notices they have company. He is sitting by the window. An athletic-looking man in his forties. He is wearing casual clothes. Breeches and a woollen jumper. There is a peaked cap beside him on the table. He seems inaccessible, sitting there and tamping his pipe.

Ester sits down at her desk. Soon she realises that everyone else in the office knows him. Mildred and Margit talk to him, and she realises he has news from Norway. They look at her and whisper. The man answers in short sentences. Occasionally he removes the pipe from his mouth and pretends to examine the glow in the bowl. What he actually does is cast a furtive glance at her; she notices.

They are talking about my parents, she thinks. They are saying I am Jewish. They are wallowing in the tragedy that my family has been deported to Germany. She looks down without letting on that she has noticed. She realises that this man has not come from the refugee reception centre. He must have come with Sverre Fenstad.

After an hour, Torgersen's door opens. Sverre appears. 'Ester, can you come in for a moment?'

She gets up and goes in.

Four men are sitting around the meeting table. She knows Sverre Fenstad and Torgersen. The other two she doesn't know, but she is aware they are high-ranking officers in the legation.

Torgersen introduces her and says she is responsible for contact with Gerhard Falkum.

'What's your impression, Ester? How is he coping with the situation?'

Ester says what she knows. The waiting is getting on his nerves. She wonders whether to say what she thinks deep down and decides to do so. She says Gerhard is reacting badly to being inactive. He feels negative about having to hide in Sweden. For him, going back to Norway is a more attractive option. She says that, for his sake, she hopes he can soon be transported to England. That will solve everything. It is inhuman to escape to freedom and have to live like a wanted criminal here in Sweden.

The others regard her in silence.

Should she say she has seen Gerhard with a British intelligence officer? Pass on Gerhard's story that the man gets booze for him? It could be true. And what damage has it done, actually? The English are enemies of Germany, as the Norwegians are. Sometimes Gerhard does have to go into the street, and then he will, of necessity, meet people.

'What does he want to do in Norway?' Sverre interrupts her line of thought.

'Fight,' Ester says. 'He's desperate to be active. He thinks his existence here is pointless; he might as well be in hiding with Norwegian saboteurs in Norway. At the start he kept asking me if I knew when he was going to England. Now he has stopped. In my opinion he's losing confidence in us. So he wants to cross the border. He's had to move once already while he's been with us, because of the police. He thinks it would be better for everyone if he's actively doing resistance work instead of passively waiting for the Swedish police to arrest him. At least that's what he tells me. The more time that passes before he travels to England, the more desperate he's becoming.'

There is silence in the room. The participants let the information sink in and say nothing.

Ester wonders whether she has laid it on too thick. She decides to quote Gerhard's own words. 'He sees himself as a resource. He's been active in the resistance right from the very first day. He thinks it's indefensible to pack him off into a hotel when they could be using him.'

'He's absolutely right about that.' It is the man sitting next to Sverre Fenstad who says it. He adds that Gerhard would probably be well received at home. 'Falkum's a man with unusual war experience. He distinguished himself in Spain, especially in Cordoba in August of 1936.'

The others exchange glances, and Ester can see they don't appreciate the man's comments.

Ester is unsure what they expect from her now and looks at them. They look back at her.

Torgersen whispers: 'Thank you, Ester. You can go now.'

She gets up and makes for the door.

'Ester.'

It is Sverre. She turns to face him.

'Kolstad,' Sverre says. 'He's out there with you. Can you ask him to come in please?'

She nods and closes the door after her. Again she has become unsure of her role and how she was playing it. It wasn't her intention to say unfavourable things about Gerhard. She just wanted to communicate the fact that he is having a difficult time. She pauses with her back to the door for a few moments. The Norwegian in the breeches is perching on the edge of Mildred's desk now. She is laughing at something he has said. 'Are you Kolstad?' she asks.

He looks up.

'Sverre's asked to see you.' She motions with her head.

'Me?' He grimaces. 'That's a first,' he says and pats Mildred on the shoulder. He departs, followed by waves of after-shave.

Ester has made up her mind: she doesn't like him. 'Who's he?' she asks Mildred.

'Kolstad? He's a sort of bodyguard, I think.'

Oslo, November 1967

1

Sverre Fenstad raps the door knocker twice and waits.

The door is opened by a woman in her fifties, wearing a blue dress with white dots. Her blonde hair is dark at the roots, and its straight fall tells him she has just combed it.

'Grete,' Sverre says. 'I was hoping to find you both at home,' he adds quickly when he sees her confusion.

She stares at him. He tells her why he has come. The information has an impact. She steps aside to let him in.

The couple have probably just had lunch. There is a smell of boiled cod and melted butter in the house. Sverre struggles to interpret the atmosphere. He isn't asked to sit down. Nor is he offered anything. Grete stands by the window, glaring accusatorily at her husband, who has been lying on the sofa, but now swings his feet to the floor and pokes them into a pair of worn slippers.

'Why didn't you say anything?' Grete says. 'I think it would be good for her to meet her father.'

Erik looks at her without answering. Then at Sverre.

Sverre doesn't like the atmosphere and wonders if there is anything he can do to alleviate it. A loudspeaker crackles. It is Erik switching on the Tandberg radio in the cabinet beside the sofa. Erik sits up straight, still reticent.

'Answer me!' Grete demands. 'You find out that Gerhard's alive and wants contact – and you say nothing? Not to me and not to her.'

Erik doesn't seem to hear.

Grete glares at Erik, who still seems to be wondering what to say. 'We heard he'd been killed,' she says to Sverre. 'That's why we agreed to adopt Turid. And now you're saying he's alive?'

'It's a long story,' Sverre says. 'The plane crash and the death were reported by our people in Stockholm. No one was in a position to doubt the information in those days. But in fact it was incorrect. The man who wishes to contact Turid is indeed Gerhard Falkum. What I'd like to know is whether he's contacted you.'

She shakes her head.

The valves in the radio have warmed up and the news reader's voice booms through the speaker. Erik looks at the radio for a few seconds, then clears his throat: 'It won't happen anyway.'

Grete has to raise her voice to drown out the news reader: 'What won't?'

'Gerhard contacting Turid.'

Grete goes to the cabinet and presses a button. The radio dies and the silence spreading through the room is charged again.

'You can't just decide that on your own.'

The couple stare at each other for so long that Sverre feels he should leave. He backs towards the door.

'Grete,' Erik says quietly. 'We're not alone.'

Grete is about to say something, but bites her tongue.

Sverre Fenstad feels this is the right moment. 'He might've contacted her directly, but then she would've told you, wouldn't she?'

Grete eyes him uneasily. 'Would he contact her without our consent?'

Sverre shrugs. 'Anything's possible. Besides, she's old enough. She can do as she likes.'

Grete turns to her husband: 'Erik.'

Her husband doesn't answer.

'Gerhard's intentions aren't good,' she says quietly. 'I can feel that in my bones. I'm sure it was him who sent the photo of Åse to Turid.'

Sverre arches both eyebrows. 'The photo?'

'She received a letter. A photo of Åse. A few days ago.'

'May I see it?'

The couple exchange glances. Erik shrugs. Grete leaves the room.

The two men wait until she has closed the door after her. Then they look at each other. 'See what you're doing?' Erik is furious.

Sverre has decided to ignore emotional outbursts. 'Gerhard's in town, Erik. Neither you nor I can do anything about that.'

'You can do something about it, if you want to.'

'Wanting to meet your own child is perfectly natural.'

Erik glowers at him. 'So you think he's restrained himself over there for all these years, do you? Then he just comes here, on an impulse, without writing first, without so much as a hint to Turid that he exists in all the time she's been alive?'

Sverre has no answer.

'Do you really think one of God's own behaves like that? Do you? Do you? Sverre Fenstad?'

'What I think is immaterial.'

'Fine. But I still make the decisions in my house.' Erik stands up. He marches past his guest without another word. The door slams after him.

Shortly afterwards Grete peeks through the door. 'What was that?'

'No idea,' Sverre says, taking the proffered photo. He retrieves his glasses from his breast pocket. Angles the photograph so that the light from the window falls on it. An attractive fair-haired woman is sitting on a doorstep. She is laughing at the photographer. The door is in two parts. The top part is open; the bottom part closed. The cabin walls are made of logs. She is wearing pitch-seamed boots, a woollen skirt and a thick Fana-style cardigan, buttoned up to her neck. Her hands are folded in her lap. The sun is in her eyes and one is squinting. A thick plait is coiled over her shoulder.

'It was taken at the mountain farm,' Grete says. 'It's ours now. But the farmhouse there has been demolished. It was like a bake house with an oven, a fireplace and a griddle. I went there with my mother a few times to make flat bread.'

'I visited them in their flat a few times,' he says. 'Åse and Gerhard. But I'd forgotten how beautiful she was.'

'We went to the same school. She was a couple of years older than me. But that was how it was in those days. One school in every village, and only one class for all the children. Now come and look at this.' She takes Sverre to the wall unit behind the radio cabinet, opens a cupboard and takes out a thick envelope full of photographs. 'I've got a school photo.' She flicks through the photographs. 'Here.' She passes him a large photograph of a group of children in front of a white house. The teacher stands erect, posing on the far left, with a watch chain over his waistcoat and a crooked pipe in the corner of his mouth. The children have clearly been smartened up. The boys with water-combed hair, the girls with ribbons in theirs. One of the boys is wearing a sailor's outfit.

'That's me'. Grete's finger points to a little girl. 'And here's Åse.'

Fenstad recognises the girl photographed in front of the bake house a few years later. She has a slide in her hair. The clean-cut features are unmistakeable. She is also taller than most of the other girls.

'And this is Erik.' Grete points to the boy in the sailor's outfit. He is sitting on the grass and looking at the photographer sceptically. 'Åse and I weren't close friends, but we knew each other well. She moved to Oslo straight after the war broke out.'

'Why did she do that?'

'Gerhard.'

'Did she get to know him in Oslo?'

Grete shakes her head. 'They met in Fagernes. She was working as a receptionist at Fagerlund Hotel. He sold advertising for a newspaper in Gjøvik. *Vestopland*. He travelled around and got to know people everywhere. He stopped when the newspaper went Nazi. But he knew a lot of people. I think that was why he was at the centre of the resistance organisation in the area later.'

'And Erik?'

'What about Erik?'

'What was the relationship between Erik and Gerhard like?'

She takes a deep breath. 'I don't like talking about my husband when he isn't present.'

He nods and says: 'I understand.'

'Do you?' she says.

Sverre is unsure how to interpret the question, so he changes the subject. 'What's the relationship between the sisters – Turid and Arna?'

Grete glances over her shoulder. Sverre turns round.

Erik is standing in the doorway, obviously angry. Trembling with rage, he says: 'It's time for you to clear off, Sverre. Take the past with you and tell that bastard whatever you like – so long as the message is the following: keep well away from us.'

Sverre passes the school photograph back to Grete. He scrutinises Erik for a few seconds … Then, without a word, he takes his stick, turns and limps towards the door.

Stockholm, December 1942

1

For the third time today Gerhard does his abdominal curls, knee bends and arm stretches in series of four. This makes him hot. Afterwards he dismantles his gun. Performing familiar routines can stop you thinking. Thinking about what has happened. Doing simple activities, but doing them properly. He takes a penknife from his rucksack, opens the blade and carefully scrapes the metal on the inside of the gunstock. There. The little black stain has gone, and once again the steel is smooth and shiny with oil. He keeps cleaning. Focusing on the metal and the various parts. Not thinking about Oslo, not thinking about what has happened or what might happen. Once upon a time cleaning your weapon or boots was ingrained wisdom, a form of meditation, because cleaning a rifle or rubbing grease into the leather was important, as well as setting you on a journey inside yourself, away from the gunfire and nausea of the blowflies hatching in the flesh of dead comrades. Now he is in the same frame of mind. He has laid the individual parts of the gun on a newspaper on the floor. Together with a little bottle of lubricating oil and a wad of cotton waste. He twists some cotton and moistens it with oil, pushes the wad through the barrel with a pencil. Lifts the little bottle and drips oil onto the trigger parts. Pulls the trigger. Ensures that everything is working and moving easily. His fingers glisten with grease. He points the barrel and flicks away a bit of fluff. Puts all the parts back down on the newspaper. Wipes his hands on the cotton. Gets to his feet. Pats his pockets. The cigarette packet is on the table. He flicks a cigarette from the packet. Pats his pockets again. Sees the matches on the window sill. It is dark outside. As he lights the cigarette he senses a movement in an archway on the opposite side of the street. Instinctively he backs away from the window. Stiffens for a few seconds, hugging the wall. Then his head and body slowly move back into the room. He is surprised by his own bizarre reaction. By his squeezing up against a wall like a petrified hare, in this neutral country. Nevertheless, he stays where he is, smoking, pensive. The cigarette is stained with grease from his fingers. He can't dismiss his automatic reaction. Adrenalin. It has rarely fooled him. He tears himself away, goes into the room, sits down. Gets up again. Goes back to the corner. Twists back the blind and peers out. Eventually he catches sight of the outline of a person against the wall where he first saw a movement. He lets go of the blind. Stands by the room's modest sink, smoking, thinking. Drops the half-smoked cigarette into the sink. It goes out with a hiss in the plug-hole.

He avoids the window as he gets dressed to go out – jumper, scarf, winter coat, peaked cap with earflaps.

He looks at the lubricated gun. Goes to the bed and fills the magazine. Loads the magazine and cocks the gun. Sticks the weapon in his coat pocket and goes into the corridor. It is dark. He walks slowly down the corridor and turns right. There is one solitary light bulb in the ceiling. He stops by the lift. It is on its way up to the floors above. But the arrow above the door points to the basement. He opens the door to the narrow fire escape. Takes the staircase down to the lobby.

The lobby is empty. The receptionist is not there.

He goes outside. Lingers for a moment in the doorway. The cold bites at his cheeks and his breath is white. He flips up his collar and crosses the street with his hands in his coat pockets. Heads for the archway where he saw the figure. Hangs back, listening. There is no one here now. He still searches the whole area, looks behind the rubbish bins, but his conclusion is the same. There is no one there now. He goes back into the street and turns right towards a shop. Goes inside. It is well stocked. They also have cigarettes. He searches his pockets, finds some ration cards and thumbs through them. Two Norwegian tobacco vouchers. He scrunches them up. Throws them into the wastepaper basket by the door. Locates the Swedish vouchers. He buys a pouch of tobacco. Goes back. Passes the archway and checks. No one is there now, either. He leaves and walks down the street without turning or glancing over his shoulder. Goes into the next archway. Hides. Waits, holding the gun firmly in his pocket. He hears footsteps. They stop.

Gerhard peeks out. Can't see anything apart from a dark shadow at the corner of the gate. He waits. But nothing happens. There is a clatter on the stairs inside the block behind him. A door opens. A family of four come out. Gerhard joins them and goes out through the gate. No one is standing on the corner.

Gerhard stops on the pavement. Everything looks as it always does on a cold evening in this city. He crosses the street and returns to Sirena Hotel. Enters the lobby. The receptionist is back. Gerhard nods to him and goes to the lift, which is open. Closes the iron doors with a bang. The metal judders as the lift starts. Judders again when it stops.

Back in his room he takes off his outdoor clothes and blows on his fingers, which are red and cold. He puts the gun in his back pocket. Goes to the bedhead, where his rucksack is. Rummages through it for his binoculars. Turns off the light and stands behind the blind. Stares out. The street lamp casts a dark shadow over the archway. But at the edge of the cone of light he sees something. He lifts the binoculars. Puts them to his eyes. Finds the bulbous shape at the edge. It is the end of a boot. It has to belong to someone, he thinks, putting the binoculars on the window sill.

He ponders his next step. Takes the gun from his back pocket. Lays it down on the window sill as well and looks out. In the distance he can hear a hum. It is the tram in Hamngatan. It is coming this way. The single headlamp bores a tunnel of light between the houses. For one brief second it illuminates the dark archway. A brief second of light. But there is no doubt. A man's face is staring up at Gerhard's window.

Oslo, November 1967

1

The front door to Regnbuen night club opens. Out come two women, wearing pink aprons and low shoes. One uses a long-handled broom to keep the door open. Afterwards they both push a trolley in through the door. The door closes behind them as Ester unlocks her yellow Renault Dauphine parked by the pavement. She gets in but doesn't switch on the ignition; she just sits still with her hands on the wheel.

It is time for a confrontation. It can't be helped that Gerhard is avoiding her. Avoidance is his project. As for her, she can't wait any longer. A telephone conversation is out of the question. She wants to look him in the eye. She wants to be on the offensive.

The parking meter clicks, and the tab behind the glass shows red. She looks up. Further ahead a car pulls away from the kerb. It is a better spot. The view is better. She starts the engine, signals and moves out.

This parking spot is free. She manoeuvres her way into it and switches off the engine. Here, on the corner between Klingenberggata and Stortingsgata, she has a good view of the main entrance to the hotel. Here she can wait until Gerhard comes out or goes in. When she sees him she will get out of the car and shout. She has no idea if her plan will succeed, but she is going to try. She hasn't got a plan B anyway.

There, in front of the entrance, a white Volvo Amazon pulls up. A uniformed hotel employee gets out of the car, holding the keys in his hand.

The uniformed man at the entrance occasionally hails taxis for guests coming out.

This could take time, she thinks, inserting the eight-track cassette into the player. Harry Belafonte sings a slow blues:

I gambled on your love, baby, and got a losing hand...

As Belafonte makes way for the saxophonist, Gerhard appears.

She grips the door handle, but hesitates as he exchanges a few words with the man in the hotel uniform. Then he gets into the parked Amazon. That is a surprise. Gerhard must have rented the car. She deliberates for a few seconds.

Gerhard's car starts up. Then he drives past her. She turns the ignition key and follows.

Both have to stop for the lights. Ester dons her sunglasses, stretches and checks in the mirror to see what she looks like.

2

The white Amazon is parked in front of a patisserie in Uranienborgveien. Ester has found a gap fifty metres behind it. She sits at the wheel, waiting. Gerhard comes out of the patisserie with a white paper bag in his hand. He stands for a few seconds on the pavement. Looks in her direction. Ester has the feeling that she has been seen. Well, so be it. The sooner, the better. But then he walks around the car and gets in. The Amazon signals and pulls out. Ester lets it go, then follows.

At Vestkanttorget she sees Gerhard's car drive down Middelthuns gate. Harry Belafonte is singing and Ester hums along.

The lights are green. They change to yellow. Ester accelerates. The lights change to red as she crosses. They pass Frogner Stadium and the entrance to Frogner Lido, which is closed for the winter.

The Amazon turns into the car park by Frogner Park.

Ester chooses the alternative. She turns right. Finds a free spot in front of the waterworks company.

She gets out of the car and her eyes search the trees in Frogner Park. She sees him disappear through them.

She runs across the road. Enters the park. Most of the leaves have fallen. The birch trees stand bare against the yellowish-brown autumn mosaic on the ground. Only the occasional maple tree still has a faded red crown intact.

Gerhard has the same white bag in his hand. He walks in front of the fountain. It has been turned off for the winter. Gerhard continues to the bridge. Here he leans against the wall and looks down into the water.

Now, she thinks, but doesn't move, and is annoyed with herself because she has hesitated. She sits on the stone wall surrounding the square with the fountain.

He leans against the parapet. Then he turns and stares straight at her.

Ester leans back and looks up into the sun. When she looks left again, he has gone. She gets up. Goes over to where Gerhard was standing. Looks down and sees him. Gerhard has gone down the steps to the little area around a pier of the bridge. He is sitting on a bench. He has taken a bread roll from the bag and is throwing pieces to the ducks. Many of the ducks waddle up the bank towards the bench. Ester takes a deep breath, dashes across the bridge and goes down the steps to the bench.

Stockholm, December 1942

1

Stockholm's trams have a problem; many of them stand idle. It has something to do with ice on the electric cables. Ester doesn't care. She resorts to Shanks's pony. It is good to move. She has wrapped herself up well. Wound the long scarf round her neck and head several times. Few people have ventured outside. She has the pavement almost to herself. She soon warms up. Rime frost settles on the tufts of hair poking out from her scarf. She thinks about the news she is bearing and what it means – for Gerhard obviously, but also for herself. Choosing the route through Kungsträdgården Park she makes for Norrmalmstorg. The snow on the path is hard packed, and the low afternoon sun casts long shadows from the trees. A man on a kick-sled comes towards her. He is wearing a fur hat and thick mittens and sends her a sombre nod as the sled glides past with almost no sound.

She glances up at the façade of Sirena Hotel. There are only darkened windows. She walks into the lobby. The lift is on its way down. The heavy weights and the cables holding them rise slowly. Then the lift floor comes into view through the glass wall. The lift creaks. There is a shadow behind the glass. A man. The lift thuds to a halt. The door opens. And she looks straight into the eyes of Kolstad, the bodyguard.

Kolstad looks down, hurries past her and out.

Ester turns and watches the front door close behind him.

Why didn't he acknowledge her?

She has a bad feeling. The little lift reeks of Kolstad's after-shave. A pungent smell of lemon mixed with alcohol. Again she has problems with the door. It won't close properly. She gives up. Leaves the lift and uses the fire escape instead. The sound of footsteps is muffled by the threadbare carpet on the stairs. At the right floor, she follows the corridor to Gerhard's room.

Stops a few metres from the door. Recognises the pungent smell. Kolstad has been here.

The bad feeling grows. She goes to the door, raises a fist and knocks.

The corridor is absolutely still. She knocks again. No answer this time, either. She tries the handle warily. The door isn't locked. There is an audible click and the door opens. She pushes it and freezes. She finds herself looking into the muzzle of a gun. Gerhard is sitting on the bed and aiming at her.

They stare at each other without saying a word.

Finally he lowers the gun and lays it on the bedside table.

She doesn't move. Everything is unfamiliar. His eyes, the atmosphere.

'Come inside or go, but shut the door whatever you do.'

It is only now that she can feel her heart throbbing. Feel fear numbing her hand. She pushes the door to with her back. 'Isn't it better to keep the door locked than to risk shooting visitors?' Her voice is tremulous.

He eyes her without speaking.

'Didn't you hear me knock?'

He leans back against the bedhead. From this position he stares at a point in the ceiling above her head.

The room feels hot. She unwinds her scarf. Takes off her mittens, unbuttons her coat. 'Who's the man who was here?'

She might just as well have fired a shot. Gerhard recoils, swings his legs to the floor and stands in one movement. She backs towards the door. He follows her. His nostrils vibrating. 'Man? Who are you talking about? Answer me. Which man?'

They stand eyeball to eyeball. Ester is nonplussed by the situation. It is obvious that Gerhard hasn't had a visitor. What Kolstad is up to has nothing to do with her. But Gerhard's address is secret. The fact that one of the legation's people has been here is a matter she will have to take up with Torgersen, not Gerhard.

Gerhard grips her arm. Hard. It hurts. 'Who are you talking about?'

'The one from the cinema,' she says. 'Let me go.'

He releases her arm.

She pulls up her sleeve and rubs her forearm. 'Your so-called black-market pal.'

'Oh, him.' The tone is lower, uninterested. Then he looks up again. 'So-called?'

For a fraction of a second she feels like throwing everything into his face. The lies, telling him she knows the man works for the British secret service, that they practise at the same shooting range. But Gerhard seems depressed. His face has taken on a desperate expression. He turns away from her and walks to the window. He looks out. His back is stooped. He seems lonely as he stands there, and she has the impression something has happened: the gun, the suspicion and now this back-turning and despair.

Dejectedly, he gazes out of the window as he continues: 'It's not the police I'm most worried about, Ester. Not the Swedes, not the British – they're not the ones who make me uneasy.'

He walks to the bed, lies down on it. Silent and despondent.

She takes off her coat and hangs it on the hook on the back of the door. 'What is it that worries you, then?'

When he looks at her again it is with eyes she hasn't seen before. 'I'm not sure you're the right person to discuss my worries with.'

She is not sure she likes what is going on in his eyes. 'What do you mean?'

'Forget it.'

'Forget what? You imply things and talk in riddles. I'm waiting. Please talk to me.'

As he doesn't answer, she puts her hand into her coat pocket and takes out a folded sheet of paper. 'I've received a letter from Norway. From Åse's mother.'

He doesn't seem to have heard what she has said.

'She isn't any better. But Turid's fine. A young couple in the village, two people who knew Åse well, are taking care of her now, because Åse's mother's in hospital.'

Gerhard sighs with an expression reminiscent of contempt.

'What is it?'

'Who?'

She is confused. 'What do you mean?'

His voice is hard. 'Who's so kind that they're taking care of my daughter?'

'I don't know who they are.'

'So she doesn't give a name?'

'Yes, she does, but I don't recognise them. Erik Heggen and Grete Sandvik, his partner.'

He pulls a face.

'What is it?' Ester asks.

'Erik Heggen and Grete Sandvik.' He jeers. 'A couple.'

'You know them?'

He doesn't answer. He swings his legs onto the floor and sits up. 'So Åse's old mum writes to you, does she? Why doesn't she write to me?'

'You know she's ill. You mustn't blame her. She's doing the best she can.'

'But she can write. Why does she write to you and not to me?'

'No one in Norway knows where you are. It's all about security.'

He laughs now. It is a harsh laugh. 'Security? And no one knows where I am?'

She scrutinises him, unsure what he means by this cold sarcasm. 'I have a letter from Sverre.'

'Sverre? Sverre Fenstad?'

She regrets mentioning this. Everything that happens at the office is confidential. But the name just slipped out. After all, Gerhard knows Sverre well. But she is still afraid she has said too much. Feverishly she racks her brains for a way to change the topic.

'Sverre? Is he in Stockholm?'

'It's the message that counts, not the messenger.' She holds out the letter. 'Read it yourself.'

'Answer me! Is Sverre in Stockholm?'

'No.' She isn't lying, because she knows he has returned to Norway.

Gerhard still doesn't make a move to take the letter. She folds it and puts it back in her pocket.

She leans against the wall, looking at him. 'Actually, I'm here for another reason,' she says.

He is miles away, lost in unknown memories, and she realises he hasn't been listening. 'Actually, I'm here for another reason,' she repeats.

'What reason?'

Ester looks down. The atmosphere feels wrong. She has to search for the right words.

'Why are you here, Ester?' His eyes are cold and appraising.

'I've come to organise something with you.'

'Organise? A dance at the German embassy maybe? Or Christmas dinner with the Stockholm police?'

'With that attitude, nothing's going to get any better.'

His face softens. 'Come on then.'

'A briefing. You're going to Britain.'

The desired response fails to materialise. 'Briefing?' He repeats the word. His voice is dismissive, as if she has told a bad joke.

She shrugs. 'My guess is they want to form an impression of you.'

His eyes are still sceptical. 'Who do?'

'Actually I don't know.' Ester again feels hot.

'You want me to go to some interview and you don't know who it's with?'

'You're the one who's been pushing for it. Now it's happening. They're planning to move you to a base in Scotland.'

'Surely you can tell me who's running this interview. You've come here with the message, after all. Well, who am I going to meet?'

'The resistance committee will take care of that. They just say you should go on Friday. I'll be there too. After work. You can hire a taxi and pick me up, then we can go together.'

'Where?'

'Somewhere in Huddinge.' She roots through her pocket for the piece of paper. This conversation has gone very differently from how she had imagined it would. When she finds the note she has almost shredded it. She hands it to him without a word.

He reads it. 'What sort of place is this?'

She shrugs. 'Never been there. I'm not in charge of these things. We take a taxi. We go there.'

He puts the address in his pocket. 'We'll see,' he mumbles.

'This is what you've been pushing for, for weeks. Are you going to say no?'

He doesn't answer. Just looks at her. Full of suspicion.

She sighs and kneels down beside him. Looks into his doleful face. Raises a hand and strokes his hair. Unable herself to understand how she can be so bold. 'Gerhard,' she whispers. Her hand is trembling, and she thinks he can see that. He can feel what is going on inside her. 'You're a shadow of yourself,' she says.

He grips her hand.

They look into each other's eyes, and she thinks, here we go. Her heart is pounding so hard she can't hear anything else and she has to swallow, sure he can hear it too. 'Tell me you'll pick me up on Friday.'

He searches her eyes, but doesn't answer.

'Afterwards we can go to Berns,' she says. 'Celebrate it as herr and fru Larsen.'

He lets go of her hand and holds her face with both of his, pulls her to him and kisses her.

Ester responds to the kiss with closed eyes. Her hand drops. Her whole body is heavy, but she manages to raise her hand again and put it behind his neck.

When he lifts his head she stays on her knees.

Gerhard looks away. 'We have a deal,' he says curtly. 'Friday. I'll pick you up.'

Ester gets to her feet. Takes her coat from the hook, finds her mittens and long scarf. Heads for the door. Turns and watches him. His eyes are still averted.

'Friday,' she says in a voice that is close to cracking.

She leaves without closing the door after her. Takes two steps and has to lean against the wall. Åse, she thinks, please forgive me. Forgive us.

Friday, she thinks again. That is in two days' time. Two long days.

She walks to the lift. Two days. Presses the button. Two nights. Watches the arrow slowly moving in a circle on the wall.

The lift stops with a bang.

Ester doesn't open the door. Instead she turns and walks back. Looks down at the carpet and walks to the end of the long corridor. The door to Gerhard's room is still open. She looks up. He is leaning against the door frame, watching her. As they exchange looks he backs inside. She follows him. Kicks the door shut behind her.

'But afterwards,' she says. 'Are we going to Berns or aren't we?'

She doesn't hear his answer. When he pulls her to him she folds both hands around his neck and smothers his wry smile with her lips, completely, as though that is what they were meant for.

Oslo, November 1967

1

Ester keeps an eye on Gerhard at every step of the flight. She stops on the last. Still with her hands in her pockets.

He doesn't turn round.

He knows I am standing here, she thinks, and moves nearer. She stops by the bench.

He looks up at her without speaking. Then he puts a hand in the paper bag and passes her a bread roll.

She takes it. The ducks waddle around their feet. Ester leans against the railing and tears the roll into pieces. Then she throws them to the ducks.

'You haven't changed much,' he says.

'Actually, nor have you.'

'Not from the outside maybe.'

Now he finally looks at her and says: 'You never know what goes on inside people.'

She doesn't answer.

'If things had been different,' Gerhard says. 'Can you imagine it? Me sitting there with a newspaper on my lap and tired feet on the pouf. A father of a grown-up girl, good job in Gerhardsen's Norway and a photo album full of great memories.'

She throws the last bit of bread. A mallard with a fine, shiny-green head sticks its beak out and gobbles it down. Ester brushes the crumbs off her hands. 'The prime minister's name is Borten, not Gerhardsen.'

She regrets both her sharp comment and the tone at once. 'Sorry,' she says and looks at him until he lifts his head and meets her eyes again. 'So you don't have any other children in your new life?'

He continues to look at her, in silence.

'I assume that's a no,' she says at length.

'I could've spent time with my dad during the last years he was alive.
I don't know when he died or where he's buried.'

I don't know that kind of detail either, she thinks.

'I was a little surprised when I saw you up there,' he says. 'At the
time you said you'd never return to Norway, not after what happened
to your family.'

'I waited a long time.'

Gerhard stares into the distance.

'In that respect we have a fair amount in common, Gerhard.'

'In that respect?'

'Those years, the waiting, the ambivalence.'

The ducks have lost interest in them. The last ones swim away, their
yellow feet paddling furiously under the surface.

Gerhard straightens up. 'Why did you follow me here?'

'I wasn't certain.'

'Certain about what?'

'If I wanted the conversation we still haven't had.'

'What would you and I have to talk about, Ester?'

She smiles to herself. 'Yes, what do we have to talk about?'

'Make a suggestion,' he says, in such a curt, dismissive way that she
has to take another look. She says: 'About 1942, for example.'

'Stockholm?'

'Yes, Stockholm,' she says, feeling somewhat bewildered, before this
feeling gives way to irritation. 'Or what happened here in Oslo. We
were infiltrated.'

He eyes her in silence. Waits for her to go on.

'I was centimetres from being arrested. Literally. The day after you
left Åse and me in Hermann Foss' gate.'

She pauses.

'Is that all? You were almost arrested?' he says.

She doesn't answer.

'Why are you saying this?'

Because she is beating around the bush, she thinks, but doesn't say
so.

'I've talked to you lots of times, Ester, in my mind, and do you know
what we talked about?'

She shakes her head.

'I've asked you a question: why were you willing to lead me to the scaffold that December in Stockholm?'

'My version of this story's a little different,' she says.

'Ester, it was a set-up. You know it was. And what else do we know? Gerhard Falkum was a problem. One that could be solved in a number of ways. But you and the others tried to solve it the dirty way.'

'Me?'

'Don't tell me you still insist it was a briefing that was due to take place that night.'

'Perhaps it was a set-up. You know more about that than me. But one person died. And, OK, it wasn't you. But who was it? And what happened to you afterwards?'

He stretches out his legs and sticks his hands between his thighs, without answering.

'Who was waiting for you there, for us?'

He sits, gazing into the distance, still.

'Have you forgotten that the two of us were supposed to go there?'

He is silent.

'The war's over, Gerhard.'

His overbearing smile morphs into a scornful grin.

'What's important now is trust,' she says.

'Trust? Now? Unlike then?'

She doesn't answer.

'Do you remember when you wanted to organise a meeting for me, but you didn't know who I was going to meet?'

She is suddenly annoyed again. 'What do you imagine would have happened if I'd been with you? Do you think I would've stood waiting at the gate while you were gunned down?'

She locks onto his eyes. 'This isn't the conversation I want to have with you,' she says.

'You can start by being honest,' he says.

'Honest?'

'Listen to yourself. Was the nice little Jewish girl in the organisation going to be sacrificed? Who do you actually think you're talking to?'

I don't know, she thinks. In fact I do not know. She tries to lock onto his eyes again. 'I'm talking to the only person who knows what happened. Someone died. Who was it? Why did they die?'

'That's what you want to know after all these years?'

'Is that so strange?'

He sends her an odd look.

'What's the matter?'

'You believe all the clichés, don't you?'

She doesn't understand where he is going with this. 'Clichés?'

He rolls his eyes. 'In those days, war. Now, peace, with the Iron Curtain between East and West. And behind the barricades stands Ester with her trust and loyalty, her faith in the motherland and the baloney about freedom from tyranny.'

She scrutinises his face, trying to comprehend the meaning behind these words.

'I tried to find some something I could rely on in your eyes the day you knelt down and begged me to pick you up by taxi. I waited a while and was curious who would play the Judas role. It was tough to accept it was you. Well, I could've guessed they would try. But you taking the job was a lot to swallow then.'

'Judas role?'

'He might be a character in the New Testament, but I think even you know what he stands for.'

'Start getting ideas like that, Gerhard, and they'll soon spiral out of control.'

'Do yourself a favour and shut your mouth. When you knelt in front of me on the floor in Hotel Sirena, I wasn't in Stockholm anymore. I was back in Brunete in thirty-seven. There's one thing you know when you have a bullet in your body and you're bleeding to death. You know you came into this world *alone*. You live in it *alone* and you die in it *alone*. You might think you're different. But you weren't then. You rattled around alone, Ester. You didn't give a damn about me. You didn't give a damn about my child. You carried out your job without any thought of the consequences.'

Ester looks down. When she lifts her head her voice is barely audible. 'There were so many of us who had to make a sacrifice in those years, Gerhard.'

A chilly smile lurks at the corner of his mouth. 'Is this the moment to play the Jewish card? Come on. Let's see if it works.'

She swallows and remains quiet.

'I can be nice now and go back to the start,' he says. 'Let's do that, as an experiment. You know just as well as I do that my hell started when Åse's heart stopped beating. So the question is quite simply: who would Åse have opened the door to? Who would she have let in? Who would she have sat drinking with – apart from you and me?'

Ester looks away. She has no answer to this question; it's one she has asked herself innumerable times.

'The world's different now,' she says at length. 'You're different. We're different.'

'You reckon?' Gerhard stands up in front of her. 'Imagine me hearing you say that! The representative of a people who have sought revenge every single day since peace came. What did you say in May when Israel occupied East Jerusalem and the West Bank?'

'Israel may have made a mistake there, but the fact is that the war started because Egypt blocked the bay of Aqaba and wanted to starve us out.'

He grins. 'Us? Aren't you a Norwegian? Do you have a problem distinguishing between nations and causes?'

'I have a son who risked his life in that war.' Ester can feel she has had enough of this conversation. 'If you want to talk Middle-East politics, then Sverre Fenstad's your man. He's on the board of the Israeli Committee of Norway. But since you asked: I discovered here in Norway during the war what it's like to be Jewish, and that experience will stay with me forever. I don't give a shit what you or anyone else thinks about that.'

'And I have no illusions about you understanding this, Ester. And I don't give a shit whether you do or you don't, because I've waited for more than twenty years.'

'What have you waited for?'

Now he finally reveals the smile she remembers. But she views it with resignation; it is a smile filled with contempt. His smile has always been like this, she thinks. I just hadn't noticed it until now. He turns his back on her and goes up the steps to the bridge.

She watches him. When he is halfway up, she shouts: 'Gerhard!'
He stops and turns round.

'You've thought a lot during these years, haven't you?'

'What's your point?'

'I came here to find out who died on that Friday,' she says. 'I wanted to meet you to find out where you went and why it ended between us the way it did. I can understand you're bitter and don't want to open up to me. That's your business. But I could never fathom how anyone could state that the remains they found were yours. For me you've always been alive.'

He eyes her frostily. Then throws up his arms as if he were on a stage. 'And how do I compare with what you've imagined all these years?'

She sighs and studies her shoes. Searching for the right words, but she says them inside her head: right now, not too well.

She turns away, leans against the railing and watches the ducks swimming around in the pond below.

The sound of footsteps tells her he has gone.

Stockholm, December 1942

Ester hasn't been asleep long when she opens her eyes. The first thing she notices is that she is alone in the bed.

She can make out Gerhard's silhouette against the window. He is smoking a cigarette. And looking out. When he inhales, the glow brightens and reveals the profile of his face against the glass.

'Are you there?'

'So you're awake?' he says without turning from the window.

'What are you looking for?'

Now he turns to her. Smiles weakly, stubs out his cigarette in the ashtray on the window sill and comes over. He lies down. His body is still warm. They lie in a spoon position. She snuggles up against his back. Placing her knees in the back of his. She flops an arm over his waist and breathes into his neck.

✳

In her dream she is in the same room as her mother and Ada. The two of them are sitting at the table and are in conversation. Ester talks to her mother, and every time her mother sends back an affectionate look, then she turns to Ada so as not to miss what her neighbour has said. Ester can't hold her mother's attention; she becomes desperate. So desperate, she wakes up.

As soon as she opens her eyes she sees that Gerhard has gone. The duvet has slipped onto the floor. She is lying there naked and she is cold. She pulls the duvet back over herself and tries to warm up again. Lies on her side, thinking about the dream and feeling that it was about Åse, even though she wasn't present in it. Åse is dead. Life is now. What has happened is Gerhard, and it feels right.

What happened in this room a few hours ago also seems like images from a dream. She lies looking at the door in the gloom as her mind moves in a different direction. Where is he? The green light from the sign on the wall outside casts a dim reflection of the window pane on the floor. One of her boots lies upturned in the pale light.

Ester can't get warm. She gets out of bed. Goes to the window. Looks out as she buttons up her blouse. The traffic below shows that a new day is well under way. She looks down at her finger. He forced a ring onto it. She tries to remove it. The ring is stuck. That, too becomes a kind of symbol that makes her smile.

She glances over at the metal bed. Now she is wide awake. Going back to bed wouldn't be right. She puts on her stockings. Then the rest of her clothes. Opens the door. Tiptoes to the bathroom in the corridor. It is free. She has a pee. Washes. She goes back to the room. Walks to the wardrobe with the clothes hangers. His coat has gone. Ditto his boots. Gerhard has gone out into the winter weather. Why? To meet whom? Why didn't he say anything before leaving?

Ester searches for her wristwatch. It has fallen under the bed. She winds it up and closes the link around her wrist. It is still early. The shops haven't opened. But she has to go now if she is going to get to the training session with Markus before work.

She takes a pen and some paper from her bag. Scribbles a note for him. Looks down at the words, which seem childish. She scrunches up the note. Puts it into her bag. Instead she takes out a lipstick. Goes over to the mirror above the little sink and, in red, draws a big smile and two eyes. Then she leaves Hotel Sirena. Wrapped up in her winter coat, long scarf and thick mittens. She takes the staircase down. She emerges and walks to the market square. It is freezing cold. She has to find a tram going to Östermalm.

2

The ladies' cloakroom is empty and this early in the morning it is quite cold. Ester hangs up her things on one of the many free hooks, unlocks her cabinet and changes into the training kit hanging there. Ties up her hair with elastic bands and hairgrips.

The gymnasium is as cold as the changing room. And here, too, there is a stench of stale sweat. She and Markus are alone, as usual this early. They train here three times a week. Run through the schedule Markus has drawn up and she thought initially she would never manage to complete. First off: warm-up with light jogging round the perimeter for ten minutes.

As she runs into the gym she tries to get the ring off her finger again. It is still stuck.

Markus is already there. He has laid out the mats and apparatus.

He asks where she has been.

She doesn't answer.

He says he dropped by hers on the way.

She says she left earlier today. She starts jogging to avoid more questions.

He follows her.

But the atmosphere is strained and quiet now. He runs past her. In front of her now, he runs backwards and looks her in the eye. She looks down and keeps running. Hides the ring as well as she can in her fist.

For the first time they go through their programme in silence. This is circuit training with apparatus. They do abdominal curls on the wall bars, arm pulls on the beam, climbing on the ropes, two minutes' skipping with a rope, arm pulls on the rings, back stretches over a box with their feet tucked under the lowest wall bar, then finish with a minute's plank on the mat. The first time she did the programme she was close to throwing up afterwards. Today she manages five beam lifts; yesterday she managed only four.

After they have finished, they are both sweaty and out of breath. Markus still isn't talkative. However, the atmosphere feels a little lighter. She tells herself she has to do what she feels is correct. Markus has no right to know what she thinks and how she feels. No one has a right to know.

When she goes to the changing rooms to shower, Markus asks if she wants to go along to the combat training.

Ester hesitates. She is unsure whether this is for her.

'Just to see,' Markus says. 'There's a really good Englishman. Brian Pankhurst.'

Ester looks at her watch.

'You've got the time,' Markus says.

Ester says yes because it might lift his oppressive mood.

They have to go down a long corridor to reach the right training room.

Markus opens the door. They sneak in.

'We just want to have a look,' Markus whispers to the man at the door.

They aren't alone. A line of ten to fifteen men in training gear are sitting on low benches alongside the wall bars.

The instructor is on the mat. Brian Pankhurst is the Englishman she has seen on the shooting range – and with Gerhard. He is wearing glasses and his hair is slicked back. He is not in a training outfit. But he is bare-legged. He is wearing a white singlet and dark shorts with a sharp crease. Right now he is holding a pointed knife in his hand. He speaks slowly in English. Tells them the dagger is the most effective murder weapon. 'Never let the dagger rest even when you're resting,' he says, tossing it from one hand to the other while speaking.

He wants a volunteer to come to the mat. A fair-haired man in his twenties gets up. The Englishman shakes his head. 'Someone bigger, taller.' He points to the man sitting next to him. This guy stands up slowly. He is a giant, almost two metres. He trudges onto the floor and smiles sheepishly at the others, who are cheering him on.

'When you lunge try to come from behind,' the Englishman says, and in one gliding step he is behind the giant. The giant doesn't have time to turn. Pankhurst grabs the giant's hair, yanks his head back, with the point of the dagger pressed into his spine. The giant's body is arched backwards. He can't move. All he thinks about is avoiding the dagger.

Ester imagines what could happen next and feels nauseous.

Pankhurst speaks again. In a dry, hoarse voice he says this move reduces any opponent to your height and weight.

Markus and Ester exchange glances. Markus grins. She can see that Markus likes the Englishman's self-assurance and authority. But most of all she is happy to see that Markus appears to have dropped the sulks about her not being at her flat this morning. And once again her thoughts are back with Gerhard. Where did he go? Where is he now? What is he doing? And what is he up to with the man on the mat?

She fiddles with the ring. It slides off without a problem. Suddenly she sees this as a bad omen and goes cold all over.

'What's the matter?' Markus whispers.

'Nothing.' She hides the ring in the pocket of her track suit.

She looks up. The next lesson is about unarmed combat. Pankhurst tells the giant to attack him. Now the guy has something to avenge. He rushes at Pankhurst. Seconds later he is on the mat writhing in pain.

Markus grins again. Ester is still thinking about Gerhard and the eternal moment yesterday, then she shakes off the memory and concentrates on what is happening on the mat.

Pankhurst pulls the giant to his feet and goes through his moves in slow motion. With gentle movements, no power behind the punches this time, though. Like ballet steps, Ester thinks.

'First off,' the Englishman says, 'you hit the opponent's forearm hard. Then, you raise your hand to strike again – and change the angle.'

He shows how he chopped the side of his hand into the giant's face.

'To the throat or face,' Pankhurst shouts, demonstrating again. 'Practise on yourself,' he says, showing how you can perform the punches on your own head and arm.

Another lesson. Pankhurst wants another volunteer. No one moves. He points to the fair-haired man. 'Your turn.'

The fair-haired man hesitates. 'Me?'

Soon he is standing on the mat, facing Pankhurst. They eyeball each other. But it is the Englishman who takes the initiative. He stamps on the fair-haired man's foot. The latter screams in pain and grabs hold of the Englishman, who keeps his hands down by his sides. But a second later he flings up his arms, spins round and he has the fair-haired man on his knees, then he delivers a chop to the throat.

Brian Pankhurst carries on. Explaining the benefit of combining a kick in the opponent's crotch with a punch. At first the opponent doubles up. The kick can then be followed up by a hard chop to the chin.

Ester yawns. She is struggling to follow this.

'Now you can practise on each other,' Pankhurst says. The men in training gear around them stroll over to the mattresses. Ester becomes aware of the man's gaze. 'Come on,' he says, pointing to Ester and Markus. 'You, too.'

Ester holds up both palms. She wants to go.

'In an hour,' Pankhurst says, looking at his watch. 'The other girls are coming then. There's a place for you too.'

Fagernes, November 1967

1

The timbered house is coming towards her. A white Swiss-style house. Ester is fascinated once again by how concentrating on a limited part of the world gives you a false picture of what is actually happening. Soon the house is still. The train has stopped at Fagernes station. She waits until the passengers in the greatest hurry have left and there are no longer queues at the exits. Then she stands up. Grabs her shoulder bag from the seat and the wrapped bunch of flowers from the rack above the window. Gets off the train and makes a beeline for the taxis. Her shoulder bag bangs against her hip. The air seems more raw and chilly than in Oslo. On the opposite side of the station there are two taxis. The first is a black Mercedes. The driver is nowhere to be seen. She waits. A door in the station building opens and an elderly man rushes out. He opens the rear door for her. She slides in.

She says she is going to Ulnes church.

The driver looks at her in the rear-view mirror. Asks her if she has got the wrong day.

'Why?'

'There are no funerals there today.'

'I'm only going to lay flowers.'

'I had to ask. I suppose you'd like to come back afterwards?'

'Yes, why?'

'If it's convenient, I can wait.'

She thanks him.

They drive along Strande fjord. It is a clear day, but November has already cast a little shadow over the daylight. The mountains are reflected in the water. Autumn has advanced further here than in Oslo. Even though the trees have little foliage here in the lowlands, the colours across the mountainsides are still dark and solid.

The church stands on a little mound by the water. The taxi drives into the car park and stops.

Ulnes church is built of stone and has a central spire and a slate roof. Medieval, Ester thinks, getting out of the car. The annexes on the sides are of a more recent vintage and built of wood. The cemetery is surrounded by a low wall.

She walks into the cemetery and starts searching systematically between the lines of graves. She follows the wall down the gentle slope to the water. Reading the names on every grave. Then she turns and takes in the next line of inscriptions.

The shiny pate of the taxi driver is visible above the top of the wall. He is smoking a cigarette.

She walks down the next line, reading the names on the gravestones. Turns at the wall and goes up the line after that.

There are two heads over the wall now. The taxi driver is talking to a man.

She walks down again, along the next line. On her way up this time she can no longer see the driver. The black Mercedes is returning to Fagernes. She stands for a few seconds, watching the car as it disappears around a bend, then she continues up towards the church, turns round again and goes down to the wall.

At last.

Åse Lajord 14.9.1919 – 30.10.1942. Much loved – deeply missed.

It is a wide headstone, a family grave. Åse is at repose with her mother and father. Ester unpacks the roses and places the bouquet against the headstone. Stands up and folds the paper. Tucks it under her arm and reminisces. She can see her friend as a little girl. Running between the houses on the summer mountain farm in high boots far too big for her feet. The little girl turns and smiles, and at that moment Ester gives a start. A man has grabbed her arm.

2

Ester has to hold onto a gravestone to stop herself falling. She looks into Gerhard's face.

'How does it feel?' he says.

'How does what feel?'

'Being spied on.'

Gently, she frees her arm and tries to recapture the mood she was in.

'The police came for me this morning at the hotel,' he says.

She gives up. 'You're here now, though,' she says.

'Two uniforms. One on each side. The whole stupid spectacle, down the corridor, into the lift and past the lobby and other hotel guests. Onto the back seat of a ridiculous VW Beetle with blue flashing lights on the roof. They wanted to see my passport and plane tickets. They could've examined them at the hotel, but they wanted to bully me. At the police station they spent two hours studying my papers. Afterwards, no apology, just a kick up the ass – out, no explanation. When I asked what I'd done wrong, they told me to shut my mouth.'

'You don't seem to have suffered as a result.'

'It's reason enough to be bad-tempered. If I'm really lucky they'll throw me out of the hotel.'

'Bad-tempered? At me?'

'I think you know as well as I do that this performance was executed under the auspices of a certain gentleman with a stick trying to tell me who's boss.'

'Keep me out of this,' she says. 'I came here to meditate over a grave, not to hear your intrigues with Sverre or anyone else.'

She looks down at the gravestone again. Feeling annoyed that Gerhard has dared to talk about his private circumstances over this grave.

She steps away.

He follows her.

They walk side by side down to the water. They pass a litter bin and she throws away the packaging from the flowers. She is reminded of the night when she followed Gerhard to another cemetery, and thinks this must be a sign – the way death keeps forcing itself onto her relations with him. This reminds her of the Colt Cobra, which is still on the bookshelf at home. She is out of training, slow off the mark.

'Have you been here before, to see the grave?'

'No,' she says. 'This is thanks to you, actually. Seeing you again made me think of her. So I wanted to come here.'

They gaze across the still lake. The cold autumn air has a bite in it now. 'And what about you?' she asks.

He angles his head towards the grave. 'We have quite a bit in common, Ester.'

'I had a taxi waiting for me,' she says, 'but it left.'

'I sent him away,' he says.

'Why?'

'Thought you could go back with me.'

She doesn't say anything at first. There is an aggression in most of what Gerhard says and does. Is that how he has become, or is this behaviour tied to his specific situation? This is not something she wants to ask him about. His sullen attitude is not conducive to that kind of dialogue. On the other hand, paying for her taxi and sending it on its way is so invasive that he must have done it to provoke her. So what does he want to achieve? He is testing me, she thinks the very next moment. He wants to see how I react. He wants to know who I am. The thought is reassuring; she is a past master at this kind of game – in his league, even.

The November darkness is falling. If she is going to do what she has planned, she will have to start moving. 'Then I'd like you to drive up around the cemetery,' she says.

'I just came that way.'

'Then I'll take a taxi. I want to go there now I'm here.'

'Of course I'll drive around it,' he says quickly. 'You can't do a good thing too often.' He turns and heads for the car park.

'But I think you'll be disappointed,' he says enigmatically.

When they reach the rental car, he opens first the passenger door, then walks around and gets in behind the wheel.

Ester hesitates.

He motions with his head inside the car. 'Shall we go?'

Ester gets in.

Stockholm, December 1942

1

The dress is purple, plain, with shoulder straps and a modest neckline. It also has a matching belt. The buckle is clad with the same material. The dress is the second item of smart clothing she has bought in all the time she has lived in Stockholm. With her first wage packet she bought a pair of party shoes. They have hardly been worn, so there is still a risk of blisters. But there is nothing she can do about that. Buying the dress was a nightmare. She has never found it so difficult to be pleased. Her body doesn't seem to fit it, and she doesn't have the time to take the dress in. It was the material she fell for. But it is all fine now, thanks to a few safety pins. It will be a trial run, then she can take it in at the weekend. She wishes she had some jewellery. The lucky charm will have to do. And the ring.

She is still excited. She has been excited for two days.

A briefing can't take forever. Torgersen said an hour. She has reserved a table for two and is willing to pay for the whole evening for both of them. She is looking forward to this and has calculated that she can manage it with her savings. A couple of days without eating won't harm; not if she's going to experience this: going to a restaurant with someone, dancing, feeling normal for a whole evening, excluding absolutely everything except the here and now.

As the time approaches she goes to the bathroom. She puts on some eye shadow, but stops and instead critically assesses herself. Sees her nervousness and closes her eyes. Tries to breathe calmly. She raises her hand and studies it in the mirror. She has put the ring back on. They will present themselves at Berns as herr and fru Larsen.

There is a ring at the door.

It startles her. She looks at herself in the mirror. Runs a finger under both eyes. She hears a car hooting its horn. She stumbles over the door sill. Hurries to the window, draws the curtain aside and looks down. A taxi has pulled up. Gerhard is standing by the open rear door. He waves. She waves back and lets go of the curtain. Runs into the hallway. Casts another glance at the mirror. A different woman looks back at her now. A smiling person. She composes herself. Takes a deep breath. Drops her new shoes into a shopping net. Puts on her boots, woollen coat and gloves, annoyed at herself for taking so much time while he is waiting. She checks she has the house key in her pocket and closes the door. Runs down the stairs.

Outside, there is snow in the air. But the taxi has gone. She casts around. Takes a few steps in one direction, turns round. Comes back. It is a fact. The car has gone.

For a fraction of a second she thinks this hasn't happened. No one rang the bell. No car hooted its horn. He didn't wave. But then she looks down. The tyre marks tell their own story.

She goes in. Slowly, back up the stairs. Unlocks the door and goes to the window. Looks outside.

No car. She stays like that, mind blank, bewildered. Then she walks out of the flat to the telephone in the corridor.

She lifts the receiver and inserts the coin when the switchboard answers. She asks for Torgersen's number.

She stands with the receiver under her chin while it rings. She turns. The corridor is still empty and quiet.

Finally she hears a woman's voice. She asks for Torgersen. The receiver crackles as it is placed on a table. She hears them talking. Now she feels stupid. Why should she talk to the boss about this? Gerhard has probably gone on to the briefing. Getting to England is all that has any meaning for him. He just doesn't want to have anything to do with her.

She hangs up.

Stands motionless, trying, and failing, to think clearly. Returns to her flat. Stops in the middle of the room, still wearing her coat and carrying the shopping net with her party shoes in. Angrily, she hurls the net against the wall. She paces back and forth. Sits down in the armchair.

Takes off the ring. Places it in the palm of her hand. Garish. Fake. It has discoloured her finger. She rubs it to remove the dark colour. In vain. She throws away the ring. That is how much she is worth.

She stares into the distance. At a loss as to know what to do.

Is there anything she can do apart from hunker down?

Then she hears an electric click. A chill runs down her spine. Her eyes are drawn to the clock on the wall. She listens to the ticking. Watches the minute hand move. There is something familiar about this situation. She stands up, goes back into the corridor to the telephone. Her instructions were to travel with Gerhard. If he doesn't want her along, that is his business, not hers. She lifts the receiver. Inserts a coin. Asks for a taxi and waits for an answer. Tells him her address and rings off. Afterwards she goes back to her sitting room. Stands by the window, looking out. It is only now that she realises how thick the snow is. It is blanketing down.

2

The taxi leaves the town behind them. The snow is settling on the road and on a sharp bend up the hill, the rear of the car skids. She has never been to Huddinge and is relying on the driver to know the way. She can't get Gerhard out of her head. Dreads meeting him again. Dreads what she is going to say to him. Dreads what he is going to say to her. She leans against the window. A snow plough roars towards them. She is startled, lets out a cry and puts a hand over her mouth. She still hasn't quite got used to traffic driving on the left. A welt of snow hits the windscreen. The wipers thrash as if in panic.

After a while the taxi turns off the main road and into a narrower side road with wheel tracks in the snow. Then she sees a blaze of red behind the trees. The taxi slows down and comes to a halt.

The Swedish taxi driver says nothing. He just sits quietly, both hands on the wheel.

'What now?'

'I'm stopping here.'

'Why?'

The driver says he doesn't want to go any closer. 'The farmhouse.' He takes his left hand off the wheel and points. 'It's on fire.'

Ester opens the door and gets out. It is the last house on the road.

She has never seen a fire like it. Smoke seems to be pouring through the walls. She moves closer. Yellow flames are licking out from under the eaves. Several of the window panes shatter, then there is a loud explosion. She recoils. The whole house is consumed by flames. She turns to the driver. He has rolled his window down. He shouts. She is paralysed. Her thoughts are too. She tells him to wait, barely able to hear her own voice, turns back to the fire and steps closer.

The heat is immense and gusts in her direction. It is as though the fire is throbbing with its own pulse, she thinks. Within the inferno she can hear a tinkle of glass as another window explodes. There is a whoosh and then she sees him in the sea of flames, through the window. His clothes are alight. The blazing man runs to the window, but is blown back. She is standing thirty metres away and even she can feel the heat singeing her face. She calls his name, but her cry is drowned in the fury of the fire. She shouts again, but the roar stifles any other sound. He is no longer visible. The flames pop and crackle. Something gives way inside and plunges down from the roof. The whole house caves in amid the sky-high conflagration.

Ester wants to be sick. Her hands are trembling and she has to concentrate to put one foot in front of the other. The driver has left his seat. His whole body is bathed in red against the backdrop of the night and he stares with an open mouth and vacant eyes.

Ester supports herself on the bonnet of the car. Inhales and breathes in smoke. Coughs. Staggers towards the rear seat. Closes the door with a bang. The driver is standing in front of the car, mesmerised. Ester wants to leave. She leans across the driver's seat and hoots the horn. The driver comes to, turns, trudges back to the car and gets behind the wheel.

Fagernes, November 1967

1

She doesn't fasten her seat belt. Old habits die hard. In case ... He notices. Watches her as he fastens his belt, every movement deliberate. Neither of them speaks. He starts the car. Sets off.

She takes in the countryside. Wondering what he knows about her. Maybe a little. Maybe nothing. Time will tell.

It isn't a long trip. The house is at the top of a rock face on the opposite side of the road. It appears as they round one of the first bends. But the roof is sunken and the house seems to be abandoned. The paintwork is peeling and some tiles have fallen off. Some windows have no glass and gape at the world, black-eyed.

He pulls in and stops. 'I was disappointed too,' he says, indicating a more robust house further up the mountain. 'I spoke to the neighbour. He's taken over the plot, but soon they're going to use this house for fire drills.'

'Keep going,' she says.

'The mountain farm?'

'Yes, I want to see that too.'

They drive on, round the hairpin bends, up the last steep inclines and above the tree line. The Bitihorn peak arches against the sky, and soon the mountain lake is revealed. 'You can stop here,' she says.

He obeys. Drives into an almost overgrown lay-by. Switches off the engine. The lake resembles a blue stripe on a dark palette dominated by greens and ochres, reds, yellows and browns. There are mountain cabins dotted around. Most of them are tarred log constructions with grass growing on the roofs. Only the roof ridge and chimney are visible on one, only a flagpole next to another.

She sits gazing at the countryside. Eventually she opens the door and gets out. To inhale the air. To feel the ground under her feet.

It is colder up here. She walks over to a decaying stump of wood at the side of the road. Cowberries and crowberries grow here. She crouches down, takes a few berries and puts them in her mouth. Grabs a handful of moss and squeezes it in her fist. The sound of a car door opening behind her breaks the spell. A cold gust of wind makes her shiver. She stands up.

He comes up beside her.

She points to the cabin idyllically situated on a headland extending into the lake. 'The one on the headland belonged to our neighbour in Eckersbergs gate, a nice, tall, fat lady called Ada. Her husband was dead. She let us use the cabin in the holidays and so on. Or I went on my own with Ada. In the end I was here every single summer and most Easter holidays. Åse was eleven and I was nine.' Ester's hand sweeps to the left and points to a fenced-in mountain pasture. 'She was the gatekeeper.'

'Åse and I didn't come here so often,' Gerhard says.

'They called us Night and Day,' she says. 'After the name of the pansy. Åse was as blonde as I was dark.'

She turns her back on him and puts a knuckle to her eye to catch the moisture.

'Meaning you always hung out together?'

'The original Two Little Maids. I can't remember us ever quarrelling. Did she tell you about the time we almost had a fatal accident?'

'Don't think so.'

'I was fifteen years old. It was in the autumn – it was so dark outside you could barely see a hand in front of your face. We'd been playing cards in the cabin. It was late and we had to go down to the farm to sleep there that night. We walked along that cliff edge.' She points. 'We both knew the way, naturally enough, and set off. But we got lost. We were both petrified of the dark, so neither of us said anything, we just walked. Suddenly in the darkness – you might not believe this – I saw a light, a very strange light, horizontal, a bit like a neon tube in the darkness. Straight in front of me. I stopped instantly and asked Åse if she could see what I could see. Yes, she whispered, from right behind me. At that moment I was about to raise my foot. And it was stuck. I screamed, and she screamed too. And I pulled at my foot, hard. I got my foot free, but my boot was stuck there. We turned and ran back to the cabin as fast as we could. Me with a boot on one foot and a sock on the other.'

Ester smiles at the memory.

Gerhard just looks at her, not at all interested.

Ester regrets telling him the story and cannot understand why she did.

'And so?' he says. 'What happened?'

Ester shrugs. 'It's just a story, a memory. We didn't dare go out again. Åse found my boot the next morning. It was stuck between two fibres of a pine tree root, on the edge of a precipice. You can't see it from here. If we'd taken a step further we would've fallen fifty metres and been smashed on the scree below. Åse talked a lot about that incident. She was sure it had some hidden meaning.'

Silence descends between them again. Hands in pockets, he stands gazing into the distance, as though there is something pent up inside him.

'I imagine Turid comes here a lot,' he says at length. 'If she's inherited it. The farm, I mean.'

'What are you actually doing here?' she says.

'Here in Valdres?'

'That too.'

'I came here to see her grave.'

'Why?'

He fixes her with a long stare. 'She and I never said goodbye.'

'Then I was in your way, down in the cemetery, when you wanted to say your goodbyes?'

For an instant she is frightened she has gone too far.

Without another word he turns on his heel and walks back to the car.

2

The sun is so low that occasionally it disappears behind the mountain crags. More often than not it hangs behind tall tree trunks and sends its final fiery rays into the car racing through the forest. As the terrain opens up, grassland comes into view above the rapids in the river. Ester is reminded of when she was small and her family drove through Begna valley. And of looking out at the trees and imagining that if you attached a big knife to the side of the car the trees would fall and the car would leave a terrible trail behind it.

She leans back in her seat. Remembering the day after the outbreak of war. The air-raid sirens went off. There was total panic. People ran helter-skelter through the streets. Buses and lorries, packed to the gunwales with people, left Oslo and headed for the hills. She ended up on a lorry that stopped on Frognerseter meadow. She walked among the crowds there all day, searching for her mother and father. The snow was still deep. But people were everywhere – people she didn't know, frightened people. There was no food. Some had packed lunches; someone from the council was providing porridge. A market trader was handing out eggs. An elderly lady was hugging a suitcase and shouting the name of her child. People around the woman were jeering. In the suitcase she had her silverware, but she had lost her child.

It had been there, on Frognerseter, that Ester had seen Åse for the first time for more than a year. Åse told her she was living with a man in Oslo. Ester smiles as she remembers the happiness and surprise at the reunion.

Gerhard glances at her. And finally breaks the silence.

'What's so funny?'

'I was thinking about Åse. There's one thing I've always wondered. Why didn't you get married?'

Gerhard doesn't answer. He continues driving and switches on the headlights.

'You lived together and had a child. It's unusual for an unmarried couple to decide to have children.'

'So you think we decided, do you?'

'That's not an answer.'

'*We* didn't decide. She was the one who wanted children.'

Ester lets this information sink in. His words: she was the one. Implying that one of them didn't want children.

'I had a job on a newspaper. Then they began to applaud Quisling in the leaders. I quit, got a job in Oslo, and we found an apartment.

Everything was fine and we moved to Oslo. But an informer knew I'd been in Spain. He wanted my job and got me kicked out. I had to join the dole queue every morning. There was work some days, a bit of loading and unloading at the harbour and so on, but mostly nothing at all. And there were Nazis who had it in for us anti-Krauts. I didn't think it was such a smart idea to have kids.'

'Not such a smart idea?'

'It was wartime.' He looked across at her. 'I was wounded in Spain. Had a break for a couple of years and a normal life, kind of. Then the war came here. Being a civilian in those days – play-acting for the Germans, for normal people, not having a job – was pure theatre.' He says nothing for quite a while, then goes on. 'The child was her way of sorting out the mess. She thought a kid would bring us closer together. But that was before Turid was born. Afterwards Åse couldn't get me out of the house fast enough.'

Ester turns in her seat. Studies him, wondering what he really means.

Gerhard looks in the side mirror, signals, pulls over and stops.

For an instant this manoeuvre alarms her. But Gerhard sits passively staring into mid-air, ruminative, not saying a word. It is getting dark. They have stopped in some sort of lay-by. She spots a wooden table with benches, an outside toilet and an overfilled litter bin.

A juggernaut roars past. It functions as a green light. 'You didn't know her like I did,' he says.

Ester thinks back to one day in Oslo during the war. She had forced herself on them. She hadn't liked doing it, but also felt the atmosphere had gone beyond anything that her presence could affect. She leaned over their little baby while listening to Åse and Gerhard whispering outside the door. She had supposed they were quarrelling. She had believed they were talking about her, how she had barged in on them. But she had probably been wrong. They must have quarrelled often.

Gerhard keeps both hands on the wheel. Then he takes a deep breath as if he has made up his mind.

'The last person to see Åse alive was Erik Heggen.'

Neither of them speaks for a while.

'Åse opened the door to Erik Heggen the evening she was murdered. Erik and Åse had been to the same school, and he was always tagging

along after her, even after she and I got together. Do you remember
that I left you and Åse on your own when you came to ours? They'd
arrested your father. I took the train to Fagernes. When I arrived I got
a lift on a horse and cart up to the Valdres plateau. The others were
already there when I arrived. Among them Erik Heggen. He's – he *was*
– a strange man. I don't know what he's like today. When he saw me
in the mountains he knew Åse was alone. It didn't strike me then, but
I've had a lot of long evenings to ruminate over what happened during
those days. The job in the mountains was to pick up all the containers
after a British airdrop. They were scattered over huge areas and there
were provisions in them. Lots of cans and a number of items it was
impossible to get in the standard way during the war. Erik stole from
the containers and went to Oslo to see Åse.'

When Gerhard stops talking, there is silence in the car. She wants
to hear the rest.

'I'm only saying what I know and what Erik should've said a long
time ago. At least to my daughter. He was with Åse – the day before or
on the same day she was murdered.'

'How can you be sure of that?'

'Erik used to visit her. Åse's mother ran a little farm and had food.
Erik would sometimes drop by with salami and eggs and so on from
her for Åse and me. I thought he did it for her mother. Of course, that
wasn't how it was. He did it to be with Åse. That day Erik stole from
the airdrop. I knew he'd done it, but I had my hands full. Suddenly he
was gone, and I didn't give him another thought. Things were like that
all the time. Most of us in the mountains were people with other jobs,
who did their bit in their free time. What I didn't know, but should've
realised, is that he went to see Åse. When she was found dead, the police
saw two glasses and found English products. That was why Sipo took
over. They knew Åse had some connection with the resistance movement. So the whole apartment was taken apart brick by brick, and they
found a gun. Then they started checking up on me. They uncovered
all my past, put two and two together and made fifteen. They thought
I was a big-time saboteur. They thought that, because I'd been in the
Norwegian communist party and done this and that before enrolling in
Spain, the gun in the apartment was mine. But the bottles were Erik's.'

'And this is the same Erik Heggen who adopted your daughter?'

He nods. 'So perhaps you can see why I have to tread carefully?'

It was her turn to nod.

'I've spent a number of years trying to work out what actually happened. When we met in Stockholm, I was in shock. I was depressed. Didn't know where I was. Åse was dead and my daughter was somewhere else.'

'Have you confronted Heggen with this?'

'Not yet.'

'When were you thinking of doing it?'

'There's a time for everything, Ester.'

'But you've been here long enough, haven't you? You've been here for several days now without confronting the man you think is behind everything.'

'He's now the father of my daughter!'

The knuckles on the wheel whiten. But Ester doesn't want to stop there. 'It's difficult, I know. Everyone would acknowledge that. But for you there's more. There has to be. Please tell me what it is.'

When he turns to look at her it is through a blank veil, but she intends to see through it. For a moment she considers saying she followed him to the cemetery. Then she comes to her senses. That would divert her from finding out what lies beneath the surface.

'What are you actually doing here in Norway, Gerhard?'

Again he doesn't answer.

'You think you're in control,' she says. 'You think you can manipulate and tell parts of the truth. But it'll all come to light sooner or later.'

'Bullshit,' he says through clenched teeth. 'Boloney, Ester. Do me a favour and talk sense if we absolutely have to talk.'

'OK, Gerhard. I saw you with Brian Pankhurst in Stockholm – but you still think how you escaped is a secret, don't you?'

His body actually recoils. The reaction does something to her. Perhaps it is that simple, she thinks. Perhaps Gerhard's manoeuvres are because he is afraid of losing his daughter again, losing her before he has her back. She understands the dilemma Gerhard is facing, of course. But she isn't going to stop now.

'You realised the briefing meeting that Friday in Stockholm was a set-up. But you didn't have to go. You could've done as you said – gone back to Norway and joined Osvald or Pelle, or the other saboteurs. Instead you walked straight into what you knew was a trap. You dropped by my flat, but that wasn't to take me along. You just showed your face so that afterwards I could witness that you'd been there. When the fire was out and the police found the bones in the ash, you went into hiding so that you could be declared dead. Why?'

He is breathing heavily. Takes his right hand off the wheel and twists the ignition key. The car starts.

They both look straight ahead. Neither of them says a word.

With her eyes half closed, she sees his hand put the stick in gear. He drives. She looks out onto the road illuminated by the headlamps. They sit like this, silent, for a long time. When she decides the silence has lasted for long enough, she faces him and clears her throat. He switches on the radio, as an act of defiance. She looks to the front again. Otto Nielsen welcomes listeners to his radio programme.

Ester grips the volume knob and turns up the sound. Otto Nielsen sings:

He's dead but he won't lie down. He's dead but he won't lie down.

1

With all the lit and unlit windows the house-fronts look like some kind of board game. Ester stands looking first at the windows then at the red tail-lights of the car driving away. It is quiet. Again she looks at the blocks of flats in Thomas Heftyes gate. In some of the windows there is a blue glow from the TV inside. Families having supper, she thinks. They sit down in front of the TV to be entertained. And even though she is happy to be finally out of the car and free of Gerhard's sullen, angry presence, it is with a certain reluctance that she walks towards the entrance of her block to round off the evening in her own company. Then she notices that she isn't alone. On the opposite side of the street, at the bus stop, sits a figure on the bench. This person stands up and limps into the light from the street lamp. It is Sverre Fenstad. He crosses the street.

'Consorting with the enemy…' It is a statement rather than a question. His face is in darkness.

She has been slightly irritated by Sverre the whole time and now at last she understands why. He keeps his mouth safely shut, carefully filtering the information he imparts. The sudden interest he shows when he rings or shows up here is nothing more than snooping. He wants to know things, but he won't give any information in return. She can feel her irritation growing, as she realises he feels no shame in using her for his dirty little intrigues.

'Let's go inside,' she says. 'Have a chat. I've just been driven two hundred kilometres in total silence.' She takes the lead up the stairs.

She unlocks the door, switches on the light and shows him into the kitchen. Asks him if he wants a cup of tea. She pours water into a whistle kettle on the stove. Fills it up and puts it on the hotplate.

'Where have you been?'

She looks at him, long enough for him to know that he has just made a false move. 'I've been to Åse's grave. Where *he's* been you'll have to take up with him. I asked you if you wanted a cup of tea. Yes or no?'

'Have you got a dram?'

'Brandy or gin?'

'I prefer brandy.'

Ester takes a tumbler. Fetches a bottle of Martell from the cupboard under the sink and opens the seal.

'You didn't have to open one,' he says from the chair by the window.

'It's been here for years. I don't like brandy.' She fills the glass half full.

'Ester,' he says with a smile. 'You're generous. Thank you.'

She takes a tin of loose tea and pours some into a strainer. Glances at him from the worktop. With his sly expression above the goatee, he resembles a caricature of a pedlar – sitting there with his glass, scowling and planning. She guesses that he will say something innocuous at first. About Jonatan, for example. She is right.

'How's your son getting on? I think you said he was in the army, didn't you?'

'Fine. He's already had a taste of combat.'

He looks down as though regretting the question and hatches a new plan. Now he wants to get straight to the point, she thinks.

'Gerhard probably won't like it that you and I have such close contact,' he says.

She looks at him again. As though she cared what Gerhard thought about anything! 'Why are you so keen to suspect him? There was nothing unusual in his hotel room, was there?'

Sverre Fenstad swallows a mouthful of brandy.

Now, she thinks. 'Sverre.'

He looks up.

'Did you find anything in his room?'

The kettle whistles. She goes to the stove. Pours the boiling water into the tea strainer. A herbal aroma spreads through the kitchen. She adds a little milk to her tea and stirs.

She sits down. The heavy silence persists.

He puts down his glass.

They eye each other. 'No,' he says at length. 'I didn't find anything, Ester. We've talked about this before.'

And I still don't believe you, Ester thinks.

'He's come to take his revenge,' Sverre says. 'The challenge is to find out how.'

'What would he have to avenge?'

'Haven't we all got something to avenge? Life is long.'

Ester swallows her irritation again. 'Don't you think he would've wanted to come to Norway before if revenge had been on his agenda?'

'Several of the International Brigade soldiers I've met lost something vital en route. For many of them war became a job, a way of feeling alive.'

'Most of the ones I've met are still idealists,' Ester says. 'But what are you trying to say?'

'What if Gerhard lost his belief?'

'Anyone can lose their belief,' she says, looking him in the eye.

He returns her gaze without flinching.

'Gerhard was part of the resistance movement,' she continues. 'So were you; so was I. What gives you, of all people, the right to say that he or I were driven by the wrong motives?'

Sverre stares back with equal resolve. 'Just forget what I said, Ester.'

'Sverre, tell me what's bothering you.'

'Bothering me?'

'You want Gerhard to be the enemy. Has he threatened you?'

Now his eyes do wander. 'Threatened me? No.'

'You put the police onto him,' she says.

Sverre looks up again.

'In the worst way. He said he was picked up by two uniformed policemen at the hotel in front of the other guests.'

Sverre gesticulates dismissively.

'They checked his passport and travel papers. Don't tell me you weren't behind it.'

'I had my reasons.'

'So let me ask you again: has Gerhard threatened you?'

'No,' he says, with an undertone of annoyance in his voice. 'Why are you hassling me?'

'Because I want to understand what your motives were when you set the police on the man.'

'It was surveillance. And you can relax. Gary Larson's always had a return ticket to the States. In not so many days we'll be rid of Gerhard.'

Ester reflects. Gerhard had said he went to Valdres to say his goodbyes. So perhaps what Sverre says is true. But what does Gerhard's departure mean? She doesn't know. But she can feel her curiosity growing as far as the main question is concerned. What is Gerhard actually doing? Why has he booked a fixed date for his return if he has come here to fulfil a neglected paternal role and clear up an unsolved murder?

'I think Gerhard's become a bitter man,' Sverre says. 'I understand that. I'd be bitter in his shoes. He does a fantastic job here in Norway. Then Satan intervenes. Someone kills the mother of his child. From then on he's kicked around like a football, by the Germans on one side and the resistance people on the other. He's booted around until one of them, his own allies, decide to get rid of him. You might remember Kolstad?'

She remembers him, but sees no reason to interrupt Sverre now.

'Gerhard survived by killing the man who was sent to kill him. Kolstad. But that's water under the bridge.'

Ester gets up. 'That's exactly what I've been waiting for you to say,' she says.

He looks up, tight-lipped.

'I think I've had to wait rather a long time.'

Not even now does he speak.

She leaves the kitchen and goes into the bathroom.

Here, she closes the door after her. Sits on the edge of the bathtub. On the one hand, it is sensible of Sverre finally to admit to the liquidation plan. On the other, it is hard not to take the admission personally. This figure of authority comments casually that Gerhard had to be liquidated by his own side. As if he were talking about pressing a flower for a herbarium. On top of which, he takes the liberty of doubting others' motivation and integrity. It had been Torgersen who had given her the order, who had said she should take Gerhard to the briefing, travel with him. To be sure he turned up.

And there lies the personal side of the matter: what plans did Sverre Fenstad and Torgersen have for her the evening it was due to happen?

Is Gerhard right? Was she saved that night because she was a Jewish girl everyone felt sorry for? But if so, how had they planned to liquidate Gerhard but save her, the eyewitness? Ester takes nothing for granted in this case. She stands up, goes to the toilet bowl and flushes. Faces the basin. Takes the mascara from the cabinet at the side of the mirror. Checks her appearance once more before going back to the kitchen.

Sverre Fenstad is rolling a cigarette.

Ester sits down. 'As the bones they found in the ash belonged to Kolstad you must've known all along that Gerhard was alive. Kolstad was your bodyguard. He disappeared. You must've realised that Gerhard survived the fire.'

Sverre takes the roll-up out of his mouth. 'There were remains in the fire. We found that out. But both Gerhard and Kolstad were missing. Not in my wildest dreams did I imagine that Gerhard had survived and would be able to hide from both the police and the Norwegians in Stockholm. He must've definitely had help. I have no idea how he did it. He didn't know anyone – after all, he needed our assistance to get out of the Kjesäter camp. Where would he get new helpers from? Those of us still in Norway concluded that Gerhard and Kolstad killed each other or died in the fire.'

'He must've found other people to help him while he was hiding in Stockholm.'

'Well – that's how it must've been. But how likely was that in those days? He was moved around so that the Swedish police wouldn't be able to catch him. Then you say he met someone who was capable of tricking both the police and the whole of the Norwegian legation and afterwards getting the man out of Sweden? I cannot fathom how he managed it. Anyway, at the time we considered it to be highly improbable.'

'I know that Gerhard was in contact with the British secret service while he was in Stockholm.'

His eyes lock onto hers. He is surprised, she thinks, and slightly put out to find out something he didn't already know.

'How do you know?'

'I just do.'

'No one in British intelligence circles informed us. Are you sure?'

She shakes her head. 'All I'm sure of is that we at the legation were told that the bones of one person had been found after the fire. You must've been told the same.'

'The main point was to persuade the police and everyone else in Sweden that Gerhard's death was the result of an accident. But at home we knew the police had found bones in the ash. It was war. Things were happening on the eastern front and we had a lot of work on our hands. My conclusion was that both were missing. They never appeared again, so we assumed they had killed each other and that was that. But we couldn't go public with this conclusion. Torgersen was instructed to tell you and the others that the remains belonged to Gerhard. Then a story was fabricated about Gerhard's death – to bring the case to an end in Norway. The same happened for Kolstad, but it was so that his family would have some peace. Where did you get this stuff about the British intelligence services?'

'Forget I told you,' she says. 'It was probably just a rumour. There was a lot of speculation when he went missing.'

Sverre pats his pockets. Unable to find what he is looking for. 'You don't have any matches by any chance, do you?'

She fetches a box from a drawer and passes it to him.

Sverre lights up and smokes in silence.

His brandy glass is empty again. He helps himself to a refill. Puts the top on the bottle and has a sip. 'Have you had any contact with people from the group since the war?'

She shakes her head. 'None.'

'You went to Israel when it was still called Palestine, didn't you?'

'Yes, I have some contact with people there now.'

For a long while only the ticking of the clock on the wall can be heard.

'It's late,' Sverre says, putting down his glass.

'Do you know where Gerhard's father is buried?'

He looks askance at her over his glass. 'Why?'

'Gerhard made a point of mentioning it when I met him. How he had to live in a different country with a different identity. What a loss it had been. He didn't know when his father died or where he was buried.'

Sverre ponders. 'I'd guess it was Porsgrunn.'

'Porsgrunn?'

'That's where Gerhard's from. His father worked at the porcelain factory.'

'I thought he might be buried at the Cemetery of Our Saviour here in Oslo.'

'Why did you think that?'

She changes the topic. 'Just forget it. There's another thing I'm wondering about. Alvilde Munthe – does that name ring a bell?'

'No, should it?'

'She died long before the war.'

Sverre shrugs. 'It doesn't mean anything to me.'

'I'm not sure. Perhaps it's just a wild-goose chase. But I'm wondering whether she had some kind of relationship with Gerhard. She's buried in that cemetery too.'

Sverre thinks. 'She might've been a person of some significance at one time. There are a lot of fine folk resting there. But she definitely isn't a name I know.'

2

Sverre Fenstad sits in the taxi on his way home. It is late and at first he has his eyes closed, pleasantly intoxicated on brandy. But as soon as the taxi branches off at Tåsen he feels anxious. You shouldn't be afraid of going home.

On the other hand, Gerhard will soon be back in America. It is merely a question of hanging on. His mind goes back to Ester's claim that Gerhard was in contact with British intelligence. She must be right that it was only a rumour. Anything else is too crazy.

The driver slows down as they approach Sverre's street. He checks the house numbers. Sverre coughs. 'Over there. The drive with the wrought-iron gate.'

The car stops.

Sverre pays the driver and stands outside the gate until the car has disappeared from view. The house is dark and quiet. He stands still, without moving, to calm himself down, to feel the knot in his stomach loosening, telling himself, this is my home. Gerhard broke in. He did it to intimidate me, to sow the seeds of fear, but I mustn't allow these seeds to germinate and grow bigger. This is my home. I am in charge of what goes on here. And now my house is waiting for me as it is supposed to.

The windows reflect the darkness of the autumn evening. The gate is closed and the door securely locked. He hears footsteps. Turns. It is the girl who lives two houses down. She is walking the little dog with ears that almost drag along the ground. She does a little curtsey. The dog sniffs the gatepost, lifts a rear leg, squirts and then pads on its way. An absolutely normal evening, thinks Sverre. He walks in through the gate, up the steps and unlocks the door.

He closes the door and switches on the light. Tries to absorb the atmosphere of the house, as he wants it to be. He wants to be reassured by the smell of home and tranquillity.

He goes upstairs to the bathroom. Has a pee, then goes into the corridor. Standing there, he senses something he has felt several times recently. Something that has bothered him ever since the break-in. The unease is connected with the bathroom, he realises. He opens the bathroom door, switches on the light and goes in. He lets his eyes wander from the door frame, past the toilet, the bathtub, past the washstand with the mirror and the cabinet and over the rail with the towels, the medicine cupboard and back to the door frame. He does the same the other way round – and now he sees it. The stick with the hook on. The pole hook he uses to open the loft hatch. It is hanging from the wrong hook. It always hangs on the second from right. Now it is hanging from the one on the extreme right. Now Sverre knows how Gerhard managed to do everything. He is disappointed with himself. He grasps the pole hook, leaves the bathroom and goes to the end of the narrow corridor. He pulls down the loft hatch. On the inside of the hatch is the ladder, which unfolds. He climbs up. He twists the light switch and scans the cramped loft. The cardboard boxes and the rubbish he has put up here. Sees the footprints in the dust between the boxes.

Sverre can imagine it all now: Gerhard pulled down the loft hatch and the ladder with it. Then he hung the pole back on the hook. Climbed into the loft, pulled the ladder up and closed the hatch door after him. Then he waited. Sitting in the darkness and listening to

Sverre's movements downstairs. He heard Sverre go to bed. When he was sure Sverre had fallen asleep, Gerhard climbed down and pottered around in the house. Boiled some coffee. Switched on the TV. Went into his bedroom and opened the window wide. Then he left. Perhaps he waited outside. Or he went back to his hotel. He rang to make sure Sverre woke up and could see what he had done. It was a demonstration of power.

Sverre climbs back down the ladder, lifts it into position and closes the hatch.

Why hadn't he checked the loft before he went to bed?

It had never occurred to him.

What if it had? What would Gerhard have done if he had been caught red-handed?

Sverre goes numb thinking about the weapon in the cistern in the hotel room. His fingertips rasping over the sharp blade. The police hadn't found it. They had searched the room while Gerhard was being interviewed. He must have removed it, being the alert, careful person he was.

Sverre limps down to the ground floor. His hip is really giving him some pain. He looks outside. It has started to rain. Perhaps this pain is a kind of arthritis, he thinks, holding his hip.

At that moment the telephone rings. He limps over to it. 'Fenstad.'

It is Vera asking him to guess what she is holding in her hand.

'A red carnation,' he says for lack of a better suggestion.

'I have the Åse Lajord file. It isn't very fat. So I thought I'd better ring.'

'Have you been through the papers?'

'The few there are, yes.'

Sverre listens with half an ear while Vera talks. He has discovered something else that is different since Gerhard's visit. The key cupboard on the wall beside the front door. It is not unusual for the little door to be open. What is unusual is that a key is missing.

'Thank you, Vera,' he says, noticing only after he has spoken that he has interrupted her in the middle of a sentence.

'Sverre?'

'Thank you, Vera. I'll call you later.'

He sinks down onto the bench beside the telephone. The seeds Gerhard sowed are germinating. He raises his hand. It is trembling. First the lighter, he thinks, and now the key. But what does Gerhard want with an old lighter? No, he must have dropped the lighter when he wasn't concentrating. The key, however, is a different matter. Gerhard's theft of the key means he will have to get new locks for the house. He opens the telephone directory and looks up locksmiths. But then he realises how late it is. No point ringing. He can't order new locks until tomorrow.

He closes the telephone directory. Shoots a glance upstairs. He doesn't want to go to bed up there, alone in this big house. Not now that he knows Gerhard has a key.

Oslo, November 1967

1

Ester catches a glimpse of Markus Rebowitz's back as he swings into Bygdøy allé. He is almost at the bottom of the hill. So he is a bit late. Markus is always punctual. He disappears through the door of Møllhausen's patisserie. She drives into Niels Juels gate to park.

When, a little later, Ester goes through the same door, Markus is in the queue at the counter. He points towards the window. He has laid his coat over a chair at one of the tables there.

'What do you want, Ester?'

'Tea, please,' she says.

On her way to the table, as usual she chooses to step only on the dark squares on the chessboard tiles.

Markus knows her obsessive quirks and smiles. 'A bite to eat?' he calls.

'A custard tart.'

She sits down at the window table and gazes out at the traffic in Bygdøy allé.

Markus comes over with the tray. She tears the top off the envelope and dips a tea bag into the cup of hot water. Breaks off a bit of the tart. 'You should try this,' she says. 'Puff pastry and custard. This is the best in town.'

Markus bites into his bread roll with brown cheese, chews and mumbles that this is a speciality as well. He takes his coat and searches the pockets. He pulls out a small, oblong case.

He places the roll on his plate and holds out the case to her. It's a mezuzah. It is made of brass and decorated with elegant engravings. Old patina.

'It's uncommonly beautiful,' she says, examining it; she means it.

'It's for you.'

He takes it back from her and shows her how to open it. Passes the two parts back.

'I can't accept this, Markus.'

'Of course you can.'

'But I'm never going to hang it up.'

He looks at her with arched eyebrows.

'I haven't forgotten that they painted a star on our doors. Or that my father slept in the shop to prevent vandalism.'

'We were also harassed. But we're living in different times now. It's no shame to be a Jew in Norway.'

She puts the mezuzah on the table between them. 'I don't believe it has anything to do with shame. It's associated with something I'd rather forget.'

They are interrupted by a young girl with an apron and a coffee pot. 'Refill, Markus?'

He nods, holds out his cup and smiles as she swivels round to the customers at the neighbouring table.

'Do you know her?'

'Let's say I know what the custard tarts taste like at Møllhausen's.'

Ester brushes the crumbs from her fingers. They both gaze out at the traffic, lost in their own memories, and jump when the bell over the door jingles. A crowd of children flock around the counter. They all want a 'school bun': a custard bun covered with grated coconut.

She looks at Markus. He looks at her, and she decides they have chit-chatted enough. 'Have you got anything to tell me?'

He closes his eyes just long enough for her impatience to intensify. 'Why did you ask me to do this?' he says.

'I told you. What's up?'

'Red lights started flashing.'

Ester regards him without saying a word.

'First and foremost: Gary Larson doesn't run a petrol station. He never has done. And definitely not in Minneapolis.'

So Gerhard is lying, Ester thinks. That is not so surprising, in fact. Someone who has lied before will do it again.

Markus collects crumbs on the tip of his forefinger and licks it clean. 'What about the red lights?'

'Gary Larson turns out to be in the same branch as you.'

She raises both eyebrows.

'And he goes back a long way. Right to ANCIB, the Army Navy Communication Intelligence Board. The forerunner of the NSA.'

She hadn't expected that. 'Seriously?'

Markus nods. 'At any rate Gary Larson's been working for the American National Security Agency ever since 1945. But now he's no longer in such good company.'

Ester concludes that she isn't actually that surprised. There has been something measured and professional about Gerhard's conduct this whole time. All the tricks to check if he was being followed when he went to the cemetery. Gerhard's physique in relation to his age, but also the composure, the cool, watchful posture.

'Apparently Gary Larson has two weaknesses,' Markus says, collecting the rest of the crumbs in his palm and tossing them into his mouth. 'Larson is what some call a dipso. In addition, he's addicted to gambling. What are your thoughts on that?'

She doesn't quite know how to express them. 'No longer in such good company? How do you stop intelligence work in America?'

'You can't make that tally?'

'It's just that all the evidence suggests he's on a specific mission,' she says. 'He does stuff.'

'My source mentioned one Brian Pankhurst.'

Ester beams.

'Did I say something funny?'

She shakes her head. 'You've confirmed what I myself suspected. Brian Pankhurst – in Stockholm,' she says.

Markus nods. 'The Englishman who trained us in close-combat fighting back then was Brian Pankhurst. The man my source links with Gary Larson is Brian Pankhurst. The age suggests it's the same man.'

Ester finishes her tea. Pankhurst represented the British intelligence services in those days. In fact, that was all she knew about him. Apart from one other thing: he and Gerhard knew each other. She had known that, but no one else in the legation had. And Pankhurst must have been involved from the start, she thinks. Gerhard would never have walked into an ambush without ensuring he had a way out. And in Pankhurst he had the world's best-qualified henchman. She can see it now. She was the one who had given him the address. Gerhard had seen the risks it presented and was uneasy. He had left her in the lurch that night, presumably to check with Pankhurst. Who represented British interests. He was the one who would have known whether the meeting was genuine or not. Gerhard had decided to go into hiding. The two of them: him and Pankhurst. Kolstad didn't have a chance. What Markus says is logical and means that there is only one element she still can't quite grasp: why was it better for Gerhard to be declared dead than to return to Norway and fight?

Markus coughs.

She looks up.

'You say Larson does stuff. What does he do?' he asks.

'I'm not sure. But I have to find out exactly what he's up to.' She slips back into thought.

'What are you thinking about, Ester?'

'Larson and Pankhurst were in contact in Stockholm. They knew each other. I saw them together.'

'Oh? How did they establish that contact? I seem to remember Larson was in hiding all of the time.'

'They must've known each other well. So they must've had dealings long before Stockholm.' She glances up at him. 'Can you try and find out how they first met?'

Markus doesn't answer.

She looks through the window and can feel his eyes on her.

'Will you?'

He is still silent.

She interprets this as a no and packs up her things.

'There's one tiny detail,' he says. 'It's tiny and I don't know if it means anything.'

Letting the cat out of the bag at the last minute is typical of Markus, but she isn't in the mood to smile.

'As I remember it, Larson had been in the International Brigade. I think you told me that once.'

'He had, yes.'

'Pankhurst too. He went to Spain to volunteer,' Markus says. 'Among other things he led a section at Brunete.'

'Larson was injured there,' Ester says. 'At the battle of Brunete.'

Markus grins wryly. 'There's your explanation. That's how they knew each other.'

2

It is midnight by the time Grete plucks up the courage to check the sitting room. It is dark inside. Erik is standing at the window and looking out. He doesn't turn. She catches a whiff of alcohol, but she can't see a bottle. The smell could have been her imagination, she thinks.

'Aren't you coming to bed?'

He doesn't answer.

'She's twenty-five. She does what she wants.'

'Then she can live in her own flat. If she can do as she wants.'

Grete doesn't respond. She stares at her husband's stubborn back. 'It's another long day for us tomorrow. And you have to start work early.'

'Go to bed. I'll wait for her.'

For another long moment she stares at his back, then she closes the door and goes upstairs.

She cleans her teeth and puts on her nightdress. Paces the room, wondering what to do. Should she go back downstairs to talk some sense into him? She listens carefully for tell-tale clinks of bottles or glasses.

Instead she hears a faint hum from outside. She goes to the window. The hum comes from a car engine idling. A white car. She recognises the idiosyncratic shape: a Volvo Amazon. Two yellow cones of light cut through the darkness. Thank God, Grete thinks, now she is coming home, at long last. Grete switches off the bathroom light so that she can see outside better. She sees Turid's long legs. Turid is standing by the car, holding the door open and talking to the driver. Has she got a new boyfriend?

Then Turid straightens up. Closes the car door and waves after the car as it continues down Slemdalsveien. Turid walks quickly to their front entrance.

Grete opens the bathroom door and goes into the corridor. Hears the front door open downstairs. Hears the rustle of Turid's coat as she hangs it up.

Erik's voice: 'Did you come by car?'

Turid's voice: 'Got a lift.'

'Who with?'

Turid's bubbling laugh. 'Don't be so nosy.'

Turid comes up the stairs.

Erik shouts after her. 'You're still living at home. You have to obey our rules for as long as you live here.'

Turid takes no notice. She just hurries up the stairs as though propelled by the words, Grete thinks. As though he is pushing her up and away from him. Because Turid naturally feels the same as Grete. The immense pressure.

As Turid reaches the top, they exchange glances. The daughter says nothing. But they have looked at each other like this many times before. There is nothing you can say. Words became redundant long ago. Turid disappears into her room and closes the door.

Grete listens. Erik is still in the sitting room. Now there is the clear clink of a glass. Grete knows Erik won't be coming to bed. She takes a deep breath and goes into the bedroom.

Oslo, November 1967

1

It is pouring down. Raindrops ricochet off the water streaming along the pavement in Uranienborgveien. Sverre Fenstad watches the rain through the rectangular basement windows high up the wall. Occasionally he sees running legs pass by and he tries to guess which ones are heading down here, where he is sitting. But no one comes into Krølle. Sverre is still the only customer in the restaurant.

A waiter in a white jacket is cleaning cutlery by the till. There is a clunk every time he drops a knife or a fork into the drawer. Sverre looks at him. The man has a double chin and a sulky mouth. He is balding. The little hair he has left is combed back and finishes in a curl at the back. Sverre holds a finger in the air. Eventually he attracts the man's attention. Soon the waiter comes with half a litre of beer and places the glass on the table. He removes the empty one and returns to his post by the cutlery.

Sverre looks through the high windows in the wall again. For the first time he sees a woman's legs marching towards the entrance. Heels click-clack on the steps. The door opens. She stands with her back to him and shakes the rain from her umbrella before turning and coming in. Grete Heggen leans the umbrella against the door frame. She is wearing a mackintosh with a belt around the waist. She walks over to the table. Unbuttons her raincoat and drapes it over the back of the chair. Even today her hair seems fresh; she pats her hairdo lightly to make sure it is still intact.

'What weather!'

Sverre beckons to the waiter.

'No, no. I'm fine, thank you,' she says quickly, waving away the man as he makes his way to their table. 'I don't want anything. I'm going to a meeting at the Women's Public Health Association. I had to use it as an excuse.'

'Doesn't Erik know you're meeting me?'

'No,' she says, sitting down. 'He would go berserk if he knew. Erik's impossible. He loses his temper over nothing. And now it's all-out war at home. Gerhard's contacted Turid.'

Sverre takes a swig of beer. 'So that's led to a row?'

She doesn't answer at once.

They sit looking at each other. He waits. Grete was the one who asked for this meeting.

'Now he's bringing up what the Germans said.'

Sverre raises both eyebrows.

'He says Gerhard killed her…' Grete says.

'Does he tell Turid that?'

'Are you crazy? No. He tells me. I didn't understand at first why he wanted to stop Gerhard meeting Turid. The answer is that he's convinced Gerhard killed her mother.'

Sverre adopts a serious tone. 'Do you share that view?'

Grete takes a deep breath. 'I don't know. This is one of the reasons I wanted to talk to you. Erik struggles with anything about the war. You know what he had to go through.'

'February 1945,' Sverre says. 'It will never be forgotten. He was strong, Erik was. He stood up against all the brutality they could muster.'

'He held on, but torture has an effect over the years.'

Sverre's eyes soften. 'Is there anything you'd like me to do?'

She breathes out. 'Everything's connected. Of course, that all happened long after Åse was killed, but what I'm trying to say is that Erik has enough on his plate. This Åse business is just making things worse.'

Sverre nods. He understands. When Erik Heggen was arrested in the winter of 1945 he was subjected to a brutal interrogation. But he didn't crack. There are many who owe their lives to Erik Heggen. Sverre has said this to Grete and her husband many times, and is about to say it again when Grete carries on:

'Everyone was sceptical when the Gestapo accused Gerhard of killing Åse. But in many ways the Germans could never work out the whole picture because both Gerhard and Åse were in the resistance. People kept mum about what they knew.'

Sverre wonders why she has changed the subject and tries, to no avail, to catch her eye. 'Grete.'

She looks at him at last.

'What do you think now?' he asks.

'In North Aurdal we received a message to help some British soldiers who were being flown in over the mountains. But the information turned out to be incorrect. The men were dropped over the Hardanger plateau that night, not over the Valdres plain. And they were Norwegians, not British.'

He puts down his glass. Deliberates before formulating his question. 'How can you be so sure of this when you didn't meet them?'

'The men who parachuted in were from the British-trained Linge Kompani, and they sabotaged the Norsk Hydro plant in Rjukan the following year. That was a big deal, wasn't it. Or it became a big deal eventually. No men were dropped where we'd laid strips of light in the snow, only supplies.'

She goes quiet again. Looks down.

He tries to wheedle more out of her: 'Supplies?'

'Erik took some. Pinched them. That wasn't so unusual. Many of them did it to earn a bit on the black market. But you know this, Sverre. It wasn't that unusual.' She pauses to think, then carries on:

'Erik used to go there, to Oslo. Took things with him. Åse came from a farm. After the airdrop, when Gerhard arrived, Erik went down to the village. They weren't fond of each other.' She looks at her watch. 'Erik went to Oslo, to see Åse. I don't know what he took with him, but I'd guess pork, maybe some cream and cheese – from her mother, right, and flat bread, and probably also some of what he stole from the containers.'

'Like whisky and sherry?'

'I presume so.'

'The items that were found in Åse's flat were a mystery to both the Gestapo and us. If at least I'd found out they came from Erik, a lot could've been very different, Grete.'

'Now you can see how quickly you can draw the wrong conclusions. You might've suspected Erik of killing her.'

Sverre shakes his head. 'If he'd told us then, perhaps we might've got to the truth and a lot would've been different, not least the situation we're experiencing now. I have to say, I find it very dubious that Erik has kept this quiet over all these years.'

'He doesn't do dubious things. Erik's a hero.'

'For enduring the imprisonment in February forty-five, yes, he is. But now we're talking about a case where he should've been open.'

She shakes her head. 'Erik's been open. I was there when he went to Oslo to see Åse. He's known I've known the whole time.'

Grete is clearly annoyed. But Sverre feels he has to dig deeper. 'If you knew, why did you keep quiet?'

'Did you ever go behind your wife's back when she was alive?'

'So you and Erik did talk about it and agreed not to say anything?'

'Not at all. He swears Åse was alive when he left her. Happy?' Grete is breathing hard. 'But he just can't talk about it. Erik thinks he can solve his problems with the bottle. He'll never be able to talk to Turid about this. She needed a reliable father when she was left alone in the world, not a man who might possibly have prevented the murder of her mother if he'd stayed longer than he actually did. Erik has no bad motives. He's always suspected Gerhard of killing Åse. But he hasn't been able to tell anyone, least of all Turid. Now, with Gerhard meddling, this has become an impossible situation. All sorts of destructive sediment will swirl to the surface. I need your help, Sverre. Your words carry weight. What you say will mean something.'

'What do you want me to do?'

'I have a daughter who's caught between two fathers, and now there's a chance she'll lose both, just because that bastard wants to dig up the past. Talk to Gerhard, tell him to go home and let go of the past. Åse's dead. She won't come back and no one can relive a life.'

'Tell him to let go of the past? Gerhard was separated from his daughter when her mother was killed. He was driven out of the country, an attempt was made to liquidate him and afterwards he was forced into a life he had no desire to live.'

She eyes him, nodding. 'Someone tried to liquidate him?'

Sverre sighs. 'Yes, and he hasn't been able to contact his friends or family. He couldn't visit his father when he fell ill. He has no idea when or how his father died.'

'But why should he take that out on others? On me? On Erik? No one knows what happened when Åse was killed. For all we know, Erik might be right. Perhaps it really was Gerhard who murdered her.'

'No, Grete. Erik's wrong there. If Gerhard had killed her he would never have meddled, as you put it. Gerhard wants only two things: to get to know his daughter and find out who killed her mother.'

Grete doesn't answer.

'Whatever happened when Erik went to see Åse, he has to open up and say. He has to talk. Anything else destroys us all.'

Grete doesn't appear to be listening. Her gaze is miles away. 'So,' she says, as if the conclusion is obvious. 'I can see it now. Gerhard can still use Turid. *That* is the plan. He'll ingratiate himself with her, set her against Erik.'

'Ingratiate himself? This is his daughter you're talking about.'

Grete turns to Sverre. Her eyes are hard and small knots of muscles churn in her jaws as she speaks. 'Turid's *my* daughter. I took care of her from before she was a year old. I adopted her. I've brought her up. I've given her everything she lost when her mother died. So Gerhard's a bitter man? Fine. The point is that he doesn't appear to understand he's going to cause pain however this develops. He should've stayed in America. What do you know about the life he's lived? For all we know, he might have a wife and kids out there. He has no right to wreak havoc on my daughter, my family – our lives – just because of something that happened a long time ago.'

Sverre Fenstad grimaces. 'If Gerhard succeeds in pitting his daughter against Erik, I'd have to say he deserves it. Standing up to the torture in 1945 is a completely different matter. What you just said means that Erik was the last person to see Åse alive. He allowed Gerhard to be driven out of the country and took his daughter. So he's made his bed and he has to lie in it. Your husband has a few things to explain, Grete.'

Grete has gone pale. She stands up. Her hands are trembling as she puts on her raincoat. 'I thought you might've been able to help. I thought you were decent.'

Sverre watches her in silence. Sees her angry body retreat across the restaurant.

But then she spins on her heel and walks back. Leans forwards, her arms supporting her on the table. 'You sit there and think you know everything, don't you.'

He recoils. 'My dear Grete…'

'You shut up! Have you ever wondered how bad Gerhard was? Åse had a mother who was in and out of hospital. Why wasn't Åse at home helping her? Why, with a baby in her arms, did she go like a nodding dog and live in a flat in Oslo with a man who couldn't hold down a job? She wasn't given the option to do anything else. He was the big shot who deigned to leave the city for the mountains and ordered the rest of us around while she had to be a good girl and stay at home, waiting. He kept her on a short leash and could use his fists if words didn't have the required effect. You've never thought that far, have you. No, you just sit on your high horse thinking you know everything, but you're naïve!'

Her shoes pummel the tiles. The door slams. She is outside.

Sverre looks at the waiter, who meets his eye.

They both look away at the same moment.

Sverre takes a deep breath, grabs his pouch of tobacco and rolls himself a cigarette. Pats his pockets. Looks up at the waiter and asks for a box of matches. The man in the white jacket carries over a tray. On the tray is a box of Nitedal charity matchsticks. Sverre takes it and lights up. The hand with the match is trembling. He pulls the smoke into his lungs and watches the hand stop trembling. Then he blows out the flame. He sits smoking, lost in thought. Uppermost in his mind are Erik Heggen and Gerhard Falkum. There is a conflict he knew nothing about. But it is satisfying finally to know. The strategy is working. Wait. Observe. The conflict that just came to light is one he should follow. Exploit it to his own advantage.

The door opens with a bang. A woman walks in. She is soaked. Her blonde hair is stuck to her scalp and her lacy bra is visible through her blouse. They exchange glances. She turns and goes to the toilet. Swaying well-shaped hips.

Sverre rolls himself a store of cigarettes while fantasising about the woman who just came in. The toilet door remains closed. He puts the roll-ups in his breast pocket, takes his hat and goes to the cash desk to pay.

2

Sverre hunches his shoulders against the filthy weather and climbs the stairs out of Krølle. The wind has dropped a little, but it is still raining. He turns up his coat collar and pulls the brim of his hat down over his forehead. Bears right in Uranienborgveien and walks towards the church and park. At the crossroads by Josefinegata there is a tall, red telephone box. He goes in. The door slams behind him. There are some burn marks on the Televerket noticeboard. But the telephone does have a dialling tone. He rummages through his pockets, finds a coin and puts it in the slot. Dials the number. It rings for a long time. Then there is a clink in the coin box.

'Hi, Sverre here. I have some news.'

He listens.

'It's regarding the airdrop you're so interested in. Also I've had confirmed what Gerhard told you. Erik Heggen was indeed the last person to see her alive.'

He listens again.

'I can't say. It was information given in confidence. What I can say, however, is that this story will end in disaster for a number of people – because of things that have been done and not least because of things that haven't.'

He wedges the receiver under his chin. Takes a roll-up from the store in his breast pocket and pokes one into his mouth as Ester says:

'If you think it might help, I can try and talk to Gerhard.'

Sverre likes what he hears. He pats his trouser pocket again. Remembers he has lost his Ronson lighter and he left the matches on the table in the restaurant. 'You do that,' he says, taking the roll-up from his mouth and studying it.

'What was it you wanted to say about the airdrop?' she says.

3

Ester looks down into her open bag and moves her make-up bag and purse so that the revolver isn't visible. She closes the bag, tucks it under her arm and leaves the ladies' toilet. Thinking that nothing is as tenacious as an old ghost. *Because everything is my fault.* Because she did something different instead of going straight to her father and warning him. Had she done what she was asked to, he and the rest of the family would have been able to stay in hiding and they would all have escaped to Sweden. They would have escaped the gas chamber. It took Ester a long time to counteract this argument with sufficient force. But now, many years later, when she is confronted with what happened in those days, the old ghosts reappear.

She places the bag on the table, hangs her trench coat over the back of the chair and sits down. Her empty glass is still there.

When God casts a dice no one knows where or how it will land. If they were dragging him out when you arrived, Ester, they must have been there quite a while already. And if you'd managed to get to your father's shop before they arrived, there's a good chance you would've been stopped at the door on your way out. You followed your conscience and acted. That counts for something. It counts for everything.

She remembers the words, but not the face of the man who spoke them. For a fraction of a second she is panicked. But then she sees him in her mind's eye again and falls into a reverie.

She is torn out of it by an unfamiliar sound breaking the silence. The throb reminds her of the ferry that plies from Oslo to Denmark. It seems to be coming from inside the building, and she catches herself checking to see if the floor is vibrating. But the engine noise stops and the lift doors open. A woman – a prostitute, to judge by her clothing – teeters out on perilously high heels and in a short skirt. Her hair is plaited into pigtails and in her mouth she is sucking a lollipop. She waves to the man behind the check-in desk. They know each other. He asks if she wants a taxi. She shakes her pigtails and carries on out. He waves a limp hand and focuses again on the book he is reading.

Ester rotates the empty glass between her fingers. How long will she have to wait? She looks from the desk back to the Munch print, which she thinks is entitled *Brothel Scene*. It shows a woman with bared nipples at the same table as a man with a lustful smirk on his face. She also recognises *Melancholy* and *Vampire*. And a self-portrait and *The Kiss*.

She yawns and checks her watch. It is well past eleven. She is the only customer in the lounge. A woman standing behind the brown bar and cashing up has changed from her waitress outfit to a skirt and suede jacket. She bangs shut the drawer of the cash till and walks towards Ester. Stops a few metres away.

Ester looks at her.

'If you require anything else it would be good if you said so now.'

'I thought the bar closed ages ago,' Ester says.

'It's closed. This is just a polite way of saying I'd like to go home.'

Ester gets up, a little confused. 'Of course.' She shrugs on her trench coat and leaves. Nods to the youngster behind the desk. He nods back. The clock over the Odd Fellow building shows it will be midnight in twenty minutes.

A taxi veers into Stortingsgata from Universitetsgata, passes Nasjonalteatret, does a U-turn, comes back and pulls up by the entrance. A black Volga.

Ester taps on the driver's window and he rolls it down. 'Are you free?'

He nods.

At that moment the rear door opens and Gerhard steps out.

He is clearly surprised to see her. 'Why are you here?'

'I've been sitting here for hours thinking why aren't *you* here?

He looks at his watch. 'It's late. Can we do this tomorrow?'

'Of course.'

Ester gets onto the rear seat. She is about to close the door when he turns and comes back.

'Could you tell me what this is about?'

'It's about 1942,' she says.

'Oh, yes?'

This Gerhard is quite different from the sullen, fuming man who drove back from Valdres. She searches for his eyes. They are in the shadow. 'Your story about the airdrop doesn't quite tally with the timeline.'

A late bus passes, and he lifts his chin and watches it. 'What timeline?'

'I've taken the trouble to note down dates and so on. There are a few gaps.'

He unleashes his charmer smile. 'After so many years in exile there's definitely one thing I've learned: memory is loyal to the person possessing it. My memory works for me and yours works for you. We remember what's important for ourselves.' He makes a move to leave.

'Let's stick to the facts, shall we,' she says hurriedly. 'The airdrop over Valdres plain was on the nineteenth of October. You were at home. You travelled to Fagernes on the twenty-sixth.'

'Don't ask me about dates. This is many years ago, after all.'

'The airdrop was part of Operation Grouse. It's a milestone in recent Norwegian history. It was the same day I went to Åse's and your place. It's also the day several Jewish men were arrested in Oslo.'

He doesn't seem interested. 'I'll take your word for it.'

'When you arrived in Valdres the airdrop was over. You can't have taken part in that operation.'

'You know, the best riddles have no solution. Neither you nor I can do anything about reality. But it sounds like we have something to talk about tomorrow. Goodnight, Ester.'

He leaves.

She watches him, waiting before closing the door.

He turns just before he goes inside. 'Have you come here late at night to ask me about this?'

'I came several hours ago. I've been waiting.'

He goes in. The doors close behind him.

She closes the car door. 'To Frogner please,' she says to the driver, who puts the car in gear.

'No problem,' the driver says, looking at her in the rear-view mirror: 'That fella's an old soldier, is he?'

'In a way, yes.'

He coughs. 'Thought there was something.'

'Would it be impolite to ask where you picked him up?'

They both look in the mirror. He grins, and jokes: 'If you promise not to tell anyone.'

She promises.

'He hailed me in Sørkedalsveien. He was coming from Vestre Cemetery.'

Ester looks out at the windows of the American embassy as they pass by. The taxi goes up Frognerveien. She can imagine him, a shadow in the mist. Still in a cemetery and still late at night. She recalls when she was in a flat in Stockholm, examining some photographic negatives that Gerhard had in his passport. Some of them were photos of cemeteries.

The taxi slows down by Lapsetorvet and carries on up Frognerveien. The last time Gerhard was in the cemetery, he went the very next day to the vault in the basement of Andresens Bank. Ester takes a deep breath and knows what she will have to do early the following morning.

Oslo, November 1967

1

The tea leaves are the top shoots from Darjeeling. Ester lifts the tin to her nose and inhales the aroma, then fills the strainer and pours the boiling water. She has got up early. She wants to know if events will repeat themselves. She has to cancel a piano lesson, but waits until just before she goes out of the door to ring. The mother answering the telephone and receiving the message appears to be happy.

It is ten minutes past eight when Ester gets on the tram for the city centre. At a little before half past she is on the corner of Thiisgården and Klingenberggata and waiting. The bank opens. An employee in a dark suit rolls up the grille on the inside of the glass door and undoes the bolts holding it in place.

Last time Gerhard arrived at about ten. She has allowed plenty of time. She goes for a walk while she waits, keeping her eyes trained on the corner building. She strolls alongside the park. Four or five women have formed a queue in front of a fishing smack moored at the nearby City Hall quay. The worst of the rush hour is over, and there is almost no traffic by the quays. She crosses the road to see what is on offer. Shrimps. Three fat seagulls have settled on a cable on the trawler's mast. They watch, and she watches. Whiting on ice, small codfish with a reddish gleam to the skin. Haddock. If she had nothing else to do, she would buy haddock and make gefilte fish, she thinks, then walks back.

It is half past nine when she sees Gerhard rounding the corner and walking down the street with a briefcase under his arm.

She goes into Andresens Bank. To the shelf at the back where you can stand and fill in money-transfer forms. She starts scribbling on a form while watching the reflections in the window in front of her.

Gerhard enters. He goes to a counter. There is hardly anybody inside. She hears Gerhard say he would like to open his bank box in the vault.

The woman at the counter swivels round on her chair and beckons to an official. This man accompanies Gerhard to the staircase in the middle of the room.

Ester takes a pile of forms, turns and drops them on the floor. And exclaims in a loud voice, 'Whoops. Sorry.'

A female employee hurries over to pick them up.

Gerhard stops and looks at Ester. She looks back. She doesn't greet him, nor he her. After a minor eternity he looks away. He follows the official down the staircase to the vault.

Ester watches his figure disappear. She wonders whether to wait for him and goes over to the staircase, aware now of the gaze of the woman who has picked up the forms. She and another employee stare at her, then they exchange glances and stare at her again, unsure, but also on their guard. Ester doesn't want to arouse so much attention. She quickly leaves the bank. Strides down towards the City Hall quay. Finds a gap in the traffic and hurries across. The queue in front of the fishing boat isn't as long as it was a short while before. Soon it will be her turn. Fortunately there is still some haddock in the polystyrene box sitting on the cover over the engine.

Afterwards, standing with her full shopping net in her hand, she deliberates. And decides to go back. Now she is in a hurry and walks faster. Reaches the delicatessen. Seconds later there is a glint of light on the bank door. It opens. They look straight at each other. Gerhard hesitates this time too. He takes off his sunglasses. She heads towards the bank. He turns his back on her, walks away, crosses the street in the direction of the City Hall Park.

'Gerhard,' she shouts.

He keeps walking.

She follows him. A line of vehicles comes towards her. She has to wait at the kerb. 'Gerhard!'

He speeds off down the pavement. Raises an arm. A dark-red Opel taxi brakes and stops. He runs over to the rear door and opens it.

Ester stands still as they exchange glares over the roof of the taxi. Then he gets in. She watches the car going up the hill to Fridtjof Nansens plass.

2

Ester has two sinks in the kitchen – one for meat and one for milk products, according to Talmudic law. Her mother did this and she follows her example. But Ester has travelled a lot in her life and she has had to adapt her principles. In her flat she uses the same cutlery for both dairy foods and meat.

Ester's mother made gefilte fish with haddock. Her relatives in Poland used carp or pike. She doesn't know exactly why the Lemkov family chose haddock in Oslo, but carp and pike have never been considered good fish to eat in Norway. That was probably why they were so hard to get hold of. Ester's mother gutted the fish and kept the skin, which she used to wrap minced fish in afterwards. Ester makes a modern variant. She slices the fish down the spine, cuts off the fins and removes the skin. Chops off the tail. Rinses well under running water. Holds the fish head while scraping off the flesh with a sharp kitchen knife. Puts it into a bowl where she has already poured some water, flour, an egg yolk and some spices. The spine and head go into the saucepan with whatever makes the stock. Afterwards she peels some carrots and some horseradish, and grates the horseradish.

She cooks the stock, adds herbs and boils it down while she fries the fish cakes. They will cool in the stock later. Then they are eaten with a sliced carrot on top and grated horseradish and beetroot as trimmings.

Usually she likes to muse on trivialities as she cooks – like Captain Hanaas, fencing training or the dwindling number of piano pupils. Not today though. Ester can see she has lost the bet she made with herself long ago. When Sverre Fenstad stood at her door she promised herself she would not let this ghost from the past take over. But she fell into the trap at once. Gerhard is controlling the thoughts in her mind to an ever greater degree. Why has he come to Norway at all? Why precisely now? What does he do in cemeteries after dark?

The fish cakes are ready. They have to cool down. Ester washes her hands thoroughly. Afterwards she checks the revolver in her handbag, picks up the car keys and heads for the front door.

3

She drives slowly up and down the tiny streets in the St Hanshaugen district, trying to park as close to the cemetery as possible. Forced to give up, she drives around the cemetery and parks by the main entrance in Akersveien instead.

It is chilly. But the sun shines on the damp grass and wet, black stones. The only people she can see are the workmen raking leaves from the gravel paths. She enters the cemetery and goes to Alvilde Munthe's grave. On her knees she tries to scrutinise every little detail of the headstone and the general area. But she can't see any more than she did the previous time. It is only when she makes a move to leave that it strikes her. The commemorative plate bearing the engraved name and dates isn't straight. It is almost impossible to notice. Almost is enough though. The discovery sends a tingle down her spine. She looks around. Two workmen with rakes and a wheelbarrow are sitting on a bench, smoking. Ester forces herself to walk on. She does a circuit, impatient to get back, but still takes the time to look at the graves of famous Norwegians: Henrik Wergeland, Camilla Collett and Oskar Braaten.

Almost half an hour has passed before she returns to Alvilde Munthe's grave. The bench is unoccupied. The workmen have gone. She kneels down by the massive engraved metal plate. It is in two parts. The whole plate is reminiscent of a coffin lid. In the middle there is a raised oval section on which the name of the deceased is engraved. This metal ellipse is in reality a large lid. She can see that now. And it is possible to open it. She pushes with both hands. It is heavy. Bronze or cast iron. Bronze, she thinks. Because the metal hasn't rusted. She pushes with all her strength. The lid moves with a loud, piercing screech. It is the same sound she heard the evening she was first here. Beneath the lid there is a hollow. The urn containing the ashes of the deceased is here. She leans over and peers inside. All she can see is the urn.

She straightens up and has a quick scan of her surroundings. No one in sight. She sticks a hand inside and gropes. Nothing. Just dust, spiders' webs, a couple of earwigs and the urn. She pulls the oval plate back into position. It finds its level with a dull click. Another sound she recognises. There is no doubt. This is where Gerhard was that evening. He was crouching like she is now. First he removed the lid and then he slid it back.

With this Ester has her confirmation. Gerhard took with him whatever was with the urn.

She stands up. Brushes the dust and leaves from her clothes. It is quiet and peaceful in the cemetery. On the way out she passes just one person. A man is on his knees tidying the bed in front of a gravestone. A navy-blue back and two fumbling hands.

Ester stops by the gate leading to Ullevålsveien. Her mind has been on other matters and she has come to the wrong exit. Her car is parked on the opposite side of the cemetery. She turns and ambles down a gravel path. Comes to another gate. Leaves. Closes the gate behind her and on the pavement bears left. She follows the fence. Stops. Stands still for a few seconds, looking down the line of parked cars in Wessels gate.

There it is. An eggshell-white Volvo Amazon. She crosses the street and walks towards the car. The registration plate is the same. This is the car she was following. This is the car Gerhard has rented.

Ester looks around. The air is still. She can't see anyone. Well, Gerhard has parked his rental car here. So he is visiting the Cemetery of Our Saviour again. During the day?

She walks back. A bus going down Ullevålsveien passes. She steps back and at that moment catches a movement in the corner of her eye. A man disappearing round the corner of a house. It is Gerhard.

She looks at the corner.

Gerhard must have seen her. Instead of attracting her attention, he has hidden. She pauses for a few seconds and thinks. She walked past a man as she was leaving the cemetery. Someone with his back to her.

She walks back into the cemetery. Stops and makes up her mind. Turns around again, goes out through the gate, over the pavement. She walks faster now. Wanting to know. Reaches the line of parked cars.

Gerhard's rental car is no longer there.

Ester walks back to her car. Unlocks the door. Sits thinking. About Gerhard going into the bank. Gerhard stopping when she shouts. Gerhard looking at her, taking the decision to ignore her and going down to the vault. Gerhard not wanting to talk. Not to her. And now: Gerhard spying on her. She doesn't like this new development.

4

She parks by the kerb and strolls slowly up to the entrance in Thomas Heftyes gate. The door of one of the parked cars opens. Out of a Mercedes steps Markus Rebowitz. The sight is familiar, but her focus is more on the fact that it is usually a bad sign when Markus contacts her and not vice versa.

She stops in front of him.

'Are you coming up?' she asks, already knowing he will decline.

Without answering he opens the rear door and bows courteously.

She gets in and closes the door. Markus slides in on the opposite side. 'Just drive around a bit, David,' he says, and then takes the trouble to close the glass partition between front and back. 'So that we can chat undisturbed,' he says to her, leaning back on his seat.

The car moves away. She can see part of David's face in the mirror. She recognises him. The young man with the vulnerable neck. The one guarding the entrance to the embassy the last time she was there.

She closes her eyes and feels how much she misses Jonatan. Misses stroking his neck.

The car accelerates. She opens her eyes. They cross on yellow. Heading for Skøyen, in the west of Oslo.

'I didn't find out much about Gary Larson at first,' Markus says at last. 'That's why I checked out his friend instead. Brian Pankhurst. One question to start with: can you remember when Pankhurst left Stockholm?'

Ester thinks back. She and Markus had trained with Pankhurst for quite a while. Over the winter at any rate. Five months? Six? Maybe longer. 'Summer of 1943?'

'We agree so far, then. And when I started digging, it became clear that Pankhurst showed up in Tehran that year, in forty-three.'

Ester looks out. They are driving along the Frogner coastal road, towards Filipstad. Ester remembers the time they found out that the supply line to the Soviet Union from the south, through Iran, had been opened. It was Churchill who feared the Shah would sell oil to the Germans. Reza Shah Pahlavi was forced to abdicate. The invasion forces sent him into exile and put the power into the hands of his son, Mohammad. It had been an issue they discussed at the legation office. The spectacular move – invading and afterwards provoking a change of throne that would allow Soviet troops to be supplied with weapons and provisions along two routes – through Murmansk in the north and Tehran in the south.

'The Persian Corridor,' Markus says. 'Pankhurst arrived there in forty-three, and I imagine Gary Larson must've been there at the same time.' He meets her eyes and smiles, as though apologetically. 'Gary Larson must've been somewhere at this time, and Iran fits the bill. At least, if we assume that Gary Larson got to know Brian Pankhurst during the Spanish Civil War. A few years pass. Then they meet again – in Stockholm. Then Larson appears, as you say, to die in a fire. In other words, no one knows where he is. Pankhurst, for his part, keeps a low profile, has barely any contact with anyone while he is in Stockholm. Let's assume, for the sake of argument, that Pankhurst's the man keeping Larson alive and incognito during this period. Then Pankhurst is ordered to go to Iran. He works for the British intelligence services in Tehran and there he has a larger staff around him. I've tried in vain to find out who. Then, when the war's over and everyone returns home, the name Larson suddenly appears in the United States.'

'So you think Pankhurst took Larson with him to Tehran?'

'What do I know? When he left Stockholm, he must've had some destination.'

Her body is thrust against the door as the car goes into a tight bend. She looks out again.

'Where are we going, actually?'

'Nowhere. Wherever you want.'

The car stops at the lights and Markus falls silent.

Ester looks out again. A bus stop. She makes eye contact with a man waiting on the bench. He starts to stare. She turns back to Markus.

'Gary Larson's established in ANCIB after the war,' he says. 'That means Larson had worked for them for a while before. You don't get into

American intelligence services from nowhere. In fact, there's only one explanation. The route into the NSA must've gone through Pankhurst and the SIS. A few years later – ten years later in fact – in fifty-three, Larson's name pops up again, in Iran. When the Shah regained power from Mohammed Mossadegh in a coup.'

The car brakes behind a bus pulling into a bus stop outside a kindergarten. A girl hangs from a wire fence with one hand, sucking the mitten on her other.

'Gary Larson was sent to Iran just before the coup in fifty-three. And I don't think he would've been if he hadn't been there before.'

Ester doesn't disagree. Gerhard could well have been in Tehran in forty-three with the Brits and ten years later with the Americans. What Markus is saying has an internal logic, as always. Actually she doesn't know anyone better at digging into classified information than Markus Rebowitz. He has honed this talent ever since the end of the Second World War.

'Gary Larson was in Tehran when Prime Minister Mossadegh nationalised the British oil wells. Gary Larson was on the staff of Faziollah Zadehi when he had Mossadegh arrested on the orders of Shah Mohammed Reza.'

Ester leans back. Feeling she needs time to digest this, work out what it means. She takes a deep breath. Lifts her head and looks Markus in the eye: 'Could Larson know that someone has been snooping into his background?'

Markus shakes his head, brusquely and confidently. 'As I said, he isn't there anymore. Anyway, Gary Larson's never held a high-ranking position. He's a foot soldier. A useful man with a repertoire of dirty tricks for tight spots. You know the kind.'

They drive in silence until Ester breaks it. 'Come on, Markus. You don't pick me up for no reason.'

Markus takes a deep breath. 'Someone's whispered in my ear that seven or eight years ago he started on a different staff, once again as muscle. In poor countries. Larson's had an American diplomatic passport and smarmed around receptions attended by corrupt politicians with the right influence: Guatemala City, Buenos Aires and Caracas. This group used every means available to convince rotten politicians

that their nation should take out loans from the World Bank, and that
their country needed cash for children's education and hospitals and
so on for old people. When they got the loans it was through private
investment banks in America. The building contracts went to American companies. They were for big national projects, not just schools,
hospitals and roads, but also power stations, dams and factories. We're
talking enormous sums here. The point is that the business idea behind
the projects is that the countries are too poor ever to be able to pay
back the loans.'

So what, thinks Ester, who has become impatient. Expensive loans to
poor countries is just a modern variant of Marshall Aid. 'Markus, you're
no politician. Nor am I. I'm not interested in how poor countries vote
the way they do in the UN.' She looks outside again and discovers they
are going up Bygdøy allé towards Gimle cinema. 'Ask David to turn
right,' she says. 'If I'm being driven it may as well be all the way home.'

Markus presses the button under the glass partition, talks into the
microphone and asks David to drive to the top of Thomas Heftyes gate
and park somewhere.

To her he says: 'This has something to do with why he was given the
boot. Gary Larson has been a loose cannon, driven by drinking and
gambling. He has no possessions, and he has a huge gambling debt.
He had something like thirteen or fourteen serious disciplinary charges
on his record before he capped it all in Las Vegas about a year ago.
The evening had started quite normally. Gary Larson lost big sums of
money, borrowed more and lost them, too. He wasn't allowed to carry
on playing and was thrown out. In the middle of the night he was supposed to have lowered himself from a veranda, naked, his body covered
in camouflage paint, with a bayonet between his teeth, like some kind
of crazy pirate. He kicked in a window in the casino director's apartment and attacked the poor man and his lover. Almost killing both of
them. The man was skewered to the bed, bleeding to death, but the lady
escaped into the corridor and screamed for help. Gary Larson knocked
the living daylights out of four security guards before he was cuffed. He
was driven to rehab in a straitjacket. Apparently he dried out there, but
was discharged under a cloud. And his decline has been precipitous.'

The driver goes past her entrance at first, carries on to the crossroads, does a U-turn and pulls in by the kerb. Ester doesn't move. 'What's he been living off since, then?'

'Freelancing.'

'Which means?'

'I'd hazard a guess at private security companies. That's usually where they end up, those who don't have a musical career to fall back on.'

She is quiet. Markus has never been especially funny even when he tries to be.

'His speciality's always been jobs with knives.'

They look into each other's eyes, and Markus's are now enquiring, tense and serious. 'Silent killing,' he says.

'Is he married?' she asks.

'I hope you realise this man is no Sunday-school teacher, Ester.'

'I asked if he has any family.'

'Apparently he has a floozy in Mexico.'

She doesn't think it suits Markus to be vulgar. 'A *floozy*?'

'She's said to have made a living as a prostitute in Mexico City. He's lived there, with her, in between freelancing. He's still got gambling debts, quite a lot of them.'

Ester lifts her shopping bag and puts it on her lap. 'What this boils down to is…' She draws breath. 'What you're actually saying is that the Gary Larson who landed at Fornebu airport is a man looking for money.'

Markus shakes his head. 'I'm trying to tell you he's dangerous, Ester. So far that's the most important thing I've read.'

She opens the door and gets out of the car. Turns back to the open door.

'Did you hear?' Markus says. 'Gary Larson's a dangerous man.'

'We've been here before. You tell me the world's a dangerous place, and I say I'll watch out. This is where you want me, isn't it.'

She closes the door. The car glides away from the pavement. She sees the back of Markus's head through the rear window. The kippah doesn't move. He doesn't turn round.

She waits until the car has reached the end of Bygdøy allé. Only then does she go inside.

1

No 'Hi'.

No 'Good morning, darling'. Just a stiff stare at the crossword. So Robert is jealous again. Turid looks from Robert's grumpy profile to the family photo hanging above the telephone shelf. Erik, Grete and her. Against a sun-drenched wall on the mountain farm one Easter, when knee-length breeches were the order of the day, and you ate oranges and Kvikklunsj chocolate bars in the sun. Peik is there too. Gazing up at them and smiling the way a Gordon Setter should. All four of them look happy. Turid loves the photo.

But now she needs a cup of coffee to avoid getting a headache. Fortunately there is some in the machine. At that moment she remembers that the telephone rang while she was in the bathroom. Two observations this morning: a telephone conversation; Robert's sulky silence. Turid understands what has happened, but carries on regardless and goes to the Moccamaster, which is still half full. Fetches a mug from the cupboard. Her favourite is from the sixties: a Norwegian Figgjo Flint model. A Turi design CLUPEA. A short mug decorated with upright blue fish and yellow flowers. The coffee is too strong. The black colour has taken on an unhealthy-looking brown tint. Robert always makes the coffee too strong. Everything is a little too much with Robert. Too caring, too possessive of the car, the mountain cabin and her.

Turid takes the milk from the fridge, pours some into her mug and stands with her back to him, looking out of the window and trying to hatch a plan to deal with the impending outburst. She doesn't understand how Robert can be bothered to build up such great charges of negative energy. After all, they are both getting on. She is seventy-three and Robert is sixty-nine. It is at least thirty years since Turid had her last fling. It is thirty-five years since she wanted to divorce Robert and move in with Hans Grabbe. It will soon be more than fifty years since she met Hans for the first time. She and Hans used to have sex in the university reading room. Turid smiles at the thought. The first time they forgot that the caretaker did rounds and switched off the lights at night. When the door opened and they heard his footsteps crossing the floor, they tried as best they could not to make a sound. And her with Hans's organ in her mouth. As soon as the light went out he came.

Turid faces Robert. 'It was Hans who rang, wasn't it.'

He is taken aback. She sees that she has floored him. He nods.

'I asked him to do a job for me. That's why,' she says.

'Job? Hans Grabbe's a pensioner, like you.'

She takes the mug of coffee with her onto the terrace, adjusts the garden chair and sits down. The neighbours' children are jumping on the trampoline on the other side of the fence. This is what she loves best. The sound of children in the summer. Their Philippino au pair calls the children from her sunbed.

Robert comes out with the crossword magazine under his arm. He sits beside her. His face is redder than usual, unhealthily so. It might be just the contrast with his white hair, but she believes it is more likely to be blood pressure.

'What kind of job?'

'I want him to secure an item for me that I thought had disappeared fifty years ago – more, maybe. A bracelet.'

'It must be quite a bracelet. He charges several thousand kroner an hour.'

'Don't cross bridges before you come to them, Robert. Hans owes me some favours.'

She leans back with her eyes closed, listening to the children on the trampoline again. Enjoying the sun warming her forehead and cheeks.

'Hans still thinks he's God's gift to the world,' Robert says, his intonation several degrees lighter than a few minutes before.

'Hans Grabbe's one of those tenacious lawyers who can never have enough of the circus,' she says, her eyes still closed. 'Even though his sons have taken over, he still tries to have some input.'

'Grabbe's a good name for a lawyer. I'll give him that.'

Turid has heard this remark probably a hundred times.

'Grabber,' Robert says, chuckling. 'Grabbing hands.'

Before he can go into his full routine, she takes the phone from her pocket and taps in Hans's number.

She mouths: 'I'm calling him.'

'Sounded as if he was on the beach,' Robert says.

She turns her back on him. 'It's me, Hans. Turid.'

'What a husband you've got,' he says. 'What did you give him for breakfast? Lemons?'

Turid leans back in her chair again. There are seagull cries in the background. Robert is probably right. Hans is in Sørland. Turid smiles at her husband. 'Robert makes breakfast here. Do you have some good news for me?'

'Well, I have some news anyway. The auction itself can't be stopped. But there's a possibility regarding the bracelet. I've talked to the legal titleholder. He doesn't live in Norway and has no connection with the country. No family, nothing. But he allowed me to explain the case on the phone. And he was intrigued. Even if he doesn't buy your version of events. The problem is that this might take some time. As I said, he doesn't live in Norway.'

'Why doesn't he buy what you call my version of events?'

'Are you Jewish, Turid?'

'No, you know I'm not.'

'There's something Jewish about the bracelet. That's why he finds it hard to believe what you're saying.'

'Who is he and where does he live?'

'The guy lives in Jerusalem. His name's Jonatan Azolay. Does that ring a bell?'

'Not at all.'

'That's strange.'

'Why?'

'He knows you.'

Turid is dumbstruck.

'That was why he became amenable. But we didn't talk for that long. He's a hard-working businessman. But we've agreed to talk. I'll follow this up.'

'Hans!'

'This is all I have for the moment. I'll get back to you.'

Turid says goodbye and puts her phone on the table. Meets Robert's gaze.

'Was I right?' Robert asks, smiles and sips at his coffee. 'Was he on the beach?'

Turid absent-mindedly studies her husband. 'Yes, he was,' she says. 'He was on the beach.' Turid leans back again. Jonatan Azolay? The name doesn't mean a thing to her.

Oslo, November 1967

1

'The university portico is among the finest examples of classicism in Oslo. Apart from the Royal Palace, the Stock Exchange and the Supreme Court, perhaps. The best feature of this building is the way the architect Christian Heinrich Grosch uses the two wings to complete the homage to Roman architecture.'

The man is wearing a white shirt and a bow tie. He is speaking to two Japanese-looking men with glasses. Each is holding an umbrella and both watch Ester as she crosses the square towards Domus Academica.

At the top of the staircase a caretaker in a blue smock is sweeping up cigarette ends with a brush and pan. Ester asks him where she can find the MA law students. He points to the central building. Ester goes back down the stairs. Nods to the two Japanese-looking gentlemen, who nod back enthusiastically. She crosses the university square and goes through the portico. Chooses the green door to the left at the back. Walks in. The smell of the toilets hits her. She turns left and carries on down the corridor to the student cloakroom. Behind the counter is an elderly white-haired lady attending to something behind her. She turns. Comes to the counter and asks how she can help. Ester asks the cloakroom lady if she knows a law student called Turid Heggen.

The lady says she thinks so. 'Blonde, isn't she? Tall, attractive?'

Ester nods.

The lady says she can ask about Turid in the reading room, if Ester doesn't mind waiting. She points to a wooden chair beside the cloakroom counter.

Ester sits down.

A few moments go by before a woman comes down the stairs and walks towards Ester. She looks unbelievably like Åse. The same narrow chin. The same full lips. Two green eyes under pronounced eyebrows, like the outstretched wings of a big bird. Ester is moved and gets to her feet. Turid is wearing faded jeans and a green military jacket. She doesn't seem to bother with make-up. Her thick hair is parted in the middle and woven into one large plait on her shoulder. Had it not been for the contemporary clothing, she could have been Åse.

Ester dries an eye with her glove and says: 'You probably think I'm being silly, but you're the spitting image of your mum.'

Turid regards her with bemusement.

'Sorry,' Ester says, reaching out a hand. 'My name's Ester. I knew Åse well, from when we were small children.'

They stand taking each other in. Ester wonders if Åse's daughter will react to being addressed so informally. Deciding to continue in the same vein, she says: 'Can I invite you to eat something?' She points to the swing doors of the basement café and leads the way.

She asks Turid to find them a table while she goes to the counter. She takes a tray and remembers she didn't ask Turid what she wanted. Can't be helped. Ester is nervous and doesn't want to appear clumsy. She takes two Danish pastries and two Cokes.

She spots Turid sitting at the back by the window, at one of the long tables. 'Sorry,' she says. 'But the coffee looks dreadful and I was a bit thirsty.'

Turid says a Coke is fine.

The pastries have been freshly made and are very crispy. Bits flake off and both try to eat with a certain dignity, but they end up grinning at each other.

Ester puts the rest of hers down on her plate, wipes her fingers on the serviette and tells Turid she got to know Åse when she was very young. 'My family spent their holidays in a mountain cabin in Valdres, not far from where your mother lived. We became good friends and stuck together. And we did the same during the war, when she lived in Oslo.'

Ester tells her she was a courier for the resistance movement in the war and collected illegal newspapers from Åse's flat. 'You were just a baby.' Ester says that she fled to Sweden a few days before Åse died.

'I never knew my mother,' says Turid. 'But I still love hearing people talk about her.'

Ester says she was about to flee to Sweden in the clothes she was standing up in. She had no other possessions.

'Then along came Åse with food and a set of clothes for me. So I had something to change into. Even though everything was rationed, she shared what she had. Your mother was a good person.'

Ester talks about her own mother and father and grandmother, who were killed in Auschwitz. Gassed to death. 'Mum and Gran were killed the day they arrived at the concentration camp. Apparently my father almost held out until liberation. He was one of the last to be killed.'

When the war ended Ester felt she had nothing to return to. All her family was dead. Åse was dead too, of course.

They look at each other. Ester can see that Turid's eyes are moist as she blinks. She is moved. That surprises Ester. She reflects on everything she has said. She told it mechanically. As a case officer might have done. The bare details. Unemotionally. It shouldn't be like that. Mustn't be like that.

'What's the matter?' Turid asks sympathetically.

Ester looks down. And decides to dismiss this self-reproach.

'There are things happening right now,' she says, 'things that are bringing back memories of your mother. Someone I know, who also knows your parents, told me you were studying law. That's why I've come here. I hope that's alright.'

'Of course. You said things were happening. What?'

Ester mounts a little smile. 'For example, I saw your mother's grave a few days ago.'

'My father's been there too, in Valdres. Did you know him too – Gerhard?'

Ester nods.

'He sent me a photo of Åse.' She puts a hand in the breast pocket of her military jacket and passes the picture to Ester.

She studies it. Åse looks very alive. Ester recognises the mountain farm and the barn, even if the land around it is barer than when she was there a few days ago. It makes her feel solemn to see a photo of the past. She has no photos of her own, not of Åse or anyone else from the pre-war days.

'I changed my hairstyle when I received the photo,' Turid says, holding her plait.

Ester passes back the photo. 'As I said, you're the spitting image of your mother.'

Turid says: 'And a couple of days ago my father contacted me. We'd always thought he was dead, but he's been alive the whole time, in America.'

'And now he's here?'

Turid nods.

'That must've been quite an experience.'

Turid nods again.

'Not a single sign of life for all those years?'

'He's suffered psychologically. He spent many years getting over my mother's death, and the way she died.'

Ester feels a rush of fury when she hears Gerhard's lies being served up in this way. She motions to Turid to carry on:

'First of all he had to escape to Sweden, then to America.' Turid looks up. 'That's why he's not been in touch.'

Ester nods again. 'What did you think when you realised it was your father standing there, here in Norway, and alive?'

Turid fills her lungs with air. 'It was very, very…' she searches for the words. 'Very odd,' she says.

'You weren't angry? Or fed up?'

'Why would I be?'

Turid laughs and Ester smiles.

'What do your mum and dad say?'

'Only my mother knows. And she's concerned for me, as always. Dad gets angry whenever I talk about Åse or my real father.' Turid says Erik is still struggling with his memories of the war. 'He was arrested by the Gestapo and tortured. He was told he was going to be shot, and then they didn't shoot him.'

'When was this?'

'February forty-five. Just before the end of the war. They shot someone else. They'd threatened to shoot Dad if he didn't talk. But he kept his mouth shut, so they shot the man in front of his eyes. He feels guilty. He still wakes up in the middle of the night. Thinking he can hear shots.'

Ester registers this. She closes her eyes and tries to let her sympathy for Erik Heggen overshadow her inner fury. She fails and again is uneasy about herself. She opens her eyes. Her gaze is drawn to Turid's wrist.

Turid asks if she can tell Erik and Grete that she has met Ester.

'Of course you can. I knew your mother, but not your foster parents.'

They sit in silence, and again Ester looks at Turid's wrist, but the bracelet is covered by the sleeve of her jacket now.

Turid asks Ester again why she has contacted her now.

Ester concocts a lie; she says she met Gerhard again and her memories of Åse came flooding back.

But she can't square lying to Åse's daughter with her conscience. She decides to be honest. 'I've been thinking about this for so long. About seeing you. But I really believe Åse would approve. I think she would've liked us to meet.'

The swing doors open. A group of students go to the counter. Ester watches them, wondering if Åse ever imagined that her daughter would study law. 'I'm sure your mother would've been really proud of you.'

Turid smiles.

'I should've contacted you before, but I only came to Norway on short trips after the war. I didn't move back here until 1960.'

'Where from?'

Ester lowers her eyes. 'Israel.'

'Why did you come back in 1960?'

'Because of a grand piano. During the war all the Jews in Norway had their possessions confiscated. All my family's things were taken too. Some were sent to Germany, some were shared out among Nazis. I don't know a lot about that. But seven or eight years ago I received a letter. The only item the authorities had managed to trace was the grand piano. They asked me what I wanted to do with it.' She breathes in. 'Dad wanted me to become a pianist.'

'What a terrible story.'

There is nothing Ester can say to that.

'Can you play well?'

'The war came between me and a career. Now I make a living from music lessons. When I came here, seven years ago, I bought a flat for me and the piano. I was lucky and found a tiny shoebox place in the district I grew up in, not far from the street where I lived, in fact.' She goes quiet as Turid pulls up the sleeve of her jacket and raises her glass of Coke.

Ester stares stiffly at the bracelet around Turid's wrist.

Turid notices and says something.

Ester doesn't hear her words. They are drowned by an inner rush of sound she can't control. All Ester can do is stretch her hand across the table. When her fingers touch the metal the rush fades and she can feel she is perfectly calm. She says it is a special bracelet.

'It's all I have from my mother. I wear it now and then.'

'Can I see it?'

Turid undoes the clasp and passes it across the table.

The bracelet is heavy. A round, patinated piece of gold with an inset stone attached to it, a thick ring covered with inscriptions.

Ester avoids looking Turid in the eye as she asks: 'What do you know about this piece of jewellery?'

'Nothing, except that it was my mother's.' Turid points to an engraving on the ring: *AL*. 'Åse Lajord,' she says.

Again this situation overwhelms Ester and she has to stare at the ceiling to regain her composure.

Turid asks: 'Is there anything the matter?'

Ester gulps. She points to the symbols engraved on the outside of the thick ring. 'Do you know what they mean?'

Turid shakes her head. 'Do you?'

Instead of answering, she looks at the bracelet. She manages a smile and says: 'I have to be off now, Turid. It was really lovely talking to you.'

Turid fastens the bracelet around her arm. 'I hope we can meet again.'

Ester gets up and looks at her. 'Of course we can.'

Ester turns. When she goes out it is as if she is walking blindly. She closes the portico door a little too hard. The plaster on the wall reverberates. She doesn't notice. Nor is she aware of the two Japanese tourists standing behind a pillar and waving as she steams past.

2

Ester walks to the City Hall quays, stands by the edge of the middle pier. Gazes at the sky while the noise from Akers Mekaniske Verksted shipyard mingles with the gurgling of the water below her. She tries to stay calm, tries to think clearly. When she hears someone cough directly behind her she is startled and almost falls into the water. There is a man sitting with his back to the shed on the pier. He is wearing a roll-neck jumper and a cap. His trousers are wet and filthy, and the sole has come off one boot. He lowers a bottle of export beer and raises a trembling hand with the butt of a cigarette between his fingers. He asks her if she has a light. Ester doesn't answer. She walks back to her car. She knows what she has to do. She has to talk to someone who actually cares about what she and her family were subjected to.

After unlocking the door to her flat, she doesn't even kick off her shoes or remove her coat. She lifts the phone and calls Markus Rebowitz. It takes time to transfer her. But finally she has his voice in her ears.

'It's Ester. I have to ask you another favour. I need access to the Liquidation Office papers. I want a copy of all the ones relevant to my family.'

'Don't you have those papers already?'

'No. All I have is a letter sent to my kibbutz. It's about my grand piano. A walnut Steinway. It turned up in 1960. A collaborator died and one of the heirs had demanded a public division of goods. Then the papers pertaining to the piano were produced. This man had been given the piano as payment for some work he did for that Nazi, Hagelin in 1944. Now there's something I need to check.'

'You've whetted my curiosity. Has this anything to do with Gary Larson?'

After some hesitation she decides to tell him the truth. 'I've just seen some of my mother's most valuable jewellery. It hasn't been seen since the Nazis confiscated my childhood home.'

At first Markus is absolutely silent. Then he coughs quietly. 'Oh? Where?' His tone is a little excited, which is positive.

She decides not to answer. She needs his interest; she will have to exploit it.

'They confiscated the shop, too,' she says. 'So they took goods from the flat in Eckersbergs gate 10 and Paschal Lemkov's jewellery shop in Kirkeristen.'

She puts down the telephone. A second later there is a ring at the door.

3

She goes to the front door. Takes the revolver from the bag hanging on the hook. Holds the weapon in her right hand while opening the door. Goes out onto the step and over to the balustrade. Peers down. Recognises the figure of Sverre Fenstad and his heavy gait. Backs inside, puts the gun into her bag and waits.

'You again,' she says, holding the door open. 'Hungry?' She walks ahead of him into the kitchen. Opens the fridge. Puts out a plate of gefilte fish, grated horseradish and beetroot.

He sits down and inclines his head with interest.

'You can use your fingers.' She shows him how to do it.

He takes too much horseradish. But she says nothing. He gasps for air and holds his nose.

'You get used to it.'

'Lovely,' he assures her. 'Bit special, but fine.'

She sits watching him until he is breathing more normally.

He primes himself to say something.

She waits.

'You and Gerhard drove here all the way from Fagernes?'

'Yes.'

He eyes her. He is formulating a question, she thinks, and decides to put her oar in first. 'I didn't meet Gerhard Falkum until after the outbreak of war. Did you know him before the war?'

Sverre's eyes widen. And he shakes his head. 'When we met he was one of the many keen, young ones who wanted to throw his cap in the ring. He joined up early, as far back as April 1940. We didn't know each other very well, but he seemed like a solid patriot. I know he was from Porsgrunn. At least that was where he grew up. His mother died prematurely, from Spanish flu. He's a couple of years younger than me. I was born in 1911, so he can't have been very old when she died – four or five maybe. I think he lived with his father for many years. His father was a factory worker. Gerhard went to sea. Don't know when. But I do know he was on a Wilhelmsen boat in the mid-thirties. Must've been twenty-odd when he enrolled for the International Brigade in Spain. They were a pretty radical lot in the Seamen's Union in those days. I'd guess he was, if not a communist, then definitely red. Jonas Lie, the chief constable, had Gerhard's name in his private archives. I didn't know anything about that side of his past. It was only when we tried to get Gerhard into Sweden that I found out he'd fought in Spain. And it was actually his political activities that made the resistance ambivalent about him while he was in hiding in Sweden.'

'Not so easy to imagine – Gerhard as a red-hot socialist.'

'I wouldn't've believed it, either. But what do we know about anyone? Only six months ago Stalin's daughter applied for asylum in the United States.' Sverre helps himself to another fish cake. He manages better this time. He chews and nods his approval. 'Politics and ideology are transient entities,' he says, licking his fingers. 'What some people say they believe one moment is forgotten the next. And for some it becomes a kind of disease. They start out hoping for a better world, but are poisoned by their own rhetoric and ultimately refuse to acknowledge it's flawed.'

'It? The rhetoric?'

'The politics.' Sverre smiles wryly, but becomes serious at the sight of her expression. 'What is it?'

'I'd like to know if it was you personally who ordered Gerhard's liquidation.'

He freezes, and for a moment the world stands still. 'Why do you want to know?'

'Because that order also included my death.'

I am being too brutal, she thinks, when he is unable to meet her eyes and studies the table. I am beginning to be mean, she thinks. That is not good. I have to remember that I am a mother. My soul should be running over with charity, compassion and forgiveness.

He takes a deep breath. 'You mustn't get this out of proportion, Ester. You'd lost your family. You were an agent in training. No one would've done anything to hurt you.'

'I was instructed to go to a house where a man was waiting with a weapon, and no one told me what was going to happen.'

'It was Kolstad who ran the show, and he decided who should know what. But you were off limits, Ester. Nothing would have happened to you. I really hope you understand that.'

'Shouldn't I have been informed?'

'The fewer in the know, the better. If you'd known, Gerhard would've smelt a rat.'

'He smelt a rat anyway.'

'We acted in the way we considered best.'

'I was an investment and a decoy?'

'It was war.'

'But it isn't war anymore. You've been steering the ship the whole time. Was that why you planned the break-in at the hotel? Have you been scared the whole time about what Gerhard knows and what plans he has – for you?'

'There's no point trivialising things that have happened. If I could live my life anew, there's a lot I would do differently.'

'You could've sent him to England back then.'

Sverre shakes his head. 'The Germans used the same strategy in this case as in everything else during the war. And they succeeded. They won the propaganda war. We had very little we could strike back with. The Gestapo stayed low and left the dirty work to the police. There was no search for a resistance man. People in Oslo – those pro- and anti- the Nazis – went around thinking Gerhard Falkum was a perverted criminal who'd murdered the mother of his own child. The police used the child. They painted a picture of an evil bastard. What you say is right. We didn't want him back in Norway. Had he crossed the border, he would've been reported to the police before he could blink. The torturers at Victoria terrasse would've taken turns to batter all the information out of him.'

'You could've sent Gerhard to England,' she repeats. 'Was it a defeat for you to give Gerhard "the communist" a chance?'

'Chance? You're saying things you know nothing about. As I said, the Germans won the propaganda war. Gerhard was portrayed as a sewer rat. Our people in England wouldn't touch a man like that with a barge pole.'

'So his life became a calculation. Why should I believe that you didn't calculate the price on my head at the same time?'

He heaves a sigh, as though she were a child. 'Ester, the decision was reached. Action was taken. The consequences were what they were. And here we are.'

She goes to the cupboard for the bottle of brandy. Puts it on the table in front of him. 'Here you are.' She also fetches a half-full bottle of Chianti. The cork is stuck. She locks her teeth into it and twists the bottle until the cork comes out. Pours herself a glass. Knocks it back and pours another. She lifts the glass and rotates the liquid slowly, fascinated by how the wine sticks to the inside.

'What did you and Gerhard talk about when you were driving here from Fagernes?' he says.

'You already know. Nothing. There's one more thing I need to know, and now I demand that you're straight with me.' She puts down the glass and searches his eyes.

He doesn't flinch.

'Did you find or see a knife or some sort of stabbing weapon when you were in his hotel room?'

Sverre Fenstad's facial expression is answer enough.

'And you've kept that quiet the whole time. Why?'

'I didn't want to unsettle you.'

She takes a deep breath.

Sverre raises his hands in defence. 'It was a kind of knife, yes. Considering his and my pasts, of course you'll understand that I'd like to know what his agenda is.'

They sit eyeballing each other in silence.

'Did you find anything else?' Ester says at length. 'Anything else you want to spare me?'

He looks away this time. 'Believe it or not, he's got rid of that weapon. The police didn't find anything in his room. Two men went through his room with a fine-tooth comb when he was brought in for questioning. They found nothing.'

The NSA, she thinks. Gerhard hasn't got rid of his weapon. In certain areas the American secret service is superior to the Norwegian police.

'What did they live off?' she says.

'Who?'

'Åse and Gerhard.'

Sverre clears his throat. 'I think it was tight. Gerhard came from Spain in thirty-seven or thirty-eight. He had a bullet wound, but recovered and got a job in Gjøvik. When he met Åse they moved to Oslo. When I met Gerhard he was working for Oslo Council, but he lost that job to a Nazi. Afterwards he was unemployed a lot of the time.'

'What was his job for the council?'

'Cemeteries Division.'

'Cemeteries Division,' she repeats. Lifts her glass and sips the wine. 'What do they do?'

Sverre Fenstad shrugs. 'We all have to die one day. Someone has to sort out the practicalities.'

'Did the resistance give them anything?'

'No.'

'You didn't give Gerhard any money when he crossed the border?'

Sverre shakes his head and takes a roll-up from his breast pocket. 'I've lost my lighter and keep forgetting to buy a new one.'

She doesn't want to let him change the subject. 'Gerhard had loads of money when I met him in Stockholm. US dollars.'

He shrugs. 'He was given the transport. The money was his. We couldn't give money to every man and his brother crossing the border. Obviously.'

Ester goes to the cupboard and fetches a box of matches. Throws it to him. She strokes her chin, thinking.

He blows smoke out through his nose. 'What's on your mind now?' he asks.

'I want to see the case file from the war,' she says. 'The murder of Åse Lajord. You can help me there.'

'Why do you think I can help you?'

'Intuition.'

'What do you want with the file?'

She takes another sip of wine. 'Turid, his daughter, has a bracelet she insists belonged to Åse. I'd like to know if this piece of jewellery was in the flat, or if Åse was wearing it when she was found.'

'Why do you want to know?'

'Because it's a bracelet my father gave my mother as a morning gift – the day after they were married.'

Sverre sits up. She has his full attention.

'It's kabbalah jewellery – protection against the evil eye. Turid's wearing the bracelet now.'

Sverre says nothing. He gets up and flicks ash into the sink. Sits down again.

'It's a very special bracelet. The jewel that's meant to protect you is the gemstone alexandrite. It's green in ordinary daylight, but changes to red indoors, with the lights on. The bracelet itself is forged from the five kabbalah metals: gold, silver, copper, tin and lead. On the outside there's an engraving in Hebrew of all the words for God listed in the Second Book of Moses, and on the inside there are the initials *AL*. Turid claims the bracelet's from Åse.'

'*AL*. Åse Lajord That fits.'

Ester shakes her head. 'The owner was Amiela Lemkov. If it was found on Åse, why wasn't it confiscated? You said yourself the Gestapo were involved in the investigation. The Nazis confiscated anything of value that was in any way Jewish. This bracelet's a Jewish work of art. The engraving on the outside is in Hebrew! The wording of the law was clear enough. All Jews' wristwatches had to be confiscated and handed over to the Wehrmacht. Gold, silver and jewellery also had to be confiscated and placed at the disposal of the German government via the Norwegian Sipo.'

'I've read the case file. There's nothing about a bracelet in it. It must've been Åse's mother's.'

'Are you hard of hearing? The bracelet was a gift from my father to my mother. She was the owner when it went missing in October forty-two. I intend to find out how this work of art made its way from my mother's jewellery box to Åse's daughter, Turid. And I need any help you can give!' She bangs her fist on the table so hard her glass tips over.

Fenstad hurries to the sink. Drops his cigarette in it and moistens a cloth. Mops up the wine. Wrings the cloth over the sink and wipes the rest. Then he refills both their glasses.

'Right,' he says. 'I promise you'll get the file tomorrow.'

Oslo, November 1967

1

Ester pushes the seat forwards and throws her fencing bag onto the back seat. Gets in. Lays her handbag on the passenger seat and starts the car. Looks in the mirror. Immediately notices a green VW Beetle pulling out fifty metres behind her.

She drives up Kirkeveien, passes the wrought-iron gate of Vigeland Sculpture Park. Stops at the lights where the road meets Middelthuns gate. Looks in the mirror. She sees only the outline of the driver's head. The windscreen of the VW reflects the sun. Ester opens her handbag.

When the lights change she turns into Middelthuns gate. As she passes Frogner Lido she sees the VW has fallen behind. She accelerates up Sørkedalsveien and across the Smestad intersection.

Now she should go straight on to Makrellbekken and Njård Sports Hall to train. Instead she veers off towards Holmenkollen.

With her right hand she gropes in her bag. Her fingers find the revolver. She releases the safety catch and puts the gun in the glove compartment.

She passes the grass pitch. Quick glance at the mirror. No VW.

So she should take Stasjonsveien to the left and drive back to the sports hall. But she wants to be sure. She carries on over the crossing and up the mountain. On the hairpin bends she still can't see the green VW. But as the road straightens out, she sees it, a couple of hundred metres behind her. She turns off at Besserud and follows the narrow roads up to Voksenlia and the back of Holmenkollen hill.

The VW is hanging on.

She heads for the Krag statue and the sightseeing point above the city.

As she approaches she sees a tourist bus has stopped in the car park by the sculpture. A crowd of Japanese tourists is admiring the view and taking photos.

She drives to the side of the statue and parks by a group of tourists. A woman is photographing the monument of Hans H. Krag leaning against a pillar of granite, a wide-brimmed hat on his head, one hand holding a walking stick and the other on his angled hip. Not unlike Sverre Fenstad, she thinks, looking in the rear-view mirror.

The VW drives in and stops right behind her.

Ester opens the lid to the glove compartment and leaves it down. Sits with the engine idling, looking into the mirror.

The driver's door of the VW opens. A squat man comes out. He hitches up his trousers and trudges towards her.

The man stops by her door and leans over. Ester rolls down the window.

'You don't remember me,' he says. His breath reeks of alcohol and his eyes are swimming. 'But I saw you many times when we were teenagers.'

Ester keeps a hand on the gear stick and a foot resting against the accelerator.

He lifts a hand and extends it towards her. 'My name's Erik Heggen.'

Ester switches off the engine and pulls on the handbrake. She opens the door and gets out.

The man moves back and almost falls.

'You're drunk,' she says.

He shrugs and smiles sheepishly. 'When you're at my level, being drunk's very different from this.'

The Japanese tourists are making their way back into the bus.

'You shouldn't be driving a car in your state,' Ester says.

The bus doors close. The engine starts.

He watches the bus through watery eyes. 'She talked a lot about you,' he says. 'Often.'

'What do you want?'

He ventures another smile. 'Perhaps we should talk about what's important?'

'Which is?'

'Someone we both knew well. Åse.'

2

A butterfly is on the window sill. It doesn't move even when she rattles the stay. Its wings are stretched out. It is a red admiral. Brown wings with reddish-orange stripes and white spots. She leaves it in peace, carefully lifting the stay, opening the window a fraction and securing it. Then she stares at the butterfly, which appears to be glued to the wood. Presumably it is dead.

She turns away from the window and sits at the grand piano. Opens the lid and lets her fingers run across the ivory and ebony keys. The piano tuner came several times over several weeks to make sure the strings were in order. Presumably during the years she and the piano had been separated it had never been played. The thought that the piano had loyally waited for her fingers strengthens her feelings for this instrument. And when she plays, the feelings appear to be mutual.

This is her private piano. It is not demeaned by bum notes or children's sticky fingers; it does not have to endure shaky tempos or rhythms. Coping with work in the adjacent room, carrying on her life, confronting children's battle against music – their submission to parents' ambitions and desperate struggle for something they don't understand – is one thing. However, her grand piano has to be spared that. She closes her eyes and allows her fingers to find the keys by themselves. They play the opening to the 'Andante Sostenuto' movement from Schubert's *Piano Sonata D960*. She has dealt with explosive emotions in this way many times before. It is a difficult piece, psychologically; it is dramatic – a hold-yourself-back and stay-cool and don't-go-mad piece. But then a growing fury enters her consciousness and however much she fights, she can't restrain this feeling. The only solution is to stop playing. To sit still and allow this new silence to subdue the fury as far as it is able.

As if on cue, the outside world intrudes. The telephone rings.

Ester glowers at it. Gets up, fairly sure she knows who it is. She is right.

'Sverre here.'

She asks where the case file is.

He says he has it in his hand. There is mention of an engagement ring, he says. And also a pair of earrings with inlaid pearls.

She interrupts. 'You were supposed to hand the case file over to me.'

'A filigree brooch,' he says as though he hasn't heard her. 'And some other traditional silver adornments, which have been given back to her mother. But there's nothing about a gold bracelet. Nothing.'

Again Ester is irritated by how Sverre always wants to be in charge and take control. She tries not to let her anger show.

'I've spoken to Erik Heggen,' she says.

'Did you hear what I said? No kabbalah jewellery was found in the flat. Did you ask Erik Heggen about the jewellery?'

'No.'

'Pity. He's probably the person who knows how his daughter came to have it.'

She doesn't want to discuss the mystery of her mother's jewellery with Sverre. She doesn't want his opinion on this entangled issue. 'And you're sure you have all the documents in this file?'

'Not all of them, no.'

'What's missing?'

'Some of the interviews, as well as the pathologist's report.'

'Åse had a post-mortem?'

'I suppose they wanted to determine the cause of death.'

'What was the pathologist's name?'

She hears him take a deep breath. His voice is low and condescending. 'Ester! She can't have eaten a bracelet.'

'I have no preconceived notions. I want the name of the pathologist.'

'The man might be dead.'

'What's his name?'

The silence ticks away for a few annoying seconds before she hears the rustle of papers.

'Sveen. Torkel Sveen.'

'Thank you. By the way, Erik Heggen insists that he and Åse started up again.'

'That very day? When he was with her in the flat?'

'He admitted to me that he visited her that evening at the end of October because he knew she would be alone. Apparently she was complaining about her relationship with Gerhard. Because he refused to work; because he only wanted to play soldiers in the woods. "Play soldiers" are Erik's words. Åse and Gerhard didn't have much money. On top of that, her mother was seriously ill. She wanted to move home and help her, but Gerhard had said no, Erik says. Gerhard didn't want to live in Valdres and slave away for her mother. Erik says he left Åse early in the morning and she was alive.'

'That's a very convenient confession. Do you believe what he says?'

'I didn't at first.'

'What made you change your mind?'

'You said there were American cigarette butts in the flat. And the Gestapo reacted as a result.'

'That's correct.'

'Neither Åse nor Erik smoked.'

His silence grows now. She takes the telephone directory, starts looking for addresses of pathologists.

At last Sverre clears his throat. 'Did you ask Erik if he took cigarettes with him?'

'He did.'

'But he didn't smoke them?'

'He's never smoked.'

'What was he going to do with the cigarettes then?'

'Black market. That was why he stole them. One of the cartons he took to Åse's was gone and there were butts in the ashtray on the table.'

Silence again.

Ester leafs through the directory, runs a finger down a page then flips it over. 'I know someone who smoked in those days,' she says.

'Erik Heggen told you he was there and left her. So when did the cigarette butts end up in the ashtray?'

'It happened in the middle of the night. Åse had woken Erik. She'd been almost hysterical and told Erik he had to leave before Gerhard returned. He'd tried to calm her down, saying Gerhard was in the mountains. But then she'd shown him the ashtray and the cigarette ends. She said Gerhard had been in the flat while the two of them were asleep. She said he'd been in the sitting room, smoking while the two of them were still sleeping in the bedroom. She'd been woken by a door closing and she guessed it was Gerhard leaving.'

All Ester can hear in the receiver now is a faint crackle. She continues to flick through the directory.

Pathologists came under Rikshospital. She takes the pen beside the pad and makes a note of the telephone number. Puts down the pen.

'Erik Heggen *may* of course have been lying about this,' she says. 'But someone who's definitely lied about this all along is Gerhard. When I met him in Valdres he claimed Erik was the last person to see Åse alive. This was his conclusion, he told me. He'd come to it after all the years he'd spent thinking about what happened. Of course it's a possibility. But what Erik told me is a much better explanation of how Gerhard knew Erik was with Åse. And it should also be to Erik's credit that he finds me on his own initiative and tells me everything.'

'But why would Gerhard kill Åse? Their child was in the very next room!'

'Now at least there's a motive. Jealousy.'

'Surely that's a bit banal, isn't it?'

She doesn't answer. Death is never banal. If someone can live for more than fifty years without realising that, then it is beneath her dignity to teach them any better. 'The water's boiling. I'm making tea,' she says. 'Let's talk later.'

3

The desk is of the British variety, with an inset leather section for writing. It is green with gold embossing around the edge. The shiny woodwork is red and polished, and there isn't a single speck of dust. She would guess the desk is made from cherry wood. It is quite similar to her father's – the one that was taken. She catches herself wondering whether the Nazis repaired the broken drawers before they sold it on. Perhaps it is the self-same desk, she thinks a second later.

The portrait of Levi Eshkol on the wall is reflected on the shiny surface, beside the only object on the desk. It has been carved from redwood – an elephant with four arms and a big stomach. It is riding a mouse and is called Ganesh – the Hindu God of intellect and wisdom. A typical quirk of Markus Rebowitz's, she thinks. Markus is a rabbi who would like to be winked at by Buddha. She hears him in the corridor, his breathing. This has never happened before. Maybe he is catching a cold. He comes in carrying a big file under his arm. He places the file on the green-leather section in the desk. He sits down, making the chair creak, and starts thumbing through the file without even so much as a glance at her.

Ester thinks back. To the day she and Åse met on the Frogner pasture. 10th April 1940. The strange feeling of happiness in such an alarming situation. They were standing on either side of the large terrace; she was walking up the stone stairs, Åse was on her way out through the door when they spotted one another and both stopped for an instant to digest what their eyes beheld. At that moment the bomb threat was unimportant – their latent panic was forced to cede ascendency. What meant something was the pleasure of knowing that Åse lived in Oslo and that from now on they could meet as often as they wished.

'Here,' Markus says. 'The confiscation papers for Paschal and Amiela Lemkow's property.' He looks up. 'I thought you spelt Lemkow with a "v".'

She nods. 'I do.'

He looks back into the file. 'Here's an inventory of everything in the flat, down to the smallest fork. Did you own a rag toy, a donkey?'

'Yes.'

'There's a note of it here.' He pushes the file over to her.

Ester leans forwards. But when she sees it all in black and white – the list of woollen socks and trousers, the crossings out and the spelling mistakes – she closes her eyes and leans back in the chair. She can't bear to immerse herself in the callous administrative machinery that bureaucratised her life and her family's death.

'As far as your father's shop in Kirkeristen is concerned, all the watches, magnifying glasses and binoculars were confiscated and registered together; in other words, the number of watches and pairs of binoculars. But only in exceptional cases were specifications such as a manufacturer's number and so on noted down. As regards items pertaining to the flat in Eckersbergs gate 10, there's also a reference to a police investigation.'

Ester opens her eyes and looks at Markus in surprise.

'Let me see…' He runs his index finger down the sheet, turns over the page. 'Lots of valuables here. A couple of Munch lithographs, a somewhat controversial Monet and a miniature by Anne Marie Grim-dalen, plus a Steinway grand piano. A chandelier ... furniture ... Of these items you say only the piano has been located since?'

'What sort of investigation?'

'Break-in. Property owned by Lemkow. Jewish. Footnote on how few valuables there are among the kitchen utensils – such as silverware. It's assumed that whatever valuables of this nature there may have been were removed during the burglary.'

Ester goes ice cold at once. 'A break-in,' she says in measured tones, and leans back in the chair again. Markus removes his glasses, rubs his eyes, opens a drawer in the desk and takes out a black cloth. He begins to clean his glasses with it.

'Do you think it wasn't Quisling's Hirden who broke into our flat?'

'I'm not saying that. But I doubt there are any papers regarding the burglary. Otherwise there would've been references to them in this file. I assume the police put these things at the bottom of the pile back then. But yes, I'm sure it was the Hirden scum who broke in, stole items of value and sold them on the black market.'

Ester is back in Ada Vinje's hallway. When they clung to each other while the Hirden paramilitaries talked outside and pointed to the splintered wood in the door.

'This sort of thing went on,' the rabbi says. 'The Nazis removed gold fillings from the teeth of corpses in the gas chambers.'

'Thank you, I know what they were capable of doing,' Ester says in a hard voice. She springs to her feet.

'I'm sorry, Ester.'

At the door, Ester breathes in. 'Thank you very much.'

'Can I offer you anything?'

She shakes her head at first, but then changes her mind. 'I'd like to use your telephone.'

4

Markus pushes the telephone towards her.

She walks back to the chair and sits down. 'May I be on my own?'

'Naturally.' He gets up. 'Dial zero first.'

She waits until he has closed the door behind him. Then she dials the number for Information.

'I'd like the number of Supreme Court Advocate Sverre Fenstad's office please.'

Markus has left his biro on the file. She takes note of the number, says thank you and cradles the telephone. Dials zero, gets a different dialling tone and calls again. Asks for Fenstad. As soon as she hears Sverre say his name, she says: 'Ester here. You said Gerhard has a return ticket. When does his plane leave?'

Sverre says he doesn't know.

'But the police checked his ticket, didn't they?'

'Sorry, but I didn't ask. I was just pleased he was going.'

'Could you find out?'

'Perhaps you'd like us to break into his room again?'

'I'm not joking, Sverre. I'd like you to stop him leaving.'

'I can't refuse to let anyone leave the country. Especially not if I don't know when the respective individual's leaving.'

'You can use the police.'

'Believe me. I can't.'

'This is all about Åse's murder. Gerhard could clear the case up in an interview. That must be reason enough to stop him leaving the country.'

'No, Ester. The statute of limitations has expired on that case. The Norwegian prosecuting authorities are unable to charge anyone with the murder of Åse. If you want to stop Gerhard leaving the country, you'll have to dig up a better reason.'

'Statute of limitations? When did it expire?'

'Åse was killed on 30th October twenty-five years ago. The case was dismissed forever on 30th October this year.'

Ester looks at her reflection in the window. She can't be bothered with polite phrases. She rings off.

She calls Hotel Continental and asks to be put through to Gary Larson's room.

The answer she receives is short and neutral. 'He's checked out.'

'When?'

'Today.'

Ester presses the plunger.

So Gerhard is possibly on his way already. He has slipped away this time too, like a lump of slime. Admit it, she tells herself. There was no final reckoning. All that is left is the truth. Accept it. Forget Gerhard. He doesn't exist. He died many years ago. He died long before you gave his body a new name.

Oslo, November 1967

1

Two workmen from Oslo Parks and Gardens are taking in the benches from Studenterlunden park. They grab hold of either side of one and lift it onto the back of a small lorry. It is a good day to do this, Gerhard thinks. Bare branches stand out against the sky. Sticky leaves meld with the tarmac and make walking unsafe for hurrying city folk with slippery soles. A third workman in rubber boots and a sou'wester trundles along with a square wheelbarrow. On top are a shovel and a piassava broom. He takes the broom, sweeps up the remaining leaves and shovels the heap into the wheelbarrow, then carries on. The two men with the benches shout to him. The man grunts something incomprehensible back. He drops the wheelbarrow beside Gerhard, who is leaning against a tree. Gerhard moves out of the way when the workman starts sweeping. Gerhard tucks a newspaper under his arm and focuses on the portico of the university. A caretaker in a blue smock is walking up the steps with a wad of letters under his arm. He stops and gives way to a young woman coming down. She exits between the columns and crosses the university square.

He watches Turid as he waits until there is a pause in the traffic, then he crosses Karl Johans gate and goes to meet her.

They stop and look at each other, and he is unable to conceal his emotion as he says: 'Every time I think it's your mother coming towards me.'

She gives him a hug.

They start walking.

She asks what he feels like doing. They have reached the corner of Domus Academica, and Gerhard looks up at the clock in the window. He checks the time against his own watch.

'Have you eaten?'

'Not since breakfast.'

He asks where she would like to eat.

She havers and shrugs.

He asks if she is in a hurry.

She says she has the whole day if necessary.

Then he suggests they drive somewhere he hasn't been for years.

2

Leafless branches from huge birch trees hang over the road. It is like going down an avenue, but there is only a single line of trees. On the opposite side there is a steep rock face. Soon the terrain opens and the road winds through farmyards with sloping fields on either side. There are still rows of hay racks scattered across the meadows, which in some places gleam with the golden hue of autumn. A white church comes into view on a hillside. Ester pulls over and stops the car when she reaches the side-road to the church. There is a milk ramp here and beside it stand a group of farmhands, chatting. That is, she assumes they are farmhands because of the boots, overalls and peaked caps. They all turn to look at her as she approaches. She asks for directions. One of the men doffs his cap. The others grin. The one who doffed his cap points up at the church and draws a map in the gravel with a stick. The others joke and criticise the map.

'Don't listen to what he's saying. He's full of lies.'

The map-drawer ripostes in dialect. Ester understands neither the dialect nor the humour, but smiles politely, gets in her car and drives up the hillside. The road goes through a few hairpin bends; the view of the lake is impressive. She branches off the gravel road and continues along a narrow tractor track. The deep ruts lead under a barn bridge, just as she was told. The track ends in another farmyard.

Ester stops the car and gets out. The grass is wet and the ground is covered with puddles. She tries as best she can to reach the white house with dry shoes. Wooden steps lead up to a porch and a grey door. She knocks. Steps back two paces and glimpses a face peering at her from behind a curtain in the window. She knocks again. She hears a door open inside. A man in his seventies opens.

'Sveen?' she says.

The man nods.

She proffers a hand. 'Ester Lemkov. I rang you.'

In the kitchen it is as hot as a sauna. Providing the heat is a wood-fired stove in the corner. A blackened coffee pot stands between two hotplates. Above the stove are three strips of fly paper, thick with dead flies.

Ester greets his sister. She seems to have a back problem because it is bent and she squints up at Ester from an angle.

She and Sveen sit down at the table. His sister is busy by the worktop. She unpacks a large wholewheat loaf from a cloth bag, cuts some slices, butters them and adds brown cheese. The lid of the coffee pot rises and Sveen's sister shuffles over to the stove and saves the pot from boiling over. She asks Ester if she wants any coffee. Ester doesn't want to upset her by asking for tea, so she nods.

At that moment a fly collides with her forehead and she recoils.

As if it were going for my eyes, she thinks, and raises a hand to wave it away. But the fly is long gone. Above the table hang more strips of fly paper, covered in insects.

Ester asks Sveen whether it is correct that he used to be a pathologist. He answers that it is. She asks if he considers it strange that someone should call him about an autopsy that he carried out on a young mother more than twenty years ago.

He ponders the question. 'It doesn't happen often,' he admits finally.

His sister has her say. It never happens. She is the one at home during the day. She is the one who answers the telephone. She points to the wall telephone. An old model with a hand crank at the side.

'So you have some questions about Åse,' the man says at length.

'You remember her, sir?'

'We can drop the formality,' he says. 'You're in the country now. I can tell you this: I'll never forget Åse.'

'What are you talking about now, Father,' his sister says, putting a plate of wholewheat sandwiches on the table. She pours the coffee. It is black and there are some light-brown grains floating on the surface. She leans back and looks up at Ester. She has curly grey hair and most of it is tied in a bun behind her head. 'Eat up now,' she says. 'You look as if you could do with it.'

'Could do with it?'

'Don't listen to her,' Sveen says. 'She just blathers.'

Ester takes a sandwich and tries it. Wholewheat with currants, butter and sweet brown cheese. She suddenly realises it is a long time since she last ate. 'Lovely,' she says, and she means it. She wolfs the rest down. Unable to stop herself, she reaches out for another.

The sister smiles with satisfaction. She has two top teeth missing. Ester melts when she sees the gappy smile amid all the wrinkles in her face. 'Now have a drink,' she says, motioning towards the coffee cup.

Ester raises the cup and pretends to take a sip. 'Lovely,' she says, setting down the cup.

'Now you can go, Mother, and leave us to talk in peace.'

Ester wonders whether there are other siblings who call each other Mother and Father.

The sister takes some knitting from the worktop and lifts a fly swat from a hook on the wall. She says she will go to the little room. She closes the door behind her.

Now the roar of the flames in the stove is all that can be heard.

Ester lifts the cup and sets it down again. Finally, she asks him why he can't forget Åse.

He hesitates. 'What do you want to know?' he says at length. 'And why?'

'Åse Lajord was my best friend,' she says. 'I had to flee to Sweden only a few days before she was killed. I couldn't go to her funeral and never found out what had happened.'

'The police weren't interested in the body,' he says. 'They didn't give a damn about the dead woman. They were only interested in what she represented. What they liked to call terrorism. I rang them and reminded them, and they asked me what I was nagging them for. I asked where I should send the report. They said I could file it. I rang because the poor girl's mother was waiting. She wanted the body so that she could bury her daughter. She was a simple woman from the country. Her daughter lay on the zinc table with her stomach open, and I couldn't show the body to the mother in that state. I remember telling the policeman that the deceased's mother was there and wanted to bury her. So he said to me: "Why are you bothering me with this? Can't you just do what she asks?" It was a scandal. Nothing less.'

A couple of flies have started taking an interest in the plate of food and Ester is no longer hungry. The heat inside the kitchen is becoming unbearable. They must have animals on this farm. Sveen's woollen jumper smells of cowshed, and now Ester is finding the odour unpleasant and acrid.

'So she couldn't have the body until I'd finished. When you rang you talked about a piece of jewellery.'

Ester looks up.

'I found a bracelet. Gold chain and a precious gemstone. I gave it to her mother.'

'You found a bracelet. In her stomach? Had she eaten it?'

'No.'

He gets up. Crosses the floor and opens a blue wooden box by the door. From it he takes two narrow birch skis. Opens the stove door and adds them to the red glow. He straightens up. 'That's how she died. She was choked to death. But the police weren't in the slightest bit interested.'

Ester nods and coughs. 'I heard she was suffocated. That's what they wrote in the press.'

He stares into the air. 'But they didn't say how she died.'

The man sits down, takes a sugar cube from the bowl on the table, puts it in his mouth and sips some coffee. Smacks his lips. 'The murderer forced the bracelet down her throat. The hyoid bone was broken and the larynx was badly damaged. She couldn't get any oxygen.' He takes another sugar cube and sips coffee again. Smacks his lips and glances at Ester. 'But he must've been holding her down. I presume she was struggling violently. It must've taken her quite a time to die. We're talking premeditation here. He had the opportunity to let her go. He had more than enough time to change his mind. That was what made this case so repulsive. I examined her nails. We pathologists like to reconstruct the crime. But there was no skin under her nails. I remember there were clothing fibres, ordinary wool. It must've been from his clothes because the bedding in the flat was linen. The strange thing was that the victim was naked while the murderer was fully dressed. Well, I didn't get any further. I didn't say anything to her mother. I just gave her the bracelet. Said her daughter had been wearing it. It was hers.'

Ester leans back against the wall. The stove is roaring. She is sweating and thinking this cannot be possible. She says: 'In her throat. Surely it's impossible to do something like that?'

'If someone's strong enough and angry enough, they can do it. A couple of her teeth got a battering. They were cracked.'

They look at each other. He carries on talking. 'A beautiful young woman is killed in her bed by a man wearing a woollen jumper or woollen fabrics, maybe knee stockings. She's naked, apparently in bed asleep. Then she's murdered like this? How could it have happened? If she – excuse my frankness – if she'd been sexually attacked and the murderer wanted to conceal the crime, wouldn't he have been undressed as well? I saw no signs of rape. The sole indication of sexual violence was the fact that she was naked. So what led to the murder? I couldn't imagine it, but the scandal was that the police couldn't give a damn. They'd made up their minds. They went after the husband and they did so because he was a resistance man. He was their lead. In my eyes the case could never be cleared up because the police weren't interested in reconstructing the sequence of events – what actually happened before she died.'

3

Despite the grey cloud cover, Oslofjord lies like a huge photograph behind the glass window. The islands are called Hovedøya, Lindøya and Nakholmen. Gerhard is impressed by his own memory. The two islands to the left are more difficult. He can't remember whether Bleikøya or Gressholmen is closer to the shore. The Nesodden headland is like a green tongue, he thinks, forest green, and catches a movement in the glass on the table. The reflection is Turid coming back after powdering her nose, as some women say in the States. She sits down and he asks if she wants any dessert. She says she has to watch her weight. He roars with laughter and says she doesn't weigh a gram too much.

She says perhaps a vanilla slice then with her coffee. 'I've got a bit of a sweet tooth.'

'Your mother to a T,' Gerhard says, beckoning the waiter. After the man has left Turid says she has met one of her mother's friends. Ester. They got on well and she can understand how her mother liked her.

He says it isn't hard to like Ester. 'We knew each other then, many years ago. That is, Åse and she were close. They almost grew up together.'

The waiter came with the vanilla slice.

He says it looks delicious.

She tastes it. Nods her approval. Asks him if he would like to try a bit. He shakes his head. Instead he tells her about how he waited in a corridor at Aker hospital when Turid was born.

She asks where he and her mother first met.

He says at Fagerlund Hotel in Fagernes. Åse was working in the reception area.

'She was as blonde as you. She also wore her hair in a big plait over one shoulder. We both talked at once, and stopped, and started again. Three times in succession. Then we burst into laughter.'

Turid laughs and he smiles at the memory.

He says he travelled around selling advertising for a newspaper. He stayed at Fagerlund Hotel whenever he was in Valdres, even if he, strictly speaking, didn't need to stop over. He did it so that he could talk to Åse. And even though the chemistry was there he had to ask her out four whole times before she would agree. She thought it wasn't done for staff to go out and eat with guests.

A group of four people sit down at the next table. They are Americans and enthuse loudly over the view.

The two of them exchange glances. 'Everyone can hear where they're from,' she says.

He grins. 'Is it the same with me?'

Turid shakes her head, raises a hand to take a lock of hair from her eyes. The sleeve of her blouse opens and reveals the bracelet she is wearing.

Gerhard grips her hand and looks at the jewellery.

'What is it?'

He lets go of her hand. 'Your bracelet,' he says. 'I haven't seen it for a long time.'

'One of the few things I have of hers,' Turid says. 'Tell me,' she says. 'Was it a present from you? I've always thought you must've given it to her.'

She takes off the bracelet and shows him the engravings. He sits there for a long time, eyes downcast.

'Yes,' he says. 'It was a present.' He looks up. His eyes are moist.

'Dear me,' she says, drying a tear in her own eye. 'Sorry, but I'm so sentimental. I cry at the least thing.'

Gerhard composes himself and says he is happy she has taken care of this keepsake.

She squeezes his hand and says she is happy he is here, with her. She has done a lot of thinking and imagining.

He says he has something to tell her. 'First things first, though,' he says, and asks her whether she showed the bracelet to Ester.

Turid nods.

He asks what Ester said.

Turid frees her hand and points a finger at the engraved symbols and says Ester asked if she knew what they meant.

'And what did you say?'

'I said I had no idea. I'd always thought of them as decoration, nothing symbolic.'

'What did she say to that?'

Turid laughs. 'You and Ester are so similar. You're obsessed by the same things.'

They exchange glances. 'She said nothing,' Turid says. 'She said she thought the bracelet was lovely. And of course it is.' Turid smiles again. But she is serious when she sees his expression. 'What's the matter?' she asks, slightly unsettled.

'Moments like these are the most difficult,' he says.

'What do you mean?'

'I have to say goodbye.' Then, when he sees the sparkle in her eyes go out, he quickly adds, 'For this time.' He places his hand over hers and squeezes it. 'I have to go to town before the bank closes.'

'What do you mean by goodbye?'

'I'm leaving tomorrow. But we should stay in touch and I'll invite you over. The main thing is that we've met. You're the most important thing that's happened to me.'

They sit gazing into each other's eyes.

'I'll go to the plane with you.'

He shakes his head.

'I insist,' she says.

'I'm leaving very early,' he says. 'Don't even think about it.'

'I'll drive you,' she says. 'It doesn't matter how early it is.'

He makes an effort not to show his annoyance. Snatches a look at his watch and says: 'Don't think about it now.'

He raises a hand to attract the passing waiter's attention and asks for the bill.

That is when Turid pushes the bracelet across the table. 'Take it. Please.'

He looks at her in amazement.

'This bracelet will be my guarantee,' she says. 'As long as you have this, I know you'll come back.'

Oslo, November 1967

1

Gerhard opens the car door and gets out. Night has fallen over Oslo. It was evening the last time he left this city and then it was hidden under cover of darkness and mystery. Now it twinkles and shines with the thousands of lights in the Oslo basin and up Mt Ekeberg. He stands in contemplation like this for a long time, then turns to walk the few metres back to and around the car. There is a click as he opens the boot. The lid creaks. But it stays open when he lets go. He lifts out a small, red metal container. Closes the boot and takes the container.

The windows in the house are dark and have been for some time. Gerhard puts the key in the lock. It won't turn. Gerhard smiles. Number Thirteen is observant. The lock has been changed. So Gerhard switches to plan B. He tosses the key onto the grass, slowly ambles round the house and into the garden. The street lamp casts a matt sheen over the lawn. His silhouette flits towards the house wall, merges into the shadow from the eaves. He draws the bayonet from the sling under his arm and inserts the blue steel blade in the crack between the frame and the veranda door. He leans on it with all his weight. A little click is all that he hears as the lock comes away. The door slides open. He goes in.

Inside, he listens. But Sverre can't have heard anything because the house is as still as before. Gerhard closes the door. He removes his shoes. On stockinged feet he walks through the sitting room and into the hallway. He puts the container down. He pulls out the telephone cable.

He tiptoes soundlessly upstairs.

The ceiling light in the corridor is lit. He carries on. The door to Sverre's room is ajar. He pushes it open. A sweet smell of sleep and stale air hits him. He notices that Sverre doesn't have the nerve to leave the window open at night.

The room is in darkness, only a faint stripe of light steals in across the duvet and the man asleep in the bed. Sverre Fenstad smacks his lips in his sleep. Gerhard tiptoes into the room. He crouches down by the bed. On his haunches he sits staring at the sleeping man. Sverre's breathing is rhythmical and calm.

Finally Gerhard gets up and slips out of the bedroom. Continues down the stairs as quietly as before.

He fetches his shoes and puts them on. Then he takes the red container. Opens the cellar door without making a sound. Goes down the steps and in through the door to the hobby room with the stuffed animals. He switches on the light. Opens the container and splashes the contents over the walls, on the carpet, on the stuffed animals.

He puts the empty can down on the floor.

To make a fire there are three prerequisites. The first is combustible material. The second is air. Gerhard opens all three windows in the cellar.

The third condition is a source of fire. He goes halfway up the stairs, flicks the silver lighter and throws it to the floor. The result is explosive. The blast wave bursts through the door and Gerhard has to sprint up the remaining steps so as not to catch fire himself. He leaves the cellar door open, runs into the sitting room and out through the veranda door. As soon as he opens it he hears the draught give the flames on the cellar stairs a surge of energy.

Outside the house, he stands watching. There is a red glow behind the windows. The curtains flutter through the open veranda door. As the smoke belches out, black and impenetrable, followed by fiery-red destruction, he turns and goes back to the car.

2

This evening Ester lies in bed unable to sleep. Because of a fly. As sleep steals upon her, so does the fly. It settles on her forehead. One touch of light fly-feet and she is awake in an instant. A fly in her flat in November? It must have crept into her hair when she visited the pathologist. She imagines the fly sitting quietly in her hair the whole long way home, then it extricated itself when she went to bed, and now it will torment the life out of her. She feels her eyelids going again. Then the light pressure of the fly's feet as it lands on the tip of her nose. This is no good.

She gets out of bed, goes to the kitchen and takes the fly swat from a drawer. Goes back to the bedroom. She leaves the bedside table lamp on. Hides under the duvet with her hand gripped tightly around the handle of the fly swat. Waits. Keeps an eye on the light and waits for the fly to land on the lampshade so that she can kill it. But she doesn't see it land on the shade. Nor she does feel her eyes closing. She only feels that something is different – even if it is an old dream. It is a reunion. An old nightmare that has sneaked out of an archive deep in the brain. Now it is back. Yet Ester is at her ease. She knows this dream, knows what will happen when she crawls into the train carriage, knows she is asleep. She is equally calm when she hears running footsteps on the stairs. She knows the train doors will close before he reaches the bottom of the stairs, and she is right. The doors close. She sinks to the floor of the carriage and knows he won't be able to get in. The man prowling around outside, the man banging on the window. That is when she feels there is something different, but she can't see what it is. She is sitting with her back to the wall, hoping. That is when the glass smashes. It shatters with a piercing sound as his hand bursts through and opens the door. He comes in. He grows into a giant figure towering over her, and now there is only one escape possible. And that is to wake up.

She looks at the lamp on the bedside table, her heart pounding. He had smashed the glass. This warning sent a feeling of terror through her that she had not experienced for many years. She tells herself the war is over. Everything finished a long time ago. You are at home in your own flat. You haven't been on active service for several years.

But there is something else.

There is a sound. The telephone. She looks at her watch. Sits up.

She swings her legs onto the floor and goes into the hallway.

'Gerhard here.'

Ester places a hand on the wall. Leans against it. 'I thought you'd left,' she says. 'They said you'd checked out.'

'There are a few hours left before the plane goes.'

'What do you want?'

'I want to see you before I leave.'

'Then you can come here.'

'Let's meet in town.'

She is silent.

'I have regrets, Ester.'

'What regrets?'

'That I allowed myself to be tempted. That I couldn't stop myself.'

'What couldn't you stop yourself doing?'

'You told me your flat was empty. Do you remember? Your father had been arrested, your mother wasn't there and you came to ours. I left you and Åse for Eckersbergs gate 10 that day. I broke in.'

Ester breathes through her mouth. The voice in her ear. This is like a radio play.

'When Åse talked about you, she always said how rich you were. She said your father kept diamonds and other gemstones in a desk drawer.'

'You took much more,' she says.

He doesn't protest.

'Money. My father's savings.'

He is quiet.

'You took my mother's jewellery.'

Still silence.

'It was you who tipped off the Norwegian Sipo about the handover of the *London News* at Valkyrie plass,' she says. 'You weren't content with robbing me. You also wanted me arrested.'

The voice that answers now is unaltered, as unaffected as before. 'I was pretty surprised when you showed up at the camp in Sweden – you of all people. I had quite a shock when I saw you.'

'You hid the loot. You hid it in other people's graves,' Ester says.

Silence.

'You took a bit of a gamble. Old graves are destroyed.'

'Not all of them,' he says. 'But then I didn't plan to be away for half a lifetime. The rest took care of that. But you're right. I was nervous. One grave has in fact gone.'

'You come back after all these years, sneak out at night and collect the stolen goods to deposit them in bank boxes. What is it you actually regret?'

'I want you to have it back.'

'I don't believe you.'

'It's true. That's why I'm calling.'

'Why do you want to give it back?'

'For a long time I thought it didn't matter. I thought that you and your family wouldn't be allowed to keep anything anyway. The Germans would take everything. I took the things only because it was better they went to someone who needed them.'

Ester is speechless.

'But it wasn't right of me.'

'Why have you changed your mind?'

'We can't plan our lives. You know that as well as I do. But something good has happened to me for once. Something I said goodbye to many years ago. I have my daughter back. For me this is a new chance, an opportunity to start again, and I want to grasp it with both hands. I know I can't recompense you for what I did to you, but I'd like to do what I can.'

Ester falls quiet again.

'Alvilde Munthe,' he says.

She is still silent.

'Meet me at Alvilde Munthe's grave, now.'

'We can meet tomorrow.'

'Tomorrow I won't be here. My plane leaves at the crack of dawn.'

'What do you think your daughter will say when she finds out you killed her mother?'

Silence again.

'You let yourself in. You saw Erik and Åse in bed together. You went back out and waited until he'd gone. Then you went back. I've spoken to the pathologist who found the bracelet. He says you took your time. She put up quite a struggle and you had plenty of opportunities to let her live, long before she stopped breathing.'

'I'll wait for you there. By Alvilde Munthe's grave. We can talk about this then.'

3

The wisest move would be to say no, she tells herself, to allow common sense to prevail. But the Ester who is getting ready to go outdoors is a practical thinker. She has to be able to move. So she chooses stretch pants and a jumper, trainers for her feet. Ties the laces. Double knots. Can't take the risk of them coming undone. Thinks about his story of an early plane – it is probably a fabrication. On the other hand, is she willing to take the risk? Her stomach is knotted. She had thought she would never go there again. Never feel the knot, never avoid eye contact with her own reflection. And all of a sudden you are there again. Even though you don't want to be. Not under any circumstances. But there you are, and there is little you can do about it now. This is how the world is. You can hide, you can move to an island, build a hut and wander on a beach for years, lonely. But when the past comes calling you are the same person.

She automatically goes into the closet behind the bedroom. Searches out the brown bag. Goes into the kitchen. Here she opens it. Inside there is a bandolier and a holster. She takes the revolver from her handbag. She ejects the cylinder; it rotates easily and soundlessly. She clicks it back into place. She straps on the holster. Stands in front of the mirror. Puts the revolver in the holster under her arm and tries on various jackets in front of the mirror.

There is a bulge every time. In the end she takes off the holster. She puts on a trench coat and slips the revolver into a pocket. It is half past two in the morning.

She stops on the way out of the door.

Turns and goes back, into the kitchen. Searches through the drawers. Finds what she is after in one of them. A candle and a box of matches. When she closes the front door twenty minutes have passed since Gerhard rang off.

His car is parked in Frimanns gate.

Early flight, yes, very likely. Ester drives past the car and parks a few blocks away. She imagines he is watching. He has seen the car lights and her car. He is waiting and has the advantage over her.

She gets out of the car and walks slowly along the fence to the cemetery. Stops. It is almost inaudible, the movement inside the fence. He is good.

She takes three steps. Stops.

The footsteps inside stop too.

The branches of the spruce hedge inside the fence move almost imperceptibly and are still.

The house walls along Ullevålsveien are dark. Only the street lamps with their round domes form an illuminated string of pearls over the pavement.

She walks on. Glimpses her own shadow on the pavement. Casts a glance over her shoulder. A car is driving towards her at a snail's pace. It turns out to be a police patrol car. It stops. Ester stops too. The window of the VW beetle is lowered. She can't see the officer inside, but she can hear his voice. 'Everything alright?'

She nods. 'Yes, everything's fine. I've been to a party and want to walk home. I ate too much.' She ventures a smile, but doubts he can see it.

The window glides back up. The car carries on. She watches it. As the car approaches the crossroads by Akerbakken, it puts on a blue light and accelerates. Then it is gone.

She peers into the dark cemetery. She can't see him, but she knows he can see her. He is watching and waiting, she guesses, like a lion deep in its cave. She turns her back on the cemetery and crosses the street, undoing the lowest two buttons of her coat as she walks. As soon as she is hidden behind a house she breaks into a run, into Nordahl Bruns gate, bears left, out of sight from the man in the cemetery. Finding her rhythm and breathing evenly, she jogs gently but quickly round the block and runs back, up Akersveien and past the main entrance to the cemetery. Swings her legs over the wire fence and shelters behind a big tree. Not stirring until she has her breath back. Not a sound comes from the cemetery. A window closes somewhere behind and above her, and Gerhard must be annoyed now, at having missed her, she thinks. Either he will give up and leave or he will wait at the agreed spot – by Alvilde Munthe's grave.

The sound of a car engine grows in volume. She sees the cones of light moving along the hedge and disappearing.

4

She moves from tree to tree alongside the fence. Her footsteps are soundless on the grass. Between the shadows a mist lingers, brushing the gravestones as though it owns them and wants to demonstrate this, she thinks. And again she presses forwards, slowly moving to the centre, away from Alvilde Munthe's grave. She has targeted the rock behind the high buttress wall. She counts her footsteps and stops now and then to listen. If she doesn't hear anything she goes on to the next tree towering against the black-and-grey sky. A shadow resembling a man emerges from the mist. She stops again. Doesn't move a muscle. The shadow is static. She steps two paces closer. It isn't a man. It is a bust on a plinth. She walks past the statue. Stops and looks back. The statue is no longer visible. She carries on, more slowly now. Gropes her way forwards in the darkness between the graves. There are sudden patches of light over the grass. She looks up. Dark clouds are drifting across the sky. Revealing the moon for brief instants. The blaze of light allows her to determine her direction. She slips a hand into her pocket. Her fingers find the handle of the revolver. She takes it out of her pocket. Releases the safety catch. Holds the gun in her right hand and lets it hang downwards. As soon as the darkness is impenetrable again she heads for the rock. She finds the path leading to the top. Now she doesn't care if her shoes crunch on the gravel. Every time the moon shows itself and casts light over the ground she stands still. Then she is finally at the top. She takes out the candle she brought. Puts a finger in her mouth, lifts it in the air to determine the wind direction, but there isn't a breath. Props the candle up with the help of two stones. Crouches and lights a match, looks away so as not to be blinded by the flash of light. The wick catches and she backs into a tree trunk. Watches the little flame taking hold as it is fed by the wax. Now to wait.

She holds the revolver with both hands and listens. He can't miss the light. Only the wind can spoil things for her now. Ester feels as if she has all the time in the world. She doesn't have to catch any plane. She is going nowhere. She has waited eternities and can easily wait another for what is about to happen. The person who definitely is in a hurry is out there somewhere.

Soon the silence is broken by a twig breaking. The sound comes from the bushes above the wall. It is not surprising that he prefers to avoid the path.

She looks to the right. But now the silence is total again. She looks up at the sky. The moon is just an outline behind cloud cover that is becoming more and more transparent. Then it bursts forth and she sees a figure freeze in the light.

He is holding a knife in his right hand, away from his body, in reverse grip. Attack position.

The moon goes in and the figure disappears in the darkness.

She fixes her eyes on the place. Her eyes do not deceive her. Slowly, slowly, the contours of his body form. Gerhard is still standing quite motionless. She wonders whether he has realised now. Their roles have been reversed. He is moving into the mouth of the cave unaware of what awaits him.

The figure is only four or five metres from the little flame.

So he hasn't seen her yet.

She calculates the distance between them. Maybe fifteen metres. Slowly she lifts the weapon with both hands.

'Here, Gerhard.'

He is as agile as a cat.

For a tenth of a second she is paralysed by his speed. He has covered half the distance by the time she fires.

She is blinded by the tongue of flame, but hears what sounds like a clink above the thud of his fall. She still can't see anything, but crouches down and moves towards the sound. Gropes her way with her free hand over the rocks and gravel. Unable to find what she is looking for, she stands up and steps back two paces.

Slowly her vision returns. The candle flame helps. It flickers. She has her eyes trained on the ground and sees the matt metal sheen. She kneels down and grabs the bayonet. It is heavy and double-edged.

She scans the mist, but can't make out where he is lying. She moves in a large arc towards the flickering flame. Waits and listens, the revolver in her right hand and his bayonet in the other. He is still stunned by the shock, she thinks. He still hasn't begun to feel the pain. He still thinks he can do it. He still thinks he can get back to his car, bind his leg wound and carry on. That is the only logic for him now.

A gust of wind blows out the candle.

The new darkness gives her better vision. She listens. Hears scratching noises. Goes over to the path. There he is. Hands claw at the gravel, get a hold. Then he hauls his body after him in one long, drawn-out movement. His left foot is lying at an impossible angle and drags after him, so he hasn't felt the pain yet. She lifts his bayonet. Looks at the gleaming steel blade. Tells herself that people in the houses around here lie awake at night. The sound of one shot can be explained away as a backfiring exhaust pipe. Two shots are one too many.

But the darkness is still on her side.

She walks towards the bundle of clothes on the path. Stops.

His wriggling stops too.

He is lying perfectly still on the path, with all four limbs outstretched. Like an insect that wants to make itself invisible. He can hear me, she thinks. He knows what is happening and that is absolutely fine. Slowly she lowers the hand holding the revolver until the muzzle is pointing a few centimetres above his neck. Then she shoots. Waits until the death convulsions stop. Searches through his jacket pockets. Finds a passport and a wallet. Can't get to his trouser pockets. Rolls the body onto its back. Avoids looking at the exit wound in his mangled face. Rummages through his pockets. All she can find is car keys.

She straightens up, walks down the path, turns right and continues towards Alvilde Munthe's grave. She is in a hurry now. She drops what she is holding, kneels down and pushes aside the lid of the urn vault. Puts his passport, knife and wallet inside. Stuffs the revolver and car keys in her pocket. Then pulls the lid back into position and hurries down the line of gravestones closest to the buildings in the east.

As soon as she is in the trees by Akersveien, she swings her legs over the fence.

She slows down on the pavement, hugging the houses as she merges into the shadows.

She has the key at the ready when she reaches his rental car. Unlocks the door and gets in. Opens the glove compartment. Nothing.

The headlights of a car racing at high speed cut through the darkness. Black and white VW beetle. Police.

The car passes. She sits still, staring at the bend. She can't see the car any longer. Only the light that shows it has stopped. Then it slowly drives on. Shortly afterwards she sees a torchlight in the cemetery. There is only one torch. Maybe it is the same police officer who spoke to her through the car window. Maybe it is someone else. At any rate, it will be a long time before the dead man is found.

Ester sits, calmly watching the dancing beam moving through the cemetery. Only when it has completely gone does she switch on the ignition, put the car in gear and drive away. A little later, turning into Fredriks gate towards Drammensveien, she switches on the headlights.

She drives to Fornebu airport. The big car park would be perfect. It will take them a long time to find the car.

1

Dear Turid,

I hope you remember me and the conversation we had when you were a student at the law faculty in Oslo. I visited you at the university because I knew your mother. I have long wanted to meet you again, but life has taken me on other paths and I have been in Israel more than Norway during the years that have passed since.

Some years ago I received a letter from the Norwegian Justice Department. They informed me that a bank box had been opened at a branch in Oslo because the owner was presumed deceased. In the box there were several items that were traced back to a Jewish couple who had settled in Oslo before the Second World War. They were my parents, who, as you know, died in the gas chambers. As I was their heir, I was asked if I recognised any of these objects. I did. They were things that had belonged to my mother and father. They were sent here, to my address in Jerusalem. Among them was a bracelet, which belonged to you. It is a great mystery to me how it could end up in this bank box. But I saw it as a sign. I am sure you were wearing this bracelet when we met in the university cellar almost fifty years ago. I have tried to trace your whereabouts so that I could give it back to you, but without luck. I am happy to say why. I have missed your mother, Åse, ever since she passed away. I think I can honestly say, hand on heart, that I have thought about her almost every day since the day we parted company. She was my best friend at a time when friendship was my most precious possession in the world. Both her dying and the way she died were a terrible blow to me. The bracelet was a vivid reminder of her. But I also suffered pangs of guilt because I knew that it meant so much to you too. For this reason, in all modesty, I have inserted a clause in my will to secure this bracelet for you upon my death. I have instructed my son

*Jonatan to try and find you and, if he should, to hand over this item of
jewellery as the memory it deserves to be, not only of your mother, but
also of someone whose greatest sorrow it is that she never had the chance
to get to know you.*

Yours forever,
Ester Lemkov

Turid lifts her head and looks at the man facing her across the table.
He is a few years younger than her and overweight. This is not so easy
to discern as the suit is tailor-made and elegant. The shirt is exclusive,
presumably from Egyptian cotton. The tie is silk, the knot bouton-
nière. He has that determined expression one finds with successful
businessmen.

He puts down the coffee cup he was given by Hans's secretary.

She speaks to him in Norwegian, but switches to English when she
sees his reaction. 'How on earth could the bracelet be among your
grandparents' possessions?'

The man shrugs. 'I don't know.'

'Who owned the bank box?'

Jonatan smiles apologetically. 'I don't know. You're forgetting that I
haven't read the letter. I don't know what's in it.'

'Your mother writes that this bracelet was in a bank box.'

He nods. 'That may well be true. I know nothing about it.'

'And you don't know who owned the bank box?'

'That's correct.'

'And she told you to find me?'

'Yes. But that was easier said than done. There were two possibilities left. Either you were dead or you must've married and taken your
husband's surname.'

She nods.

'So we tried the newspapers. The personal columns.'

Turid sighs. 'Do they still exist?'

Jonatan Azolay smiles. And Turid recognises this smile. One front
tooth slightly longer than the other.

'It's an unusual column, but they publish messages on request. That was how my mother wanted it, and so that was how it was. She's old-fashioned in some things.'

'So when you didn't get an answer you decided to sell the bracelet?'

'It wouldn't be sold.'

'It wouldn't?'

'It was a last attempt. A Norwegian business connection had the idea. He tipped off a journalist in a newspaper. They took photos of the bracelet and wrote an article. I was hoping you'd read it and contact us.'

'I hope you understand that I'm happy to have the bracelet and grateful to you,' Turid says. 'But I'm left with more questions than answers.'

Jonatan laughs out loud. 'Welcome to a small but exclusive club. As you can imagine, I've collected a lot of questions over the years. My mother's a woman with many secrets.'

'You talk about her as if she were still alive.'

Jonatan Azolay gets to his feet. He shakes her hand. 'Meeting you has been an absolute pleasure. Now I can say with an easy heart that my mother's mission has been accomplished.'

Turid sits, weighing the bracelet in her hand. It is the same bracelet, of that there is no doubt. But she feels no pleasure at holding it. She feels only sad.

She rereads the letter. Noticing the formulations: *Some years ago … have tried to trace you … but without luck … as the memory it deserves to be…*

There is a knock at the door.

Turid puts the bracelet in her bag. 'Yes?'

Hans comes in. 'Everything alright, Turid?'

She nods.

'Did he come alone?'

Turid raises her head, enquiringly.

'There were two of them yesterday. Him and quite an elderly lady. She appeared to be the boss.'

Hans is standing by the window. He looks out. 'I suppose she was sitting in the car. Not so good on her pins, I imagine.'

Hans turns. 'But you're happy, Turid. That's the main thing. I'll get one of the ladies in the office to write an invoice.'

Turid jumps up.

Hans laughs. 'That was a joke, Turid.'

Turid has no time for Hans's jokes. She dashes out of his office, through the ante-room, onto the stairs and down. The front door is locked. She casts around in desperation. There – the switch on the wall. She presses it. The lock clicks. Turid pushes the door open. There is hardly anyone around. She looks to the right, then to the left. Sees the elegant man sitting on the back seat of a black saloon further down the street. The car sets off. It goes about fifty metres, but has to turn round because the street is blocked off. It comes back, towards her. Turid sticks out an arm to stop it. The car drives past. A glimpse of shadows behind darkened windows. But she can see quite clearly. There are two people sitting at the rear. A tall man and a sunken, petite woman.

The dark car signals and bears left. Turid sees it come into view again, in the gap between two buildings. Then it is gone. Turid takes a deep breath. Looks down at her bag, opens it and checks to make sure. The bracelet is there.

So at least *that* is real.